THE GENESIS

The *Vampyr Snyper* Series:

The Genesis
The Vampire's Son
Divided They Fall
The Servant
Blood of Ages

Also by K. L. Kerr:

Jeremy (A Story of Real-Life, Only…Not)

THE GENESIS
A VAMPYR SNYPER Novel

K. L. Kerr

PENREFE
PUBLICATIONS

First published in 2006
by Lulu.com

This edition published 2009
by Penrefe Publications

Copyright © 2000 by K. L. Kerr

The Author asserts the moral right to
be identified as the author of this work.

Second Edition.

ISBN: 978-0-9559845-0-1

Printed by Lulu.com

For Steph

From the Precipice of Chaos, a Spirit Stirs...

A light breeze swept through the monolithic crypt like a lost child.

The building had long since been abandoned. A family crest embroidered on the scarlet-red curtains was obscured through centuries of settling dust. The cracks in the floor and wall said that a great battle had once happened here.

A spirit walked through the bare-stone walls, barely discernable against the darkness.

Something will come soon, it thought to reassure itself. *And I will be ready this time.*

PROLOGUE

Moonlight spilled out through the parted clouds. Its ghostly silver shimmer was overshadowed by the garish synthetic lights of the city it overlooked. Pockets of life sprang up on every street. In these early hours, the only places still open were the clubs, all packed with eager hopefuls out for an exciting night.

A tall, dark-haired, pale man in indistinguishable black clothes stood motionless on the rooftop of an apartment building. His treacle-coloured eyes cast over the people on the street below, funnelling into the opposite club. Above the entrance was a red neon sign, flashing the name 'Eterniti' into the street.

The man dropped the butt of his latest cigarette and crushed it under his boot. The faint sound of static broke his concentration, and he reached into the lining of his coat to take out a vibrating mobile phone. The display read: 'Rose'.

'What?' he asked. The caller spoke in a sprightly voice, and he said nothing in return. After a minute or so of listening, he hung up. A change in expression left faint worry lines on his otherwise flawless skin. He put the phone away and headed towards the fire escape.

The girl bolted like a startled deer across the street. She twisted out of the way of an oncoming vehicle. The man closest to her wasn't so lucky. She heard the crunch of metal against flesh but didn't bother looking back. At least now there was one less to deal with.

She darted into the nearest alley, listening to the screams of her closest attacker as he lay dying in the street, and the heavy footsteps of the others still giving chase, none of whom seemed to have stopped to aid their fallen ally.

Pain shot up her biceps as she clambered the wire mesh fence. Upper body strength had always been her Achilles heel. Running was easy, considering all the practise she got, but anything that required power was her downfall. Four men, all of whom probably spent half their lives in a gym, were right behind her. Adrenaline coursed through her bloodstream and forced her over the top; her muscles burned as she tumbled over the fence and landed with a thud.

Three of the men in pursuit clambered over the fence with relative ease, although the thing bent a little under their joint weight. The first over caught sight of the target disappear around the corner, her long chestnut waves streaking along behind her like a beacon.

The fourth man couldn't get any decent footing on his climb attempt. Cursing loudly after the others, he took a few steps back to try again.

The pale man leapt from the shadows as the man started towards the fence for a second time. He charged at the man's back and wrapped one arm around his thick neck. With his prey in his iron grip, he crushed his arm together until he heard the muffled *snap* of the spine beneath unbroken skin.

He dropped the limp body to the floor and ran at the fence, clearing it without making contact. As he steadied himself on landing, he thought he felt something. Over the sound of rushing footsteps and cars passing in the distance, a lingering breeze seemed to pass by him. Something else was there. He turned but saw nothing but shadows. He was the most dangerous thing there. He shook his head and the ominous feeling dispersed. He continued to trail the girl and her attackers.

The streets were overcrowded with old, decrepit buildings, creating a maze of alleyways and alcoves. The girl cut through them, zigzagging around broken bottles and taking small leaps over garbage cans. She didn't look back; the irate shouting and footsteps said that the men who wanted her dead were still close.

The second man died running through the narrow alleys. The pale man grabbed him by the hair and rammed his head into the wall. His skull burst against the brick and one strike was enough.

He couldn't resist the smile that crept over his face as he let the second corpse slide out of his grip.

The girl wore down after the initial pump of adrenaline ran dry. She turned into the small alcove of a building's side door. She tried the handle, but it was locked. Pressing her back against the wall, she tried to clear her mind and listen. Footsteps were still getting closer. She held her gun against her chest, feeling it move with the immense thud in her chest. She could die here.

She readied her weapon, as a figure ran past. The gunfire was loud, as her gun wasn't fitted with a suppressor. The bullet hit its target in the back of the neck. It split through the skin and tore out his throat on exit.

She set off running, leaping over the man as he lay choking on his own blood. She had no time to make his death quick and painless, nor did she have any real desire to do so. He wouldn't have been so considerate had the situation been in his favour.

With her heart beating ever faster, she darted down another alley. Her biggest mistake was that she didn't check first for other signs of life. She ran head-on into the last man. Stephen McCann. His initial surprise at having her charge right into him quickly subsided into blind rage.

Instinct brought her arm around to hit him with the handle of her gun. He was too close to get a shot in, and he was too quick for her to manage a successful hit of any kind. He wrestled the weapon out of her hand. The sound of it clattering to the floor echoed through the silence. She'd never been much of a bare-knuckle fighter; everything was in the weapons she carried. This didn't stop her bringing her knee up. It hit him square in the groin and he keeled.

She took her chance and ran. She didn't get far.

A few staggered and panic-stricken steps and he was upon her again. Despite his obvious advantage of size and build against her petite frame, he wasn't lenient with his physical punishment. Then again, she *had* been sent to kill him. Mere minutes earlier, she'd had him on his knees, covered in his own sweat, tears and urine, begging for his life. How was she to know a man built like a tank carried a personal panic alarm?

He hooked his arm around her neck and dragged her backwards. He lifted her clean off the ground. She struggled fiercely but felt his grip tighten over her windpipe. She tried to cough but it caught in her throat and started to choke her.

She heaved and her body struggled, partially without intent, to get free. Precious air was being denied. Of all the ways she thought she'd die, this wasn't one of them, and it certainly wasn't worth the two grand she'd been offered to do the job. Consciousness started to fade, spots marred her vision, and she struggled less vigorously. She knew he wouldn't stop once she was unconscious. She could smell it in him. He was a killer, too.

He let go without warning. She hit the ground, her legs gave way on impact, and she crumbled. She couldn't see clearly but tried to crawl away. She fell short of getting to her feet the first few times. He didn't come after her.

Blind curiosity turned her around. The guard was pinned against the wall by the shadow of a man, who had one hand gripped diligently around his neck. McCann was choking, and his feet weren't touching the floor.

She leaned over, nauseated by the recent asphyxia. She felt faint. A silver streak sliced through the air, and across McCann's throat. The blood spurted from the wound, which the mystery assailant dodged. She gagged and swallowed the vomit rising.

She scrambled to her feet. When she tried to breathe normally, there was a wheeze in her chest that hadn't been there a minute ago. She swayed and stumbled forwards, seeing only a glimpse of the dark-haired mystery coming forwards, with his arms held out to catch her...

CHAPTER ONE

Catrina took a swig of beer. She could hardly taste it through the bile clinging to the back of her throat. Her head pounded from where it'd been slammed against concrete; the music and constant drone from the bar's occupants didn't help.

No one noticed she was injured; her dark clothes hid the blood. It wasn't all hers. Clotted in her long waves of chestnut hair and stuck under her fingernails was the blood of a man she'd killed that night. Her own contribution to the scarlet stains happened during her less-than-graceful retreat to what was possibly her worst performance on record.

The man sitting across the table was a stranger to her. He'd saved her life less than an hour ago. This drink and her company was all he'd asked for in return.

He'd admitted openly that he hadn't been there by coincidence. His organisation had been tracking her work for 'some time'. Her initial hesitance had already subsided into suspicion, reinforced by the man's composure.

He didn't touch his drink— a double shot of whiskey neat in a tumbler glass—and tended not to focus on her for very long. He hadn't spoken since their arrival.

After more than fifteen minutes of relative silence, listening only to the constant thud of bass tones and drone of chatter from those surrounding them, she cracked. 'What did you say your name was?'

'I didn't.' He offered his hand across the table. 'It's Fox.'

She shook his hand out of courtesy but was eager to pull away. 'I'm Catrina.'

'Catrina Malinka.' He went for his drink. 'I know who you are. I know a lot about you.'

'Do you? Like?'

'Like what you do for a living.' He leant in closer. 'Like what your business was with Stephen McCann. Like why you have that Beretta tucked in the back of your jeans.'

'So you knew I'd be there.'

He nodded. 'I was a little disappointed. I thought you were capable of a simple contract killing.'

'I had it under control.'

She didn't know this man or where he'd appeared from. She hadn't wanted his help. Sure, she *could've* died otherwise, but that was a risk she was willing to take, something that came with the job description. Things went wrong. People died.

He took out a cigarette. The flame from the lighter caught a distant gleam in his eye. 'You don't trust me.'

'Why should I?'

'I just saved your life.'

'That's not good enough.' She went for her bottle of beer.

'What more do you want?'

'You could tell me what you were doing there.'

He leant back in the seat. 'Just be thankful I was. I was going to leave you to deal with it, until he started to strangle you.'

Damaged pride spurred her. 'I *had* it under control.'

'It didn't look that way to me.'

She folded her arms, a gesture shy of stomping her foot. 'Maybe you should've left me, then. Now we'll never know who was right.'

He smiled, an odd expression to his pale and serious face. He took the cigarette from his lips and exhaled a cloud of smoke, watching it drift towards the ceiling. 'Maybe.'

'So, how long is some time?'

'I'm sorry?'

'In the alley, you said your organisation have been watching me for some time. How long is 'some time'?'

'You don't want to know.'

Her eyes narrowed, and she decided right there that she didn't like him. Past his chiselled features and impressive physique hidden under thick clothes, he had an arrogant manner. And he'd barely said a word.

She didn't like the little she'd gathered from him so far. She realised he was watching her and stiffened.

'If you're not going to tell me how long your people have been watching me, you can at least tell me why…'

'—First of all, it hasn't been my people watching you.' He paused to tap excess cigarette ash into the already bulging ashtray. He leant over to the next table and took a clean one. 'It was just me.'

She put up her hands. 'Okay, fine. Why?'

'I need another drink first. Can I get you one?' He was already walking away. She must've been drowsy; she didn't see him get up.

She shrugged. 'Sure.'

She watched him head towards the bar. His pale features were more accentuated within a crowd, but the people were too engrossed with themselves to care about a passing handsome stranger.

Yet he didn't avoid walking into people. He didn't have to. They moved aside without noticing. The whole crowd parted for him to pass like a shadow.

She sighed heavily. Without his presence as a distraction, she took the time to take stock of the situation. Everything had happened so quickly. One minute, she'd had McCann on his knees, crying and begging to keep his life…

She didn't remember much after that. She *did* remember being underneath him, close enough for his stale breath to nauseate her. Then, without warning, he'd let go.

Within seconds, McCann was pinned against the wall. His feet didn't touch the floor, as her 'saviour' pulled a knife and slit his throat.

Fox returned with more drinks.

'You alright?'

'Reliving the moment.' She took the bottle he was offering. 'Thanks.'

'Where was I?' he asked as he sat down.

'You were about to tell me why you've been tracking me.'

He lit up another cigarette. 'I was?'

'Yes,' she said through clenched teeth. 'Look, I'm grateful for your help so far, but I need an explanation.'

He opened his mouth but then decided against saying whatever he was about to. His eyes drifted to his glass. The discomfort of the silence slid over her shoulders, and all she could do was wait. The closer she looked at his face, the more concentration she put into examining his features, the older he appeared. It hurt to stare too long.

She blinked.

'Three years,' he said. Her eyes wandered up to his. 'You wanted to know how long I've been watching you. I've been doing that for three years.'

As she took in those words, everything around her went very quiet, and all the air was sucked out of her lungs. Her brows knotted.

Three years, a little voice inside her head repeated. Her fists clenched in her lap. *All you've done in the last three years*, the voice added. *All he could've seen…*

She vaulted forwards. The chair was knocked back behind her, as she charged straight for him. She had one knee on the table and one hand around the bottle about to smash it across that perfect jaw, before she realised that her body had stopped.

Fox still sat at his side of the table, with one hand raised, having caught hers mid-swing. He rose out of his seat slowly, still holding her by the wrist. The sheer power behind his movement forced her back.

She slid off the table. Her heart—now lodged securely in her throat—was so loud she thought everyone would be watching them. When she moved, her body didn't follow.

Fox still had his hand around her wrist; he took a moment to prise the bottle out of her grip and spark up another cigarette, all with ease. She watched him do this with equal amazement and disgust. It was the latter that showed.

'Who the *hell* do you think you are?' she growled, while trying to wriggle out of his grip. He moved when she did. 'Let go of me!' She tugged again, but this time he pulled back and dragged her to him without any effort. Twisted amongst the thoughts of the violation of his observations and the shock of how long it had been for, she was stunned by his power.

She stopped struggling and straightened up. It was only now, this close, that their physical difference became obvious. At five three, she'd always been considered petite, and against this man—over six foot at least—she should've felt overpowered by him. She just glared straight up at him, blue eyes ablaze.

The few people who had stopped to watch the drama returned to their business.

'Are you done?' His voice was slightly agitated, but his expression hadn't changed.

Catrina nodded. 'Let go, please.'

He did so immediately and sat back at the table. She wasn't imagining it; he was moving quicker than she could see.

She sat opposite, wiping the beer she'd managed to spill on herself into her jeans. She took a deep breath and braved herself to look him in the eye.

'Alright…Fox,' she said. 'You want my interest?' She spread her arms. 'I'm all ears. But three years is a long time. I need you to tell me why you've been watching me, and I need it *now*.'

Whether her tone had the effect she'd intended or he'd simply tired of the games he thought he was playing, Fox sat back in his seat and put out his cigarette.

'We know you've been in the business from a young age,' he said. 'My mentor was actually the first one to come into contact with you.'

'Your mentor,' she repeated. 'You mean your boss?'

He nodded. 'You were sixteen at the time, just starting out in the contract business. Something about you interested him. He couldn't explain it, but that was when he gave me the assignment of watching you.' Her eyes asked for more. 'I only watched you work. Your personal life was of no interest to us.'

That reassured her somewhat. 'You were headhunting?' He nodded. 'But…why?'

'Because your skills are interesting. You never had formal training, did you?'

'People say I was meant for it. Like how you can just 'fall into' the right career.' She shrugged. 'Not exactly a clerical post, is it?'

'Was it your choice to do…what you do?'

She shrugged again, but a thin smile crept into the corner of her mouth. 'I don't have any complaints. I'm good at it. You'd have seen that in your observations, right?'

'Without taking tonight into account?'

The smile dropped. 'Mistakes happen.'

'You could've been killed.'

'So you've said.'

'Putting your mistakes aside, we *are* interested in your work and your potential for the future.' After a moment's pause, he added, 'We want to hire you.'

'That's the first direct thing you've said to me.'

'Are you interested?'

'That depends.' She crossed her legs and silently revelled in the fact that the conversation was under her control. 'I'll need a pretty sweet deal to draw me away from what I've got now. But I'm guessing you already know that.'

'I know your situation with Tony.' The name passed his lips with slight acidity. 'But you've been looking for a way out for a while.'

Her eyes widened. 'How did you…?'

He lifted one hand to stop her. 'I didn't need to be watching you privately to know you were getting lax in your responsibilities as a killer. That usually means one of two things…either you're too old for your station, which you're obviously not…or else the work isn't challenging enough, because you're outgrowing it. I'd say it could be down to you being in the wrong line of work, but…'

'It's not that,' she agreed.

'So you *are* looking for something more?'

'Well, sure, as much as the next guy, but…it's complicated.' She started to pick the label from the bottle-neck. 'I owe Tony more than just a job.'

'I know,' he said. 'You let him control your life for the best part of nine years.'

She didn't deny it. 'I was happy being a daughter to him.'

'And he was happy with you as a replacement child.' It was not posed as a question.

Her fingers curled around the chair arms, nails digging into the wood. 'Where do you get off with this shit?'

'I didn't come here to argue with you.'

'Then what did you come here for, *Fox*? This proposition sounds more like an excuse to criticise me.'

He held up his hands; she had no idea whether his submission was genuine. 'It's not intentional. I just wanted you to know that, despite your flaws, we're still interested in taking you on.'

She exhaled. 'I'm flattered.'

'You should be. This isn't an offer open to anyone, and I haven't decided how long you've got to make a decision yet.'

'You still haven't told me why,' she said, catching him slightly off guard. She saw it in his eyes and smiled. 'You've said you want to snatch me from my current employer, but you haven't said why.'

'Do I need a reason, other than what I've observed?'

'For someone like you, yes,' she replied. 'You're not just your average organisation. I saw you pick a guy up with one hand. Something like that takes special training. What I want to know is why someone of your *obvious* abilities would be interested in me.'

He opened his mouth but no words formed. He checked himself. 'It gets complicated. If it helps your decision, you'd get the same training.'

She considered that. *She pinned her attacker against the wall and lifted with ease. He tried to cry out, but his voice never made it past her grip at his throat, feeling his throat quivering under her palm as she went for the knife...*

'You don't expect me to make a decision right away, do you?' she asked. She couldn't guarantee that—*should* he offer her the job right then—she'd turn it down.

'Of course not,' he replied. 'I wanted to make you aware of the offer, that's all.'

She tried to keep a composed mentality. 'So what's the catch?'

He hesitated. 'We would only ask one thing from you. You would have to give up your identity as it stands. You're coming into a world of people that don't exist.'

'That wouldn't be a problem. If I was leaving the Gostanzo business, it wouldn't be safe to go around with the same name, anyway. Is that it?'

He hesitated. 'There are certain 'restrictions' when it comes to leaving our organisation, once you've accepted.'

'Meaning?'

'Meaning that you don't leave once you've been taken in. It's a job for life.'

She thought about this carefully. 'But what if I started to look for something more challenging, say, some years down the line?'

'You wouldn't.'

'Humour me.'

'If you became unsuitable for your post for some reason, for example mental instability or the inability to carry out assignments, you would be removed. Other than that, you're in it for life. But trust me, Catrina, you'd never find a reason to look elsewhere.'

She sighed. 'A couple of years ago, I would've said that about Tony.'

'I understand if you want to take some time to think about it.' He took a few seconds to light up another cigarette, as though his very being revolved around the small white sticks. 'It's a life-changing decision.'

'A minute ago you wanted nothing more than for me to accept right here and now.'

'I know. But you need to be aware of the requirements and I have to enforce our rules.' He didn't sound enthusiastic.

'Isn't there a probationary period?' she asked. It was unusual for an organisation to accept a new employee outright.

'It's been three years,' he clarified. 'We've had all the probationary period we need.'

'I don't appreciate the fact that I've been watched like a lab rat being shoved in my face.'

'Well, for such a renowned killer, you're not all that difficult to track.'

She exhaled loudly and bit her lip. 'Sure, for someone of your abilities.'

'For anyone, actually,' he retorted.

She fell silent, rapping her fingernails on the tabletop. Her mind was clouded with emotions—mainly a conflict of interest and hatred for this man.

'What are you thinking?' he asked casually.

She continued to tap the wooden surface. 'I'm thinking that three years is a long time. I'm thinking...sorry, *hoping*, that, should I accept this proposal, I wouldn't be reporting to you. And I'm thinking that if you keep demeaning my abilities, you can shove your job offer right up your ass.'

He let his underhand smile slip and checked his watch. 'And I think that's the perfect end to our conversation.'

He was standing before she blinked. He didn't wait for her to get up after him, so she was a few steps behind as they headed through the crowd. The mass unconsciously parted for Fox. They moved in again once he'd gone, leaving Catrina to barge her way through the tight-packed bodies.

Away from the bar's horde, she welcomed the cool night air to her lungs. Fox threw his latest cigarette butt out into the empty street.

'Where do we go from here?' she asked.

'That depends,' he replied. His eyes were burning with more intensity than before. 'I don't expect you to make your decision now, but you can appreciate that an offer like this can't be kept open indefinitely.'

She nodded. 'I understand.'

He took a business card from the lining of his thick woollen coat and handed it to her. On the front was just a phone number; the back was blank.

'I want you to think about your decision carefully, but call me as soon as you've made it. I'll give you three days, is that fair?'

'I suppose,' she said, turning the card between her fingers. 'Even though you haven't told me anything about you *or* your company, *or* what I'm supposed to be doing for you.'

'I've told you all you need to know. Your intuition should fill in the rest.' As though he'd said all he'd ever need to, he started to walk away.

'That's it?' She took a few steps after him. 'Thank you and goodnight?'

He turned back. 'What else do you want? A nightcap, maybe?'

Her face flushed red. 'I want more information.'

'You don't need it.' He continued to leave, and she didn't try to go after him. 'You're looking for an excuse to escape. We're offering it to you. Call me with your decision.'

He turned the corner and was gone.

She was left in the quiet street, alone and none the wiser. She passed the card between her fingers. She was wary of him, but there was something more to him that drew her interest, something beyond his distracting good looks and conceited nature.

Fox made his way farther towards the outskirts of the city. A car horn blared from behind. As he stepped into the road, a black Mercedes came hurtling towards him. The driver hit the breaks so hard that the tyres left a trail of burnt rubber and smoke behind. His hand instinctively reached out to touch the front end, as the car slowed, stopping inches from him.

He opened the back passenger door.

His mentor—African-American in decent and far into his thirties—stepped out of the car. His soft brown eyes and gentle smile likened him more to a friend than a leader.

The driver barely gave Fox time to close the door. The engine roared and the heavy vehicle sped off into the distance, overshadowed by the constant thud of the driver's music.

'I suggest we walk,' the mentor said in a deep, calm voice. 'You can tell me what happened.'

They started down the deserted streets. Fox straightened his thick woollen jumper, pulling his coat tighter around his broad chest to guard from the cold. His mentor's eyes drifted upwards to watch the stars dance over the black sky. While Fox was slightly taller than his mentor, it was obvious who held the influence.

He resisted the urge to light up a cigarette. 'I put the offer to her.'

'So soon?'

'It seemed like the right time. She was in danger.'

'There was no more danger there than usual.'

'She could've died.'

'Do you honestly believe that? It was dangerous, but her life is a constant threat. You accepted that a long time ago.' His attention returned to the sky, immersed with the grandeur of the heavens. 'You'd think they'd lose their appeal after all this time, wouldn't you?'

Fox tilted his head briefly to look. The stars did not cast the same spell over him; he looked on with slight disdain and instead thought of her. 'Some things you never tire of.'

He did not see his mentor smile. 'I'm assuming your persistence stems only from her abilities and not your fascination with her?'

'If I hadn't been there…'

'But you were, as you always are.'

'And if there comes a time when I'm not?'

'There is always that chance. Considering her life to this point, I'm surprised she has made it this far, even *with* your protection.' He glanced to his friend with an astute look this time. 'I'm starting to wonder if your reasons for taking her are as justified as you perceive them to be.'

Fox pretended not to hear. 'I assumed it would be in everyone's interest to offer it while time isn't against us.'

The mentor let out a weary laugh. 'Time is not always on our side, is it? How ironic.' The smile crept back on his face. 'Her life has always been your occupation, Fox, not mine. Do as you feel is necessary. I will stand by your decision.'

Fox bowed his head. 'Thank you.'

The two parted ways at the next junction. Fox would head home, but the dark-skinned man had something he wanted to do first. He waited until the sound of Fox's boots against asphalt faded, before he went to the nearest building and ascended to the roof.

There he was at peace with himself, looking out beyond the slums to the urban skyline. He listened to the night. His smile made lines to crease his features. The stars remained out of his reach for a few seconds while his mind endured the matter at hand.

CHAPTER TWO

Catrina's apartment was immaculate, mostly because she spent so little time in it.

Her bedroom was different. Clean and worn clothes created a makeshift carpet. Another pile gathered at the bottom of the wardrobe. An inconspicuous pinewood cabinet was built into the side door of the opened wardrobe. A sniper rifle and sawn-off shotgun hung there, barely used. The same could not be said for the Colt AR-15, scratched, dirty with trace remains of blood on the handle, discarded behind the door. The Beretta—her favourite—was underneath a magazine on the bedside table and in a better condition. It had been a gift.

Catrina awoke from an unsteady sleep. After taking a few painkillers for her headache, she sat down in front of the bed, slipped her toes under the frame and started sit-ups.

The repetitive motion helped clear her head and shake the feeling that the ghosts of her victims were watching her. During the day she had more important things to think about and they were buried in her subconscious. At night, her defences dropped and they returned.

Remembering bulging eyes and panicked hands gripping her coat always woke her with the sensation of being choked. It was one of the reasons she didn't sleep much.

She thought of Fox; his offer, the circumstances surrounding it, but mostly, she just thought of *him*. He was unlike anyone she'd ever met; stronger, faster, *better*. She couldn't stop considering the idea that he was the result of some Secret Service experiment.

She wouldn't find out the truth unless she accepted the offer, and if she declined, it was safe to assume they'd never meet again. Not to say he'd stop watching her...

She stopped exercising. It dawned on her how long three years actually was. She'd been a professional contract killer for as long. She'd been involved in the business for closer to seven, but Tony hadn't given her a gun until she'd turned sixteen. The things she'd done as part of the job was enough to send shivers up her spine. Fox could've seen it all.

This 'organisation' wanted to take her on because of her performance so far. She was flattered at the attention, and the intrigue of the whole thing was immensely alluring. Fox had been so confident she'd say 'yes' without giving any real persuasion.

She went into the bathroom for a glass of water. Catching sight of herself in the mirror, the tank top she slept in rode up to her ribcage and showed the thick scar over the left side of her pelvis.

It was faded silver now, but she still remembered it red raw, and how much she'd cried. She got it the night she'd met Anthony Gostanzo. He'd hit her in his car.

She was ten at the time, and Tony—having a son of a similar age—took pity on her. After the accident and realising she was a runaway, he took her in. It started so easily. Before the age of thirteen, she'd shot a would-be assailant in the kneecap and pushed a man out of a ten storey window.

Catrina had very few scars, as her skin was quick to heal. But the older ones, such as this one, stayed to remind her of the past.

Tony was the biggest issue she had to overcome, not just from a professional standpoint but as a father. She had no family and refused to talk about her parents. Tony was the only family she knew.

She'd be a fool to let Fox's offer slide. She'd been looking for other work for a while, but never actively. She *had* been lax in her assignments, but mainly it was in the hope that Tony would fire her. It would make it easier to walk away when he was angry.

Unfortunately, a Gostanzo never gave up on a child, even if the family ties were not by blood. He just assumed she was struggling under the pressure.

The previous year, she'd carried out a kill on Robert Dyne, a boss to a rival organisation and a personal enemy to the Gostanzo family. That had been the pinnacle of her career, yet she'd felt little elation—except on a personal level—at having the honour of killing him. It left her feeling hollow, and her work had taken a nosedive ever since.

Fox wouldn't wait. No doubt there were other people with natural abilities that rivalled hers. She climbed onto the bed, cradling the Beretta in her lap. It helped her think.

This was a once in a lifetime opportunity. If she turned it down, she'd be with the Gostanzos until she died. She understood how important it was; she was just taken aback at how quickly she had to decide.

Settling back into her existing profession wouldn't suffice. She wanted something more challenging, something more dangerous, more exciting. Even Tony wouldn't pass up an offer like this.

The scars told stories, and there was no time she wouldn't remember them. A change of scenery couldn't change memories. She wanted this. She was interested in Fox and his abilities; more interested in how they'd benefit her.

She finally got into bed, slipping the gun back under the magazine. She curled up under the sheets. The LCD on her alarm clock flashed 03:47, which left her a few more hours before she had to leave.

She set her alarm for nine o'clock every morning, whether or not she was working. She exercised or went to the nearest café and watched people passing. The world moved so quickly, she never liked to sleep for too long for fear of missing it.

Her reasons for getting up that morning would be different. She hadn't returned to the office that night to report on the McCann assignment. Tony would be worried, and had she not signed in by the next morning, he'd send out a search party. If she was planning to accept Fox's offer, she'd have to be out of the apartment—if not the city—by then.

She'd decide in the morning. If she were to stay, she'd make up a story to excuse her absence and sign in as usual. If she were to go, she would gather a few belongings and go before she was found.

Without windows, the room was pitch-black. A slit of light slid under the door. It was cool inside, blanketed in silence with the exception of steady, deep breathing.

A shrill telephone ring sliced through the serenity; the darkness shattered as the room's occupant switched on a light.

Fox took a few seconds to wake up, rubbing at his eyes with thumb and forefinger. He sat up in bed and checked his watch. It was seven thirty. He'd barely been in bed half an hour. The sheet slipped off his bare shoulders, as he dragged himself up to reach the phone. There was no number on the display.

'Good morning, Catrina.'

'How did you know it was me?'

'I don't know anyone else who'd call at this time.'

'I know what I want to do.'

'Go ahead.'

'I'll do it. I'll do with you.'

His smile was sincere, but it was not articulated. 'What persuaded you?'

'I know this isn't your average job offer.'

'No, it isn't.'

'That and curiosity.'

'I'm glad,' he replied. He ran his fingers though his hair and considered his next move. 'I can't get to you until tonight. Do you have a problem with safety?'

'Not yet, but it's only a matter of time. I didn't sign in. They'll be looking for me soon.'

He gave her an address and instructions over the phone. It was the name and location of the nearest safe house. 'Got it?'

'Every word,' she replied, scribbling the last thing he had said on the Post-It by the telephone stand.

'Bring as many of your things as you want or need to. Leave your bigger weapons, and don't be offended if they take your gun when you go.'

'If they threaten to take it, I'm not going in.'

He sighed and pulled off sheets. Since she had woken him, he might as well get up. Half an hour was not bad. He took his cigarettes from the table and lit one as he circuited the small room.

'I'll let them know to expect you, then. Don't be aggressive with them, Catrina. In fact, if you're going to be courteous with anyone, make it them. I'll be there at eight thirty.'

He hung up at that, but he continued to pace and smoke. There was an excited gleam in his deep brown eyes. The hardest part was over, all that there was left to do was *take* her. He sat down on the bed and wished he could get there sooner. But what was one more day? He fell back and rested his arms on the back of his head, moving one to take the cigarette out of his mouth. He watched the smoke rise from his barely parted lips. He was still tired. He had to reserve his energy. It wouldn't be an easy job.

The line went dead in her hand. She stared at the handset a few seconds before placing it back in its cradle. That had been easy; it just meant that now she had no right to be in the apartment. Tony would be in his office before eight. If she had not signed in, first he would try to call her. She checked her mobile phone was off and put it back in her pocket.

When he couldn't get her on the phone, he would send someone to check her apartment.

She set about packing. She left most of her clothes and belongings; it'd be more convincing that she'd been abducted if her items had been left behind. For the same reason, she didn't pack any guns other than the Beretta. Tony would've expected her to have taken it anywhere she went.

When the search of her apartment returned nothing, the search would spread across the city. By then, she would be initiated into Fox's organisation and too far for anyone to pick up the trail.

She read the Post-It again and again until she could recall it from memory. She went into the kitchen, fished a disposable lighter out of the drawer and set the note alight. She dropped it into the sink and watched it burn before washing the ashes away. No one else was to know where she was heading.

She left the apartment without looking back. She hadn't been there long enough to set roots or have any sentimental attachments. It was just a series of rooms in a lifeless building.

The safe house was a few miles away, but it was still early. She was in no rush to get there, since Fox would not be there until gone sunset.

She ended up at the safe house just after one. There was an intercom on the steel-enforced door. She pressed the button.

'Look into the camera,' a stern voice commanded.

She leaned away from the door and looked straight into the camera jutting out of the wall. The intercom crackled.

'Who are you?'

'Fox sent me,' she replied to the camera.

Another silence, longer this time and more uncertain. 'Hang on.'

The lock clicked back and the door opened slightly of its own accord. She pulled it with supreme effort. The door slammed shut behind her and for a few seconds she was enclosed in the tight space between the enforced door and the entrance. She braced herself and went inside.

The inside of the safe house was nothing more than a run-down motel. A long corridor ran from the front door, splitting into corridors, rooms and stairs. There was a cheap desk a few yards in from the security door, and a man sitting behind it who fitted the scene.

He was a dumpy-shaped man in his forties. There was more hair on his face than his head, all grey and white. He looked Mexican, maybe Hispanic. She neither knew nor cared, but he was the first port of call.

'I'm here to meet up with a man called Fox. He said you'd be expecting me.'

The man continued to chew his gum nonchalantly. He made his way around the desk.

'Hands on the desk,' he droned. 'Godda pat you down. Don't look at me like that. You get a pat down or you walk out.'

'Firstly,' she said, scooting back. 'Fox was meant to tell you not to search me, and second…' She whipped the gun from the back of her jeans. The man jumped as though she had shoved it in his face. She slammed it on the desk. 'You could just ask me to show you what I'm packing.'

He read over her face carefully. 'Is that everything?'

She smiled. 'If I wanted to use it, it'd be enough. But I don't need it. I just carry it for comfort.'

There was a long hesitation on his part. Her face betrayed nothing of her intention. 'You're Fox's?'

'I'm here to see him, yes.'

'Right, right, sure. Whatever. Well, okay, if you're here for him, I guess I can let you go on ahead.' He went back to his side of the reception. He took a key off a board full of identical keys. 'Forty Three.'

She took the key with a nod, picking her gun back up as she went.

She settled in her room; no doubt once Fox arrived, she'd be busy. There would be so much paperwork to go over, they would probably be there until the early hours of the next morning.

She opened the curtains to get a view of the area, only to find the windows were boarded up. In a place like this, she didn't think maintenance was high on the list of priorities.

She decided to get a few more hours sleep, just one or two, to make sure she was alert for when he arrived.

She was dragged from the nightmares of shadows and monsters by the sound of someone knocking on the door. She groaned and rolled over, and only then did she remember that she wasn't at home. She sat up quickly and checked her watch. It was eight o'clock exactly.

'Shit,' she cursed quietly to herself, dragging herself off the bed while trying to straighten her hair and look more presentable. 'It's not locked!' she called.

The door opened carefully, but it creaked all the same. Fox avoided meeting her gaze as he entered.

'You should always lock the door,' he said. She barely heard him.

'Mmm,' she said. 'I usually do. You must have a heap of papers for me to sign.' She looked at him and frowned. 'You haven't brought anything?'

He said nothing.

Although she barely knew him, something in his expression was off. She refrained from questioning him and instead started to get her things ready. She was nervous and not quite sure why. It felt like excitement. Or foreboding.

She grabbed her backpack from the windowsill and quickly threw a few things in it.

'I'm not ready yet,' she explained, trailing her own discarded items. Each time she caught sight of him in the corner of her eye, he was getting closer. 'I was just so tired when I got here. I was only meant to have an hour. But I didn't sleep well last night, and I figured we'd have a lot of business to cover, so…'

She turned around to come face-to-chest with him. She looked up, doubled back and raised one arm to create space. He stepped warily back, and after a few moments of staring, she went back to packing.

The Beretta went into the bag last. She fastened the bag and put on her coat. She caught eyes with him. His expression didn't change, but his entire stance was tense, uneasy.

She straightened up. 'There a problem?'

He shook his head; the motion itself seemed to prove a challenge. 'No. No problem.'

She shrugged the bag over her shoulder; with all her worldly possessions inside, it was heavier than she remembered.

She attempted a smile his way. He didn't respond, keeping his distance, back to the door. Had she offended him somehow?

'I'm ready when you are,' she offered.

His eyes drifted up to meet hers. Breathing appeared to have become a challenge for him now, as well. He cleared his throat. 'You're sure about this? You can't go back on your word.'

She looked at him carefully. 'I know.'

'Alright, then let's go.'

He moved aside and she went to the door, only then realising it was locked. She hesitated. 'Did you lock this?'

She turned; he'd moved right up alongside her again, so she had to crane her neck to look into his eyes. They were darker than she remembered them. She tried to re-establish her own space with her arm. This time he resisted.

She pushed against his chest, but it was like pushing against a stone statue. She tried to slide to the left, but he moved his arm to the wall and cut her off. She was half afraid, half irritated, and—perhaps not wisely—it was the irritation that showed.

'What do you think you're doing?'

She moved to the right; his other arm was already there to box her in. Now she had nowhere to go; the door handle pressed against the small of her back and forced them closer together.

Her eyes widened; with her bag containing her only gun now jammed against her spine, she was unarmed and facing what was increasingly becoming 'the Terminator'. Her heart pounded her chest so hard she could feel him being moved by it. The motion only made him move closer, so close she could feel his breath on her lips and his hair as it brushed against her cheek.

And then—for a split second—he was gone. The pressure let up, allowing her to breathe, and all she could see was the room. She tried to move forwards, and reality returned. Fox grabbed her by the wrists and forced her against the door. The wood strained against their weight.

She tried to speak, either to scream for help, hurl insults, or to reason with a man who had obviously gone mad. Nothing made it past her throat.

He stabbed what felt like a needle into the side of her neck. God only knew what he'd put in her; sedative, poison…a feeling more potent than blind panic took over. She shoved her entire weight against him, and for a second she felt his grip lessen. But it returned, and with his entire body forced against her, he slipped his hands up her back and pulled her away from the door.

She refused to go down like this, and if she didn't fight, she *knew* he'd kill her.

She tried to kick him. Her brain told her limbs to move, but nothing happened. She tried again. No reaction. Again. Nothing. In her mind, she shoved her knee into his groin and slammed his skull against her raised knee. In reality, she just stood there.

All the muscles in her body abandoned her, and she started to slip into Fox's expectant arms. The hot sting around her neck where he had started felt like it was about to slide down her throat and into her chest.

Her face was wet. It took her a few seconds to realise she was crying. She could not hear herself, because whatever Fox had injected into her had muted everything.

The world started to turn dark. It returned a few seconds later, but she knew this was the onset of unconsciousness. White spots danced tauntingly across her vision. Her body convulsed. She wanted to wipe her eyes, stand up straight and kill the man who was trying to kill her first.

He lessened his grip on her, which made no difference now. She couldn't hold her own head up, let alone fight back. He guided her carefully to the floor.

Darkness remained for longer this time. Her eyes fluttered fitfully. She was losing the fight. Whatever he'd done to her, he'd done it well. Her blood was burning with whatever drug he'd used.

Still crying and going into shock, her body surged and her back arched. His hand went over her chest and pushed her back to the floor.

He leant closer, looking into her eyes. He said something that she couldn't hear. He should've *known* that much. His eyes were completely black. She felt him press against her more urgently. Her own consciousness receded. The last thing she saw of him was a set of fangs, covered in blood, as he went back for more…

She woke up screaming. The sound resonated in her head and forced her forwards. She opened her eyes to shake the images. She was met with the dreary drab of the safe house room. Nothing had changed, and she was alone.

She untangled herself from the sheets and threw herself out of bed. Her heart was racing, leaving her short of breath and light-headed. She staggered to the wardrobe for support. Her head throbbed with a terrible ache and she slid down to the floor. She checked her watch. It was five o'clock, but she was none the wiser whether it was morning or evening. She wasn't sure which would be more strange.

She could hear her heart like never before. The soft thud as it surged the blood around her body was surprisingly calming. It also meant she wasn't dead. She tried to stand but failed. Her body was so tired. Slowly, she headed back to bed. Her feet itched whenever she moved. It was as though the carpet was filled with thousands of tiny spikes. She may have been coming down with a fever.

She slid under the sheets, lay back and tried to relax. The beating of her heart was not getting quieter; it started to annoy her. She rolled over and pulled the pillow over her ears. The feeling shifted in her chest; she felt and heard it all perfectly.

As she sat up again to get her painkillers, she heard the key turning in the lock. She hadn't locked the door. Fox had. But Fox had not been yet. Had he?

She went for her Beretta only to realise it was not there. Her bag was tucked in the opposite corner of the room. She hadn't packed yet, either…

She was out of bed in a shot. The carpet scratched the soles of her feet. She fell by the bag, fumbling with the ties.

The door opened. She was momentarily blinded by the intense white light from outside. It burned so fiercely, she thought her eyes would burst. She raised her arm to protect herself and ended up falling over.

Fox closed the door quickly, and gave her a few seconds to readjust to the dim light and sit up. 'You're awake.'

She stood up so quickly it shocked her. When she blinked, the light lingered behind her eyelids and dazzled her. She took a deep breath and stood firm.

'How are you feeling?' he asked eventually, moving towards the chair beside the bed. He sat down and waited for her to join him.

'How am I feeling?' she repeated, moving forwards cautiously. She tried to get some answers from his expression and saw nothing. 'I'm not sure. You're early,' she added, tapping her watch.

'Actually, you're late,' he replied. 'It's five o'clock in the morning. You've been out for nearly nine hours.'

She edged back towards the bed. 'Why didn't you wake me?'

'I did.'

She stopped. 'What?'

'You remember what happened.' It was not a question, more an urge for her to bring back the memories she had been so quick to stifle.

'That…didn't happen.'

'Yes, it did.'

'It didn't.'

'Catrina.' He stood up. His eyes lacked both their ungodly blackness and their dangerous gleam, but it didn't calm her. He gestured to the bed. 'Sit down. I need to explain.'

She made no attempt to move. 'What did you do?'

'Sit down.'

'No, tell me first.'

His eyes softened a fraction. He went into his coat pocket and took out his cigarettes. Lighting one, he gave a sigh. Without taking his eyes from hers, he stated, 'I turned you into a vampire.'

She let out something in between a laugh and a scream. 'I'm sorry, *what?*'

He took a step closer. 'It's not easy to believe…'

'You're *crazy.*' Her legs were going to give way. Sheer determination kept her standing. Her heart pounded. She felt dizzy. 'You're crazy and a liar.'

'I'm not lying.'

'You have to be,' she argued. She staggered to the side, feeling nauseous. The last thing she saw before she passed out was Fox moving to catch her.

She woke up again in bed. This time Fox was already sitting in the chair beside her. He was not watching her. He sat with his arms rested on his thighs, staring at the opposite wall, deep in thought.

The feeling that he'd been there with her all that time infuriated her. She didn't feel well as it was, and his presence didn't help. What was she doing back in bed? What had he said? She sat up, arms folded.

'Feeling better?' He was smiling.

She could have screamed. 'You think this is *funny*?'

'Not at all.' He sat up straight and let the smile drop.

'What's going on here, Fox?'

'I've told you.'

'Well, I don't believe you.'

'And I don't care. It doesn't matter whether you *believe* it or not.'

Her body ached. It felt longer than one night. Maybe she'd been out for days. She needed to stretch, to crack her bones; maybe do a few exercises or go for a run. She didn't want to let him know she was in pain, because inside she was still fighting away the notion that he'd done something terrible to her.

'I want to get out of here,' she said.

He shook his head. 'That's not a good idea. Your body's going through some changes. It's not wise to move around too much.'

'I need to move.'

'It's normal, trust me. The best thing is rest.'

'But my legs…'

'—You're going through a change,' he cut her off. 'I know what it's like. I've been there, we all have.'

'All?'

'Other vampires. Most turnings take a few days.'

'Vampires? Turnings?' She hunched her shoulders, tried to move. 'I'm going for a walk.'

She got one leg off the side of the bed, before Fox was by her side. The concerned gaze didn't suit him. 'Just lie back. The pain will pass.'

She tried to stand. 'I'm going for a *walk*.'

She made it half way, before he wrapped his hand around her throat and forced her back down. 'You're not listening to me.'

'Why should I?'

He sat back down, willing to give her space, as long as she didn't get up. They stared at one another. Her eyes blazed, but it subsided into another dizzy spell. She shuddered and felt herself passing out again. 'God damn it…'

This was not the best start to her new, 'exciting' career.

Catrina awoke, as something was stabbed into her arm. She screamed and tried to fight. Fox pulled the needle out quickly.

She lashed out, throwing a severe punch to his gut.

He doubled back and let out a growl. His grip lessened, but not long enough for her to attempt an escape. He turned her over and caught her leg as she went to kick him. His fingers dug into the skin around her ankle. The blow must have shocked him.

He moved back. She sat bolt upright in bed, overcome with vertigo. He took something from a carry-all by the door.

'…What are you doing now?'

He didn't answer but came back to the bedside holding rope. Despite her fragile state, she attempted another mad rush for the door. He went after her, so much quicker than she could fathom. He hooked one arm around her waist, lifted her up like a giant feather, and carried her back.

He shoved her onto the chair. The sting ran from her tailbone right up to her skull.

'What's your preference?' His voice was sharper; at last her behaviour was pushing him. 'The chair or the bed?'

'*Excuse* me?'

He wrapped the rope around his hand. 'You're going to accept this sooner or later. I didn't want to spend long doing this, but you're *obviously* having difficulty with it. I'll need to keep you from causing any harm to yourself.'

'You are *not* tying me down.'

'That's my decision,' he replied, less patient by the second. 'Do you accept that you're a vampire?'

He waited. She wondered what he was expecting her to say. In the end, she shrugged. 'No.'

She let him tie her wrists and ankles. The rope burned where it touched; every microscopic fibre scraped against her skin. She lay down on the bed and tried to keep still. The sheets were itchy. The light burned her eyes. Her heartbeat drummed its constant rhythm in her head.

'How long are you going to keep me here?'

He sat down on the chair and tilted his head to look her in the eye. 'As long as it takes for the hunger to kick in. You won't be able to deny it then.' He got back up.

'What hunger?' she asked, trying her best to follow his gaze without moving.

'The body stops changing within forty eight hours. After that, it becomes stronger, more attuned. Your sight, hearing, smell...all the senses will improve. But your new strength will need a new kind of nourishment to keep those abilities at full power. Without blood, you'll become delusional, and your body will suffer.' He took a small vial out of his pocket. 'I have a few of these to hand. It's blood. Your body needs it now. Will you let me inject you with it?'

'I don't want that thing in me.'

He shrugged and put the syringe back into his jacket. 'Fine. But eventually your body will force you take it.'

'I didn't know vampires were injected.'

'You can't drink from the vein until you've accepted what you are.'

His words sent shivers up her spine. 'I can't.'

'You say that now...' He headed to the door.

It was a task in itself for her to roll over on the bed to look at him. 'Where are you going?'

'You'll benefit from some time alone,' he said. 'The hunger will start to show itself soon. I want you to experience what will happen if you deny your body what it now needs.'

She woke up some time later to an empty room. The light did not sting her eyes as fiercely as before. Her heartbeat was not so loud. Either she was tuning it out, or it was not beating as strong.

Something else was thudding in her ears in its place.

A shadow cast over her face for a second; she focused on the ceiling. She heard the thud again and discovered the perpetrator.

A determined little moth flew into the bulb. The flap of its furry little wings brushed air against her face. She could see every single hair on its back. She could see into its eyes. She watched the insect, fascinated by it, hypnotised. Nothing else existed in that moment but the two creatures; one an insignificant little moth, the other not quite sure what she was at all.

She drifted in and out of consciousness. Each time she awoke she wondered where she was and had to remind herself how she'd ended up there. And as she woke up more frequently, she wondered why Fox hadn't returned.

She was starting to feel irritable and the ropes were burning her skin. Although the aches and pains were lessening, she still wanted to get up.

She thought of ways to retaliate when Fox came back. She would let him think she had let all this go, then take him down when he least expected it. She thought about him as she drifted back into sleep.

The dreams she had were stranger than usual. The faces of victims had gone, replaced by people she had never met. One, a man dressed in a simple woollen cloth robe that obscured his face, hefted a broadsword on his shoulder. The second was barely a man at all. Built like an ox and standing on legs that—while sturdy—shouldn't have been able to carry such a huge frame. The hunch in its back put more emphasis into the decorative crest over its leathery head, where a thick snout and canine fangs hung over a protruding jaw.

Neither man nor beast spoke, and in the moments she saw them, they looked stunned to see her looking back.

The sound of heavy breathing brought her around, and she listened to the deep rumble before she opened her eyes. It was a soothing sound, gentle and constant, like the sound of a father's chest as a child slept upon it.

Her closed eyes scrunched up. The sound was deeper than she was used to. Slowly, she opened her eyes.

Standing at the end of the bed, watching her through eyes that glowed like torches, was this same creature. Its clawed hand was held out expectantly; did it expect her to shake it?

She sat up in bed. She took a precious few seconds to realise what she was seeing. Its eyes were set deep back into its skull and glowed amber, no pupils. It lowered its hand.

It stopped, tilted its head in a universal gesture of curiosity. 'Interesting,' it said.

She froze in place; every fibre in her body was ready to flee. The creature disappeared in smoke and sparks that shocked her awake…

She sighed at the effect this was all having on her. Her body wasn't aching now, but her eyes still stung and her mouth was dry. She stared up at the ceiling and watched the tiny silhouettes of passing lint cross the bulb. Footsteps constantly came and went; she listened until she could discern the men from the women.

She tried to ignore the constant gnawing in the pit of her stomach; the thing that craved its fill. It surged through her arms to her fingertips. When she couldn't bring her arm around, she discovered that Fox had chained her to the bed. She fought against the shackles, her body contorted and she grew angrier with each ferocious heave.

The alien feeling inside crept through her veins and between the pores in her skin, searching. It became more frequent and sharper; it wasn't happy that it couldn't find what it was looking for. Her eyes felt drawn to her wrists. It was only when she struggled up to the metal bed frame and locked her jaw around her own wrist, knowing even then that she was looking for a major artery, she pinned herself against the bed and screamed. The thing inside wrought against her bones and tissue, threatening to break her into pieces. She screamed and screamed, beyond when the lining of her throat begged her to stop.

When Fox came in, she lay on the bed trembling and sobbing. She didn't hear him come in, but her senses heightened when the door clicked shut. She opened her eyes wide, forgetting momentarily that she was bound. She lunged forwards, until the chains locked and threw her back down. She curled her fingers into fists and punched the surrounding area with all her strength, already forgetting Fox was there.

'Catrina,' he said.

She glared back at him. Her breathing was shallow and her chest was closer to vibrating than expanding. The sharp, short noises coming from her mouth said her throat could take no more screaming, although she still wanted to.

'Fox.' She hadn't spoken since he'd left, save for the light mumbling to herself. Her voice had never sounded so hoarse or loud. She tried to cover her ears, but—still chained to the bed—she didn't get far.

Fox moved closer. 'How was it?'

She glared up at him. 'I tried to eat my own arm!'

'Are you going to take the blood?'

She sighed agitatedly. 'Does it look like I have a choice? All I know is I can't hear you properly because people are walking around outside, and every time I breathe, this *thing* acts like it wants to break my ribs.'

He sat down on the bed and turned to her. There were dark circles under his eyes. 'It'll pass. Relax.' He took out a syringe and prepared the blood. She took a few deep breaths, but the hunger could sense a release to its pain and surged forwards. She screamed as it jumped into her throat and started to choke her. Fox moved quickly but without so much as a flinch. He pushed her hard against the bed and, as her body went into a spasm, he jammed the needle into her bicep and plunged the entire elixir into her system.

Her eyes flashed open, pupils contracted until they were no more than the size of pin heads. The effects were instant; the hunger was beat into submission by the strange substance Fox injected. The rush flowed like liquid ice through her burning blood, soothing and invigorating all at once. She felt as though she could lift a ten tonne truck with one hand, if she wanted.

The feeling of unquestionable euphoria was very short-lived, lasting barely more than three seconds, but as it subsided, it took the agony of the hunger with it. She breathed more steadily, letting her body relax in itself once more.

She looked up at Fox. 'That was good.'

He nodded but passed no comment of his own, as he unlocked the chains and helped her to sit. She pushed him away. After a few unsuccessful attempts, she stood without falling.

She turned to him. They'd never really looked at one another without some hidden agenda. Now that she looked at him, he seemed more real.

'What now?'

CHAPTER THREE

They left the safe house with a gracious 'thank you' to the owner. He just nodded. He had seen their kind come and go so often, their social niceties fell on deaf ears. He sat back in his chair, watching her as she left behind Fox.

He shook his head, gave a grunt, and muttered grumpily under his breath: 'Damn vampires are everywhere these days.'

Fox had so much he needed to tell her about the situation, but at that moment he said nothing. He could tell by the way she looked around that she wouldn't hear a word he said. Her deep eyes sparkled with child-like awe in the overwhelming magnificence of the world through the eyes of a vampire.

Every stone had a thousand marks that told stories of where it had been. The leaves on the trees were decorated in exquisite veins. Sounds were even better. In the distance, when she strained, she heard the screech of an owl diving for its meal. In the back of her mind hung the constant low hum of cars. Even the stars were brighter, no longer diminished through the low hanging clouds of the city.

She tasted at the air; it left traces of freshly cut grass, the refreshing chill of a winter's night, the leftover breeze that unravelled through the buildings. She walked ahead of Fox to take it in.

There was something else when she took a breath and let her senses take flight. A metallic but not altogether alien taste stirred all manner of reactions from both her body and mind. It was both warm and cold, angry yet placid, stirred and resting. She stopped and looked to Fox for an answer.

Fox paused momentarily to take her bag. She didn't ask him to but was quietly charmed by his chivalry. He hunched her heavy bag over his carry-all, and still walked without as much as a lean or limp.

'It's the blood,' he explained, as they continued to walk. 'From humans nearby.'

'Will I always sense it?'

He shrugged. 'In a way, but you start to ignore it. In time, your senses distinguish between animals and humans. Right now, your hunger is picking up on every living thing for around a hundred yards.'

The statistic stunned her. 'Jesus. Why didn't I get this in the safe house?'

'You were just born. You probably *could* sense it, but you chose to ignore it. Enjoy this perspective.'

'Which one?'

'Where the world seems *bigger* than you remember,' he said. 'It's something that all newborns go through. It'll pass, so enjoy it while you can.'

The ancient beauty of the new world was wasted on the dark-haired mystery. He had seen far too much of it, and while he would never favour the grey drab of the human mind, sometimes he still thought the world as he saw it lacked the grandeur it deserved. The only thing he watched with quiet admiration was the young woman beside him with a new glide to her step.

He was proud of what he'd accomplished, and for the moment he found it surreal. He expected at any moment to wake up and for none of this to have happened. She was now a vampire; the wheels of Fate were starting to turn.

She walked with mesmerised grace, listening and looking, smelling and tasting, and revelling in senses she had never truly appreciated.

After a few minutes, she stopped and waited for him. 'Where are we heading?'

'Home,' he replied.

'Where's home?'

'You'll see when we get there,' he replied. 'I thought you'd enjoy the walk, since it'll give you chance to grip this new world.'

She thought of the monstrous creature she'd seen, but she was too full of new information and exciting feelings to care about the horrors of a delusional mind.

'Thank you.'

He nodded. 'Besides the blood, the senses are the most difficult aspect of vampire birth to accept.'

She didn't comment. For a minute, her mind was elsewhere. Her head began to hang, as she remembered the situation. 'Did anything happen with Tony?'

'Your apartment was torched.'

'They burned it? Why?'

'I guess it was his way of letting you go,' he replied. 'He thinks you're dead.'

'No,' she said, more to herself. 'He won't be satisfied that I'm dead until he has my body buried in the cemetery. You say it was torched?'

'They made it look like someone had been disturbed while robbing the apartment and panicked. It was believable. No one else in the building even knows who you were, so the police are at a loose end.'

'It was just a warning. He's saying 'If you're dead, you'd better stay dead'.' She looked up at Fox, shrugged. 'That's just his way.'

'Then I recommend you don't disappoint him.' He started to pick up the pace. 'Let's make a move. There are people waiting to meet you.'

She kept a step or so behind him all the way. She could relax and observe the new world. This was all so strange, yet she was accepting it already. Was it wrong to? Perhaps she should've been planning an escape, to find the nearest psychiatrist and tell

them how she was a vampire. But she was enraptured in it all;
even the way she walked was stronger now. She was suddenly
less of a being and more a presence.

They walked for a good two hours. Fox remained silent, only
speaking when she asked him questions. It was natural to be
curious, and he didn't mind going over facts. He identified the
facts from the fiction quickly; she had to know the basics.

She would be living in a vampire 'Clan'. The hierarchy was
similar to a military base. It was a completely self-sufficient unit,
complete with doctors for the wounded and training rooms for
the restless.

Drinking blood was the only thing a vampire had to do
without question. Failure to do this would destroy them. It
wouldn't kill them, as a vampire was beyond mortality, but living
while in a state of perpetual loss would be a fate worse than
death.

Fox didn't go into detail, despite her willingness to learn.
Perhaps he thought too much would confuse or frighten her. Or
maybe he just knew that she'd turn on the attack if incensed with
terror, and he wasn't ready to invoke such feelings. Not yet.

'So going out in the daytime's not such a good idea?' she went
on.

'Not particularly, although there's nothing to stop you.'

She couldn't tell whether he was being serious or making light
of a rather severe handicap. 'And no reflection?'

'We have reflections,' he corrected. 'The stories come from
millennia ago, when the ancient, born vampires didn't have them.
It was said that it was because the reflection was the window into
the soul, and the old creatures simply didn't have them. I don't
know the real reason.'

The makeshift lesson was stopped short as they rounded the
corner to the latest street. While she was not a stranger to the
city, everything here was new to her. It could've been a whole
new city, for all she knew.

Floodlights kicked into action as they approached a derelict-
looking factory. The lights shone from the front doors; two thick
steel doors, old but sturdy, painted terracotta and years overdue

for a fresh coat. There was nothing particularly inviting about the place.

The factory was dead; no lights—save the security ones— emanated from inside. Fox stopped and she walked straight into his outstretched arm.

'We're here,' he announced. She sensed pride in his tone, although she had no idea why. The building looked ready to be torn down.

'This is it?' she asked, coughing immediately to hide her disappointment. 'So this is it,' she repeated, much more neutrally.

'You'll understand once you're inside. The exterior is for cover. We don't want to publicise what we are to the world.' She took a step back at his words. He gestured to the building. 'Let's go.'

They went past the main doors. The building stood apart from others in the area. The ominous leer said without words how much an old building needed space. Catrina automatically thought of Tony and suppressed a laugh.

The path led around the side of the building and headed towards an underground parking lot. There was a full security system installed at the entrance barrier. They went half way down the path. There was a smaller, more concealed entrance here, complete with security key pad and swipe machine.

Fox put the code in. The door clicked open, and the congregation of hundreds of life forces hit her with a reeling blow.

Fox caught her mid-fall and half-carried, half-dragged her through the door, kicking it shut behind him.

Catrina struggled to get away from him. She was quickly losing her serenity; whatever the drug was he'd injected into her was wearing off. She suddenly didn't like being close to him and instead forced herself to walk alone.

The noise of people talking pierced through her ears and into her brain. Yet there was nothing to see but a long corridor, surrounded by a multitude of doors that branched out into the building. There was only one anomaly that struck her. The senses were heightened, as she was accepting for the time being without question. She could smell the press of bodies, excited sweat of people at any kind of social gathering. She could hear hearts beating everywhere, but something was missing.

'I don't sense any blood,' she said aloud.

Fox took the opportunity to reply. 'Do you sense it on me?'

'No.'

'Why would you think that is?'

She didn't have to think very hard. 'Because you're…the same as me.'

'Exactly. You don't sense my blood, as you don't sense your own, and you will not sense the blood of any other vampire.'

She was about to comment, when a sharp pain ran from her spine up into her brain. It crushed at her temples and reminded her again of the trouble she was in. Now the way everything looked and sounded was not so magical.

'I don't feel well.'

'What's wrong?' His voice said little to suggest he was concerned.

'A *lot*,' she snapped suddenly. 'This whole thing has gone straight over my head. I'm just about *now* realising the mess I'm in. I don't even know where I am. I don't know you, I don't know how I got here, and I feel like my head's about to explode.'

He stopped in the middle of the long corridor. 'If you have something you want to get off your chest, I suggest you do it before we get in the main hall. You have an audience waiting.'

She hesitated. '…a what?'

He held back his all-knowing smile. 'Think about it. I've just closed a three-year deal.'

'Don't talk about me like that,' she spat.

He started walking again without waiting for her to follow. 'I'll arrange for you to visit the Infirmary in a minute, but we have to do this first.'

'Do what?' She stumbled slightly as she went after him.

'You have to meet the Clan leader.'

The main hall was at the end of the latest corridor. A rush of raised voices emanated from behind the door. Fox checked himself subconsciously, before he opened the door and led her inside.

The room was nothing more than a huge concrete box. Any signs that the place had been a working factory had been cleared out long ago, covered with industrial concrete fill and badly plastered walls. The ceiling perimeter, a metal-frame walkway, was all that remained of the building's history.

Now the room was a makeshift club. There was a small bar at the back wall, manned by a single barman, whose efficient nature meant he was more than capable. A few comfortable armchairs and circular mahogany tables were dotted across the room. This was not the kind of headquarters she was used to.

There were in excess of fifty other people in the room. They were all chatting idly in their own small circles. Not many of them noticed the two arrive, but those who did stopped what they were doing and gave them their full attention.

Catrina was still looking around, catching a few of the curious gazes. It took little more than a few seconds worth of Fox's glare, and everyone was back to their own business.

At the bar, the man who had been waiting for her over three years put down his untouched drink. Fox's mentor turned on the seat, a soft smile starting in the corner of his mouth. He rose and started towards them.

They met half way across the room. Catrina's eyes stopped wandering and set on the one she instantly knew was the one in charge. He had a look that said his true age clearly surpassed his thirty-something body.

She didn't notice Fox leave. He headed for the bar, where he and the barman exchanged a few quiet words. The barman looked towards her with a smile on his face.

The black man held out his hand in a fluid motion. He took less than a second to analyse and evaluate her and to reach a conclusion.

He drew his hand to his chest.

'I am Attilla.' His voice was absent of real emotion, and yet every syllable was overpowering with each breath. She could tell that he was critically studying her, thus far giving no indication that he'd found flaws. 'I'm glad you are finally with us, Catrina.'

The silence that fell between them was not tense. It lacked the apprehensive moments that she and Fox had already shared. She spotted Fox by the bar.

Attilla noticed. 'I trust he was not too abrupt with you?'

She smiled at his choice of words.

'He was…' She glanced again. He was holding a tumbler of double neat whiskey in his hand and taking short drags of his latest cigarette. '…assertive.'

He smiled at the description of his colleague's character. 'That's just his way.'

The words put her at ease the second they fell from his lips. Attilla watched her looking towards the bar and saw that she was uneasy. 'Is something wrong, Catrina?'

'I've not come to terms with it yet.'

'No one expects you to so quickly.' He motioned to the bar. 'Would you like to sit down?'

She nodded and let him take her through the crowd. The place and people were welcoming enough. In time she could see it as home. A few eyes followed them across the room. She assumed the attention was due to the vampire she was with.

Attilla remained standing as she sat down beside Fox.

The barman clicked his fingers to grab her straying attention. He was a young man, twenty at the very most; his little grey eyes glistened with the candour of youth. His thick mop of unruly black hair fell into them, and he had to cock his head back a few times. She took in every tiny motion he made. Her perceptions were giving her a headache. 'You strike me as a beer drinker.'

'Please,' she replied with a grateful smile. He pulled a bottle from under the bar and flipped the lid off in one quick arc of his hands. He had remarkable technique for one so young. He barely had chance to put the drink down before someone else wanted his services.

As she put the bottle to her lips, a stomach-churning nausea washed over her. She swayed marginally but kept her composure, hoping no one would notice.

Attilla was the first one to come to her aid.

'How are you feeling?' He spoke quietly so her behaviour drew minimal attention.

'I'll be fine,' she assured him, hooking her hand around the beer bottle. She threw Fox a quick but very sharp look, who stood to join Attilla.

'She hasn't fed, has she?' he asked Fox directly.

'I didn't think she'd cope,' Fox said to justify his actions. 'She wasn't receptive as a whole.'

Attilla said nothing in response to his own student's opinions. He went back to Catrina.

'The nausea you're feeling is caused by starvation,' he explained gently. 'Fox believed your body could not take blood to begin with. He was right not to force it and you should not be angry with him.'

'I'm not angry at him for that,' she said.

Attilla let the comment slide. 'We were going to give you a room, but I think you'd benefit from a night or two in the Infirmary.' He turned slightly. 'Fox, a word, if I may?'

He led Fox discreetly away from the bar so quiet words could pass between them. Without their eyes on her, Catrina let her mask slip and clutched her head.

The barman noticed. 'You okay there?'

She looked up and feigned a reassuring nod. 'Hmm…fine.'

'You don't look…'

His sentence was cut short by the sound of a loud door slam. Catrina looked over to the north side of the room, like most had, where a young woman stood. She posed for the stunned looks she was getting. She grinned; Catrina had never seen a smile so wide. She looked like a Cheshire Cat, with an unruly bob of curled red hair that fell into her bright green eyes. She waited, hands on hips and cocked to one side, posing for an invisible photographer. Suddenly, it all dropped and she walked across the room, oblivious. Everyone else went back to their business. Catrina, however, ignored all her principles and continued to stare.

The girl spotted Catrina, and the grin spread back across her rounded face. She trotted over. The barman took to wiping the bar surface.

Once closer, the girl's walk turned into a swagger. Catrina tried not to stare once she realised she was the only one in the room doing so. The redhead sat down beside her, grinning from ear to ear, and held out a hand that she shook politely.

'The name's Bond,' the girl said in a bad Scottish accent. '…James Bond.' With the girl's hand wrapped around hers, there was little Catrina could do but smile politely. '…That's a joke…I'm Rose.'

'…Catrina.'

'I know, I know. You're like a celebrity around these parts.'

'Fox mentioned that.'

'Uh huh,' she agreed. 'While I'm on the subject,' she took a digital camera from the backpack she carried. 'One for the yearbook.'

Catrina's expression darkened, as her picture was taken with a quick flash. 'What was that for?'

'Archives,' she explained, turning the camera on herself, pulling a face to capture the moment. 'Nothing personal. Everyone has to have one.'

She threw the camera back into the bag. She met Catrina's worried gaze, laughed lightly to herself.

The barman felt it was time to intervene. 'She doesn't feel well.'

'Can't you see we're having a conversation here?' she said, raising her hand to emulate ignorance to his statement. She turned to Catrina. 'You're feeling under the weather? Yo, Fox! Your urchin's not feeling too peachy.'

Fox looked over from his conversation with Attilla and nodded. Others had turned at Rose's statement, and Catrina suddenly wished she had not mentioned anything.

'Attilla suggested she's to be taken to the Infirmary,' Fox said. 'Will you do it?'

She stroked her chin to ponder the request. 'I guess that would be the courteous thing to do.' She hopped off the stool. 'Come on, Shorty.'

Rose linked her arm and guided her away. Catrina knew she had to leave Fox and Attilla to discuss her arrival. They went through the furthest door on the north wall with a number of curious eyes on them.

There was another corridor, only there was little chance of getting lost here, as there were only two places to go, no side-passages or complex networks in sight. This was here for the sole purpose of whatever was inside the one room that was there. The door at the far end was an exit to the building. The only other room was accessible via two replica swinging hospital doors.

'Can I ask you something, Rose?'

'You can try.'

'Well, I was thinking...'

'I find myself doing that sometimes. It always passes. So what's on your mind?'

'Is Fox always so...?'

'Pissy? Why, yes he is. I wouldn't worry. He's just on his period.'

Catrina hid her smile. 'I get the feeling I've done something wrong.'

Rose shook her head. 'Trust me, it's not you. Fox...well, Fox has issues. And even though he'll never tell you what's bugging him, he'll always make sure you're aware of it.'

'Sounds great,' Catrina said sarcastically.

'Doesn't he? He's not so bad. Compared to Jessie, he's a walk in the park.'

That was a new one. 'Who's Jessie?'

Rose smiled. 'You'd be better off not knowing, really. But hell, who am I to withhold information? Jessie's a kid vampire. Fifteenth Century, I think, maybe earlier. I've never asked. Don't really care.' She shrugged and let out a laugh. 'Anyhoo, she and Attilla started the Clan in the early twentieth. Jessie's the second in command. But...' She looked around carefully to check no one could hear. She whispered into Catrina's ear. 'You wanna listen to me when I say that Jessie is not the kind of vampire to get on the wrong side of. And Jessie is a *very* easy old woman to get on the wrong side of. She's crabby and doesn't take much of a shining to anyone. Watch yourself around her.'

Catrina didn't like the tone in her voice, but before she had a chance to question in detail the presence of a 'child-vampire' further, they had reached the doors. The vampire linking her arm doubled back to shove them open with a kick.

The walls inside were pasty white. Test tubes bubbled or rested in their racks. Various liquids sat patiently in numerous beakers waiting to be used. The faint smell of leftover chemicals drifted through the sterile air.

Even *more* doors networked out from this laboratory. It was a central area to other parts of the building because of its location within the factory.

'Corey!' Rose yelled. 'We got a new specimen!'

Corey, a twenty-something man, wandered into the room. He looked at Catrina over the rim of his glasses that had slipped down his nose and smiled warmly. He had a usual 'scientist' look about him: a little gangly but not without his charm. His dusty-brown, shoulder length hair took no particular style. He removed his glasses to show bright hazel eyes.

'Sorry?' he asked. 'Didn't quite catch that.' He smiled at Catrina. 'Hi there, you new?'

Catrina nodded. 'Apparently.'

'Corey, this is Catrina...Catrina, Corey,' Rose said to introduce them, crossing her arms over one another to simulate her words. He joined them and shook her hand graciously.

'What seems to be the problem?' he asked.

'She's not feeling too bright,' Rose said on her behalf. 'You know how it is...girl meets boy, boy turns girl...girl doesn't get enough of the red stuff...girl feels all cranky...'

'Thank you for that, Rose,' Corey said, humouring her as he motioned for Catrina to follow. 'Are you alright for walking?'

She was grateful for his concern. 'Yeah, I'm okay.'

'And I'm going,' Rose added, unlinking herself from Catrina. 'Places to go, people to kill.'

With that as goodbye, she left them to it. Corey led Catrina to an examination table and helped her to sit down. The metal was cold. She watched Corey take her blood pressure, while he continued to smile with fixed reassurance.

'Am I going to live?' she asked lightly.

'You'll be fine,' he said with a laugh. 'At least you're taking this all with a pinch of salt.'

'I'm not,' she said, more sullen.

He stopped smiling, lifting his head to look her square in the eye. 'If you're struggling with it, it's best you talk about it sooner rather than later.'

'I'm aware of that.'

'Are you feeling okay?' he asked. She sighed and opened her mouth to argue. Corey smiled and interrupted. 'I know, I know, you feel like shit.'

'Is that the scientific term?'

They smiled at one another. Corey sat down on the chair opposite the examination table. 'What you're suffering from is like a very mild form of anaphylactic shock.'

'An allergic reaction?'

'In a sense,' he agreed. 'Chances are you've rejected the blood. It'll take a few more days for your body to get acquainted with your new feeding habits.'

'I was given an injection.'

Corey nodded to himself. 'I know, Fox took it last week. It's known as 'the city's best kept secret'. Very potent blood with sedative properties. It can be very powerful...' He paused. 'Sometimes it's too much, especially for newborns.'

'And that's what I am?'

'That's right.'

'Are *you* a vampire?'

He stood up, smiling. 'Yes, I am. I'm also a doctor, but I'm guessing that means nothing to you right now.'

'So you *are* a vampire,' she checked.

He let out a laugh. 'Just like hundreds of people in this building. Just like you.' He lifted her head and shone a small torch light in each eye to check her pupil reaction. 'You're a vampire, too.'

'Just like that?'

He flicked the torch off. 'Just like that.'

He searched around the table for another instrument. She looked at the palms of her hands as they rested on her thighs.

'Can I ask you something?'

'Shoot.'

'Am I acting like a person who's just been turned into a vampire should?'

He took another smaller torch and tilted her head to one side while he checked in her ears. 'Turning affects everyone in different ways. Judging on the number of newborns I've seen come in here, I'd say you're taking it pretty well.'

'My head hurts.'

'It's a side effect of the drug. I'll get you some painkillers.' Again, he smiled. She could tell he loved his work in helping people. She tried to picture him with fangs, but it wouldn't form. Right there he was a hardworking doctor, a helpful medic, and just a man.

He helped her off the table. At the back of the lab was a door with a blocked-out window. He took her inside to a room that resembled a small hospital ward.

The walls were adorned with a few watercolour pictures to lighten the dull atmosphere. There were a dozen or so beds, each one laden with basic eiderdowns. One bed was already occupied. The man recovering there was motionless, save for a diminutive motion when he breathed. His viciously inflicted wounds were covered in bandages, and a patch covered one eye.

Corey led her to a bed at the furthest end and helped her to lie down. He presented her with a small syringe wrapped in sterile plastic. She flinched as force of habit on seeing it.

'I'm not a huge fan of needles.'

'Not many people are.' He removed the plastic wrap. 'It'll help you sleep. Deep breath.' He gave her the drug, swabbed the needle mark and threw the syringe in the nearest bin. 'It'll take a while to kick in. Just relax. I'll check on you in a couple of hours, but that should see you through to tomorrow night. Tomorrow I'll give you a check over and probably let you out.'

'Thanks,' she said uncertainly, lying back. The nausea had diminished now, but with what she'd been through, she reasoned that spending the first night under the watch of a doctor was for the best. He left her to get acquainted with the surroundings with a light 'goodnight'.

She closed her eyes and briefly relived recent events. It was a lot to take in. Everyone was being very receptive, she noticed, towards her arrival. This idea trudged the memory of Fox's initial conversation, where he had said they had been following her for three years. Her eyes opened. She glanced around warily. He hadn't explained why it had been so long, and it didn't make sense. Most probably, the choice of who would become a vampire was strict, but she was certain that no one would spend three years carefully monitoring her every motion, only to have her do the same thing she had done as a human.

These questions would have to wait, as she felt her eyelids trying to close. The night had been long, and she could feel the drug having effect. She lay back on the sheets, feeling each crease against her skin. She was too exhausted to care, and before she knew it, she was asleep.

*****

It was an uneasy rest, and she woke up feeling worse than before. She was alone in the Infirmary: the man who had been in with her was gone. The absence of sound left her uneasy. She went to the door and leant out into the laboratory. There was no sign of life.

'Corey?'

The air gave no reply.

She was back in the factory's main hall in moments. It was so quiet now. The blacked-out windows gave no indication to how long she'd been sleeping, and as she checked her wrist she realised she wasn't wearing her watch.

She made it halfway across the empty room. A light breeze picked up from behind and urged her forwards. Driven by curiosity, she wandered further across the floor. Her feet sank into the concrete with every step.

A few cautious steps in, and a low rumble shook the unsteady ground.

She stopped in her tracks; this wasn't where she started. The walls had a life to them, they moved as if breathing, and the low hum hooked her attention. It was more than a feeling; the walls expanded, drawing in breath.

The surroundings changed with their presence, a sultry, surreal painting that shifted reality to its own.

She turned, and came face to face with the amazingly monstrous creature she'd seen in the safe house. His glowing celestial eyes fixed on her. His stump-like neck and heavy, square shoulders helped support the wide crest of bone atop the unusual head. Almost two feet taller than she, the creature crouched to compensate.

He took a second to rub at the shackles bound at his wrists. The chain that would've held them together was snapped, but the shackles were made of iron, something the creature couldn't remove.

She staggered backwards, poised between confusion and stark fear. Whether this thing was trying to disguise itself as a man and failing, or if this was his true appearance; neither option seemed effective.

He shuffled precariously on his feet, which—like the wrists— had once been bound. He stood as straight as he was able, saw her anxiousness and stepped back.

He dipped his head graciously as greeting. She backed up to watch him in his entirety, partially wanting to return the gesture.

'Who are you?' she asked. If this *thing* was not going to attack, she had every right to learn more.

'You ask as though you care.' His tone suggested he was offended, though she wasn't sure why. She was also not sure why she cared. This thing was a monster.

The creature took another step back, straightening his hunched back with a loud crack of bones. He must've spent a long time restricted.

She looked at him, watching the smallest of motions become giant signs that he was genuinely confused. She would venture to saying he sounded bitter, as though she had no reason to ask.

'I want to know who you are.'

But then he laughed, and she shuddered at the harrowing tone that chilled her more than anything she had ever encountered. It was a tortured noise; whatever pain he'd endured came through his voice.

'You don't understand,' he said. 'You *don't* want to know. You long for nothing less.'

The world around her was gone for an instant with a thud, but it returned with the creature still staring at her. She could see it in his eyes: the world was losing its grip. He smiled again, moving closer. She didn't move away.

'To understand the mystery of this world, you must know the truth.'

There was another heavy thud, and it felt like someone had punched her in the stomach. The world disappeared for longer this time. He was still there: she could hear him breathing through the void. 'The truth will invoke fear in you, and that is what you do not want to know. You long to know what the mystery before you is,' he continued questioningly, as the images flooded into each other; his leathery skin merged with the surroundings. 'I am nothing more than the consequence of a chaotic mind.'

When she finally woke up, she wasn't lying in a cold sweat, her heart wasn't racing, and she wasn't afraid. She was, however, already sitting upright in the Infirmary bed.

The images drifted away, replaced with undesirable confusion. She wanted to find some way back into the dream to finish what the strange creature had started. Regardless of what he said, she was convinced that he was more than a figment of her imagination.

CHAPTER FOUR

The daytime silence in the factory's main hall was shattered by the clip of heels against the concrete floor. A young child walked through the room like a ghost. She was no older than ten, yet she carried herself with more grace than any noble. It was a wonder the air did not part for her.

Her auburn hair rippled in long curls over a delicate Victorian dress. Her mouth was open just enough to show flawless petite fangs. Her skin was ivory-white and did not have the smallest hint of a blemish. She was the perfect specimen of a child in all respects, save for her eyes, which reflected only pure animal ferocity.

Jessie turned at the sound of a door opening elsewhere in the hall. Her smile was disconcerting, as Attilla joined her.

'One would almost be suspicious of your afternoon wanderings, Attilla.' Her voice was young and old, naive and wise, dangerous and beguiling. She had a strong British accent. A born aristocrat, she had maintained her lineage completely through her centuries of life, not an aspect about her appearance had changed.

He was accustomed to her behaviour and the dispassionate way she addressed him. The two had been together too long to surprise one another.

'I take these quiet times to think,' he replied with a courteous smile.

She nodded her little head contentedly, as they walked towards the bar. 'You are such a pensive creature. If I did not know better, I would assume you a lost soul. But I understand your restlessness. It is this monotonous waiting, is it not?'

He nodded with the shared understanding they had about the situation but gave nothing in reply. She did not give him time.

'The means to an end can often make existence seem wretched.' She touched one of the leather barstools. Her nails clawed deep lines across the material. When she caught his gaze, her eyes were dancing. 'But I am willing to have patience for the consequence.'

She was the picture of innocence, a perfect little girl, but the way she spoke, the way she scratched the leather like a cat; it was otherworldly and savage.

He coughed gently. 'Will you hunt tonight?'

Melancholy shadowed her face, turning away at the question. 'Of course. I have no desire to remain within the building's confines, no matter how unacceptable I am to the outside world.'

'My apologies, Jessie.'

Her smile this time was lighter and more civil. 'There is no need for apology. What is said…is said.' She took a deep breath, looking towards the main doors. 'Is it not yet evening? I awoke this afternoon and found myself wandering as blindly as you. Time may have escaped me.'

Attilla checked the vintage clock that hung behind the bar. 'The sun will still be out.'

'Ah.' There was bitterness in her utterance. 'I understand the Vessel is amongst us now.'

His hesitation was so brief she did not have chance to catch it. 'Fox brought her last night. Perhaps you could meet her this evening?'

'I have no conscious desire to *know* her, Attilla. As long as she serves her purpose, she is no more important to me than any of the others.'

His lips parted to comment, but he held his tongue and nodded impartially. 'As you wish.'

'One other thing,' she said, moving away from him. 'A stranger came here yesterday. I had him contained until you could see to him.'

She moved away without any farewell gesture. She stalked with ancient grace, and he knew she was with her own thoughts now.

Ever the gentleman, he waited until she was gone before moving on to tend to his latest errand.

He went quietly and unobtrusively into the laboratory.

Corey was sitting at one of the workbenches and did not notice Attilla arrive; his mind was rightfully occupied with the delicate procedure he was undertaking. He placed a disc of thick, maroon-coloured liquid onto the worktop, reached for a pipette and extracted a sample. Attilla waited for the man to place the apparatus down before he spoke.

'Corey?'

He looked up. His momentary shock passed with a brief nod. 'Attilla.'

'Have you been working all day?'

'No, no, I caught a few catnaps, don't worry,' he said. 'I'm not handling dangerous chemicals while suffering from sleep deprivation…again. What can I do for you, sir?'

'How's Catrina?'

Corey shrugged. 'She seems fine. Just had a rough start. She didn't have any surface wounds.' He gestured to the nearest chair.

Attilla did not take the seat offered, more concerned over Jessie's report. 'I've been told someone was brought in yesterday.'

Corey laughed. 'Dragged kicking, screaming and cut to the bone. It was horrible, sir. She's losing her grip, if you ask me.'

'You shouldn't question her.' There was a hint of warning in his voice. 'Perhaps her actions were justified.'

'I'm sorry, I'm sure they were.' Corey sat back and indicated towards the Infirmary. 'We saw to his wounds and he'll make a full recovery.'

'Can I see him?'

Corey laughed again, this time as though to a personal joke.
'Sure.' He slid the glasses back over his nose.

Thrown by Corey's smirking, Attilla nodded as politely as was
necessary and strode across the room.

He took a second to notice Catrina resting in the far corner. Her
face was contorted, as though she was in an unpleasant dream.
He expected no less; anyone with her experiences would suffer
while sleeping.

He turned his attention to the man who Corey had tended to.

The man was late twenties, a shaved head and small
moustache forming on his upper lip were his only distinguishing
features. His faded skin was mixed race. Attilla knew him. The
face that looked back with an attempt at a smile was familiar.
One eye shared Corey's amusement, the other was covered with a
patch.

His pleased reaction was suppressed from the severe beating
he had taken. One arm was broken, but he still outstretched his
other and managed to smile.

Attilla shook his hand politely. 'It has been a while, Ice.'

'It's good to see your security's tightened,' Ice replied, a well-
timed pain shooting through his arm, as he went to clutch it. He
seethed, his fangs protruding slightly, before the pain passed.

'This is not the best of times,' Attilla said gently.

'It never is.' It was not a harsh remark, merely a statement of
fact. 'Don't worry, I'm not asking to stay. But Christ, man, she
nearly had my eye out.'

'You're on her ground. You know how territorial she can be.'

'I know,' he said. 'I just…didn't know where else to go. I
got chased out of my city.'

Ice was a vampire who lived on the edge, which was why he
spent most of his life running. The last the Clan had heard, he
had set roots in a popular city, drawn by the lifestyle and
vivacious nature of the people there. Most vampires preferred
more unknown cities, where they could hide in obscurity,
disguised by unrelated crime and violence. Unfortunately for Ice,
his choice of lifestyle had landed him in the same district as the
Slayer Headquarters for the entire country.

Attilla knew, just by the implicative way he spoke, that his problems would be connected in some way to their most feared enemy. As his expression changed to one of understanding and empathy, Ice gave a slight nod.

'I didn't really *want* to come here, either,' he reiterated, which was taken good-naturedly. He sat up again, causing the sheets to slip. It showed a few more surface wounds that were worse than the rest. Attilla's frown deepened. Ice was not a threat; Jessie knew that. 'I wasn't expecting much of a welcoming committee.'

'Did you go to your mother?' It seemed reasonable to assume that he would have gone to family before risking his safety by returning to a Clan that felt such negativity towards him.

'I don't know where she is,' he replied with a shrug. 'I tried to find her, but you know what she's like.'

'She won't be found unless she wants to be.'

'Yeah, and she doesn't want to be found by me.' He paused to arrange his thoughts. 'I wanted to see my sister. Ebony said she'd help me out, but Jessie was the one I ran into first.'

'It's understandable for Jessie to be cautious,' he said in her defence, which she would not want but certainly needed. 'You were never much affiliated with one another.' Again, he looked at the wounds. It had been a day, but some were so deep that they had not started to heal. 'But I do not condone her actions against you. This level of hostility was unnecessary.' He stood back and looked the rogue vampire over. He gave a gracious nod when he had finished. 'I will give my consent for you to stay here until it is safe for you to return home, or at the very least, until you find residence elsewhere in the city.'

'Thank you, Attilla.'

Attilla nodded but left the room without a word.

Corey looked up on hearing him emerge from the Infirmary. He was not acknowledged, and Attilla walked across the room in short, aggravated steps.

'Are you alright, sir?' Corey asked.

He kept walking, giving him a small respective look to acknowledge his concern. 'She wanted him *dead*.' The scientist bowed his head. Attilla stopped at the door and commanded: 'Watch over them both.'

He left the room before Corey had a chance to reply. The room fell into an uneasy silence, and Corey knew that Attilla was on his way to find her.

CHAPTER FIVE

Corey gave Catrina a quick check up when she awoke the next night. After giving her the all-clear, he directed her towards the main hall. As she neared the door that gave passage to the area, the flare of excited noise said other people were already up.

A mass of bodies greeted her. She could distinguish they were all vampires from the lack of blood. They came as varied as any other race, all with individual faces to match their lineage and clothing to suit personal preference.

They went by with slight regard for one another. A few gave her a friendly nod when she caught their gaze, and in return she gave them a pleasant yet bewildered smile. It made her feel insignificant to walk amongst so many immortal beings; it took the suggestion of speciality away from the entire concept.

The barman spotted her and raised an arm to gesture her over, but someone else had her attention.

'Cat-*rin*-a!'

Her own name pierced through the air. She turned to see Rose bouncing through the crowd. A few vampires gave her a disdainful look, most an amused one, all of which she ignored, shoving through the horde.

She threw her arm over Catrina's shoulder and dragged her towards the bar. 'So, how was night *numero uno?*'

Catrina recalled the creature staring at her in the dream. The imperial glow of his amber eyes remained when she blinked the vision away.

'*That* exciting, huh?' Rose's voice struck through Catrina's thoughts. 'Where's the enthusiasm? Be proud, Shorty, you've taken a step up the evolutionary ladder!'

The factory hall had doubled the number of vampires it had accommodated the night before; there was so much noise. With one arm around Catrina's neck, Rose indicated to the people. 'This is our Clan...me casa su casa.'

'I didn't think there'd be so many.'

'We're the biggest Clan in the city. You'll get to know people in time, but jeez, most of these guys even *I* don't know, and *I've* been here over half a century!'

Two vampires dressed as bouncers stood at the opened main doors. The streetlights cast a warm glow across the room, as a small throng of people headed out. Not many vampires left. Most crammed around the bar to get served from the solitary barman.

'Are we going out?' Catrina asked, casting her eyes to the exit.

'Not me and thee, no,' Rose replied. 'You're still a newborn, and...no offence...but you ain't my responsibility.'

A vampire politely offered Catrina his seat. Rose leant on the bar, palming the top to get the young barman's attention. Catrina focused carefully on him. There was something different about his scent. It was musty; not so much old as just *aged*.

Rose shouted 'Sonny!' after her patience left her. He abruptly finished serving and turned around to face her.

'Patience is a virtue, you know.'

'Bullshit.'

'What'll it be?'

'I don't...' she pondered, '...know.'

The barman rolled his eyes, distracted by the vast number of others calling his name. He served a few more people, and when the inevitable crush slowed, he returned to Rose and the new vampire sitting beside her.

'How are you feeling now?' he asked Catrina curiously, trying to get her attention. She didn't hear him, straining to find Fox or Attilla through the horde. 'It's Catrina, isn't it? Hello?'

'Yep, that's Catrina,' Rose said, filling in for her.

Catrina blinked. 'What?'

Rose motioned towards the barman. 'This is Sonny. Demonic entity of the jackass dimension.'

His rounded little face scrunched up. 'Excuse me?' he said sharply, placing the cloth he used to clean the glasses on the bar.

Rose already had her hands up defensively. 'You know I'm only jealous of your career choice.' She glanced over his shoulder to the shelves. 'I'll have a double vodka.' She nudged Catrina in the shoulder. 'How 'bout you?'

Catrina shrugged carelessly. 'A beer's fine.'

She didn't really want a drink. She was still adjusting to the noise. Everything was amplified, from the shuffle of the feet to the creaking of the steel doors as they were constantly closed and opened.

Rose jerked a thumb at Catrina. 'And a beer for the fledgling, my good man.'

Catrina watched him go, with Rose's description of the young man repeating in her mind. Once he was out of earshot, she spoke up. 'He's a...demon?'

'Yeah,' Rose replied, with tight smile in the corner of her mouth. '...and he's a little...' She tapped her forehead with one finger. 'Over the rainbow, if you know what I mean.' She looked at Catrina expectantly, but her brows knotted.

'No, I don't.'

'Couple of sandwiches short of a picnic, apples short of a basket, got a few loose screws, lost his marbles, the lights are on upstairs but nobody's home...you know, *crazy*?'

Catrina resisted the urge to laugh at the irony. 'What makes him different from a vampire?'

'Not much,' she replied. 'It's more a status thing these days.'

Catrina wanted to ask more, but her senses were taken with something else, an overpowering yet so faint a scent that she was surprised she noticed it. She turned to see Fox walking across the room; his cologne and general appearance were distinctive enough to turn anyone's head. He had the same effect on the vampires: others made a conscious effort to move out of his way, which gave him evident authority. She wondered if it effected his ego.

Sonny returned with their drinks and welcomed Fox into their company with a short nod. 'The usual?'

Fox nodded as acknowledgement of the welcome and an affirmative gesture to the question. Rose waved her hands frantically in the air at someone she recognised and left without any goodbye. Fox's eyes drifted after her for a moment, while he took out his first cigarette of the evening and lit it.

Sonny passed him the tumbler of double neat whiskey, before someone else wanted his attention.

'How are you feeling now?' Fox ventured.

Catrina took a deep breath to tell him about the dream, but then thought better of it. '...Fine. Fox, Rose said I wasn't her responsibility.'

Fox's gaze shifted from the clock. 'That's because you're not.' He tasted at the liquor, while she tensed. He saw her tiniest defensive movement. 'You're a newborn. You can't face the world head-on yet.'

'Whose responsibility am I then?'

'Mine.' His look said more than words.

He finished the whiskey in a single mouthful and could feel her glare burning into him. He gave her a sideways glance but said nothing.

Before she had chance to think of a response, Fox straightened his posture and looked around. She was soon to follow, as she noticed the noise in the hall dim a fraction before continuing at its current level.

Attilla walked amongst the vampires like a god among men. He gave a few of the congregation polite nods, which they all returned immediately. His eyes moved towards the bar, face betraying nothing of his thoughts, but it brightened on seeing the two of them. He was stopped every now and then by a well-meaning vampire with a problem. Sonny brought Catrina and Fox another drink while they waited.

It took the leader of the Clan over ten minutes to make a twenty second walk, as he dealt with every enquiry that came his way. Everyone was respectful, but soon they surrounded him. After a while, and at his quiet command, they let him pass. It was reverence in its purest form.

Fox got to his feet, and she felt obliged to do the same. She had spent enough time in Tony's company to know when to show respect.

Attilla stopped in front of them, nodding in the same polite gesture he had to the rest. His eyes drifted past Fox, more interested in her.

'How did you sleep?' he asked her. Again, she saw the creature standing there. She couldn't tell Attilla about it, either. He wouldn't understand.

'Fine,' she replied, quickly adding 'thank you', to which he smiled and shifted his attention to Fox.

'And you?'

Fox just nodded.

Attilla smiled to himself and glanced back to the crowd of vampires that had clamoured for his advice. 'There isn't enough time in the world for me to support their burden.' He directed his next comment at Fox. 'More concerns come to me every night now, because of the Awakening.'

Catrina's ears pricked up.

'What can I do to help?' Fox asked.

Attilla shook his head appreciatively. 'Nothing. I'll deal with them all. You have enough to worry you for the moment. But I doubt any of us will rest much over the next few months.'

Sonny shuffled over. 'What can I get you, sir?'

He shook his hand dismissively. 'Nothing, thank you, Sonny,' he said, and just as quickly, the barman left. Attilla looked back at her. 'We should introduce you to some of the others.'

He started across the hall. Fox gestured for her to follow, waiting until she had begun walking before following. She saw the congregation watch her. She wondered how she was viewed within the Clan, hoping that it would eventually be with some of the same admiration they showed those she walked with.

Attilla held the door open for them both, as Fox led her off into the network of passages. They stopped at a door that lacked any distinct markings. People were talking inside, and she could tell that one of them was Rose.

The room was designed for conferences and meetings, furnished with a single, long, rectangular table. In the far left corner was the monitor of a surveillance camera for the parking lot. The pictures were not very clear, but her new eyesight meant she could see every detail perfectly.

Everyone was quiet. All eyes set on them, or more specifically, on her. Before she could analyse the strangers, Attilla stepped into the room and addressed them.

'These are your colleagues,' he said, gesturing to the four vampires at the table. 'In time, you will become familiar with the other Clan members, but I don't want to overwhelm you.' He motioned to Rose. 'You have already had the pleasure of meeting Rose.' His hand indicated Corey, who chewed contentedly at the stem of his glasses. '...and Corey,' he added. Corey sat upright and put the glasses into his pocket, looking at Catrina with a civil nod.

Her eyes fell of their own accord to the woman sitting beside the doctor. A dark-skinned beauty, arms folded, only half-attempting a hospitable look. She was very beautiful, with long black hair and treacle-coloured dark eyes, but she kept it behind the cold spark she was emitting. If anything, she showed a lack of interest.

'Ebony is one of our more gifted associates,' Attilla continued. 'She is a temporary addition to our Clan.' She looked Catrina over once without showing much other than indifference, but she nodded all the same.

Attilla's eyes drifted to the last vampire. The introductions were not over, but he looked more confused than welcoming now.

The vampire's physique was medium but masculine, with nothing short of supermodel looks. Waves of dark blonde hair fell to his broad shoulders, a chiselled jaw without a trace of stubble, and stunning green eyes that looked at Catrina over the rim of purple-tinted glasses. With one arm slung over the back of the chair, showing off his gold Rolex, he was not what a vampire was expected to look like. Catrina realised she was staring.

'And Louis,' Attilla said in a slightly bemused tone, to which the young man smiled. 'He doesn't live with us, but he helps out with certain matters he's rather talented with. Unfortunately, his presence is not appreciated by many Clan members, because of his choice of lifestyle.' Attilla turned to him more directly, forgetting Catrina for the moment. 'We weren't expecting you tonight. It's probably best if you leave as soon as you can.'

Louis sighed. He caught Attilla's glance and lowered his gaze. 'I know, I'm sorry.' He indicated to the book Ebony was reading. 'Just came to get this. We can finish most off this at my place, but there are things we need to go over, when you get some free time.'

Attilla said nothing but nodded. His schedule would be even busier than planned.

Louis smiled in return, satisfied, and his eyes slid over to Catrina. He moved towards her, offering his hand. She accepted his social nicety with ease. Although he'd been perfectly respectful to Attilla, he had a rebellious edge that made him less deferential than the others.

'You must be Catrina.' He looked to Fox, a smile playing about his lips. 'She's cute.'

Fox gave no response, as the clean-cut vampire sat himself back down and continued to pour over the book with Ebony. Catrina was left open-mouthed at his audacity.

Fox took a seat beside Rose, who was playing a game on her mobile phone. He had barely sat down, before Rose's hand was under his nose. She wasn't looking at him, but he knew what she wanted. He took out his cigarettes and handed her a spare. He also had to pass her his lighter, both of which she took without giving him as much as a glance.

Catrina remained standing with Attilla. As he was about to motion her to take a seat, the door behind them opened.

Tension rose like heat from hot coals. Everyone stopped dead. Rose slowly put her phone down. Fox had considered lighting another cigarette, but now it could wait.

Catrina didn't notice the change at first. She was too shocked at seeing a child below the age of ten in amongst vampires. She guessed it was the same child Rose had warned her about and forced herself to avert her eyes. Jessie headed straight for the stack of books in the far corner, either oblivious to or merely ignoring the presence of everyone else.

The rest of the present company cautiously watched her.

'Jessie,' Attilla said, drawing the attention of the entire room.

She spun on her heel. 'Yes?' There was clear-cut tension between them, but Attilla gave a gentile nod and motioned to Catrina.

'This is Catrina.'

Slowly, the girl's sparkling eyes drifted over the newborn; Catrina shuddered. It was momentary, as Jessie's attention was quick to fade with a disdainful shake of her head.

She locked eyes with Attilla. 'And?'

Attilla gave no response. He didn't assert the same kind of authority over the child. She snatched a book from the stack. 'Another vampire is of no concern to me.' She made her way back across the room without glancing in Catrina's direction. It was probably for the best; no doubt the thing wouldn't have appreciated Catrina's scowl. She stopped beside Attilla, giving him a final contemptuous look. 'Do not plague my mind with inconsequential matters.'

She left with the same disapproving attitude she'd entered with. The room brightened as soon as she'd gone, but no one spoke of the 'experience'.

The rest of the vampires began discussing something Catrina was quickly lost with. She tried to follow the conversation, but it was incomprehensible at best.

A hand touched her shoulder. She turned to look into Attilla's beguiling eyes.

'Walk with me a while.'

The hall was as full as it'd been before. If any had left, more had arrived to fill their place. Sonny was busy. Although it was curious to see the demon working alone, he was coping.

Several people watched the two of them, whether through jealousy or admiration, she couldn't tell. There was an air of demanding regard about Attilla. Catrina had never been one for social order; if he was unpleasant, she would've treated him with the insolence she saw fitting. But he was a gracious, amiable man, and with his obvious troubles as head of the Clan, she had to respect his behaviour.

'I understand how bewildering this is for you,' he said, leading her through *another* door she hadn't been through. 'Change is rarely taken nonchalantly.'

'Hmm.' If 'change' involved dreaming about monstrous creatures, she wasn't going to take it well at all.

'You must have questions?'

'Too many to mention,' she replied with a smile.

A wide metal staircase spiralled up onto the second floor of the factory. The top of the staircase gave entrance to a long corridor, lavishly decorated, giving it an aristocratic look that didn't fit into the factory setting.

There were only three doors in the corridor, one at either side halfway down, and a third at the end. The floor was finished in a fine mahogany, covered with a red and gold patterned carpet down the centre. The walls were papered in soft cream; a mahogany panel ran along the sides to match the varnished floor. It resembled a stately home.

'Your questions?' His insistence was welcomed, but she had no idea where to begin. Too many thoughts plagued her, and despite his obvious intelligence, she was confident he couldn't answer them all.

'Well…' She started laughing, redeeming herself by clearing her throat. '…I'm sorry. This is so strange to me.'

'Perhaps I should start from the beginning, then. No doubt, with your disposition, you would like to know what you will be involved with as part of our Clan?'

'Fox didn't go into much detail,' she admitted.

'He was right not to overwhelm you. Of course, the matter of your work is not what bothers you. It is this conversion to a new species, which I can empathise with, but there is little I can say to comfort you in that respect. The change is not as harrowing as you would imagine. I understand you haven't fed yet?'

She swallowed hard. '…Fed?'

He continued as though she hadn't spoken. 'Feeding is a necessity, something we all have to do. It is possibly the most unpleasant aspect of vampire life, but it is also the core, and it cannot be avoided.'

'I understand.' Actually, she was far from understanding. But she let it pass, in no hurry to concentrate on the small matter of drinking blood until it was *absolutely* necessary.

'In terms of your work, although your situation is more complex, you will initially be working directly with Fox, in the control of the Slayers.'

'Slayers? They're a real threat?'

'Wherever there is something unusual, there will always be something opposing it. In our case, there are humans whose knowledge about our existence has led them to become enemies. Their inability to understand causes them to fear us, which has driven them for centuries in eliminating our kind. As you can see, they have not succeeded.' He took a deep breath. 'Unfortunately, neither have we, and we must fight to survive as they fight to destroy us.'

She could understand the situation quite easily, but it seemed like a hollow existence to always live in hiding. 'You'd think we'd be above them.'

He was smiling; his eyes drifted ahead. 'There are the few of us who think we should not be forced to live in shadows.' He glimpsed at her again. 'But we are an elusive species, Catrina. It would be hard to imagine a world in which we do not hide from the human race. If they knew the truth about us, there would be chaos.'

'So I'm here to help against the Slayers,' she said to herself, looking at him for agreement. He nodded. 'Why is my situation more complex?'

He smiled at her perceptiveness. 'I don't think you'll understand those reasons just yet.'

'I'd still like to know.'

Before he had chance to respond, her new senses took over. The trace essence of blood touched the tip of her tongue. She took a few cautious steps ahead, drawn wholly by her senses. She headed towards the doors half way down the corridor. The door on the left was made of glass. Even closed, she could sense that there was blood behind it.

The room was a delicate and tenderly made makeshift garden, lit by tall lamps. It spanned across the entire side of the second floor of the factory. The entire ceiling covering it was like that of a greenhouse, made out of Perspex, giving sight to the late evening stars. It was nothing short of a masterpiece. Catrina's concern was not with the craftsmanship of the garden, but more on the woman sitting on a smoothed rock, reading.

Catrina frowned, as Attilla stopped with her at the garden's entrance. She waited for an explanation, but he just watched the woman leafing through the book, oblivious to their presence, with a small notebook and pen beside her. There was a worn but tireless look about her, as though every movement was done because it had been done so many times before.

'Who's she?' she asked eventually, slowly realising that he was not going to give her any answer unless she provoked one. 'She's human, right?'

He turned his gaze, giving a nod that looked sorrowful. 'Can you sense the blood?'

She nodded. 'So what's her story?'

'Her name is Maria la Graziano,' he said. 'She is a scientist and a physician.'

'...La Graziano. Is that Italian?'

He dipped his head in response, although it was questionable if he was listening at all. The woman was not a stereotypical Italian, if her golden waves of dark blonde hair were anything to go by. Catrina cast her eyes about the garden, the lure towards the woman and the blood she could sense coursing through her veins was replaced by a curiosity over her presence.

'Why is there a human living here?'

'A series of circumstances brought her here. The reason she is human is something that requires a more comprehensive explanation to the purpose of the Clan itself.'

He'd lost her with that, something she wasn't about to admit. She only hoped that he'd elaborate on it in due time. No doubt he wanted to explain things, it was just a matter of waiting, which she had no choice but to get used to.

'I take it we'll get to that, then?'

He gently touched her shoulder, urging her away from the door. 'Come…I'm sure she does not like being watched.'

They continued down the corridor to the far end. The area's sophisticated feel must have been Attilla's doing and privilege. He gestured her inside.

CHAPTER SIX

It was unquestionably Attilla's living quarters, a large room with one other door, closed so Catrina couldn't see what was on the other side. The décor was more exquisite than outside, with polished wood furniture that matched the door; thick, red velour curtains held by an untarnished brass railing over windows that glared out into blackness, far blacker than the city's night could ever be, corresponding with the ornamental lamps that hung from the cream walls.

Attilla indicated to a bureau desk. 'Have a seat.'

She made her way across the soft carpet. She wished she hadn't been wearing her boots and was consciously aware of every speck of dirt trailing behind her.

'This must be like Hell for you,' she commented, sitting down. He stopped pacing; a look she couldn't fathom passed over his face, but it was gone before she could think much into it. 'Do you have to explain these things to all the new arrivals?'

He shook his head. 'Considering the circumstances within our Clan at present, I thought it best that everything was explained to you directly, and as soon as possible. I believe we have kept enough from you as it is.'

'Fox never got around to explaining why you were tracking me for so long.'

'Your tone tells me you were not impressed with his revelation.'

'Would you be?' she asked. 'I think it was out of order.'

'Apologies for that situation will have to wait,' he said, and for the first time she noticed him hesitate. '...because while our existence is a shock in itself, your situation runs deeper than most. It is more than I can explain in one night, and I honestly doubt you will be able to accept it at this early stage. Will you trust me when I say that it will come in time?'

His eyes spoke of nothing but his sincerity. 'You're saying there's more to my being here other than being an extra set of hands?'

He gave a cautious nod. 'I believe so. But first I want you to understand more of our Clan's purpose, which will be enough conversation for now.'

She sat back and managed a smile. 'Go ahead.'

'...Very well.' He still paused. '...I think first I should explain a little about vampire history, if it will not be too difficult for you to believe?'

Although she nodded, in the back of her mind, she was still a human being. This man was asking her to learn about the history of a race that didn't exist. But the hunger clamped down on her gut; that *definitely* existed. 'I can listen.'

'As vampires, we have a beginning, a source...his name was Aisen, the creator of the Vampire Nation.' He said the name with such admiration, she wondered if she should've bowed at the very mention of it. 'He was the first of our kind, and is still considered the most powerful vampire of all time. He was known as the *Genesis.*'

'The Genesis? Because he was the first?' She could picture him already: sleek black hair, long, black cape, pale face, sharp eyes, and a tiny stream of blood trickling down his chin from his last feed...

Attilla's nod was accompanied by a questionable sigh. 'In part. The name carries more implications than that.'

'Where is he now?' She wanted to meet him, his mere name, *Aisen*, was so alluring, any doubt about the upheld opinion of the Vampire Nation vanished with his name alone.

'He's dead...killed millennia ago.'

She bowed her head for a moment of respect, before continuing. 'I thought vampires couldn't live without their

Master.' She knew the myth of vampires that they revolved around their creator; Mina Harker was 'saved' once Dracula was slain. 'I take it that's not true?'

He shrugged in response. 'We will never know.'

The pieces of the puzzle he'd handed her so far weren't fitting together. If he'd been killed, surely the fact they were there talking about it *proved* they didn't need a Master.

'By the time he was killed, he had already begun what is now known as the Vampire Nation, by creating the bloodline of the Trine to continue his legacy.'

'The Trine?'

'The first people, and according to history, the only people Aisen himself turned. They were his lieutenants, his guardians, his council and his consorts. They became stronger than family. They became his children. It was the Trine that turned humans, but it was Aisen's power that made vampires what they are.'

'So his life was in his children?' she tried.

'...Perhaps,' he said, with uncertainty that still suggested she was wrong. He took another breath. '...When he was murdered, the Trine were there. Their refusal to lose their father was almost strong enough to save him.'

'Almost?' Disbelief laced her question. Although history had its inconsistencies, it only stretched so far before it became unbelievable.

'I cannot say what happened,' he admitted. '...but it is said that his body, though desecrated, did not die. His body is kept under heavy guard in the Crypt of the Noble. His children now exist for the sole purpose of watching over him, waiting for him to live again.'

'Who killed him?'

'Our enemies now were the same back then,' he said with a sigh. 'And vampires were as susceptible then as they are now, even Aisen himself.'

'...*Slayers* killed him?' To think that they would be a danger to vampires in general was understandable, but to say that the source of the Vampire Nation was as weak to human 'Slayers' as the rest was doubtful to say the least. Even suspicious.

While the story so far struck her as more legend than historical fact, to think that children could have such literal 'undying' love for their father was impressive enough.

She edged forwards in the seat.

'Do the Trine know when he'll be brought back?'

He withdrew from the question. This only made her lean closer. There was a twist to the tale.

'The history texts have cited an instance when his body was freed from its stone prison, by rituals performed by the Trine.' There was darkness to his tone that suggested something had prevented Aisen from rising. It couldn't be so simple. It never was. 'It happened at the turn of the last millennium. Everything was prepared. The Trine knew he would be weakened by the years trapped in such an indeterminate state, so they provided him with sustenance. Instead of his body returning to its true state, his spirit passed into a young woman sacrificed to act as a vessel for him.' He cleared his throat and continued with a slightly . ' Of course, the Slayers would never allow the Master to rise. They stopped the ceremony before it could be completed. His spirit was returned to the statue, the Slayers stole the book used to cast the Ritual, and the Vessel was killed. They have never tried again.'

She could only attempt at conceiving the reasons why the Trine had only tried to revive him once. She didn't think about it long, still not feeling much involvement in the tale, although it was now *her* source he was talking about as much as it was his.

Leaning back in the chair, a thought came to her, something that had been mentioned earlier, and was being discussed in the conference room. She hadn't understood it then, but it seemed to make sense now.

'What's the Awakening?' She had jumped to the right conclusion. He held that surprised look with her for a little longer than usual; his face gave away the truth, and she smiled with fresh insight. 'Why has *this* Clan taken on the responsibility of raising Aisen?'

'Circumstance,' he replied softly. Her eyes asked him to elaborate. 'The book,' he continued, 'used by the Trine to raise Aisen was…misplaced by the Slayers, a rather foolish gesture on their part. It spent centuries in the hands of unknowns, passing to kith and kin. Over eighty years ago, I met the last vampire to carry it. When he passed on, his belongings became mine.'

'*You* have the book?' This had all very quickly become much, much too close for her liking. As a story, she could listen easily enough. To consider it a real possibility would take some convincing. 'And when will this 'Awakening' be performed?'

'When the Ritual is deciphered.' Although at first there was a look of anticipation on his face, by the time she looked again, it had fallen into a frown. 'It has taken some time. It is written in a language known only to the Trine, their own creation, as it were.'

She took a double-take at the implication. 'They don't know the Clan's performing the ceremony?' His eyes lowered. 'Why not? Why don't they know?'

'That is Jessie's request.' His tone was low. 'Jessie is a very powerful vampire…but her need for respect and recognition is her greatest driving force, which is her only weakness. She asks that the Trine are not to know.' He saw her open her mouth to ask why, but he quickly held up his hand and continued before she had chance to speak up. 'She believes that when Aisen is Awakened, his praises will be bestowed on those who raised him. She does not want him to think that this was the Trine.'

Catrina frowned. How did Jessie expect to get away with it? Surely, the Trine had a good reason for not attempting this thing again. Maybe it was dangerous. Maybe Aisen's body was so fragile that another attempt would destroy it for good. She hauled herself to her feet. Attilla stepped aside.

'They won't be happy in their offspring stealing their Master's body, only to perform something that they themselves won't do,' she said while pacing, catching him a wary sideways glance. The look he returned said he wholly agreed. She could only assume that Jessie held more power than she'd seen. The reaction from the others had been one of fear. She didn't doubt that Jessie's word was binding. 'You don't expect them to just *let* you take the body?'

'Most of the Clan is in disagreement to her idea towards the exhumation of Aisen's tomb,' he replied. 'I have to agree. But she will not be dissuaded, so I have taken no involvement in it. I do not question her behaviour.'

'But if it goes wrong, the Trine would see it as the Clan's strategy.'

Attilla shook his head. 'No, the Clan would not be held responsible for Jessie's mislaid plans. We would all make sure that she took punishment for her own actions.'

Catrina had spent the last nine years under the impression that it was the job of the underlings to stand in the path of any danger to their boss, whether a political backlash or a bullet. What he was suggesting didn't sit right. 'Wouldn't they protect their leader?'

He shook his head again, his expression growing ever more grim. 'I will not force conduct on my people. They are free to draw their own judgment, and to act on it as they see fit.'

She continued to pace the room, waving her hands slowly through the air in an attempt to ponder. Eventually she stopped in her stride, turning to face him.

'And how does all of this involve me?'

He didn't answer. 'I think this will be enough for tonight. You must be enlightened to your own abilities before I can even begin to explain the true circumstances you are under.' She silently begged for more. Grave robbing and resurrections? This was just getting interesting. And now, still knowing that there was a reason she'd been tracked for three years, but that he wouldn't tell her yet, she itched for answers. It could've been anything, from assisting in the body snatch to guarding the body. Attilla shied away from her stare. 'Catrina, please.'

He headed for the door.

At least now she was aware of the Clan's drive, the concept of the first vampire to have lived, and the fact that the Clan were going to attempt bringing him back from the dead. It was a lot of information to process in a few minutes.

It sounded ridiculous, farfetched, but to her, so did drinking blood. All of it would come in time, and inside, she already knew that.

He opened the door for her.

The scent of blood was strong and abrupt. She didn't see a person, all she could see was the blood rushing through them. A yearning inside catapulted her forwards towards the unsuspecting victim. Her mouth stung, as a set of fangs forced themselves through her gums. She reached out for the fragile neck. In that moment, what she was doing felt like the most natural thing in the world, and the hunger led the way.

Then the moment passed, as a calm yet forceful hand pulled her away. When the world came back into focus, she realised what she'd almost done. She stared at Attilla, who subsequently released his grip.

'I'm sorry,' she stammered, turning to her would-be victim. 'I…had no idea…'

'That's alright,' Maria replied, raising her hand. Her voice trembled a little. 'It's not the first time it's happened.'

Catrina smiled apologetically and quickly took it as her cue to leave, as Attilla motioned Maria inside.

She headed down the corridor in a daze. She pushed her thumb up against her canines. Everything felt fine in there; nothing new and razor-sharp, at least.

While this entire situation of being a vampire was a complete joy to handle, at that point it was towered over by the new information. Bodysnatching; a new story of creation; a *Genesis*, whatever that really meant; a resurrection; and—the part she wanted to think about the least—the mysterious role she had to play in it all.

She made it back to the hall. Sonny welcomed her to the bar and got her a beer without a need to ask.

'…What?' she asked eventually, once she realised he hadn't moved.

'Just wondering if you've been through the process yet.'

One eye narrowed; the eyebrow raised on the other. 'You mean feeding?' He nodded. 'Not yet.'

'Jesus, you must be feeling the strain.'

'I nearly attacked that woman that lives here.'

'The hunger can take over like that,' he reassured gently. 'I wouldn't let it get to you.'

'It hasn't.'

'Yet,' Sonny pointed out. 'I expect you'll be feeding tonight, so you'd do better getting yourself psyched up for it.'

'And how would I do that?' she asked sharply.

'Well, I...Fox,' he said, looking past her to the vampire whose appearance came like a shadow creeping over a wall. She gave a brief nod as welcome, as Sonny set about getting Fox's complimentary drink.

'I've been looking for you,' he said.

'Attilla wanted to explain a few things to me.'

He didn't reply straight away, reading over her expression. She tensed immediately. 'What did he tell you?'

'A lot of things.'

'Such as?'

'Aisen's history.'

'And?'

'The Clan's involvement in the Awakening.'

'...And?'

'And Slayers.' She sat back. 'That's it. Why? Should I know more?'

He cleared his throat. 'No. I wanted to know whether he explained the details of your work. I'm assuming he concentrated more on the history lesson?'

She looked him over, looking for signs that he knew more than he let on, but there was nothing. 'He tried to go over it,' she said. 'The most I gathered was that we get jobs on whoever, these Slayer people, and we deal with them.' She liked the way that sounded; she would always be a killer, and a killer was the same, regardless of immortality, once the target was dead. The vampire aspect would simply make her job more interesting. 'Is that what you wanted me for?'

'That too,' he replied. 'I've been assigned someone, but I need to take you out for your first feed. I thought you could do both tonight.'

'I get to kill someone already?' she asked with a coy smile. 'I'm honoured.'

Fox reached into his side pocket and handed her a photograph. It was very blurred; the most she could see was a mass of bleach-blonde curls flailing, and the face of a girl about Catrina's age.

She wafted the picture in front of him. 'Who's this?'

He smiled, letting the cigarette hang precariously in his mouth. 'You know how these situations work, don't you?'

'Well, I *gathered* she was the target, but *who* is she?'

'A Slayer.' He took the photograph back.

Ignoring the fact that the blonde in the picture hardly seemed like the type who *could*—let alone *would*—kill vampires for a living, she took out her own gun. The magazine was empty on inspection. 'I hope you have some sort of weapons facility.'

He actually laughed at that. There was a dark, mocking quality to the sound. He put his hand around the barrel and lowered it. She watched him through narrowed eyes. She wrenched it back, holding it tightly by her side. No one touched her gun.

He pushed open the door, and they were standing in a silent corridor near the laboratory and Infirmary.

They came to yet another door. Since the rest of them had lived here for years, she was fairly certain that she was the only one to get lost in the seemingly endless passages. Fox unlocked the door and motioned her inside.

A set of metal stairs led down to a warehouse underneath the factory building, filled with shelves stacked full of weapons. Knives, daggers, and an assortment of exotic armaments. She took each step unconsciously, drawn by the arsenal displayed in glass cases.

Fox followed. His interest in this place seemed much the same as his interest in everything else.

She walked through the passages, running her fingers over the smooth glass, feeling each minor imperfection between the panes. Fox headed to a far wooden cabinet, much larger than the rest, and opened one side of it. It was stocked with ammunition for every type of weapon held by the Clan and more. He took out sufficient ammunition and closed it again.

They left the room up a different set of stairs and emerged at the back of the laboratory.

He stopped. He didn't appear to be looking at whatever had his attention, so Catrina strained her ears. There was nothing at first, but then it became as clear as day. A subtle rattle of an inward breath, then the wheeze. Nearby, someone was snoring.

There was only one person already in the lab and that was Corey, who was managing to find the time to catch a doze on the pile of scattered papers over his desk.

Fox moved up alongside him and yelled, 'Corey!'

Corey jolted in his chair, his head jerked upwards. He pulled the sheet of paper stuck to his left cheek, while trying to keep his composure. When his eyes focused onto Fox, he gave a deep sigh of relief.

'Jesus Christ,' he said, wiping his hands over his face, leaning back in the chair and giving a slight yawn. 'I thought you were somebody important for a minute there.'

Fox stubbed out his latest smoke in an ashtray on the desk. 'How's the work?'

Corey groaned. 'We're getting by, but she's getting harder to work with.'

Before he could elaborate, the doors swung open again, and Maria walked in, bringing with her the hunger in Catrina's system. She hated feeling so drawn to a person simply because they were full of blood.

She glanced at Fox, whose composure had changed. His shoulders hunched and breathing became shallow, although his expression stayed exactly the same. She wondered whether his hunger had caused the same reaction as hers.

Maria halted upon seeing them. She avoided Fox's gaze and instead looked at Catrina, who was sure the smile was done for her benefit. The atmosphere wasn't comfortable.

'We meet again,' she said lightly, and Catrina nodded in reply. Whatever the woman's reasons were for being there was still a mystery. Catrina wasn't in a position to judge. The same couldn't be said for everyone. She could sense the chilling vibes emanating from Fox, as he nodded politely at Maria.

'Fox,' she said as a greeting.

Maria broke the stare and focused on Corey, almost thankfully. 'What've you got for me?' She moved over to him and looked through the papers he'd been sleeping on. His scientific diagrams and complex formulas had long since been drawn-over by doodles and song lyrics.

Catrina wanted to go; she couldn't understand Fox's reaction. Yes, Maria was human, but she seemed amiable enough. Even if they had problems, he could've at least hidden it for her benefit, since he hid everything else. His narrowed eyes glared at Maria's back as she directed Corey with a few plain commands.

'Did you find out what was wrong with Catrina?' he asked whoever wanted to answer.

Maria stopped working and straightened before turning to face him. 'She went through a traumatic experience.' She looked at Catrina. 'You'll be fine. It was just a difficult turning.'

Catrina was about to thank her, when Fox fiercely said, '*I* turned her.'

Catrina felt like she could choke on the air; it was so thick with tension.

Maria spoke diplomatically. 'Then you should get checked over to make sure you're okay…'

'—I'm fine,' he growled and turned his back on her. 'Come on,' he said to Catrina, 'We've wasted enough time.'

He stormed out without another word. It took Catrina a second or two to realise he'd gone. The others only shrugged at her silent question.

Fox was waiting in the corridor.

She glared. 'Are you a complete bastard with everybody?'

'When did you meet her?' he asked bluntly.

'When I was with Attilla…I almost attacked her.'

He smiled to himself unpleasantly, and she didn't have to hear him speak to know what he was thinking. 'Pity. Save her, did he?'

'What's your problem?'

'She doesn't belong in this Clan.'

She took a step to the side; clearly this was one of those things she shouldn't have questioned. '…Why?'

'Because she's human.'

'What's wrong with that? We've all been there.'

He tilted his head to the pitiful nature of that statement. 'Don't make assumptions until you know what you're talking about, Catrina.'

'Then explain to me why you were a complete dick with her. Because she's human?'

'Because she's *still* human.'

'Why doesn't she just get turned, then? Would that make you happy?' She considered her words: she doubted anything would make Fox 'happy'.

'It's not as simple as that. If you want to know why she's human, ask Attilla. He's the only reason she's still alive.' His voice echoed a whole variety of undertone, most of it bitter.

'What do you mean by that?'

'They're both adults, Catrina. Figure it out.'

That comment opened up a new world of thought towards the complexities that came from a relationship between the Clan leader and the only human there. Fox was in a sour mood now, and there was so much she needed to find out from him. If he was to be her mentor, his attitude was going to be a difficult obstacle to overcome.

CHAPTER SEVEN

The black Mercedes veered dangerously close to the curb, as it turned the corner. In the driver's seat, Rose hooked one hand around the wheel and used her other to skip music tracks. The blare of heavy metal music turned heads of the crowd queuing outside the club, as she brought the car to an abrupt halt outside the main entrance. Catrina got out first, and Fox—who hadn't spoken since the Infirmary—followed closely behind.

The music inside the club was much the same as in Rose's car: harsh, raw…alive. Rose didn't go with them; she waited outside and started a conversation with the bouncer. He let Fox and Catrina inside without looking at them, although the heavy steel entrance suggested that the place was protected.

Inside, the gathering danced into oblivion. Fox led Catrina to the bar. Her head ached with the deafening sound of a hundred hearts, thumping with the pounding bass. As they slipped through the crowd, she noticed the path being created by people was wide enough for the both of them.

The traces of blood that hung in the air taunted her taste buds, and a half-new feeling came in a quick, powerful rush. The lure of blood. She couldn't hold it back. Just like in the safe house, just like with Maria, the hunger craved for its fill.

She didn't notice that Fox had sat her down at the bar and had begun a conversation with another man, who—while listening intently to every word Fox was saying—watched the crowd carefully. Fox nodded at the man, who returned the gesture and disappeared into the crowd.

She mustered the energy to focus. 'So…where are we now?'

'A Moderator Bar.'

She looked out into the crowd; the people all as oblivious as each other. No, not all of them. There were a few people there that stood out. Their movements were more fluid, more calculated. Even from this distance, she knew she couldn't sense blood on them. These were others like her.

Fox stood by her side and watched the congregation move. He tapped excess ash from his cigarette and pointed towards the man he'd been speaking to. 'The Moderators make sure humans aren't killed on their ground. Most vampires, especially clan vampires, don't kill their victims. The rogue community isn't so forgiving, and *some* of our Clan's vampires kill, regardless of consequences.' She felt as though that comment was aimed directly at her. After all, killing for nothing other than profit had been her life until the turn. 'Humans are relatively safe here.'

'Relatively?'

'As long as they stay in the bar.'

'But outside they can be killed.' Averting her eyes from both her prey and her maker, she added: 'Am I meant to kill them?'

Fox stubbed out the cigarette. 'That's your choice. Being a vampire doesn't make you a savage. Most vampires don't kill their prey unless it's necessary, which it rarely is.'

'So why get me to work for you?'

'Because sometimes it *is* necessary.'

'Like these 'Slayer' people?'

'In their case, killing's *always* necessary.'

The Moderator headed back through the crowd. His black hair was artistically combed back to compliment his inviting eyes. People didn't need to stand aside for him; he slipped gracefully amongst them.

His eyes fixed on hers, a stare so deep that she could do nothing but return it. Eventually, the Moderator offered his hand. When she turned to Fox for an answer, he just nodded.

She took the man's hand.

'Is this your first feed?' the Moderator questioned, with such a soothing tone it immediately took away any anxiety she felt. She nodded. A pulsing sensation burned her insides, roused by the question. 'The pain you are feeling is the hunger. It will torment your system until you give it what it needs.' He looked down at her. 'I've seen the young many times. I know how difficult it is to voice concerns you don't understand. It is not the most pleasant experience to begin with,' he added gently, leading her through the people. 'There is one thing you must remember. Blood is the giver of life to your vampire self, but not to you. As such, the hunger works of its own accord. In time, you will learn to succumb to it whenever it needs to feed. Only then will it become a part of you, and only then will you be able to control it.'

'And until then...?'

The Moderator smiled. 'Until then, you will feed just like the rest of us.'

He led her through the crowd. The hunger was beckoned by the abundance of blood that surrounded it; it urged its host through the crowd, held at bay only by the old vampire that held Catrina's hand.

A man was dancing in the doorway to the back of the club. He swayed out of time with the music, eyes dilated like saucers and mouth open wide.

The Moderator released his hold; the hunger led on. She didn't need to be instructed. The hunger drove her in quick steps to the waiting victim.

It guided her towards the vein.

She hooked her hand around the man's neck. The hunger writhed, eagerness forced her fangs out. Her stomach churned, but the desire drove on. The second the fangs pierced the skin, the burning pain receded with a surge of pleasurable intensity. It was close to unbearable. The warm liquid enveloped the churning spasms, and the pain receded immediately.

She felt a rush of adrenaline, the power inside her was growing with every sip of the man's blood. She felt his spinal cord underneath his skin. She—or rather, the *thing* that was in charge right then—didn't want to let him live…

In the instant the hunger subsided, the Moderator pulled her back. Her eyes were wide with shock.

'That is the nature of the thing,' was all he said. 'Learning to calm it is a challenge worth taking.'

They didn't share any goodbyes, save the small thankful nod that Fox gave, leading her back towards the door. The Moderator watched them leave, releasing the man, who wandered aimlessly back towards the dance floor. Where she had fed was nothing more than a slight bruise now. It was a successful first time.

Following her experience in the Moderator bar, the Slayer assignment was an anti-climax. In the latest bar, she could still sense the blood in those around her, but it was different now. There was no lure about it. The hunger was satisfied and required no further fill. She was glad; that would only distract her.

The Slayer assignment was simple; if the girl identified in the photograph made a show, they were to kill her. She'd been warned away on two previous occasions.

The only drawback to the simplicity was that she and Fox could do nothing but wait. It could last all night, and there was no guarantee the girl would show at all.

They were on their second round. They'd chosen a table on the balcony to gain the best vantage point. She'd watched Fox when he'd gotten the drinks. They'd barely spoken since their arrival. At least when he argued with her, words passed between them. This perpetual silence was agitating.

'Catrina?'

She shifted her weight off the balcony rail and sat back in the chair, taking the bottle of beer he offered. 'Thanks.'

He sat down opposite, holding his regular tumbler of whiskey on one hand and a half-smoked cigarette in the other.

'How are we sure she'll show?' she asked.

'There's always the chance that she won't. She's still new…she'll want to impress her superiors. She's barely out of training, which is why she's been assigned such a simple task.'

'How do you know all that?'

'A mixture of informants and theory.'

There was nothing to suggest he was joking. It was understandable that informants would pass through the enemy lines. But if there were those who betrayed the Slayers, no doubt there would be vampires who did the same.

She hoped he'd continue some conversation. He was still a mystery, and she wanted to know about the man she'd be working with. He picked up the whiskey and took another sip.

She picked at the bottle label, glancing up to him without quite meeting his eyes. Her curiosity was too difficult to fight.

'Can I ask you something?'

He looked across the table. 'Go ahead.'

'How old are you? How long have you been a vampire?'

He withdrew from the question. She had to wonder about his true nature, if it was anything more than the short-tempered, condescending personality he had shown. There had to be more. Attilla wouldn't take someone under his guidance unless they were something exceptional. She couldn't imagine Fox would've been trained as well if there were only this constant darkness to him.

'I'm thirty two,' he replied, breaking his own trance as well as hers. 'I've been a vampire going on eleven years now.'

Just knowing his true age, his face suddenly had a new diversity, more of a *knowing* that he was older than just *seeing* it. She understood why she couldn't look at him analytically, as with each moment she was looking back over the years towards his human self.

'So it's true,' she clarified, braving his attitude in the hope that he would talk to her. 'Vampires don't age.'

'We age,' he replied, warming to the conversation now the attention was not solely on him. 'But not in the way you'd assume. Humans…get older. They begin as infants, change to adults. After they've reached their peak, they're then forced to witness their own decay. It's the law of nature, everything is born to die. As for us, we're outside of nature. When we *age*, we reach our peak, and then we stop.'

She watched his eyes blaze with an awareness she hadn't seen in him before. It troubled her to think that vampires would never grow old. She'd always feared old age, losing the use of her most basic motions, but it didn't remove the twisted undertone of the notion. To think that she would be nineteen for all eternity had its attractive appeal, but she could not shake the feeling that there was something wrong with it.

'...Why?' she asked.

'Why?' he repeated mockingly. 'You want to know why we're the closest thing this God-forsaken world has to perfection? Humans are born to die. That is the *only* definitive role they play without question. We exist without the fear of the inevitable, living only to accumulate the knowledge of ages until, for all intents and purposes, we are perfect.'

She knew immediately that she shouldn't argue. Still, she had her opinion. She took a swig of beer. '...What gives us the right?'

He leant closer. 'Did Attilla *tell you* about Aisen?'

She looked at him uncertainly. '...Briefly.'

'Perfection was his gift to the Vampire Nation.' Again he sat back, taking a short drag on his cigarette. 'He believed that the world should be in the hands of those who are worthy to hold it. To be worthy, there should be no flaws. He created vampires to carry out his ideas of perfection in material form.'

She scoffed. She had nothing against Aisen, but those ideas were wrong, because vampires didn't rule the world. 'Looks like he failed then.' He looked up, eyes narrowed, but she disregarded it. 'Humans have control. Vampires have to live beneath them, even if they are their food. They have to conceal themselves, because they'd be destroyed if mankind knew the truth. If he was trying to fulfil a dream of perfection, it must have died with him.'

'Aisen's dreams died when the first human was turned!' he snapped.

She put her bottle down. She took a deep breath and noticed he copied. 'Seem to have hit a nerve there. I don't suppose I'll get an explanation.'

'What did Attilla tell you about Aisen's death?'

She knew as soon as the question was asked that Attilla's history lesson had some holes. 'The Slayers...' He shook his head to disagree, opened his mouth to explain, but she stopped him. 'Why would Attilla lie to me?'

'Why would I?' He spread his arms. '...Vampires killed Aisen.'

'Why would they kill their creator?'

'Because he tried to kill them first.' He composed himself before continuing. 'He tried to destroy the first blood, because he felt they didn't deserve his power. They defeated him instead. It proved to him that they were capable, but it cost him his life. But it left the Vampire Nation in a state of confusion. They had destroyed their creator, but they had not managed to take his power. That was when we began to strive for perfection.'

She peeled off the last shred of the beer label and started to roll it between her fingers. 'So you're saying we're failures.'

He blinked and finished his whiskey. He shook his head while sparking up off the butt of the previous smoke. 'I wouldn't go so far as to say failures,' he rectified, folding his free arm back over his chest. 'But we're nothing like he imagined vampires to be.'

'Then how do we become 'perfect'?' Despite his obvious cold attitude towards her difference of opinion, it was more than could be said if they hadn't spoken at all. At least they were finding out about each other, even though it only seemed to drive them further away from any sort of understanding.

'Time,' he replied with a shrug. 'We're outside of nature, but not time. Our opinions as humans, our emotions, what makes us as we are...we take those with us, along with the preconceptions of the world we've always lived in. It affects the way we grow, and over time minor deficiencies can become severe.'

'You say that like emotions are bad.' His returned gaze said that was exactly what he meant. 'That's why you act like you do, isn't it? You try to show that you have no emotion. You mean to say that nothing positive can come from having a soul?'

Just by listening to him speak, she discovered his behaviour was a façade, something he used to mask his disgust at once being human.

'That's not what I said. Certain emotions, such as guilt,' he looked quickly back at her, 'can make us weak.'

'You'd rather everyone was like you and not feel a thing?'

'I have emotions,' he said quietly. 'I just know to control them.'

She raised her eyebrows. 'Really?' she challenged. 'Because I haven't seen anything that even *resembles* emotion from you.'

'You don't know anything about me.'

'Yeah…' she retorted. 'Well, other than your 'observations', you don't know shit about me, either.'

He backed down at that. He tapped at his cigarette, eyes shifting across the room. 'We've all got pasts. Events that stick in the back of your mind resurface when you least expect it, but you can't be influenced by them. People who let their emotions and pasts overshadow their present actions end up as liabilities and can often get people killed.'

Another silence passed between them, this one uneasy. She scrunched the torn label in her fist and focused all her energy into not throwing it at him.

'Is that your way of saying I'm a liability?'

His brow wrinkled. 'No, that's not…' He held his breath a moment. 'I just…wanted you to be aware that in this life there are a lot of dangers. And if you show that you are a slave to emotion, which before you say anything I *know* you are, others can manipulate it to their advantage.'

A very long moment passed between them, which ended with a sad smile on her face. 'At least that came from you,' she said, looking away. 'I'd rather be put down by you than Attilla.'

'Attilla would never demean you. His beliefs are too strong.'

The mistake showed on his face, she caught it all too quickly and leant forwards. 'Beliefs?'

As though a gift from Heaven to release Fox from the sudden pit he'd walked into, his mobile phone began to ring.

He was frowning as he took it from his pocket and flipped up the cover. His eyes routinely surveyed the room; they might have company.

'...Yes?'

CHAPTER EIGHT

Rose had no issues about driving and using her phone at the same time, either practical or ethical. Her face was flustered. She pulled up the instant Fox and Catrina emerged from the building.

'Slayers?' Fox asked.

'Like a Burger King burger, you got it,' she replied. 'Get in.'

Catrina looked at Fox, expecting an explanation. He didn't give one, and Rose started to drive before the doors were closed.

'Where are they?' Fox's voice was quiet.

'Not home, don't worry.' She jerked a thumb towards the back seat. 'What about Shorty? Is she coming?'

She looked towards Fox, who in turn looked at Catrina, then back to Rose.

'How many are there?' he asked.

Rose shrugged, and Catrina continued to stare at them both. She didn't belong there again; the conversation, although easy enough to understand, wasn't directed at her.

'She'll be okay,' she replied. 'Strength in numbers and all that shit.' Rose eyed Catrina in the rear-view mirror. 'You'll be okay, won't you, Shorty?' Catrina managed a nod, as Rose tried to turn around to face her. In doing so, she released her grip on the wheel, and the car began to veer towards the curb. It was nothing to worry about, as Fox had his hand on the wheel straight away, guiding the car back on track. Rose grinned. 'You wanna send some Slayers to the seventh circle, don't you? Yeah, sure you do...'

Rose turned back to the front and scowled when she noticed Fox's hand on the steering wheel. She slapped it away. 'Do you want to drive? No, didn't think so, so you just keep your hands off the merchandise, capisce?'

Rose slammed on the brakes and mounted the curb outside the Moderator bar. When she opened the door, the sound of gunshots and screaming flooded into the car. She leapt out with a gun already drawn and went in without them. Fox checked his gun with one hand, a skill that must've taken years to perfect. Catrina took her Beretta out and held it guardedly to her chest.

The sounds became much louder as they drew closer to the bar's entrance.

Fox pointed his gun inside first in case anyone was heading down the corridor. But it was desolate; the attack was in the bar itself.

'Be mindful of bullets,' he instructed. 'The Slayers coat them with a drug called Themisium. If you get hit, you won't get up again.'

'How do we go about this?' she asked.

He glanced back to her. 'Kill as many as you can.'

Bodies were strewn about the floor or slumped over tables inside the bar's main room, all of them vampires. Their fangs protruded from their inanimate lips. Each dead vampire, regardless of any other wounds, had a single puncture wound to the chest.

The Slayers were easy to distinguish; fearless, skilled...and something else. The smell of death itself clung to their clothes and emitted from their hands as they drove the stakes to kill.

She was snapped out of the shock when someone swung at her. She saw their clenched fist in the corner of her eye. She instinctively slapped away the flailing hand. But the attacker's free fist swung out and caught a sharp blow to the face.

Releasing her grip on the hand, she stumbled and heard a girl shout, 'Someone throw me a *fucking* stake!'

Catrina quickly regained her stance. She looked at her attacker and was ashamed to admit that the punch hurt. It was a teenage girl, not even Catrina's height. The girl raised her fists, after sweeping her tousled hair back into place.

She would've felt guilty about raising her gun to such a young girl, but the Slayer must've been aware of the dangers her job entailed. That was always the problem when you killed for a living; it looked like not much would change on that front, either. The bullet hit the girl in the torso; she went down. The blood oozing between her fingers was almost black: a liver hit. Catrina raised the Beretta barrel towards the girl's head.

Someone else ploughed into her side, sending both her and her new attacker to the ground. The young man wrapped one hand around her neck and raised the stake he held in the other. Wild fascination flared in his eyes. He hesitated. She took this as her chance to put her gun to his temple.

'Put it down,' she commanded fearlessly. 'I'll shoot you before you get that thing in me, so just *put it down!*'

He didn't move. His hand trembled as it held the stake over her heart. She could feel his pulse racing through the hand he still had around her neck.

'You're going to kill me anyway.' His voice trembled with his body, but his mentality was composed. 'I might as well take you with me.'

He raised the stake. By the time she fired a shot, he's been thrown half way across the room. A hand reached out to her.

'Thanks,' she said to the Moderator, who helped her up before returning to the fight.

The vampires outnumbered the Slayers, but that didn't seem to be affecting them. They were skilled in their 'trade'; they knew exactly what they were doing. She raised her gun to try and pick off any wanderers, but they were all surrounded by vampires. She had her fair share of luck, as the other Slayers seemed far more able than the two she had encountered. They were effortlessly batting back the barrage of attacks.

She heard a safety catch click back behind her, and she spun around to face the teenage girl. That was always something Tony had insisted on. If she didn't shoot them in the head, she had to assume the target was still alive.

The girl fired the gun. There was such a short distance

between them, Catrina could do nothing. Feebly, she put her hands to her head and tried to duck.

In the back of her mind, she heard the low rumble of the creature's growl. It felt as though she was making the noise herself. She wanted to open her eyes, but when she tried, she saw nothing but blackness. She wasn't there at all, the Moderator's bar was gone, and all she saw was the creature.

'What…'

He held up a hand to silence her.

'If you die, you will never know,' he said, speaking so softly, so knowingly, as though the universe existed around him, and only him. She felt a sharp stabbing pain shoot through her system; the creature smiled as if expecting it. 'If you never know, you will never become…'

He and his 'world' collapsed, and she fell back into her own world with a sharp blow to the head.

When she opened her eyes, she was on her knees, gasping for air and choking on her own blood. Having no idea what had happened, she tried to stand. She slipped in something and fell back again. When her eyes finally managed to focus, she realised that she was kneeling in blackened blood. Her hands were covered in it. The Slayer lay dead a few feet away. Now there was no doubt that she was dead. The girl's neck had been broken, as if snapped by a savage beast.

She stared wide-eyed across the room; her eyes met Fox's. He just stared back; quiet alarm whitening his already pale face.

The blood on her hands said that she'd killed the Slayer, and it made her wonder how long the creature had kept her in his world. She wanted explanations, but no one was even watching, except Fox, who just stood there, stunned.

She was about to move, when shotgun fire suspended all action. The fighting ceased. The Slayers grouped by the door, headed by a man in his late twenties with black curtained hair and cold blue eyes. He was strange to look at, if she didn't know better, she would assume him a vampire, too. He was very pale but otherwise in good health; muscles showed beneath a slender build. He rested the shotgun on his shoulder, as a few Slayers dragged the convulsing bodies of injured vampires to the doorway.

'This is your warning,' the leader spat, pointing his shotgun in the Moderator's direction. 'I suggest you take it. Next time, I won't be so good-natured.'

He didn't acknowledge the fact that one of his own was dead at Catrina's feet, preoccupied in making sure the Slayers had some 'prizes' to take with them. The vampires caught were weakened by this 'Themisium' drug and were carried out with ease. The Slayers vacated the building, and the vampires in the bar could do nothing but let them. They were fortunate to be alive.

Rose dragged herself from under the body of another Slayer.

Catrina couldn't take her eyes off the Slayer's body. Eventually, Rose noticed.

'Nicely done!' she said. Fox approached with an unsettled frown on his face. Rose mocked his expression. 'What's your problem?'

Catrina shied away from his stare. Whatever she'd done, he'd seen it, and if it was anything as worrying as his expression suggested, she didn't want to know about it. Rose disappeared into the crowd of remaining vampires who were reliving the attack.

'I don't know what happened,' Catrina said quickly, partially in her own defence. Maybe if he could understand, she would find it easier to come to terms with whatever she'd done.

She didn't like the look on his face, or the response he eventually gave: 'Neither do I.'

'Why wasn't I shot?'

'I don't know.' They stood there in uneasy silence, until he spoke up again. 'Dodging bullets is possible if you're fast enough. But you...you stopped it.' He waited for a response. What was he expecting? An explanation? 'You didn't look like yourself.'

She wanted to laugh and say 'I wasn't', but the shock was too strong to let her do anything but stare back at him. It must have been the creature; he'd performed a feat outside of any vampire's ability. Was he protecting her? Holding back the desire to smile at the strange beast's honourable actions, she blinked.

Now would be a perfect time to tell Fox about the strange spirit that kept guard over her, even if he wouldn't believe her. When she opened her mouth to speak, nothing materialised.

The car journey back was sombre. The music was off and Rose just drove; something had moved her that night.

'I take it that's a regular occurrence?' Catrina asked, when the mood had settled enough. She was aware of the sensitivity of the subject but was too eager to steer her mind away from what had happened to care.

'Regular as clockwork,' Rose replied. She slammed her fist on the wheel. 'If I could get my hands on that piece of shit Head Slayer, I swear...' She eyed Catrina in the rear-view. 'Did you catch a glimpse of the guy with the boom-stick?' Catrina nodded. 'Remember the face. Nathaniel Rae...the biggest son of a bitch in this city, if not the world.' Her shoulders hunched, focusing on the road again. She sighed. 'Ah well, at least we got some. How many d'you notch up, Foxy boy?'

He gave her a withering look for the name. 'Four. They're getting weaker but increasing in number.'

'Yeah,' she said, thinking for around three seconds. 'But quality always beats quantity.' She glanced to the backseat. 'How bout you, Shorty? Kill any, except for that major deal you did on that girl?'

Catrina looked towards Fox, but he said nothing in any way to help her. He just looked out of the window.

The factory was as busy as ever. Rose checked her watch and glanced up to the clock above the bar to make sure it was right, before she disappeared in the crowd. She turned and gave a brief farewell salute. Fox motioned towards the bar, but Catrina shook her head this time.

'I need to get some rest.'

'Alright.' He glanced at her. 'I'll show you your room.'

He took her through the middle door on the north wall. Everything was bare, but there was still a sense of home to it; she couldn't put her finger on what made the factory feel more than just a building.

The corridors snaked around, splitting into countless passages, all full of doors where the only identifying marks were faded brass numbers, dully lit by the bare bulbs hanging from the ceiling. It would take some time to get used to the labyrinth, with each corridor looking just like the last. The factory was much bigger than its external appearance gave it credit for.

There was nothing to distinguish the corridor he stopped her on from the others. Getting lost inside the factory was the least of her problems, but she was taking each as it came along.

She tried to look thankful, moving into the grey box, and Fox began to close the door.

He hesitated. 'Will you be alright? You don't need me to stay a while?'

She turned from inside the small room and tried to be thankful for his efforts, but the closest thing that came over her face was a feigned reassuring smile. She needed to be alone, to have time to think over what had happened. She wanted to dream that night; the creature had some explaining to do. '...I'll be fine.'

He nodded and closed the door behind him, leaving her in her new box of a room.

The wardrobe was empty, as was everything else. Her eyes fell on her bag, which someone had brought up. Checking the contents, she realised nothing had been disturbed and smiled. She remembered the carriers that went into Tony's building; they would come back in tatters after the rigorous security checks. Then again, it wasn't as though there was anything she could've brought with her that would do any damage to the other occupants.

Fox returned to the hall; Sonny had the whiskey ready before he'd even sat down. He took it graciously and sparked up again. They helped him think.

'Rough night?' Sonny asked.

He raised his eyes from the glass, tongue resting on his still protruding fangs. 'You could say that.'

'I do say that.' He was about to say more, but someone else shouted his name, and he was dragged back to work.

Fox sat in silence for a moment, replaying the event in his mind. He tried to block it out, flicking the cigarette irritably. It was too soon to see a change. Too soon. He wasn't ready to accept the fact that she could be something so...distinctive. He'd led himself to believe that he was ready, he'd even convinced Attilla, but with facing it, he knew the truth.

He realised he was being watched, turning to face his mentor. Attilla stood still for a moment.

'I did not want to take you from your thoughts,' he said with a gentle smile. The words had barely passed his lips, before Fox realised that something was wrong, a strangely vigilant expression covered his mentor's usually composed face. 'Come,' Attilla said, moving towards the main entrance. The two never spoke about sensitive matters within the factory walls, knowing their discussions would attract unwanted attention. Many of the Clan were envious of Fox, as he had the strongest bond with Attilla, something they could only ever hope to achieve.

As they made their way to the factory roof—a place used almost exclusively for their conversations—Fox explained what had happened that night. Attilla's expression never changed, his smile stayed until Fox had told the entire story. He was clearly shaken by it, more than Attilla expected.

His smile receded once Fox was finished. 'You found it troubling to see her act in a way we are expecting and hoping?'

His inquisitive look was not met on Fox's part. 'I didn't think it'd happen this soon.'

'...How did she take it?'

Fox leant against the wall, switching his attention between Attilla and the city at night. He needed a cigarette; this was about as much as he could handle without the aid of nicotine. 'All things considered, she took it well. I don't understand how she did it.'

'Chances are she feels the same,' Attilla said. 'It was a risk to her life. The power would have acted without her knowledge. As difficult as this is for you, it is something you must come to terms with, Fox.' Their eyes met; Fox's were stubborn. He didn't want to come to terms with it. 'She is something more than she or anyone else is aware. And, in time, she will supersede us all.'

That hit hard; Fox looked away. 'It's too soon,' he repeated. 'She didn't even know what she'd done.'

Attilla nodded to himself. 'Then perhaps it is time to enlighten her.'

CHAPTER NINE

It was still dark when Catrina opened her eyes. For a few seconds, she couldn't see. But she could hear. Heavy footsteps clipped across concrete in a feral rage. The sound came nearer. She opened her eyes just in time to see a complete stranger hoist her off the hard ground she'd been resting on.

'You fool!' he screamed. She tried to gather her thoughts before the man strangled her. She didn't know him; his pale olive skin, thick glossy ringlets of black hair and dark eyes were all new. His first impression wasn't a very good one. 'You are in allegiance with him, aren't you!'

He threw her to the ground; she bounced like a rag doll.

'What, I…' she stammered, trying to stand. Words didn't come easily, as she was only half-aware of the situation. She'd only just about gathered that they were not in her room. It felt too real to be a dream.

'You have disgraced me,' he growled, going for her again. This time she eluded him. Whatever she'd done was driving him mad. The man swept the heavy cloak he wore from around his feet. He moved with ancient grace. His expression fitted more that of a rabid dog.

She tried to catch his eye, to calm him with a look, but he wouldn't look at her. His beautiful face glowed with rage she didn't understand but could clearly see.

He went for her again and again. She was the quicker of the two, and it only enraged him more when he couldn't let his aggression out on her.

Eventually, he fell back. He lifted his arms to the ceiling, tilted his head back and screamed: '*Usurper!*'

He charged at her. She neither knew what to do nor what to expect, and beyond all reason, she waited for him to attack.

Called from the dark fear resting over her heart, the creature appeared in front of her. The figure ran straight into him, as the creature raised his heavy hand. It hit the man square in the face; he screamed and stumbled back. No sooner had he taken the blow, the figure pounced again.

It was like watching a dog pit itself against a bear.

Catrina's immediate fear for her life was stifled for the moment while watching the strange fight. The man, though clearly no match for the beast, was unwavering and determined. But every time he threw himself forwards, the creature swung its girder-like arms or sunk his long fangs into the man's soft flesh. The figure was soon floored. He staggered back on his haunches.

'Usurper!' he screamed at them both.

The creature's growl was lower than before. He lowered himself to the floor; the huge muscles rippled under leather-like skin. He sprang forwards.

The figure tried to get out of the way, but it was pointless. The creature, while tank-like in physique, was unbelievably agile. He leapt upon the man, who was—despite his ferocious nature—just a man. Catrina surrendered to the natural urge to look away, as the beast broke the man's neck.

The heavy snap echoed through an otherwise dead space. The creature's breathing was forced, uneven. He fell to his knees beside his challenger.

When Catrina opened her eyes, the mysterious figure was gone, and the more mysterious creature was all that remained. He stood up proudly.

'What did he tell you?' the creature asked.

She looked up to the creature, as he came closer. He was too tall to look into his eyes from so close. He accommodated this by lowering himself to her level.

'I…I'm not sure.' She looked into the creature's iridescent eyes. 'Usurper,' she repeated. 'That's all he really said. Who was he?'

The creature looked around. 'Who *is* he,' he corrected. 'The man is a spirit, beyond the call of the dead. You have seen him before.'

She waited for further explanation but got none. 'I haven't…' Then she remembered. She *had* seen him before: in the dreams at the safe house. His face had been shrouded by the hood he wore, and she'd paid more attention to the broadsword, which he no longer carried.

'I don't understand,' she said. It sounded desperate.

The creature nodded. He lifted a heavy hand and rested it on her head. Despite the horrible feat she had just witness him do, she welcomed the touch.

'There is no reason you should,' he assured gently. 'The more you search for your truth, the further you will be from finding it.'

The world crumbled in a matter of seconds. The creature watched her, eyes glazed in momentary sadness over her leaving.

She couldn't get back to sleep after the encounter. The creature invoked questions in her and the new company—this brash figure—unnerved her. Whatever demons were playing tricks on her mind were winning.

Her first night in her own room had been no less harrowing than her first night at the Clan. There was something about this factory, or else there was something about her…

She took the time to get her bearings. She followed the numbered doors back towards the main hall.

By the time she was there, her mind had diminished the images. Concerns over the creature's origin was dwindling, but she hadn't yet confronted him about his assistance in the Slayer attack. Since these 'dreams' were completely beyond her control, she doubted she could ask him either way.

'Expecting Attilla?' a voice asked. It was Sonny. He had to be able to *feel* her glare. 'Sorry, I just assumed…you're up early.'

Her eyes softened; at least people here were considerate. 'Couldn't sleep.'

'They say alcohol's a great tranquilliser,' he replied with a smile, opening his arms out to his bar. 'Beer, right?'

She was about to decline, to say that it would be best if she could keep her head clear for once, but then he took out a bottle and waved it at her.

'Thanks.' She perched on the nearest barstool.

'I heard about the Slayer-fest,' he said casually. The image of the dead Slayer clouded her vision; she had to tread carefully for fear that he'd see her differently. It made her wonder why Sonny had assumed she'd been looking for Attilla.

'What about it?' she asked.

'That kind of thing happens too often. Slayers are a plague on this planet.'

'They must see us in the same light.'

'That's objective of you.'

She had a few mouthfuls of beer, but it didn't agree with her. She put it back on the bar while trying not to offend. He picked it up, tipping a little back himself.

'Why did you ask if I was meeting Attilla?'

'Deductive logic. He's looking for you, I just assumed...'

'What does he want?'

'Ask him,' he said, at the same time gesturing behind her, as Attilla approached from across the hall. She could see in his eyes that he knew what she'd done.

When Fox had told him what had happened in the Moderator bar, Attilla had stayed on the roof to think. He stayed as long as the night endured, and when the sun threatened on the horizon, he retreated into the sanctuary of his private office. There, he considered the situation and the difficult task he had to prepare.

Catrina had shown signs of being an anomaly from the start; he had expected no less. But Fox was right to say it had showed itself alarmingly quickly.

Attilla knew that telling her the whole truth so soon would create a defensive retaliation on her part. She did not take to change well. But he had no choice. There was no plausible lie he could placate her with, and she would be even more eager to know the truth now she had witnessed such a phenomenon.

They did not speak on their way to the conference room, and he could sense her unease. He sat her down at the empty table.

'Fox told me what happened,' he announced, sitting in the opposite seat.

She tensed. 'He did?'

'I expect you were shocked?'

'That's about right.'

'Would it shock more you if I said I'd expected it?'

She scanned his face. 'You know what happened?'

He answered with the question: 'Were you afraid?'

'Wouldn't you have been?'

'With your experience and knowledge your only comfort, yes. But it didn't concern me when Fox explained the event.'

She looked away. 'It concerned him, though.'

'He was surprised, but I expected that also. While he appears to be an impenetrable man, he is still relatively young and as such is naïve to the ways of vampiric divinity.'

'I'm sorry, I don't follow.'

'I am going to explain what I believe happened to you, and you want to listen to every word as if your life depended on it.'

She nodded to an unspoken question, granting him her full attention.

He took in a careful breath to give the explanation he had been preparing all day.

'Aisen…was a great man,' he started carefully. This was all so new to her, he had to take it slowly. It worried him to be giving so much away already. He hoped she would have heard this sometime later, when she would be more receptive to vampiric concepts as a whole. But he could not deny Fate; it had already dictated her path. 'His power was so great that it had a consciousness of its own. It became his constant companion, a well-intentioned wraith that was his battle shield. Many, many people tried to kill Aisen in his lifetime, but everyone who tried to attack our lord hit nothing but air. His power protected him when his life was threatened. They called this power the 'Genesis', because Aisen acquired it *before* he became the first immortal being. The 'Genesis' *was* his beginning. Do you see?'

She looked back with a naïve stare. 'I get what you're saying, but what does that have to do with me?'

'Think,' he said gently. 'Did you save yourself from the shot that would have killed you?'

She disguised her shock through ignorance. 'I don't know anything about a vampire's ability. How was I to know what I'd done was so strange? The last couple of days has been nothing *but* strange.'

'I understand.' His soft tone calmed her. 'But I am telling you now, what happened was not an accident. Something else was protecting you.'

When she neither argued nor agreed to his suggestion, he took it as incentive to continue.

'The Genesis was Aisen's stronghold, but ultimately it was also his defeat. When he grew too strong for the power to control as well as assist, the Genesis abandoned him.'

'That's why he died.' There was no question. She understood, even if it was subconsciously. 'This 'Genesis' power was his foundation.'

He did not hide his pleasure and smiled broadly. 'Exactly. Without it, he was as susceptible to attack as any other of our kind. But he was not to know that until the moments he had between the living and the dead.'

They sat in silence for a moment; a quiet epitaph to the lord neither of them had ever met. The silence lingered.

'This is all a great story,' she said eventually, after their benevolence to the same god had bonded their train of thought. 'But I still don't know how it effects what happened to me.'

'Then I'll tell you,' he replied with simple smile. 'The Genesis, after abandoning its master, became an arcane spirit that wandered this plane in search of a kindred. Legend says it still searches for one to protect that deserves and will accept its intentions. I believe that search ended nineteen years ago, and it has merely been in hibernation until the host's potential was realised.'

She stared at him, not sure whether to laugh at him or scream. She couldn't deny that an outside influence had saved her from certain death, but she wouldn't admit that the outside influence was a monster.

'You think I'm this…'

'Genesis,' he finished with a nod. 'Whatever takes the power of the Master assumes title of the Genesis.'

She wasn't prepared for this and felt her pulse rise. She tried to keep her demeanour fairly composed, she was sure Attilla wasn't falling for it.

'I don't believe you,' she said defiantly, braving his stare.

'That is of no consequence,' he replied. 'You were a witness to your own actions, Catrina. You cannot deny what you did.'

The problem was that she *could* deny it very easily, but there was no one else to lay the blame on. She could hardly say it was a creature she'd been seeing in her dreams that stopped the bullet. Unless he was the spirit Attilla had spoken of. There was nothing to say this creature was not the Genesis himself; she'd just not asked him.

Her frightened stare made his imploring gaze soften. 'Forgive me, Catrina. I had these beliefs imposed on me before this city was built. It was what brought me to you three years ago.'

'Is there any way you could be wrong?'

He smiled. 'Of course. Everyone makes mistakes.' He held up her hand before she had chance to argue. 'However,' he warned, 'I doubt I am wrong in this case.'

'This is a lot to take in.'

He nodded. 'I know. I only ask you keep an objective opinion throughout your stay within my Clan. Many a member's belief challenges my own, and as a leader I have to honour them all.'

She straightened in the seat. 'What aren't you telling me?' It was a bold assumption, but hit the spot, as he let out a slight sigh.

'Indeed, if it were all as simple as I am suggesting, you would have your crown and no one would contest it,' he admitted. 'But it is not so. This Clan is full of totalitarians and you would do well not to challenge them yet. The rest of the Clan have another route for you to take, and I cannot stand in the way of their beliefs.'

She let out the breath she'd been holding. 'Explain.'

'I want to you understand that I do not believe this to be your Fate.'

She nodded, albeit agitatedly. 'I get it.'

'You remember what I said about the Awakening?'

'When Aisen will be brought back? I remember.'

'The Clan believes that a strong-willed woman will die in the name of his resurrection, to be Vessel to his spirit,' he recited. 'As in legend.' He must've seen the change in her then, because he quickly added, 'but they are ill-informed of the possibility of a new 'Genesis'.'

After he'd run out of assurances and she'd heard all she could take, a long silence overcame them. Eventually, she brought herself out of a very long and incomprehensible train of thought.

'I think I get it,' she said. His look urged her on. 'You've been after me for years to make sure I'll be suitable to die for your god.'

He stood at that, shaking his head. 'You haven't been listening. You have the chance to be the greatest prodigy of modern vampire history, and yet you stifle yourself in the belief of others.' He went to the door without gesturing her to follow. 'In the end, your own belief will shape your future, nothing more. I have told you all I am able on the subjects that need precedence. I cannot and will not provide any more information until you realise what is happening to you.' He looked back at her from the open doorway. 'I ask only one thing of you, Catrina. Be alert in the beliefs of others. Irrespective of what you are, others must believe their own truths or you will put yourself in jeopardy.'

Catrina stayed in the conference room long after Attilla left. The air was neither tense nor friendly. She had so much to think about but nowhere to begin.

Some time later, she found her way back to her room. While the idea of having some divine power sparked her intrigue, it was too fanciful for her logical mind to grasp, and it seemed less likely than the very real possibility that she could die in the Awakening. While she tried not to doubt Attilla's beliefs, it was his viewpoint against the standing of the entire Clan.

Only then did she realise the hypocritical behaviour of everyone she'd come into contact with. They'd welcomed her to their home, while in the back of their minds they were going sacrifice her.

This extra realisation was the one that kept her from sleeping, so when Fox came to wake her the following evening, she was already up.

'Attilla told you?' he asked cautiously. His manner was different, more sombre than usual. Maybe she wasn't the only one affected by this.

'He did.'

'He didn't mention how you took it.'

'How the *fuck* do you think I took it?'

Fox let himself in. 'It's not a good idea to draw unnecessary attention to yourself.'

She growled and took a few steps away from him, ignorant to his demand for compliance. 'As if attracting attention is top on my priorities list! All I've been able to think about is that the people who've been so goddamned *nice* to me so far are actually a bunch of backstabbing *bastards!*'

'You don't know enough to make that assumption,' he argued. 'And you need to calm down.'

'*Calm down?* What would you do in this situation?'

'I'd be honoured.'

'You'd be honoured to die to a god you don't even know exists?'

He averted his eyes. '*I* would, but I don't expect you to understand that.'

'Stop trying to be honourable. It doesn't suit you.' He didn't respond. 'Or there's the other option,' she went on. 'I could've stolen his power.'

'I'm feeling the repercussions of this as well,' he said. 'I didn't expect to see the power so soon.'

'Oh, I'm *so* sorry. My heart bleeds for you. I could *die* because of this!'

He stepped back and took a deep breath. When he finally spoke, his tone was sharp. 'Do you *honestly* think I'd stand by and let anyone so much as *touch* you? I've spent years protecting you. I'm not about to stop now.'

His voice was spiked with insult. Not once since she'd been turned did she consider that Fox still felt obliged as her protector to stand in the way of anyone who might cause her harm. That included his own Clan. She was still under his protection, a duty he undertook alone. Because the Clan envisioned that she would die meant that he'd fight *all* of their beliefs.

With this thought, regardless of how he acted or spoke to her, she bowed her head. '...I'm sorry.'

He hesitated. 'I know this is hard for you, but you are something more than anyone else or even you yourself can comprehend.'

She could read him for once, and he was uncertain of something, although she could not pinpoint exactly what it was.

'What about you?' she asked with a curious tone. 'I know what Attilla and the Clan think. Where do you stand on it?'

'My opinions on the Genesis?' He gave a sceptical shrug. 'It's an interesting concept. You?'

'I don't believe it. Besides, I don't think it's right for anyone to just be handed some kind of ultimate power for no reason. And if it was Aisen's, it should've died with him.'

'Aisen had no choice. The power was stronger than him. He had to let it go.'

'That doesn't mean it should be passed to someone else.' She scoffed. '*Especially* not me.'

'Why not?'

'Because I don't deserve or particularly want them.'

'That's because you're afraid of being more than your own mind will let you.'

'I'm not afraid of it,' she said. 'I'm just against it.'

Fox smiled, leaning a touch closer. 'How can you be against something you don't believe in?'

Her eyes cast about helplessly in an attempt to search for an answer she didn't have. She knew there was something behind it, a deeper meaning to 'it all', something that intrigued them enough to track her for three years. But that was their justification, that *they* believed she was unique. It didn't explain why she had gone against her better judgement and accepted the proposition on a whim, when she hadn't been fully informed of the truth.

She knew something as powerful as Fate, if not more so, had made her accept the offer. And why *was* she so against the idea of the Genesis?

She was barely coming to terms with the fact that she was vampire blood. Each night following her conversations with Attilla and Fox, she started to fall into the vampire routine. She would wake each night and find her way to the main hall, with the help of everyone else heading in the same direction. She would sit at the bar and wait for Fox to come and get her. She would feed under the Moderators' supervision night in, night out.

This was a constant, and Fox explained at every opportunity how the routine wouldn't change, until the day came when she'd no longer be his responsibility.

CHAPTER TEN

Louis traced Attilla's footsteps, as the two headed to the nearest conference room. His arms were full of folders, loose papers and field notes. Attilla had already offered to lighten the burden, but Louis politely declined.

There was a space between them that reached further than contact; the two did not associate with one another very often.

'How's Maria?' Louis asked quietly.

'Overworked, but she will insist on working herself into the ground, no matter what alternatives I suggest.'

Despite himself, Louis laughed. 'She won't change.'

They made themselves comfortable in the large, cold room and started to read over the stacks of information, research and theories.

Louis's work was in the stars. Having been in training to become a lecturer in astrology as a human, natural selection left him to his own devices after the vampire blood was in him. He was rarely called on, as vampires had all but abandoned the concept of the Heavens having any say in their lives.

However, the Awakening wasn't of recent times, and its proximity was having an effect on the night sky. As soon as Louis had proven that something was happening out there, everyone was suddenly interested in his so-called 'hobby'.

He lavished every minute of attention.

But it meant now that Attilla was involved in his business, not to mention *Jessie*. While Louis had only reverence for Attilla, which he knew on some level was mutual, the child vampire had nothing but utter contempt for him.

He assumed she was jealous of his freedom. Being a rogue vampire, Louis was confined only by the loose laws of the city's rogue community, which meant he was free to do whatever he wanted and kill whoever he pleased. Clan vampires had rules and regulations imposed by their leaders, which they had to follow. Even vampires like Jessie couldn't escape all the impositions, bound by the technicality of being 'Clan'. If it were not for the control, Jessie would have long since abandoned them in search of more fulfilling prospects.

Attilla went over a particular star chart with him a third time. 'This shows great progress.'

'It's amazing how quickly the last month's been,' he agreed. 'The symbol is almost in the second phase already.'

Attilla had always been the receptive party at these meetings. If for nothing else, then he respected that this was Louis's forte and he was not one to challenge.

Louis took a notepad from the pile and turned to a page he used for constant reference. On it was a pencil sketch of a symbol, or a hieroglyph that preceded the Ancient Egyptians.

He ran his finger over the long curvatures of the strange V shape, dashed over a backwards two. It was more than a symbol; it told a story.

Known in vampire history as the Mark of Divinity, this symbol was supposedly branded on Aisen's chest. It was said that the Slayers had done part of it to display proudly that they had killed the vampires' god. The backwards two was said to have been added by the Trine, a way of defying the Slayers' attempt. Together, it simply said: 'this destroyed god will live again'.

Much speculation surrounded the symbols meaning and even existence at all, but when it was reported that the stars were starting to show a very faint replica of the mark, Louis had been called in.

Louis believed that the stars were a countdown to the time when Aisen would be ready for the Awakening. He called it Aisen's 'clock'; no one questioned his theory.

'Do you ever wonder what kind of animal could do this to someone?' He traced his finger over the sketched symbol. He wasn't speaking to Attilla, who answered the question anyway.

'It was a test to Aisen,' he replied. 'He earned it as a reminder to the ordeal he endured.'

Louis coughed. 'I know, I'm not still a student.' He immediately wanted to take it back and bowed his head. 'I'm sorry, I…I've been under a lot of stress.'

Attilla smiled. 'Haven't we all?' He paused to let the tense moment pass. 'Will you participate in the Tournament this month?'

'It's one thing to watch, but I wouldn't feel right taking part, so I'll have to say no. But thanks for offering…sir. It means a lot to me. Really.'

Attilla nodded in understanding. Not many people welcomed Louis, but the Clan leader would never turn away a man who clearly craved some kind of company.

'Rose will not be pleased,' Attilla commented. 'She claimed adamantly that you would fall under her fist.'

'Were those the exact words she used?'

They looked at one another and smiled.

When they'd discussed all the implications of the stars, the symbol, and the relation of it all to the Awakening, Louis piled his papers back together and readied himself to leave.

'I'll forward the findings to Jessie myself,' Attilla offered.

Louis nodded gracious thanks and left quietly. When he was sure he was alone, Attilla sat back at the table and traced the symbol over the desk with his finger and considered the Tournament.

The competition was how the Clan bonded with each other through very basic instinct: survival. Attilla had always insisted on them. In the scale of importance, social gatherings should have been rock bottom, but Attilla understood the need for a common diversion for his people to follow.

The Tournaments were the best way for his Clan to forget the pressure they would be under when it became their responsibility to raise their creator.

CHAPTER ELEVEN

Catrina and Fox made their way through the main hall, which—
for once, and to her surprise—was completely empty. Even
Sonny didn't man his post.

The constant flow of raised and excited voices echoed from
elsewhere in the building. They headed towards the conference
rooms, but soon Catrina was as lost as the first night she'd
arrived.

They went into a room marked 'Training Room 6'. The
interior resembled a gym. The walls were painted in white gloss
that reflected the glare from the halogen lights hanging from
chrome strips on the high ceiling. The pinewood floor was
highly polished, so everything *glowed*. She squinted as Fox guided
her through the entire Clan that packed into the room. The huge
space could barely accommodate them all.

There was a makeshift area in the centre of the room, an
improvised arena; the vampires were careful not to step into the
circle. Fox had mentioned the Tournament concept to Catrina,
but he hadn't mentioned the excited reality of one hundred
people crammed into a room, waiting. It was electric.

She and Fox reached the ring's boundary. Someone punched
her in the shoulder. She opened her mouth to hurl abuse at the
culprit, but she just smiled once she saw who it was.

'You okay, Shorty?' Rose asked.

'I'm good.'

Another touch on the shoulder turned Catrina's head. She saw someone's hand reach over to shake hers.

'We haven't been properly introduced,' Louis said.

'It's Louis, isn't it?' she checked.

His smile was charming, and he knew it. 'That's me. And you're Catrina, right?'

Rose stuck two fingers in her mouth to emulate her feelings. 'Oh, Christ, is there anyone you *won't* hit on?'

'...You?'

She just grinned. 'That's only because I'm too much *woman* for you to handle.'

Louis held up his hands with a laugh. 'You got me.'

Rose pulled Catrina away from him and put her hand over the side of her face. She whispered, 'He thinks he's God's gift...I can't see it myself. He just looks like a pretty boy to me, if you know what I mean.'

Catrina couldn't help but smile. Fox was now standing opposite her at the circle; he was too sharp in his exits that she never noticed him go. He was talking intently with a young man she'd never seen before.

She nudged Rose in the arm. 'Who's that?'

'Fabian. Fox's been training him. This is his match.'

Fabian was tall, with a very slender physique, a crop cut of jet-black hair and glittering green eyes. He didn't seem anxious, only excited.

'Are they fighting each other?' Catrina asked.

The question seemed logical enough, so she was slightly offended by Louis's laugh.

'I'm sorry,' he apologised immediately. 'It's just...Fox doesn't get involved in these matches in any other way but to train students. He's too good for anyone to fight...other than Attilla, of course.'

Catrina looked across the ring to Fox. She'd seen him in action before now, but she hadn't realised just how untouchable his abilities actually were.

Attilla stepped out into the centre of the ring. She was about to question Rose further, to get all the information on this new stranger, when the chatter amongst the others died down to an expectant hush.

'Is Fabian fighting Attilla?' She asked Louis, whispering so as not to break the silence.

Louis leaned closer to her. 'No,' he whispered back. 'Not yet, anyway. If he wins the Tournament, *then* he'll fight Attilla. Fighting Attilla is the prize of the whole event.'

'Uh huh,' Rose agreed in an equally hushed tone. 'You're either very honoured or one hell of a bad guy to fight Attilla.'

Attilla motioned the combatants forwards. Fabian nodded a final time in agreement to Fox's last words and took his place to Attilla's right, while the vampire Ice approached on the left. Attilla motioned the two to face one another.

'I assume you are both aware of the rules?'

They turned to him. Catrina watched on, as captivated as everyone else. The fighters nodded at their leader, who stepped back again.

'Who's your money on?' Louis whispered to Rose, whose eyes flitted away from the fighters.

'Flip-coin kinda odds,' she replied quietly. 'You got Ice on the one hand, he's got the born vampire thing going on...but Fabian's been trained by Fox, that has to be in his favour.' The look on Louis's face said that she had not answered. 'Oh, you mean me myself and I...who we want to win? We'll be cheering for Fabian.'

'...Why?'

'*Because*,' she whispered. '...*I* wanna kick his ass.'

She opened her mouth to add something, but the air shifted and the entire room readied themselves for the start of the fight. Attilla stepped back to the sidelines. The opponents were left in the middle of the ring, watching him, waiting.

He gave a slight nod, and the fight was underway.

The silence turned to ravenous cheering, when Ice initiated with a frontal assault. Fabian deflected the hit. He attempted a counterattack, but it was knocked away with the same disregard. Rose screamed, raising her fists and wishing she was part of it. Ice returned the deflection with an assortment of automatic punches. Fabian was expecting them; their arms connected no matter where Ice swung, until Ice caught his opponent a single punch to the face. Fabian seethed, taking a defensive step back; he didn't attack, waiting instead for Ice to launch at him again.

Catrina's eyes moved to Fox, who was carefully watching every manoeuvre his student made. He must've taught a defensive strategy; it was working well.

Ice tried a critical blow to Fabian's face, but his arm was caught by the wrist. Ice's instinct was to swing his other arm to break free of the lock. Fabian had preordained and relied on such an attack, his other arm reached out to grab Ice's flailing fist. While Ice was restrained, Fabian pulled back and kicked Ice in the chest. The force sent Ice across the floor, while Fabian took a few precautionary steps to the side, his fists raised, ready to defend again. Ice skidded across the varnished floor, rolling backwards onto his feet.

The crowd was in uproar over the feat. Ice's eyes burned at falling for such a trick. Fabian saw it and grew more cautious; humiliation stoked fury. That second of concern was registered all too quickly by Ice, and he took advantage.

He dropped to the ground. His legs caught Fabian by the knees, knocking him over. The crowd cheered. It was surprising that Fabian hadn't seen it coming.

Catrina looked again at Fox; he was unmoved by the actions. But he'd taught Fabian well. As he fell, he thrashed his legs out, and Ice was back down. He found his feet before his opponent, taking an instinctive step to attack, only to remember his training, and he consciously stopped himself. Ice leapt to his feet, defeat sending him further into a rage.

She could see how important these fights were, as the finalist would put their skills against Attilla. She looked across the circle to him, only to find that he was looking back. Her eyes quickly averted back to the fight.

Ice finally had Fabian at a disadvantage, hooking his arm around the waist of the young vampire, throwing him over his shoulder with the strength that only a vampire could muster. The crowd gasped, some in shock, most in amazement. Fabian hit the floor hard, the arm he held out to break his fall gave a painful crack but didn't break. He remained on the ground while trying to recuperate.

Attilla moved, thinking it may be time to end the fight.

A small drop of blood fell from Fabian's mouth. On sensing it, his eyes narrowed. Now his tactics failed to hold him back. He rolled forwards, as Ice came at him. Fabian effortlessly hooked one arm under his opponent's, forcing him onto his back yet again. Ice retaliated in hauling Fabian straight over him, using the momentum to stand.

'*Kick his ass!*' Rose yelled, with just a hint of innate rage in her eyes. Other vampires shouted the same; the rest just cheered. The two continued to fight, oblivious to the fact that they were being watched.

Both were on the offensive now, one would throw a punch and the other would retaliate with much of the same. Catrina considered that a fight of two so similar could last a long time, and she was about to pose such a question to Louis, when it was interrupted.

Fabian grabbed Ice's arm and spun him around. It was a highly aggressive motion; Catrina would be the first to say she was surprised seeing Fabian on the attack. Of course, having seen so little of his fighting abilities, she didn't know what was expected. But, catching Fox's eye, Fabian's actions were a shock to all.

Fabian wrapped his arm around Ice's elbow and hooked his other through, until they were interlocked. It was a bold step to take, and it could have gone either way. Fortunately for Fox's student, Ice realised too late. Fabian hauled him over his back, flinging the secured opponent down to the ground with a loud slam.

Had he been human, his spine would've snapped. The force of impact was enough to stop him getting up again. The only movement was the rising of his chest as he breathed. A little blood spilled from his head where it had hit the floor. His arm was broken. The crowd went quiet.

Fabian gasped for air, sweat pouring down his face. His eyes drifted around to Fox, who subsequently turned to Attilla. A collective breath came from the crowd; they were all anxious to know whether the fight was his. Attilla stepped into the ring, scanning over Ice. He looked up to Fabian and nodded.

Corey and another vampire rushed forwards, before the crowd had a chance to realise the fight was over. They picked Ice up off the floor and began to haul him in the direction of the Infirmary.

It took less than a second for the whole place to explode; the circle disappeared as people moved in to congratulate Fabian. Fox effortlessly made his way to his waiting pupil, and they were talking by the time Catrina and the others approached.

Rose wrapped one arm around Fabian's shoulder; something he seemed as used to as anyone else was in her company. 'Kudos, Fabian...seriously.'

'Thanks...I wasn't sure which way it was going for a minute there.' He had a soft leer in his accent. It was not the deep, hoarse tone that most of the city's men had. He spotted Louis, frowned momentarily at seeing him, but nodded all the same.

'I'm still gonna kick your ass,' Rose said.

Fabian smiled. 'We'll see.'

She tousled his hair. 'Quiet confidence won't get you shit.' She let him go, gesturing an invisible sword towards him. 'You'd better get training...*we'll* be using weapons.' She swung her 'sword' at him, which he deflected effortlessly with a smile.

'Congratulations,' a voice said. Fabian turned towards Attilla. 'Your performance deserved its reaction.'

He dipped his head. 'Thank you, sir.' He looked across to Fox, who remained indifferent to his student's victory.

Catrina noticed Attilla watching her; she didn't meet his eyes.

'Maybe you could learn from Fabian,' he suggested. Fabian hadn't noticed Catrina until that moment, and Attilla took the opportunity to introduce them. 'This is Catrina.'

Fabian blinked, his smile lessened a fraction, and he nodded. 'I gathered...hello.'

'Hey.' She immediately disliked him but tried to hide it. From the look he was returning, he wasn't all that interested in her, but his words suggested he'd heard her name mentioned a few times before. Possibly from Fox.

Fabian looked at his teacher, waiting as he had been since the fight was over for his reaction. When no response was given, he coughed. 'How did I do?'

Fox's face remained stern and his arms folded. '…Your performance was mediocre,' he commented. The others pretended not to hear him; it was not the best thing to have an audience while being humbled. Fabian nodded, but Fox wasn't satisfied by the meagre response. 'You let your defences down too early, and you opened yourself up to an attack on more than one occasion.'

'I think overall…' Fabian tried to argue, which was clearly a mistake. Fox took a step closer, eyes sharpened as they did when his opinion was disregarded or challenged.

'—Overall?' Evidently, he had expected more from one he had trained himself. 'Do you think Slayers care about 'overall'?' Some of the vampires who were still making their way out of the room had stopped to listen. 'One mistake is all it takes, you know that.'

Fabian looked outwardly ashamed at the reaction his performance was given, eyes averted from his mentor. Fox stepped forwards to continue in the irritation at the performance, but he was moved back by Attilla.

'Fox,' he warned. 'Not here.'

Fox looked at his mentor and nodded, but it was forced. In trying to keep himself calm, Fox quietly stepped through the parting crowd and left.

Attilla led Fabian towards the more optimistic of his supporters.

Louis moved over to Catrina. 'And *that* is why Fox doesn't get involved in these things.'

She watched Fox leave. The others moved hurriedly out of his way. He was angry, and what made her want to follow him was the curiosity behind why. Fabian's performance may have been less than perfect, but even she doubted he'd deserved such a demeaning reaction.

'Where's he going?'

'He'll have gone training,' Rose replied, grabbing her by the shoulder. 'You wanna go watch?' Catrina looked back unsure, but nodded regardless. She was guided away by the wild vampire, giving a quick smile as goodbye to Louis.

Rose escorted her down more corridors; it was a wonder anyone could find their way around. She stopped outside another training room, opening the door. She pointed further down the hall.

'Go down there, take a left, and he'll be in three...' She tried to think for a moment, shrugging carelessly as she did. 'You'll want to wait a while...he's a bit bitchy after a bad fight. Wanna test match?' she added, waving her inside.

Catrina shook her head. 'Thanks anyway, but I don't think I've got much...'

'...Pep?' Rose offered. 'Your loss. Later...'

Heeding Rose's warning, she headed back to the main hall. Sonny was cleaning the bar surface and serving a few people when she arrived; he took out a bottle of beer and left it on the side for her.

'It's pretty intense, isn't it?' he said casually.

'The aftermath's pretty intense, too.'

Sonny just shrugged. 'Fox doesn't accept anything less than perfect.'

'I take it his reaction wasn't much of a shock to anybody?'

'He was more disappointed than angry,' he pointed out. 'You won't see Fox get angry over something like a bad fight.'

'I didn't think Fabian was that bad.'

'The point isn't whether the outcome was in his favour...not really.' He sighed. 'The Tournaments are a recreational activity, sure...but that doesn't mean you should let your guard down. I've seen Fabian fight with Fox, and his skills are much better than what he showed out there tonight.'

'He was probably nervous.'

'If he doubted himself, he shouldn't have done it,' he replied. He paused, thinking for a moment that they should not be talking about such a sensitive topic, but it was quickly disregarded. 'Whatever, the point is...he could've been better, and Fox knew it...and you don't only give your second best, especially not when your teacher's watching you. Can you imagine how Fox must feel, to watch his student only give something like fifty percent?'

'But he *won*.'

Sonny shrugged again. 'You wanted to know if Fox usually gets like that. I'm just saying he gets like that when someone he's taught doesn't show what he's learned.'

As he hadn't told her anything she could have easily picked up herself, and she doubted that he would, she allowed him to change the subject.

He asked the usual questions: how she was fitting in, how everyone was treating her, but after barely a minute, she'd stopped listening. All she could think of was what Sonny thought she was. She wondered if she was even answering the questions he was asking.

Only Attilla and Fox believed her to be the Genesis, which meant that everyone else, *including* Sonny, thought she was going to die. She watched his face, finding it infuriating that he would consciously try to get to know her, if that were true. It made her hurry her drink. She thanked him for the polite gesture, made her excuses and went back to the training room.

She wanted to be in the company of someone who she was sure didn't think she would die, even if he was short-tempered. She didn't want to find Attilla; his beliefs were too much to contend with. She could lose her temper with Fox and not care.

Fox didn't hear her enter; his attention was taken with a punch bag. Although he looked reasonably calm, the aggression his fists struck the bag with was disturbing. His movements were graceful, if grace could be something so fierce; every punch was meticulously planned and choreographed.

He must have spent a lot of his eleven years as a vampire in a room like this; she thought it alien to be able to perform the same routine for years without losing the ability or interest to do so.

He stopped with one fist still touching the bag. She readied herself for anything; she didn't know if his anger had subsided since the fight.

The first few beads of sweat were starting to form on his brow and across his chest. He must have been attacking the bag since the fight had ended to get so worked up.

She took a moment to look him over, merely a precaution to ensure he was approachable, before she went to him.

'I thought vampires didn't change?' she commented, pointing to the apparatus in an attempt to explain. 'If we're not going to change, why bother training?'

He considered the question; she thought that he hadn't understood. Before she had chance to rephrase the question, his hand went up with abrupt swiftness around her throat. Her instincts brought her arm up to stop him, but his hand jutted down to grab her wrist. She swung her other arm around, but he had pre-empted the movement. His hand was waiting to grab hers before she could stop herself. With her arms wrapped over one another, he pulled her closer with mockery in his eyes.

'Because we can still learn what we don't know,' he replied. He held onto her in the same way he had done that night in the safe house, that same gentle touch that could snap her wrists, if he felt so inclined. He let go with a wry smile, which she responded to with a most unimpressed glare.

She rubbed her wrists. 'You could have just said so…I wasn't expecting a live demonstration.'

'That's the point.' He levelled his fists back up to the bag, giving a few wary jabs against the material. 'You need to know the things you don't.' He reconsidered the scene and motioned to the crash mats to the centre of the room. 'There's no harm in learning.'

Hesitating at first, she followed him, taking off her jacket so it would be easier to move. She scooped her hair up into a ponytail. When they were standing opposite one another, he readied himself for the first lesson.

'You have a very brutal style of fighting,' he stated, while she watched him and tried to concentrate. She could smell his cologne mixed with the angry sweat of his body and watched his muscles tense underneath the dark grey vest. His presence was much more noticeable when he was angry. She tried not to stare. 'But brutality is often badly planned and can leave you open to attacks.'

She sighed. 'Is it your job to condescend everything I do?'

'It's my *job* to protect you.'

He raised his fists, which she mimicked automatically. She knew how strong he was, and although she doubted he's intentionally hurt her, accidents happened. He moved forwards slightly, and a very intimidated feeling washed over her. 'We'll start with you on the attack...go ahead.'

After waiting a few seconds to be sure he wasn't going to try and catch her off guard again, she swung at him. His arm was already there to deflect it. He made no attempt to grab her. Instead he shook off the attack as if it were nothing. She tried again, aiming for his stomach, but his arm was there to block before she had made her initial movement. For every punch she was about to deliver, his hand was already there to knock it away.

After a few minutes, her attention dwindled. He grabbed her wrist again. Her other arm swung around instinctively, which he caught. She was trapped again. Unable to admit falling for the same trick twice, she brought her left leg around. He swept his leg aside, catching hers as she brought it up. He let go of her arm just in time to let her hit the mat with a thud.

The shock went up her spine and rang out in her ears. She noticed his hand reaching out to help her up. She just leant on her elbows, staring up at him with eyes of defeated scorn. She crumbled and fell onto her back, adding insult to injury. She let out a disgruntled sigh at losing so quickly, and to such a simple attack. He held out his hand again, and this time she let him lift her up.

She was not sure when the turn happened, but the more Fox taught her, the more she wanted to learn. The change was welcomed, and Fox's behaviour was slightly less arrogant while teaching something he was very skilled in.

As the minutes became the entire night, she felt different, and it wasn't just because of what she was learning. She started to feel like she was the same as him, as anyone else. Fox made no mention of the Genesis; very little talk arose of individuality, and only minor criticisms of her abilities, which she started to overlook. She realised, although the remarks that came from him were usually sharp, they weren't deliberately so, and that underneath it all, it was well-intentioned.

She tried to talk to him, but he was reluctant to discuss anything that wasn't related to what they were doing. He steered away from topics that ventured into him; he completely ignored anything about his past.

He was more interested in her, anything he hadn't learned over the years. He wasn't interested in her abilities, as he could see that from the speed she picked up what he was teaching, but he asked more about *her* past. The more he questioned, the more she realised that—aside from her skills as a killer—he knew very little about her as a person.

She found it difficult to talk while defending against his attacks. While he was being lenient, she was still far from good.

The nights that followed her introduction into training finally began to let the lifestyle fall into as much order as could be expected for a vampire. Fox would accompany her when they left the Clan to feed; he wouldn't let her go anywhere alone.

They roamed the streets for victims as they'd done before, while the Moderator's bar relocated after the Slayer attack. They spent the nights trying to manage in one another's company without starting an argument. Succeeding at this meant that few words passed between them, as their interest in each other came from their differences.

Time drifted; she grew more and more accustomed to feeding on blood, and she continued to be trained. Fox took each lesson slowly to ensure she understood.

She hadn't been 'visited' by the creature or the cloaked figure since she'd dreamt of their fight, and she was thankful for that much. She questioned her own memory, eventually putting the experiences down to the harrowing nature of the change from human to vampire. But in the back of her mind, the idea that she *had* to speak to the creature about his knowledge of the Genesis and exactly how he'd protected her wouldn't go away. But without the dreams, she couldn't ask him.

The rest of the vampires became acquainted with her, all taking their own approaches. Ebony had barely spoken to her from the first night, but when they passed in the hall, she'd acknowledge her. She got the same response from most. She liked Sonny's company, mostly because he gave interesting insight into most of the other Clan members, although it took her a while to coax gossip out of him.

Whenever she saw Attilla, he was always busy: discussing some issue regarding the Awakening, or even more trivial things such as feuds between Clan members. She talked to him on a few occasions and valued his words. Attilla was not as closed as Fox; he was comfortable talking about his past, although he kept it vague.

He'd spent close to two centuries as a vampire, and through his recollections, he regretted nothing. He held a constant admiration to his teacher and maker, which Catrina realised must've had an impact on his leadership ability.

Then there was Jessie. Catrina hadn't spoken to her once since the cold reception she initially received. The child wasn't seen amongst the others; on the few times she did emerge, no one dared approach. Her attitude only changed, Catrina noticed, when she was in Attilla's company.

A few weeks in, Fox explained another concept to her, something that she was only attracted to because it removed the need to wander the streets, a necessity that hardly appealed to her taste. It was known as the Feed, which was another form of the Moderator's bar, but was only for members of the Clan, as the factory was the base for the event. It was like any other human and vampire occasion; the humans were oblivious to the underlying purpose. It worked under the same principles as the bars: a vampire could bring as many 'guests' as he or she wanted, and there was always an inevitable queue of people outside who hadn't even been invited. The idea thrilled her, but Fox soon added that the events were only occasional, and they were rigorously organised as a test of ability, as well as some form of recreation.

The nights went by unhindered. There were no Slayer attacks to report, nothing out of the ordinary, and everyone seemed—if just for a little while—to relax.

CHAPTER TWELVE

A distorted static noise shattered the silence. It emanated from the conference room, where Rose sat alone at the table. She held a chewed biro in her hand, tapping it in time with the music that blared from her earphones. She guided the biro over symbols inside an old, leather-bound book, listlessly spinning the executive chair on its pivoting stand.

A hand appeared from behind her and pulled one of the earphones out.

Her blazing glare didn't lessen when she registered the perpetrator. Louis smiled down at her.

'What do *you* want, pretty boy?'

He took a seat. 'Nothing, really…what're you doing?'

She leant back and stopped her music, concluding that any company was better than none. 'I'm working on the Awakening ritual, dumbass, same thing I've been doing for the last *month…*' She waved the hefty book in front of him before throwing it on the table with a sigh. 'And if it doesn't start making sense soon, I'll tell Jessie to go shove it.'

He laughed. 'You wouldn't dare.'

Her face spread into a wide grin. 'Yeah, I know, but still…every time I look at these symbols…' She gave a careless sweep of her hand over the book's content. '…they change. No bullshit.'

'Ever consider the possibility that you're looking at them too much?'

'Well sure, but you try telling *her* that. Why the hell she gave me this shitty assignment…I don't know. Maybe she's got it in for me.'

'She's got it in for everyone.' Louis took the book and leafed through it; he was looking for something, and a smile crept over her face as she realised. 'It's towards the middle.'

'I know where it is,' he replied, voicing his offence.

'I'm just saying…'

Her sentence fell short as Louis found what he was looking for and placed the opened book on the table. It was an artist's rendition of a bloodbath. It was a very crudely-drawn piece, and yet there was a senseless air of divine power that drew their eyes:

There was no accurate description of the central point of the picture, as for all intents and purposes, it was nothing more than a box. Perfectly shaped through the rest of the wild strokes, corpses surrounded it, all fallen into a circle. The dark lines suggested that life-giving blood had spilled from the torn flesh. Three shadows hovered around the box, loyal guardians watching over it, the absence of black lines around the faces of these wraiths emanated a ghostly presence.

He and Rose stared at the drawing for longer than either noticed; Louis was the first to stop.

'Still sends shivers up my spine.'

She gave a sympathetic shrug. 'Yeah, well…the explicit foretelling of Aisen's return has a tendency to do that to people.'

'You know what always gets me?'

She put one of the earphones back in her ear and switched the music on. 'Nope.'

'It's this…' He put his finger onto the picture of the perfectly crafted box. 'These symbols. No one's ever worked these out.'

'Why would they?' she asked sceptically. 'It's Aisen's tomb. It'll be some mishmash of his last words or something.'

'How do you know?' he challenged.

She sighed. 'Because I'm God, and as God I say that doesn't mean shit. Besides, we have everything we need in the ritual itself.'

'But how do you know?' he repeated, more desperate this time, as though his question was not getting through, which was true. 'You haven't even deciphered it yet. Maybe this text right here is the last piece to the puzzle.'

'Then I'll come to it when I've finished deciphering the ritual. Look, Louis,' she said, close to ripping the earphone out of her ear. 'I got a deadline to work to…I don't have time to piss around looking at the writing on the doodle of Aisen's lament, okay?'

'It's just a suggestion.'

'Yeah, well, your suggestion sucks.'

One eyebrow rose. 'Have you ever considered anger management classes?'

She let a crude smile pass her lips before giving him the finger. 'Fuck you, pretty boy.' Still smiling, he took the book off the table and rose to his feet. She leant after him. 'Hey, where're you going with that?'

'I'm curious,' he said, walking towards the computer that soldiered on in the background. The machine was decades old and didn't consist of more than a few basic programs, a printer and a scanner. He went to the scanner, lifted the lid and placed the book inside.

'Hey, be careful with that machine, it's like a relic.'

He typed a few commands into the computer and the scanner hummed into motion. 'If you're not going to look at this, *I* will.'

'Don't you have anything better to do in your spare time, like visit a gay bar or something? You lead one *controlled* life, Louis. Speaking of which, where is Ebony?'

He folded his arms and turned. 'Left her back at my place…she's had some epiphany about the time span between now and the Awakening…' He saw the disinterest on her face. 'I know, I was the same. That's why I've left her to it. She's great…in small doses. Then she gets too…'

'Up her own ass?' she suggested. Before he could remark on her slur, she added. 'Hey, I'd be up my own ass, too, if I had the privilege of being *born* a vampire.'

'Yeah. So anyway, the symbols…' he said, quickly changing the subject. 'The one's you've managed to work out…where are they stored on the computer?'

'They're not,' she said, scouting around the mess of papers strewn across the conference room table. 'They're on disk. And...ah...' She found a piece of paper covered in similar markings to the rest. Some were accompanied with the appropriate translated English letter or word. 'And this...it's all presumption...like here, it's got the Mark of Divinity, I'm guessing they're talking about Aisen...'

The scanner finished it process, and Louis took one of the disks stuffed alongside the body of the computer, slotting it into the machine. 'I'm borrowing one of these.'

'Be my guest,' she said. 'What do you think it means?'

He glanced back. 'I have no idea, but it looks like I found a new pastime.'

'You party animal.'

'This means I'll be spending more time here.'

'Sonny won't be happy.'

He sighed. 'He's *still* pissed at me?'

'Louis,' she said carefully. 'You know he is. It's one thing to go around trying to shack up with anything with or without a pulse, but he liked *her*. You didn't have to sleep with *her*.'

'It's not like they were together.'

She tittered, 'Just because you can't go one night without 'rigorous exercise'.'

'Is that what you call it?'

She just stared at him. 'Whatever, I don't care. Here.' She handed him the accompanying disk and sheet of paper as he passed.

'Thanks, I'll take these back and give it a once over before I start trying to work it out.'

'I'm happy for you.'

He shook his head and headed for the door. 'I'll let you know what I find.'

'Whatever, sure, okay, bye now,' she said, waving him off.

He was still smiling and shaking his head as he left, and she went to the computer and took the book back from off the scanner bed, sitting back down while putting the earphones back into her ears all in one fluid motion. She let the aggressive music fill her head, falling into the serenity of solitude once more.

*****

The Tournament room was more crowded this time. Word of Fabian fighting Rose spread fast and attracted more interest.

The thick square of padded linoleum in the centre of the room was the designated area this time. Vampires surged around it, their energy infectious.

Catrina stood with Louis at the front of the hustling crowd. While Fox tended to his other student, the rogue vampire was more than happy to keep her company.

Attilla stood on the boundary, waiting to begin. Fox passed on last minute advice to Fabian, who nodded obediently to everything he said. Rose was beside them, stretching in an absurd and useless fashion.

A large vampire entered the ring, carrying a cylindrical metal basket filled with an assortment of rapier swords. He dropped it in the centre and checked the contents. He gave the all clear to Attilla and left.

'How's this work, then?' she asked Louis. 'Is the winner the one that doesn't get killed?'

He laughed. 'They're judged on the principle of swordsmanship. They're not allowed to actually hurt each other...course, if it happens by accident, it's overlooked. The aim is to immobilise the opponent. The winner then wins on the assumption that the loser'd die if it wasn't stopped.'

The fighters walked towards the basket; Fabian gestured for the lady to have first choice. Rose carefully picked one, gave it a testing swipe, scrunched her nose in disdain, and put it back. She weighted the second for its durability, gracefully spinning it over her wrist, taking a preparatory stance. She nodded to Fabian and stepped back, allowing him to make his choice, whose selection process was much the same but slightly longer.

The remaining swords were removed and Attilla stepped into the ring, separating the combatants at arms' length. They lowered their weapons.

'I assume you are both aware of the rules?' They nodded simultaneously. 'The first to immobilise the other is deemed the victor.' The swords twitched; the crowd dared not make a sound. '...Begin.'

The swords clashed fiercely against one another. The fighters pushed against their weapons, seeing who would back off first. Rose slipped to the side, and Fabian stumbled forwards. He saved himself from falling, swinging the sword as he turned to deflect her oncoming strike.

Rose swiftly struck out, while he waited on the defence. Evidently, Fox's lecture had worked; there was no brazened confidence in Fabian's eyes.

Rose caught his sword with hers, spinning it around with such speed that it flew out of his hand. The western side of the crowd gasped louder than the rest as the sword landed nearby. Catrina thought that the fight was over. But Fabian was far from incapacitated. As Rose swept the sword to knock him off his feet, he leapt back, sliding across the floor to grab his weapon from the ground as he stood up. The crowd cheered.

She swiped her sword at him; he barely had time to lapse into defence and stop the blade from catching his skin. No one noticed how close it was. Catrina wondered how close was considered to be close enough, how severe these 'accidental' injuries had to be before the fight was over.

Fabian flipped the sword into his other hand, thinking it was safe to do so. Rose brought her sword to deflect a non-existent hit. Her blade sliced his bicep. The force of it was so heavy— she'd expected it to contact metal, not flesh—he toppled to the side, still managing to keep hold of the sword.

The crowd waited to see if it counted as a disqualification.

Attilla gave no signal.

Catrina looked to Fox, seeing his eyes worry at his student's dying composure.

Fabian held his bleeding arm, sweeping the sword around angrily. He leapt forwards. She deflected his strike, but he'd already brought down another hit. She had no choice but to defend. She parried away from him, dipping the sword to catch his low attack. He spun and the blades clashed.

Forcing her backwards, he spun the blades around and drove hers out of her hand. It sailed upwards, spinning towards the ceiling.

He moved his sword up to her neck so he could end the fight and have the victory as his, but it was not over in her eyes. Spinning towards him, she grabbed the wrist that gripped the sword handle so firmly. The shock made his grip loosen; she forced the weapon out of his hand, tripping him over her leg and knocking him to the floor. Her sword plummeted back to the ground; and in a final flourish she raised her hand and caught the hilt as it fell.

Rose swept both swords gracefully over her wrists. As Fabian tried to sit up, he saw a flash of metal and the swords stopped inches from his neck.

For the briefest of instants, no one dared move. Fabian stared into her eyes, dangerous eyes that said she could've killed him. The blades were so close to his throat; one slice and it would be over. But that animal ferocity died quickly; she blinked and the look was gone. She lowered the blades.

'Checkmate,' she said, reaching out to help him up. The crowd went wild, as she lifted Fabian back onto his feet.

He didn't look at her. Catrina followed Louis's lead and they made their way forwards, as Rose gave both swords to the vampire handling the basket. The crowd roared and swarmed around them.

'That wasn't bad,' Louis said with a derisive smile.

Rose laughed between exhausted pants, wiping the few beads of sweat from her forehead with the back of her hand. 'You watch…you learn.'

Fox turned his attention to Fabian, who was standing away from the crowd, refusing to take his eyes off the floor. As Fox approached he had no choice but to look at him. The stern expression on his teacher's face didn't change.

The others didn't listen to Fox's lecture this time, even Catrina averted her attention. They'd heard enough the last time, and that was when Fabian had won. The young vampire didn't look too diminished when Fox had said all he had to.

As Catrina listened to Louis and Rose banter, the wrench of the hunger began to rise to the surface. She hadn't fed that night. The pain had lessened a fraction in the time she'd been a vampire, but it wasn't enough to stop her from feeding every night. Besides, she craved routine.

She walked over to Fox apprehensively, as Fabian left the room amidst commiserations.

'I need to eat,' she said, shuddering at her own words. She still saw taking blood as a pure, repulsive necessity. Most of the others took pleasure in it.

Fox gave a small nod, but his eyes strayed over to Fabian by the door; his student was in need of some extra tuition and in the perfect frame of mind for it. She watched his expression and knew he was hesitant about joining her.

'It's alright,' she said. 'I'll go on my own.'

He looked at her as though she'd just punched him in the face. 'No. That's not a good idea.'

She sighed; his overprotective attitude battered her self-confidence. She was always surrounded by people here, and she was starting to miss the seclusion that came so naturally in the past.

'You can't keep treating me like I'm going to break.' She couldn't understand how Fox had seen her abilities and still insisted on keeping her under constant watch.

'I don't want you out alone. I know the dangers out there, most of them by name.'

'I know my way to the Moderator's bar,' she persisted. 'I'll be there and back within the hour.'

It was not so much a request as it was a statement. Her mind was made up, and he offered only a grimace in reply.

The gratitude she had towards him when he finally agreed to let her go was kept to herself, because he'd been too guarded about doing so in the first place. She felt as though she had to be careful for his benefit, as though any problem she got herself into would result in a lecture on his part.

But the solitude was highly welcomed; she walked the streets with her head held high. She found her way to the Moderator's bar, which had moved several times in recent weeks to avoid further Slayer attacks. She talked to the leading Moderator—the man she'd met on her first night in the Clan. He was a steadfast man, unwilling to back down, despite the threat from Nathaniel Rae. He knew the risks; so did his people. Catrina appreciated the unity.

Fox was at the bar when she returned a few hours later. While he denied it, she was resolute in thinking he'd been waiting up. When he asked how it'd been, she just nodded and went to bed without conversation.

CHAPTER THIRTEEN

She woke up in an attic and breathed in a mouthful of dust. She spat it back out and dragged herself from where she'd been lying.

The squat little room had received years of cast-offs and no attention. A dirty light bulb hung from the brittle beams that precariously held up the ceiling. Dust-covered blankets concealed everything that was discarded here.

On the ceiling of the slanted roof was a window. It gave a perfect view to the night outside, to the stars, which the creature was looking at with ancient lure.

He didn't notice her arrive, which meant for the first time *she* had to initiate conversation with *it*. It wouldn't be hard to talk; she had a multitude of questions that only he could answer. The problem was where to begin.

She readied herself to speak. Without realising, she was edging closer to the beast, so when he turned, his closeness came as a shock.

'They herald the new beginning,' he said, motioning out to the stars. 'They tell the story of the vampire lord.'

'Aisen,' she said, sharing his gaze to the black sky's flares for a moment.

'Yes. These stars tell of his return.'

'How do you know what stars 'tell'?'

'When you have spent as long in the void as I, there becomes very little that you do not know.'

She looked to the floor; his words and demeanour took her attention away from what was important. 'I have to ask you some questions.'

He nodded to himself and looked back out of the window. The pale starlight illuminated a sadness in his eyes. 'To aid your unease at my presence.'

She couldn't deny it. 'You have to understand. I'm not from a world that openly accepts you…' She thought on this. 'Or the help you give.'

His eyes smiled where his bestial face denied him the basic function. It was just as powerful. 'This is because I protected you.'

'Why did you do it?'

'Must there be a reason for everything?' he challenged. 'Can you not accept the altruistic actions of another?'

'Are you the Genesis?' she asked suddenly.

The balancing sway that kept him in constant motion ceased. He lowered himself so his eyes could look into hers. All of a sudden, she was afraid of him again. He was a beast, a machine, a small god. Who was she to challenge his presence and intentions?

He broke into a laugh; it was mocking and lewd. 'The Genesis is a presence, not a person, fledging.'

'I've been told that the Genesis chooses someone to protect. That sounds like the actions of a conscious being to me.'

'Perhaps it would appear so,' the creature agreed. 'But my reasons for protecting you are not so complex.'

'Then why did you do it?'

He smiled. 'Because I can.' He looked into her eyes. 'I have been banished to this life beyond death for centuries, and ever since I was sent here, my punishment was that I was to live it alone. I had no contact to the real world. Then you became a vampire, and the doors were open between us. I cannot explain how it happened, because *I* do not know. But we are bound together, and I felt it necessary to repay your company with protection, when I could give it.'

She read his expression carefully. She forgot that this creature was one with feelings, despite his appearance.

'So how did you do it?'

'I was a vampire once…years ago, before I died. I use my power from my world to protect you in yours.'

'Vampires don't have that kind of power.'

'No, but spirits do. And spirits such as myself, ones that were denied the release of death, gain powers greater than any living equal. A dead vampire, if left long enough, can become more powerful than any *Genesis*.' He said the word with particular scorn.

She wanted to step away from him. His reasons were not good enough. She'd never known anyone to protect another just because they 'could'.

His thick brow furrowed. 'You are not convinced.'

'No, I'm sorry.'

The light bulb blew in a quick, immense flash, the stars vanished and she was surrounded by a new type of darkness. She couldn't hear the creature's deep breathing, and for a moment, she thought she'd woken up.

The light shifted from the window to an incandescent glow, like the call of a host of angels beckoning her to Heaven. She turned, met by something now in the centre of the room covered by a blanket. She tore it away, looking into an antique full-length mirror. The heavenly glow faded inside the reflection, and all she saw staring back was herself.

The creature reappeared behind her, waiting for her to notice. He cast no reflection.

The time he took to speak completed a cycle of eternity, but she waited patiently for him to gather whatever thoughts he had. His head bowed when he spoke; his entire stance was one of melancholy.

'You fear me.'

'It's not intentional.'

'But I have to carry the burden in knowing I invoke fear in you.' He moved closer again, and held out his hand, looking more human than he ever had before. 'While you fear me, I cannot help you.'

She took it; it was colder than ice. She held it while seeing the more human qualities in him. He was unlike anyone she had known before; his nature made her take pity, but there was still that idea that he was a beast in the back of her mind. 'Why do you want to help me?'

Seeing her face cloud with familiar confusion, he smiled. 'You need me to learn what you are…you cannot do it alone, and you will know this…eventually. This, as your purpose and your understanding of it, will come in time, and then you will accept it without question. Until then, I will leave you be.' He took his hand back, held it to his chest. 'I ask only one thing of you.'

'And that is?'

'Never forget that you are not as the others are.'

He moved away as the walls began to fold in on themselves. She watched as his world crumbled, the objects turned to thick oozing wax spilling out over the wooden floor.

The creature's voice echoed in her mind. 'I will leave until you become what they will say you became.'

He vanished into nothing. She couldn't *be* whatever it was that everyone seemed to think she was without some form of guidance.

Attilla and Fox could only take her so far, but their own opinions and beliefs bound them in such a way she knew it would break them if her outcome contradicted. The creature could take her the rest of the way. But she knew—as he did—that she still needed time.

The mirror toppled and smashed in an explosion of flying glass. She was wrenched out of the world, as the tiny pieces twisted and turned in the thickening air, and all she could see was the shattered fragments of herself through the broken shards.

The presence lingered when she woke, and the thought she was being watched drove her from the room.

She didn't check her watch at first, but as she walked into the main hall, she realised that it was very, very early. Only one person shared her company in the hall, and it wasn't Sonny.

She wanted to go back, to run back to her room and wait until someone else was awake besides Jessie. She was adverse to the idea of spending any time alone with the eternal child.

Not wanting to seem curt, she made her way across the room. She would go anywhere, anywhere Jessie wasn't. She couldn't stop staring: long, curled auburn hair, faultless complexion, exquisitely tailored dress…everything was so perfect, right down to the dainty shoes. She was a very pretty little girl, but the permanently protruded fangs ravaged the idea that she was harmless. Her attention was taken by the book she carried. Catrina crossed her fingers behind her back that she wouldn't look up.

She wasn't that lucky.

'I have a certain suspicion in fledglings that wander during daylight hours.'

With the creature still in mind, and the thought of dreams and twisted realities, she thought that maybe Jessie hadn't spoken. But the child was now staring at her, dark eyes sparkling. She took a few steps forwards, carefully analysing Catrina with a fixed smile on her doll face. Clearly, the creature wasn't the only one who could sense fear.

'…Sorry?' Catrina questioned, hesitant about moving. Jessie wasn't so timid. Catrina felt half obliged to dip and curtsy or at least kneel so they were at eye level. As Catrina made up for her shortcomings by her skills as a killer, Jessie made up for her appearance in the way she spoke. It drove deeper than knives.

'Why are you awake?' There was no concern in her voice. She glanced towards the clock, and Catrina did the same. It was not even afternoon. She wished she'd stayed in the dream; at least the creature was amiable.

'I…couldn't sleep.'

'Another insomniac,' she scowled, rolling her jaded eyes with such perfect subtlety Catrina had no idea how to respond. Her lack of expression seemed to say enough for the child, who nodded to herself. 'I wouldn't take heed to what the others may have told you.' She moved closer. 'You are nothing to be proud of.' She blinked. 'What *has* Attilla told you?'

Catrina's mind raced, faster than Jessie could see or at the very least understand. Her reply was so seamless and quick, there was no suggestion that it was a lie. Another Gostanzo trait was that of deception.

'I know what I am,' she said, possibly the biggest fabrication she had ever uttered. She couldn't be further from certainty on that subject if she tried. But she knew what the Clan thought she was, what Jessie thought she was, and that was enough of a foundation for a believable lie. She nodded solemnly at the child. 'I know what's going to happen to me.'

Jessie still looked contemptuous. 'And yet you do not cower?'

'If it's meant to happen, there's nothing I can do,' Catrina replied, immediately stunned by her own words. They may have been exactly what Jessie wanted to hear—and were possibly enough to keep Catrina out of Jessie's mind in the future—but she didn't like what she was saying.

Jessie snarled. It was a disturbing sound to come from a face so sweet.

'I do not favour traits of bravery and nobility,' she said. She glared at her once more, taking as much as she could gather from the way Catrina looked back. The fear seemed to be enough for the girl. 'Well,' she added brightly. 'As long as you know your purpose, and that you are no better than the rest...'

Catrina watched her leave. She was about to do the same, still with nowhere in mind to go at such an ungodly hour, when she sensed that Jessie had stopped and was glaring at her again.

'He will try,' she mused. 'Attilla always tries.' The little child smiled wickedly. 'He thinks that individuality is important, that if you are unique, you will not die.'

Catrina didn't want to listen. The only reason she could fathom behind Jessie's acidity was that it stemmed from her own uniqueness. Being an ancient vampire trapped in the body of a child drove her from others. The only solace she now had was in destroying the spirits of those who still had theirs, making everyone as bitter as she. She was good at it.

'One piece of advice I will give to you, Catrina...' She almost spat when saying her name. 'Nobility and bravery are overrated, but individuality is the trait of a fool...'

Catrina was left in the room, arms falling limp at her sides and coughing out the breath she had dared let out while Jessie was there for fear she'd come back. Jessie's opinion weighed on her mind as she headed to the conference room. She couldn't possibly be the only vampire—aside from the devil-child—who was awake, and right then she was willing to speak to anyone.

Someone must've heard her quiet prayer, as a hand touched her shoulder. Having still been on her guard after Jessie, she spun in shock. She laughed with relief as Attilla looked back.

'You can't sleep, either?' she asked.

'I sleep when the need arises, as of late that seems to be less of a concern. Has something happened?'

She smiled to cover her shaken expression. 'I've just spoken to Jessie, or rather, listened to her tell me about those deep-set opinions of hers.' She was probably out of line to speak ill of the joint Clan leader, but she wasn't about to let it lie. She'd let enough things go unsaid.

Surprisingly, he smiled. 'Spoken like one who knows. I assume it was not an amiable gesture on her part?'

'She hates me.'

He didn't respond: despite Jessie's unacceptable attitude, it was Attilla's choice not to question. 'Did you have trouble sleeping?'

She gave a slight nod. 'I haven't been sleeping very well for a while. I'll get over it.'

'I don't doubt that you will,' he said lightly. 'If this is any consolation, quite a few members of the Clan walk the factory during the day at some point. Peace comes to each in its own way. If the problem persists, you may want to speak to Corey.'

'Thank you.' She glanced around the place. There was no one else with them, and the sun wouldn't set for a while yet. 'What do *you* do during the day?'

'There are too many modestly demanding tasks for me to mention, but when all of that is finished, the choice of activity is still confined to indoors.'

'That doesn't leave a lot of options.'

'No, I suppose not.'

'Where were you going?'

*****

The conference rooms always looked the most lived-in. Books of every shape, size and wear were strewn about the place, scraps of paper scattered over yellowed pages, scribbled notes all over them. The place smelled of work. But for the moment, it was a calm, serene environment.

They sat quietly, the only ones there. Attilla was engrossed in the book he was holding, but Catrina couldn't be taken by fiction when she had questions for the man sitting across the way.

'Two centuries is a long time,' she said casually, although her heart was racing, diverting his attention from the book. They'd briefly been over his past before, it'd been insightful but she'd never pressed before. 'You must've seen a lot of things.'

'I have. It is something you can only understand if you witness it for yourself.'

'…Such as?'

'Do you have something on your mind?'

She cursed herself for being so easy to read. While the thoughts were fresh, she had to push. 'Did you ever meet him? Aisen, I mean. Or even know anyone who has?'

He lowered the book. 'You're questioning his existence.'

She shrugged. 'Call it my sceptical side…I have to *see* things to believe them.' She looked at him carefully. 'Have you even seen him?'

'Aisen died long before I became a vampire,' he said. 'I never met or even saw him.' He scanned over her face, smiling. 'That gives neither you or I reason to believe that he does not exist.'

'…*Did* not,' she corrected. 'I can believe that someone like Aisen could have existed a long time ago. But these days…'

'We live in an unconvinced world,' he continued for her. 'Where people beg for explanations, reason, and answers to questions not worth asking.'

Everyone except her seemed to have accepted that some things didn't need answers. It left her thinking that it was somehow wrong to want to understand.

'I was part of the vampire nobility as a fledgling. One of the nobles, who I never had reason to question, saw the first Awakening. He *saw* Aisen, as did a number of other vampires alive at the time. But whether or not people have known or known *of* him, it makes no difference.'

'It doesn't stop him being real?'

He read her adamantly disbelieving face but made no motion against it. 'If you were anybody else, I would tell you your beliefs count for very little against those of the Vampire Nation.'

'But those rules don't apply to me, do they?' She sat back in the chair, reading over the cover of the book he'd suggested she read. She would take it with her; this was more important. 'What about you, Attilla? You ignore the beliefs of the rest of your Clan in regards to the Genesis and the Vessel...what do you think Aisen was?'

'When you hear the stories that circulate about the Master, it can become difficult to discern your own series of events.'

'Like the story of who killed him.' She hadn't meant to say it out loud, and from the look on his face, he hadn't been expecting a callous response. But it quickly became an understanding smile.

'I see you have been a witness to this?'

'Fox told me another version, and not to be offensive to your ideas, but...his version *was* more credible.'

'And credibility is rather influential,' he agreed, putting his book down. 'My belief in Aisen is different to Fox's, just as our stories as to his demise differ. I cannot say which is more 'credible'.' He smiled at his choice of words. 'I have no reason to doubt the story Fox told you, and with what I was told of Aisen, it seems strange that my opinion is what it is.' He sighed openly, hesitant about divulging his own beliefs. 'Fox believes in Aisen as a physical being, who once lived and will one day live again.'

She blinked to shake the suspicion in her eyes. That was what Attilla had told her, only now he was talking as though it was not his opinion. 'And you?'

He smiled, sensing her apprehension. 'Aisen, to me, is slightly different...a wonderful and powerful deity to follow, but perhaps no more than that.'

She let the words sink in. The Genesis, the Vessel, their Master...with his revealed beliefs, she could've quite a different take on them. 'You don't think he's real.'

'No Catrina, I believe in him, but...'

'But as a religion,' she said. 'Aisen's life was so far back in time, mystery surrounds it, which is why your stories differ. It's not difficult to assume that believing whether he could exist at all could come under the same doubt.' She folded her arms. 'That's why you have faith in me. You believe I'm the Genesis but not the Vessel, because I can't die for something that only exists in the minds of its followers.'

She felt she understood Attilla a fraction better in that moment. He listened to her explaining his own beliefs, making no attempt to stop or correct her. 'I suppose you believe him to be more like God than an actual person. He created vampires, after all. What about the Awakening, then?'

'That is a belief that will wait to be made,' he replied, clasping his hands thoughtfully under his chin. 'Whether Aisen will rise or whether nothing will happen because he does not exist, I do not know.'

'Which would you prefer?' she tried again, but now she realised that she had overstepped the mark. He sat back in his seat and his eyes fell on some other point in the room. She waved her hand to completely ignore her last comment. 'Never mind.'

'When the event has been and gone, ask me that again,' he said gently. The silence between them was very brief; she leant forwards again.

'...Has much changed?' she asked. 'It must have been different two hundred years ago?'

'There were differences. There was a higher sense of nobility to the Nation as a whole...vampires could be lords, their reverence came from social status, regardless of what they were.'

'Do you think Aisen was right?' she asked more pressingly, still wanting to find the answer to a question she didn't understand. She was reminded of her conversation with Fox. 'Whether you believe in him as a physical being or not, his ideals still circulate.'

'About...?' he asked, interested.

'Fox mentioned something,' she replied. 'He suggested that...I don't know, something like vampires have lost that certain...something that they had.'

'He means they are no longer noble.' He only smiled to the statement. 'His standpoint is his own opinion, and I make no attempt to change it, but his outlook on the Nation as it currently stands are very low.'

She stared at another window on Fox that she wanted prised open. 'Why?'

His lips parted slightly, and he sighed. 'He…' Attilla must never have spoken about Fox in such detail before, but then again, there hadn't been someone working so close with him before. 'His hatred for the human race has unfortunately spread into vampires who were human.' He shrugged nonchalantly at that. 'It's a common trait in born vampires.'

'But Fox was turned,' Catrina pointed out. She let a smile onto her face. 'Does he see himself as born?'

'I suspect he would like to.' The tiniest smile escaped his lips at his charge's behaviour. 'Aisen was known to say that vampires have fallen from grace. Fox thinks the same way.'

'But turned vampires don't think that?'

Attilla laughed slightly, 'Catrina,' he said gently. 'Aisen believed turned vampires *were* the fallen.'

'…That's hardly an incentive to bring him back.'

'It simply means we have a lot to live up to.'

As the afternoon went by, they spoke intricately on a vast array of subjects. He didn't have to tell her when she was out of line; she stopped herself beforehand.

They talked about the Genesis. His belief in Aisen and his belief in the concept of the Genesis were two different things; he didn't consider them linked. She was still not convinced about her fate, and he didn't mind. It was possible that he was quietly confident she'd know better, but if that was the case, it didn't show.

She tried to bring Maria into the conversation, pushed by the mention of her relationship with Attilla, which Fox had been *so* clear about. Attilla didn't mind that either, but one question remained unanswered, something she couldn't bring herself to ask. It was early evening by the time she had gathered her nerves and the curiosity was too much to stand.

'…Stop me if I'm out of line for asking,' she said. He gave her an allowing nod. 'But…why is Maria still a human? Hasn't she been here for something like two years? You'd think there'd be less emphasis on her if she was the same species as those around her.'

'It's been closer to four,' Attilla corrected, getting up and walking around the table, running one hand over the open books as if he could absorb information through his fingertips. 'She has never wanted to be a vampire, and would not force it on her.'

'Unlike Fox?' she said, half as a joke, half serious.

'You can disguise *your* turning as you please. You can think that the choice was not your own, that it was imposed on you, and deceptively so...' He sat down at the head of the table, a position that was clearly meant for him. He raised a decisive finger. 'But...anyone who is turned, and had time, as you did, to contemplate a change, however little information is disclosed...is aware of the implications.'

'You're saying I knew?' She caught the look in his eye; the smile played about his lips artfully. She was naïve to think she had gone in blind.

'You knew that Fox was different from the first moment you laid your eyes on him.'

'And Maria...?'

'She had a more unfortunate encounter with vampires before she came here. She believes there is a line between trusting vampires and becoming one.'

'Profound,' Catrina remarked with a hint of undertone. 'Who attacked her? Rogues?'

'If I knew that, they would be dead,' he said softly.

'You didn't know her before? Then how did she get here?'

'She was a friend of Louis. When she was attacked, the only thing he could think to do was bring her to those who could protect her.'

'I'd have thought the others would've wanted her out,' she remarked. 'Stop me if I'm saying things I shouldn't, but I can understand where Fox gets his hostility towards her.'

Attilla sat back. 'Continue.'

'It's just...she's human. What kept her here in the first place?'

'I did.' He found himself smiling. 'Besides, her being here protects your identity.'

'What do you mean?'

He went to the pile of books and started to stack them. 'When Maria arrived, the new Genesis was more widely believed. I took it upon myself to convince my Clan that it was her.'

Catrina let out a scoff without realising. With a silent apology, she asked, 'Why would you do that?'

He kept his back to her. 'To protect her. That is why Fox despises her, because he is the only one who knows she is no more than a human I care about.'

Their conversation was interrupted by Rose. Catrina was surprised for not hearing her sooner.

She backed into the room, shoving the door with her shoulder, as she tried desperately to hold a folder overflowing with papers in one arm. In the other, she held a half-smoked cigarette. Her eyes were closed, lost in a world of her own, and she was trying to sing in time with the music blaring in her ears. 'Singing' was a term used loosely, as it sounded more like a ragged cry against the hiss of the music. She tapped her feet to the beat, and her voice became a very feminine hum when she didn't know the words. Rose could've made a fortune bottling and selling whatever it was that made her.

When she spotted the two of them she looked like a rabbit caught in car headlights. The moment quickly passed. She dumped the folder onto the table and took the earphones out. She stubbed out the unfinished cigarette, looked over their faces and smiled as innocently as a child. She slammed her hand down on the bulging folder.

'Been studying.' Her face glowed with enthusiasm. 'It's an interesting read.' She glanced at Catrina as though she was an alien. 'You're up early.' Clearly, Attilla being awake at all hours was nothing out of the ordinary. Rose blinked, something clicked. 'Ah, troubled sleep? Wouldn't worry…it happens to the best of us.' She pointed at Attilla to make a clear example.

'How is the work progressing?' Attilla asked her.

Rose beamed. 'Like a house on fire, Capt'n. Did Louis tell you about deciding to put his two cents towards Aisen's lament?'

'He mentioned it, yes,' Attilla asserted, sharing Rose's attentive expression. It could've passed for concern, but Catrina was too confused to notice.

'The...what?'

Rose took it as a request. She foraged through the loose papers in the folder. The one she picked up, complete with cigarette holes and torn edges. She tilted it slightly before handing it across the table.

'A witness of the first Awakening apparently tried to depict what he saw. This was it.'

Catrina took the paper and looked it over. The cigarette holes were accompanied by coffee rings and irate scribbles.

This was the first time she'd set eyes on the depiction of Aisen's tomb, and yet the same shiver shot up her spine as it did whenever anyone looked at it. It was a bad photocopy, but the sheer powerful nature of its content had that intense pull that she couldn't ignore. She didn't need to be told; she just *knew* what it was.

'It's called his lament,' Rose continued, 'because he's still trapped in that tomb and this drawing is all that's left of his glory days.'

Rose and Attilla continued to talk about the lament, as well as her progression on deciphering the Awakening ritual. Catrina slid the picture away, sat back in the chair, and listened until she lost track of what they were discussing.

She checked her watch; sunset had passed. She wasn't hungry yet, but she had to find Fox so they could go out. However, when she was in the main hall, surrounded by the other Clan vampires, she decided that she had every right to go out alone.

She was not a prisoner and didn't need Fox's permission—or anyone else's, for that matter—if she wanted some time to herself.

CHAPTER FOURTEEN

She couldn't remember the last time she'd welcomed rain so much. It was still early; she hadn't even started to think about the hunger. She could take her time, perhaps call into a regular bar. A weight had been lifted now, although she didn't know where it had gone or even what it had been in the first place. It had something to do with the creature. No matter what he believed, she had her own opinions. He may have said that her fate was inescapable, but she didn't believe in Fate.

She knew there was much more than anyone was letting on, but she couldn't have expected any less. It'd taken her four years to discover what Tony *really* did for a living. He claimed that it was a secret because she wouldn't understand and it would destroy her. She wasn't sure if it had, but she didn't think she was an emotionless psychopath.

There was an unparalleled liberation that came with stalking the streets alone. It wasn't that she detested company, but it was nice to have time to appreciate the world by herself. She looked at the clear sky; her vampire eyes let her see beyond the hindrance of polluted clouds. The air that brushed her face was fresh. The night was too inviting to let her mind be bothered by problems.

The hunger started to rise; it reminded her of her beginning. It burned somewhere in the pit of her stomach, spreading throughout her system until every inch of her craved its fill. She was a fair distance from any bar. It escalated quickly, becoming painful within minutes, and there wasn't a soul around.

She stopped, leaning against a building, clutching to her stomach in the hope that it'd make the pain subside. But it just grew; she had to find someone quickly.

She began to feel light-headed, as her eyes wandered towards the poster she was leaning against. Half of it had been torn, but she could make out that it was publicity for an underground music venue. She ran her hand over the material, where the weather had caused it to bubble and fray. She wondered how long that particular picture had been there, how long the beautiful longhaired man had been staring out into the empty street…

'…Excuse me, short stuff,' said a gruff voice from behind. Dazed, she allowed a stranger to move her aside.

As she tried to focus, she realised that whoever the new company was, he wasn't human. She couldn't make out much from the back of him, but he seemed to fit into the area quite well. He was a large man, more bulk than build, dressed in dirty black jeans and a worn, grey hooded jacket. She assumed the long strands of mangled black mess that was his hair would only compliment his face.

He started at the bottom of the poster and gave it a quick rip straight up the centre, taking the more attractive man out of the picture. The vandal carefully folded the picture and stuffed it into his jacket.

Catrina tapped him inquisitively on the shoulder. 'Excuse me…'

'Y'ello?' He was grinning as he turned. His face was chunky, as though he'd been in good shape once but had become a vampire while in the process of letting himself go. His facial hair was something to remember, a thick layer of stubble ran across his jaw line, and his top lip was adorned with what he must have thought was a moustache. He still had some sort of lure about him, something that stemmed beyond his appearance.

'…What're you doing?' she asked.

He frowned. He motioned to the advertisement then gestured to the paper inside his coat. 'You never saw this, okay?'

While she gave an uncertain nod towards his request for anonymity, he moved his head from one side to the other, eyes squinting in an attempt to analyse her. He grinned again.

'…Vampire?' he asked presumably, and she nodded. She felt no reason to lie to one of her own. He must've been a rogue, although his sociability didn't match the idea she had for the behaviour in rogues.

'Yeah…rogue?' She had to ask.

His grin grew broader, tongue in cheek. 'Yah-ha…clever little Clan vampire, ain't ya?' She hesitated at his assumption. She hadn't heard him approach. Maybe he'd been stalking her. 'Chill out,' he said, seeing her expression change. 'You're not the only one who's smarter than you look.' He paused, taking a handmade roll-up and a box of matches out of his pocket. He offered it to her first.

'I don't smoke.'

He snorted. 'Good for you.' He lit up and discarded the match, all so casually. She tried to be offended at his gestures, his remarks, but found it impossible. He reminded her of Rose; everything he said could only be taken light-heartedly. He folded one arm and bit his thumbnail. He was looking at her slightly pallid complexion. 'You don't look too hot…you hungry?'

She nodded. 'Are there any Moderator bars near here?'

He snorted again. 'Moderator bars…' He cleared his throat to wipe the slanderous reaction to her feeding habits. 'Sure there are, but you look like you could use something right now.' He held up one hand. 'Don't move.'

Her eyes drifted uncertainly: she hadn't intended to. He took a step back, fastening his jacket to secure the poster he'd ruined and began rooting through his pockets.

'It's important to keep topped-up, y'know,' he commented carelessly. He gave her a quick glance. 'Especially when you're just starting out.'

She looked sharply at his second assumption. 'I didn't know I was that obvious.'

He just smiled, lifting the jacket up to look inside the pocket. The torn poster of the mystery man started to slip out from underneath, but he wasn't paying attention.

'Yeah, well…' He was only half-involved in the conversation, still resolute in finding whatever he was looking for. He was amusingly disorganised, or maybe he'd just not expected to meet someone who needed his help. 'You get a nose for those kinda things, kid. You still have the smell of mortality on you.'

Before she had chance to comment on the generalisation, he laughed triumphantly and pulled a small object out of his jacket. He put the poster back into place, straightened his clothes, and presented his find. 'Here...take it.'

It was a small vial. She looked past it to his eyes and frowned, but he just manoeuvred the vial, his cigarette, and her hand, until it was hers.

'Taking things from strangers,' she said. 'There's the best piece of advice I ever heard.'

'If you don't want help from a well-intended guy, give it back,' he said, holding out his hand. She didn't move. '...just drink the damn thing.'

She popped the lid. The hunger was drawn to it; she didn't even have time to question before she'd tipped it down her throat. Suddenly, she felt the exact same powerful surge as from the drug Fox had given her in the safe house. She gasped, holding her arm out to try and find the wall to support herself. The stranger reached out first, hauling her gently back upright.

Instead of soothing her hunger with the warm feel of fresh blood, it beat it into submission. The hunger was gone. The vampire let her go once he was confident she had the ability to stand.

'...City's best kept secret,' he said, tapping his nose.

'Where did you get it?'

He laughed. 'It's my own secret recipe.' He looked at her and something clicked. 'You've had it before?'

She nodded.

Her clarity returned with a vengeance that was so quick it almost knocked her over yet again. She could make out his face all the more clearly, and now she had the time to wonder about him. He didn't seem so keen on the analysis.

'You'll still want to get to a bar, or however you planned on dining.' He gently pushed her forwards to start her on her way. 'In small doses, the effects are...not that long.'

'Who are you?' she asked curiously, turning her head to look into his eyes. She could tell from the returned gaze that he wasn't one who divulged that kind of information.

'We never met.'

He was gone before she had chance to register his movement; a whisper of wind carried him away.

*****

She'd been sitting at the table for barely five minutes when she spotted that night's choice of victim. She put down her drink and watched him. He was a dark-skinned man; the only distinctive thing about him was the hint of European heritage. His eyes were slanted, narrow slits, which he cautiously scanned the room with, looking for someone. He spoke to no one, ordered only a glass of water, and passed a business card through his fingers with a suspicious gleam in his eye.

He was a killer; she could smell foreign blood of various sources on his shirt. He must have washed it tirelessly, and the dark-coloured material disguised it well, but it was still there. Tonight, he wasn't there to kill anyone; his eyes were too anxious. This was a deal of some sort, and he was waiting for the second party to arrive.

She half-turned her head to make a comment to Fox, only to realise he wasn't there. She shuddered inwardly at how quickly she'd fallen back into the habit of working with someone. Her only other partner had been Rio Gostanzo, Tony's son, and when he was killed, it took her the best part of six months to learn to work without him.

The killer was on the move. There was no sign of a second party yet, but he was leaving for a reason. She wasn't sure whether he'd spotted his business associate, but there was urgency in his step.

The bar's bouncer stepped aside for her at the door. She looked as though she was waiting for a cab and hoped that the bouncer would fall for it.

Her eyes drifted to one side, where the killer was approaching a second man standing in the shadows of an alley. He was a fair distance away, and even with her improved vision, the darkness concealed the second man's face completely. The only hint she got at his features was when the cloud over the moon let the white light through and for a moment his stature was emphasised.

He was slender against the size of the killer, but his bold stance suggested he was more than capable. As the killer approached, the second man held out a spare cigarette. Judging from the way the killer stormed forwards, he wanted more than a smoke. He swiped the slender man's hand aside and slammed him into the wall.

Letting out a sharp laugh—albeit a choked one with the killer's arm over his larynx—the smoker wasn't concerned in the slightest.

'We had a deal!' the killer yelled.

The bouncer saw that something was happening but looked the other way. Catrina pretended to wait for her cab and checked her watch.

The slender man pushed at the killer; his motion was so precise and quick, it was enough to move him back.

'You breached your part of the contract,' he replied, his voice smooth, but with just that hint of conviction to subdue the man's tone. He flicked at his cigarette. 'Protection was agreed on the basis that you wouldn't visit the inner city.'

'I never went there,' the killer protested.

'You were seen, Stefan. We got it on tape. We got *everything* on tape.' The man's voice dropped slightly. 'We're not stupid. We keep tabs on people like you, and for good reason.'

To look at him, this killer, Stefan, seemed no more than a street thug. She could imagine him working for the second man. The slender man's voice was one she thought she knew, but despite her best efforts she couldn't place it. She knew that the bouncer, being human, wouldn't be able to hear the words passing between them. She hoped that he'd only think that she was watching them out of innocent, if not foolish, curiosity.

'I had to,' Stefan said, deflated. 'I had business to finish.'

'Then you should've finished it before you came to us,' the man snapped. He thrust out his hand, which now held a large wad of money. 'Consider this a goodwill gesture on our part.' He threw the money; it hit Stefan in the face. He cursed but still knelt down to pick it up from the rain-soaked ground.

By the time he'd picked it up, the slender man was gone. Catrina didn't notice him leave, either.

It was still raining. Stefan didn't look up as she approached.

She was surprised how easily her soft words calmed the killer. His grip tightened around her arm, as they walked down the alley. Whatever his intentions, it was sickening. If he was afraid, she was curtly amused by his human nature, that natural sense of fear. If it was something else...her stomach churned. Her fangs were in full show; she thanked the clouds that covered the moon. That would've scared him, no matter how deadly he was.

She glanced behind her, checking that they were far enough from the street to make her move. He followed her look as best he could. He couldn't see much, except a hint of a smile on her face.

'What?' he asked, eyes darting around the alley. 'Catrina, what is it?' It was strange to hear someone she didn't know call her by name.

The moon came out from behind its shadow; he caught sight of her fangs and yelled out, adrenaline giving him the strength to push her back. In his panic, he slipped and fell, hitting his head on the side of the building. She saw the streak of blood from where his head had made contact with the wall.

'Jesus!' he cried, his voice a strangled gasp. He reached for the back of his head, wiping fiercely at the cut. She advanced, as he mustered up the entirety of his energy to stand. 'Get away from me!'

She grabbed him by the throat. He fought against her, his hands gripping around her back. She drove her fangs through the tender flesh and drank; the blood pulsed through her veins until it was her own.

The lingering hunger pangs disappeared almost instantly, but she didn't care; she wanted to kill him. Stefan deserved it; she could smell death on him, clinging to his clothes.

No, not his clothes.

Not even on him.

It was the overpowering smell of death from a Slayer.

She pulled back abruptly, ripping the skin on Stefan's neck, staring at the new arrival.

That slick black hair, icy blue eyes that could be seen even with the absence of light, slightly paled skin. She couldn't forget a face like that; she'd been warned not to.

He pointed his gun squarely at her. Stefan saw him too, leaning against Catrina as his life flowed from his neck. He wrapped one hand around the wound and reached out with the other. Catrina saw this, dragging Stefan in front of her as a human shield. He was as good as dead anyway; he might as well be of some use.

'Rae,' Stefan spluttered, his outstretched hand trembling. He shook against her; she rolled her eyes. She was more concerned about the Head Slayer pointing the gun at her face.

'What are you going to do?' she snapped, holding Stefan closer. She was no expert, but she had a fair idea that a Slayer's principles didn't lie in killing humans. Nathaniel Rae hesitated for a moment, his gun flinched just a fraction. She'd built up a negotiation here, or at least bought herself some time.

Stefan gasped. He knew what was coming.

'Rae!' he yelled, a vile, guttural sound from a man bleeding from the throat. Nathaniel's gun shifted an inch, and he fired. The suppresser kept the notice from others away, and the shot to Stefan's head stopped him from screaming.

Blood splattered in an unsightly shower, which Catrina just managed to avoid. She dropped the body to the ground. The blood spilled from Stefan's neck and head into a dark pool on the ground. It mixed with the dirt and bits of stone. They turned the pool into a curdled mess; it seeped over the newspapers, and a front-page beauty queen was drowned in the blackened scarlet.

Nathaniel turned his gun back on her. She didn't have time to reach for hers, which was his first advantage. His second was that he was the city's *Head* Slayer.

He was the one Stefan paid for protection. It was a fair deal; Stefan breached his contract, so protection was withheld.

He was missing something, some look in his eye. He wasn't going to kill her; she could sense that from the outset. But his gun remained poised at her. She knew she couldn't kill him. She didn't doubt her ability, as such, more of a knowing that the Slayers wouldn't be too pleased if their leader was killed.

'Do you know who I am?' he asked. His tone was brash, over-confident. As far as Slayers went, she liked him the least out of all she had encountered. At least the others still had a human scent about them somewhere.

On him, all she could smell was death.

'Nathaniel Rae.'

He gave a nod, slight and intentionally rational. 'It always helps to know you're recognised...Catrina,' he replied, accompanied with a smile. He tapped his free hand to his ear. 'I listen.' She'd been stupid to give her name. She'd remember in future, if she lived to see it.

She tried to shrug nonchalantly, not knowing whether he believed her attitude or not. It made little difference. 'I wasn't aware goodwill came at a price these days,' she said, kicking Stefan's corpse. Nathaniel's eyes drifted to the body, and he seemed—just for a moment—to show guilt. It was short-lived. A sly grin crept back onto his face. 'If he'd paid you right, would you have killed him anyway?'

'We will never know.'

He was standing in front of her now. He'd been moving very slowly all the while, his voice playing about her so intensely that she hadn't seen his motions. He pressed the gun against her head. Her eyes darted to the side and back, a preternatural speed no normal mortal would've noticed.

'You could try.' His voice cut like sharpened blades. His breath felt warm against her skin, but it wasn't pleasant. 'But you wouldn't make it.'

His fist made contact with her face, and the sheer force behind him was enough to send her crashing into the wall. The side of her face smacked against the brick. She felt her own blood spill, saw the droplets left on the wall as she tried to stand. She put her hand against the building and lifted herself back up off the ground. Dazed, she turned to look back at him. He was strong, even compared to her. Of course, he had to be; his job demanded it.

She was raging; Stefan's blood coursed through her veins, her fangs shot out. It was an instinctive reaction: they were weapons as much as tools.

'What do you want?' she said. The demand in her voice not subdued by the low tone she spoke in. 'It's obvious you don't want to kill me, or you'd have done it already.'

There was a biting quality to his laugh. He grabbed her by the hair and hurled her across the alley. She fell against the opposite wall, managing to protect the other side of her face with her arms. The force ripped her clothes as they grated against the ragged bricks.

She collapsed on the filthy ground. Had it been anyone else, she would've attacked and killed them without a second thought. But this was a *Head* Slayer. While she hadn't been told that much about the hierarchy amongst Slayers, she applied logic she'd gained under Tony's instruction: 'Head' was 'Boss', and as boss, Nathaniel was an untouchable.

'I always like sharp wits and intelligence in women,' he spat at her. She remained against the wall, at least that way she could see straighter and not have to worry about standing at the same time.

She felt his gun handle smack against her skull. The impact made her world turn grey. Blood slid down her throat. It didn't feel so good when it was her own. He loomed over her, moving the barrel of the gun to her chest. She couldn't see clearly, lost in the power he had over her.

The sound of gunfire echoed through the alley, and she waited for the pain to set in. But it hadn't come from Nathaniel's gun. She tried to get up, but was met with a sharp boot kick to the chest. Nathaniel held her down with one foot while scanning the area. Someone else was with them, someone who had a gun and no qualms about using it.

'It was a purposeful mistake, Rae.' The voice came from the darkness. She recognised it. 'Unless you think I'm naturally as bad a shot, you'd better pray I miss again.'

Nathaniel laughed at the threat.

'She's one of yours?' he asked, recognising the pale face that looked back at him. His long, black strings of hair stuck to his face with the rain, his crude pistol poised fearlessly at the Slayer's head. Catrina looked up to see that it was the rogue from the streets, before Nathaniel's boot forced her back on the floor. She wasn't going anywhere.

The rogue shook his head. 'No, but that doesn't mean I'll let you get your hands on her.'

Nathaniel pressed his foot down. She tried to move; a sharp kick stopped the attempt. 'If she's not a Dealer, what I do to her really isn't your business.'

'I'm *making* it mine, ass hole. Let her up.'

That seemed to be an appropriate name for the dark-eyed, scruffy vampire; a Dealer. His voice was enough, that casual, laid-back tone; the sense that he didn't give a damn. She thought it considerate of him to help, but Nathaniel's gun was still on her. He could always shoot first.

'I didn't know you had empathy in your blood,' Nathaniel replied. 'You sell that too?'

'Fuck you...that 'I know everything' attitude's gonna get you killed one of these days.' The Dealer wrapped his other hand around the pistol. Nathaniel had no choice but to consider the proposition. She made no attempt to move.

The Dealer relaxed just that fraction Nathaniel needed, he moved his gun like lightning and shot her in the stomach. The scream that left her lips was loud enough to drown out the sound of the Dealer's gun as he fired at Nathaniel, hitting him in the shoulder.

In some form of retort, he kicked Catrina in her new wound. She rolled over, but he couldn't possibly finish what he'd started. He leapt to the side, clutching at his arm. He shot a look at the Dealer, who readied to fire again.

'Consider yourself *dead*, Dealer,' he snapped before disappearing into the night. The Dealer lowered his gun.

It wasn't the first time she'd been shot, but this was something different. No bullet had this kind of effect on her. Acid ran through her veins; she wheezed and coughed up blood. It bore the reminiscence of every pain she'd ever felt; it burned, chilled, and cut at her insides. She couldn't move of her own accord, but her back arched and her arms scraped at the floor, cutting through the flesh with the force.

The world darkened; she heard the Dealer's voice as he ran to her aid. But there was something else, something her rescuer couldn't see or even sense.

She opened her eyes to find herself staring into the eyes of the cloaked figure. He bent down beside her. Afraid of what he might do while she was incapacitated, she screamed and used all her energy to back away from him. He said something, but through the void all she caught was '…tragedy'.

The acid chemical swarming through her blood reached her heart, exploding in a shower of burning hot needles. It scattered through every blood cell, forcing tears to stream down her face into the marks on her cheek. It was the last thing she remembered, screaming at the figure, an image that disappeared with her consciousness.

The Dealer knelt down beside the girl and tried to get her to look into his eyes. It was useless, as she shuddered violently on the floor, hands bleeding from scraping at the ground.

He hadn't thought about the consequences of his actions, having done it out of instinct. He didn't leave a fellow vampire in danger, not from a Slayer, and *especially* not from Nathaniel Rae. It was an act of principle, and even rogues, despite their name and the nature it suggested, had morals.

In saving her, he'd put his own neck on the line. Once he'd taken her somewhere safe, he'd disappear. It wasn't unusual; he'd left the city countless times before. Being a Dealer made him one of the most hunted vampires in the city. Unfortunately for him, there was truth in Nathaniel's malicious threats.

The Dealer scooped the girl up in his arms and tried to stand. She fought against him. He stumbled but kept his balance.

There were not many places he could take her; she needed medical attention. Hospitals in the city weren't equipped to inoculate against a Themisium bullet. All he knew about her was that her name was Catrina—he also listened—and that she was a Clan vampire. He'd presumed that she was not alone at this early stage of her vampire life.

His car—an old beaten bottle-green Chevrolet Chevelle—was parked at a thirty-degree angle from the sidewalk. The car matched his clothes and his persona; clean but unkempt. Rust had eaten away at the paint above the wheels. Here and there were a few spots of more olive-green bodywork, which was the car's colour before he'd decided to change it. There were several bullet holes in the passenger door. It was a very distinctive car, and despite the imperfections, he took great pride in the old thing.

He fought with an arm and foot to open the car door and placed her on the backseat. There was nothing he could do for her. He knew enough vampires in the city, but there were none he knew who had any idea about the medical implications of Themisium or its antidotes. There was only one place he could take her.

He tapped his hands irritably with the music that blared. His movements were not in time with the rhythm, and his knuckles were white as he turned the wheel. In motion, the car was a ramshackle mess; the bodywork rattled and the engine groaned. The Dealer kept looking into the backseat, watching her shake and yell, her eyes wild. She stared out blankly; he would've been surprised if she had any idea where she was.

His jacket fought against letting him take a reefer out of the pocket. He almost crashed the car into a traffic light, as he tried to strike the match against the strip of sandpaper he'd glued to the dashboard.

CHAPTER FIFTEEN

It'd been a long time since he'd visited this part of the city; it was one of the few places business was slow—not to mention dangerous—for a Dealer. He was a liability to the biggest vampire Clan in the city, and with vampires like Jessie living there, the only way to stay safe was to keep his distance. It was also the only place he knew where the girl convulsing in the back could get help.

He spun the car into the alcove, speeding down the side of the factory, towards the underground parking lot. He slammed his foot on the brake pedal a few feet in. After making sure his passenger hadn't fallen off the backseat, and that she was still alive, he kicked his door open and ran towards the building's side entrance.

His arm reached out to pound on the heavy sheet of steel, when it swung outwards. He leapt out of the way, as a familiar face emerged from inside.

It was Fox.

He had a worried look on his face; his cigarette held thoughtfully in his mouth. His eyes trailed up the ensemble of the Dealer standing before him, his eyes brightened slightly as he recognised him. The feeling was mutual.

'Jesus,' Fox murmured, composed shock seeping through his system. He took the cigarette from his mouth. 'Long time…'

The Dealer waved his hands frantically. 'I'm not here for a reunion, Fox man…' His face broke into the quickest and slightest of smiles. 'But it's good to see you.' He forget the situation. 'You look...well, you look about the same. I guess that's the thing with us, huh?'

Fox nodded, but his mind was as elsewhere. The fact that they knew each other wasn't important. The Dealer shook his head vigorously to fix his mind back on the drugged vampire in the back of his Chevy.

'You would not *believe* how glad I am that you opened the door...' He moved closer, afraid someone might hear them. 'Is Jessie still alive?' Fox gave a short nod. 'Man, that must suck.'

'Not that I'm not glad to see you,' Fox said. 'But I've got business to deal with right now, and you're the last person I expected to run into.'

He nodded with a certain understanding, aware of how Fox could be. 'Sure, man, I get it.' He waved frantically towards the car. 'There's this vampire kid, she's O.D.ing in the back of my car...you know, the usual.' He gave a shrug and that hint of sarcasm in his voice even made Fox smile. He didn't start towards the car; it was the Dealer's business.

'What'd you give her?'

The Dealer put up his hands defensively. 'Hey, for once, it wasn't me.' He gave Fox a look that suggested only one thing.

'Slayers?'

'Try Nathaniel Rae.'

Fox's eyes narrowed. 'Themisium?'

'Hole in one.'

'And she's still alive?'

The Dealer gave a coy shrug. 'What can I say? I'm a God.'

Fox rolled his eyes, starting to move towards the car. 'What exactly did you do?'

He grinned, but the corners of his mouth trembled. 'Let's just say I'll be skipping town tonight...' He stopped Fox with his arm. 'And if you see Rae anytime soon, with his arm all shot to shit, tell him he's welcome.'

'If I see Rae, I'll kill him.'

They went to the car.

'Why did you bring her here?'

'Uh, she said she was a Clan vampire, or more…I *gathered*. And this is a big Clan. I figured if she wasn't one of yours, your chief would've taken her in 'til she got better. Anyway, I thought that woman, that human…thing, you got here.' He clicked his fingers in an attempt to strike his memory. 'What's her name…tip of the tongue…?'

'Maria.' Fox held back the urge to spit out the name.

'Yeah, that's her,' he continued. 'I don't know, I just thought…maybe…because she's had experience in this Themisium deal…and the whole *helping* people when they've been shot with it…I just thought…' He slowed his tone. 'That maybe…*may-be*…'

'—I get the point.'

The Dealer laughed hoarsely. 'Then again, I could just be attracted to you.' His smile screamed with thick sarcasm.

Fox shook his head to the comment, reaching for the car's door handle. There was no harm in taking her inside, as long as she was gone before someone like Jessie found out he'd brought in a stray.

'I think I might visit the West Coast.…' The Dealer spoke whimsically, as though he'd been planning a holiday for a while and just needed a reason to leave. 'See the sights, get laid.'

Fox set his eyes on who was in the backseat. Her convulsions had lessened, but they were still enough to keep her in a constant state of motion. His eyes widened, and he straightened, leaning against the car. His laugh was choked.

'It's Catrina,' he said to himself, turning to the Dealer.

'Yeah, that's her name,' he replied brightly. 'You know her?' He smiled at himself proudly; he had found her Clan. 'Cool…' He considered the situation. 'Well, maybe not for you.'

Fox lifted Catrina out of the car. She stopped moving, taking abrupt breaths as he held her steady in his arms.

'I'm sorry,' the Dealer said sincerely, when he saw the expression on Fox's face, as though it'd been his fault. 'I tried to get to her before he shot her…if I'd known she was one of *yours*, I'd have killed the bastard.'

'She could've died,' he replied, a scornful gesture to her actions as well as praise to her saviour. 'She owes you her life.'

'I'll add her to my list,' he said with a smile. The Dealer stepped past Fox and closed the passenger door. He walked around to the driver side.

Fox turned to leave. Catrina needed help and fast. The Dealer leant over the car's roof. His thick hair swept over his face, over that misshapen moustache that would never grow out, as he cleared his throat.

'Fox?' His voice was gentle, inquisitive. Fox turned back and gestured for him to ask any questions he had quickly. 'She's important, isn't she?'

It wasn't really a question, more of a comment. Fox looked over to his roughened friend with a troubled nod of his head. 'You have no idea.'

The Dealer smiled broadly. He clicked his fingers. 'Gotcha.' As the car engine growled, he leant over the passenger seat and wound the window down. 'Remember the drill...I wasn't here. But give Rose my best.'

Fox looked at him and managed a smile. The Dealer revved up the old engine. The music blared, and he turned the car in an unexpectedly graceful motion and sped up the ramp without looking back. It was easier for him that way.

The calmness that Fox was known for slipped through his fingers, as he headed towards the Infirmary. He passed two vampires wandering the corridors, shooting them a look that said he'd kill them if they dared ask what was going on.

They continued on their way, no enquiry made, until he was out of earshot.

'Isn't she the Vessel?' one asked the other quietly.

'I think so. Either way, she looked in the shit.'

He backed into the laboratory with Catrina in his arms. Corey wasn't there, but the scattered papers thrown carelessly everywhere said he hadn't been gone long. Fox looked for somewhere to put her. There was a workbench covered in miscellaneous apparatus. It crashed to the floor as Fox lay her down. She still wasn't moving, save for her uneven breathing.

The commotion brought Maria out of the Infirmary.

'Fox!' she snapped. 'What the hell are you…' She stopped abruptly halfway across the room, seeing Catrina lying on the workbench. 'Oh, God.'

'She's been shot,' was all he could say.

Maria pushed passed him and started to examine the latest casualty. She tilted her head forwards and tried to lift Catrina's eyelids. Her eyes didn't flinch, and closed as soon as she let go. Sweat covered her body, mixing with the drying tears and blood; her clothes clung to her like an extension of skin. Fox tried to see what was happening, but she kept moving him aside.

'Themisium. It's going for her heart,' she said eventually, her voice low but sturdy. She swallowed hard and checked over Catrina's other wounds, particularly the one on her face.

'What happened to her? How many times has she been shot?' While the professional tone did not waver, beneath it was a hint of scorn for letting this happen. His hands clamped down against the work surface. He looked straight ahead as he spoke; looking at her would only make him more furious. It wasn't the best time to be in a room together.

'I don't know…once,' he guessed, grinding his teeth. She was wasting time asking questions.

'What do you mean you don't know?' she demanded. His muscles tensed, it was a wonder his coat didn't rip. She had no right to speak to him that way. 'You weren't with her?'

His fangs protruded under his top lip. There was no one else around; it would be so easy to end it like this. But he needed her to help Catrina; he knew what'd happen if the Themisium wasn't extracted. With the Slayers, they used the drug purely to incapacitate. It was removed by specialists upon arrival at a Slayer Vicinity. If not, it would eat away at the victim. Catrina was going to die.

He slammed his fist on the surface. 'She went out on her own, I don't know!' he spat.

'Did you find her like this? Jesus Christ,' she muttered under her breath.

He gripped at the workbench, being close enough to strike out. She remained indifferent; if anything, his fury was making her more apathetic.

She sighed irritably. 'She's barely moving. I need to know how long she's been like this.' She looked away; she could see his fangs for certain now. She busied herself with equipment and chemicals at hand. 'Counteracting the balance is based on amount and time span…if you don't know either, she could die regardless of what I do.'

Catrina's body convulsed and she let out a choked cry. Maria looked down at her. 'Damn it, Fox, you should've been with her.'

He grabbed her around the neck and dragged her close enough to feel her heartbeat against his chest.

'I don't need to be told my own mistakes,' he hissed. His fangs were on full show; more than ever he wanted nothing more than to kill her. 'You must've made a fair share in your time…' She had to know that his concern over Catrina was not the only reason he gripped at her throat so tightly. 'If you don't help her, I'll kill you, I swear.'

A third person's hand came from nowhere, grabbing Fox, which was enough to let Maria go. He glared at the intruder with the same contempt, his hand suspended in the air.

'Fox!' Corey's voice was strained with shock; he gripped with uncertain yet required heavy-handedness at Fox's wrist. 'Have you lost your mind?' Maria took the opportunity to take a few steps back, as the scientist spotted Catrina. 'What the hell happened?' He looked at Maria for answers, who turned to Fox. He stared blankly back at her; she could tell Corey whatever she wanted. He didn't care if he would be blamed for what had happened; he already blamed himself.

'It was Slayers,' she said. Fox looked to the ground; she was defending him. How admirable. How he hated her. 'She was shot with Themisium.'

'By who?' Corey asked, this question aimed directly at Fox. Maria continued to see to Catrina; this was Fox's story, he had to keep it to his own boundaries.

He sighed, hoping that the Dealer' story was true.

'…Rae,' he replied. Maria tensed, but neither noticed. The strangest look came over Corey's face. It was confusion, mixed with that hint of fear, and just a slight suggestion of intrigue.

'Damn,' he said, with a tiny smug grin. He bit his lip with interest, his eyes brightened. 'And she's alive? Where were you?'

Fox shot a quick glare to Maria, who resolutely ignored him.

'...She was feeding,' he replied. It was possibly a lie, he didn't know, and in the end it didn't matter. 'I wasn't watching over...I didn't know he was there. I tried to get to her before he...he got a shot in, I got his arm...he ran.'

Corey looked over Fox's face carefully. 'At least you got her back here.'

Maria and Fox shared another look. She was glad that he was intelligent enough to make up a convincing story so fast, and he was at least thankful that she was helping Catrina. Their concentration was broken as Catrina screamed again. She was waking up, kicking frantically. They had no choice but to act.

'Hold her down,' Maria commanded. She snapped on a pair of latex gloves. The bullet's entrance wound was wide, and she could see the piece of metal lodged inside her body. 'We need to get it out.' She spoke as she moved, trying to find something with which she could extract it. There was no time for anaesthetic.

Corey put his hands around her ankles to stop her kicking. Disoriented, she tried to get up, still screaming. Fox put his hand on her shoulder, forcing her back down onto the table. She struggled against the both of them, but she was too weak. They had no trouble keeping her down, save the emotional torment that came from watching her collapse under their hold.

Maria set about quickly, gathering and mixing what she needed. Fox looked over to Corey, who was staring back. No doubt his outburst had confused the doctor. Everybody knew of his contempt against the human race, but no one really thought he'd vent his anger on someone, and *especially* not on Maria...not with her ties.

Maria hovered cautiously over the table, carefully peeling Catrina's top away from the wound; Catrina flinched to the touch. Fox and Corey's motions had been direct, Maria was trying to be cautious, and it was neither welcomed nor helpful. Catrina writhed and kicked and screamed loud enough to draw attention. She fought against those holding her; her eyes flashed open. She tried to get up again, but Fox moved his free arm over her neck and pushed her down. Her back arched, and Maria took the opportunity to get the bullet out. She couldn't wait for Catrina to co-operate; she was hardly in the condition for it.

She grabbed the nearest set of forceps and hooked them around the bullet jutting out of Catrina's gut. She pulled it out with a lightning-quick motion, and again Catrina screamed. Her arm flung out after anything she could reach, the pressure she exerted had to be some release from the pain. She hooked around Fox's arm, grabbing so hard that her nails ripped his flesh. He leant closer so she could get a better grip. He didn't care if it hurt; he deserved it.

Maria grabbed a syringe she'd filled with whatever she'd mixed before and without hesitation jabbed it into Catrina's arm. She yelped like an animal. Maria reached for bandages and antiseptic and set about cleaning the wound.

Catrina felt everything.

She couldn't understand what was happening. The last thing she remembered was Nathaniel standing over her with his gun poised. Someone had tried to help her. There'd been a gunshot, and then came the agony, and the loss of control.

She didn't know where she was, how she'd got there, and she couldn't see who was holding her down. Maybe Nathaniel had taken her; maybe she was in the Slayer's experiment centre. She tried to take in her surroundings, but her eyes didn't co-operate. Everything was white, apart from a blur of beakers and test tubes...someone was holding her down. She screamed until her throat hurt, feeling the pressure with which the people kept her still.

Her head shot up, as someone jabbed a needle into her arm. She tightened her grip on whatever she was holding.

Fox felt the urgency she grabbed his arm with, and all he could do was hold her steady. He had no idea what was going through her mind, if there was anything left there.

'I've counteracted the drug and given her morphine for the pain.' Maria took the gloves off and sighed. 'Once she loses consciousness, there's no guarantee she'll wake up again. It's all a matter of strength now. That's all I can do.'

He had to take her word for it, which was not something he did willingly.

'Get her off the table,' she said. Corey looked at Fox and stepped back; he was welcome to do it himself.

Fox gently moved his hands under her neck and her knees, lifting her off the table. He caught a look in her eye as he cradled her, but it was too fleeting to discern whether or not it was recognition.

Catrina focused on her heart beating against her ribcage, fighting to get the poison out of her blood. Her mind focused on nothing but the pain. She was lowered onto something soft, but it still felt as though it was tearing her apart. Then, whatever painkillers she'd been injected with kicked in, and she was gone. No faces, no dreams…just the darkness she might never wake from.

CHAPTER SIXTEEN

Rose frowned. With an apple between her teeth, she stared hypnotically at the computer screen, as her mobile phone vibrated from her jacket pocket.

She pulled it out, checked the small screen, and clicked the button. '…What?'

'It's Louis.'

'I know it's Louis. What do you want? I'm busy…'

'You're playing solitaire.'

She scowled at his presumption and the fact that he was right, which he naturally didn't see. 'So…? Get off the phone.'

'Rose,' he said with a touch of irate impatience.

She sighed, closing the game and sliding the chair across the floor. 'This had better be important, pretty boy.'

'It is,' he said. 'Get the book and look at Aisen's lament.'

She groaned and her head lolled; now was not the time for work. This was the first time in a week she'd taken a break. 'Trust you to ruin my breather, Louis.'

'Come on, just do it.'

She dragged the chair up to the conference table, shifted the miscellaneous notes aside to take the book from underneath. Leafing through the pages was more difficult when she had to do it with a phone in the other hand. She rested it on her shoulder. 'Right, got it. Now what am I looking for?'

'It's wrong.' His voice was edged with unease.

'What?' She looked closely at the writing on the tomb. She squinted, tilted her head, moved the picture alongside her gaze. It made no difference. She leant back against the black leather. 'Are you on drugs?'

An irritated sigh cracked over the line. 'Look at it properly.'

'I *am* doing,' she protested.

'This could be important.'

'And it could be nothing…'

'Just listen,' he persisted. 'I've been looking at the symbols, and I've worked out some similarities to what's written on the tomb, but only if the image is inverted.'

'So…?' she asked, taking a bite out of the apple. The sound of her chewing must have annoyed him as much as her tone. He didn't have her attention at all. 'You sure you didn't just flip the picture when you copied it?'

'You think I'm that stupid?'

'You *really* want me to answer that?'

'It's the same as the original,' he continued, 'and it's not just that. When you figure it out, the letters are flipped. And backwards. Like a mirror image. That's why it didn't make any sense at first. It's hard to explain…'

'—Then don't bother, since I'm not interested,' she suggested. 'I'm hanging up now…'

'Rose!' he yelled. 'Jesus, will you *listen* for once?'

She rolled her eyes, a motion wasted to one who couldn't see her. 'Fine.'

'Think about this,' he said. 'No one's ever seen the original lament, have they?'

'…No.'

'And no one's ever seen the tomb, either, right?'

She sighed. 'Going somewhere with this…?'

'I don't think that what's on the lament is what's on Aisen's tomb,' he said.

She shook her head with a loud and disbelieving snort. 'You and your theories.'

'This has foundation, and you *know* it.'

She looked again at the image; it was perfectly plausible that the strange writing on the image could've been added to it at some point. 'So what's your idea?'

'Well, whatever this is…' he said, obviously motioning to his copy on his end of the phone. 'I'm guessing it was written by someone other than the Trine.'

'But it was a unique language,' she argued. 'They were the only ones who knew it.'

'Them and Aisen,' he pointed out.

She laughed out loud at his suggestion. 'You're telling me Aisen pulled a Houdini and wrote the damn thing on his own tomb?'

A short laugh came over the line, although he tried to keep serious. 'I'm not saying Aisen did it, but…I don't know…this is still in the brainstorming phase…'

'Then why are you telling me?' she asked. '…you find out what it means before you come at me with all these *theories de fantastique*.'

'Why is what's written on the tomb in a different code to the Ritual?' he asked, trying to invoke thought in her. Whatever idea he was having, he wanted someone to share his passion in working it out. Rose wasn't the ideal choice.

'You're questioning the most famous image of the Master,' she pointed out. 'It has to be part of it.'

'But why? No one's ever paid much interest to it.'

'Have you actually worked any of it out yet?'

'It's not that easy,' he replied. 'It's like a code, and it's in the same language *you* can't even work out when it's all in order. But I'm talking the most basic of codes here…very crude. Someone tried to get this through without the wrong people seeing it, someone relying on the ignorance everyone's given it.'

'You're turning this into a conspiracy theory,' she remarked. 'Now it's your turn to listen.' She closed the book before the image drew her eyes much more, leaning further into the chair as she put her feet on the table. 'You'll drive yourself nuts trying to work out every single detail. And I say this because I care…stop being so fucking nitpicky about it. Work out the damn thing before you start going off on one, okay?'

His sigh carried over the line. 'Alright, *fine.*'

'Don't bitch just because I think your theory is as full of shit as that scribble,' she remarked. 'Just, I dunno, work it out first. I'm really hanging up this time...'

She pressed the button before he could argue.

*****

Fox focused on a spot on the Infirmary ceiling.

Catrina was unconscious on the bed, tubes stuck in her arms and throat, attached to blood packs strung up at the bedside. *She needs constant blood infusions, until the diseased blood is replaced entirely. The Themisium is eating through her system, and even with the antidote pumping into her, the drug is a powerful one to neutralise.* Those were Maria's words, her explanation when Fox had demanded further information.

He hadn't moved through the night and into the start of the new day. Only his hand moved, as he constantly rubbed his face to keep himself awake, or to light another cigarette. He hadn't fed, because he didn't want to leave her.

'How is she?'

He looked up, surprised to see Attilla there. He took an uneven deep breath. 'There's no way to know how long it'll take her to recover. Maria says she's out of the worst, but I can't see any change...'

Attilla moved to the bed and leant over her, putting a hand on her forehead. She was dead to the world. He looked back across to Fox and smiled as reassuringly as he could.

'She's in good hands,' He waited for the moment of respect towards her to pass, before he changed the subject. 'Corey told me what happened to her.'

'Did he?' His voice went hoarse. He doubted Corey had also mentioned what he'd almost done to Maria, as the look in his mentor's eyes was not angry.

Attilla smiled and gave a slight nod, giving a subtle motion to Catrina, making himself comfortable in the chair opposite to Fox. 'I'm interested to hear your version of events.'

They sat in silence. A single noise came from Catrina, startling them both when she wheezed. It lasted barely a second, but it was enough to make them both look away. Fox was on his feet; he couldn't stand to be that close with Attilla watching him. He could tell by the intonation in his mentor's question, and by the way he watched him move, that he hadn't believed what Corey had said.

He leant against the door. If anyone were to interrupt, he would know in advance. He sparked up a cigarette. Attilla relaxed in the chair, watching Fox with the same concern he had for every Clan member. This had affected Fox the same way it would've affected anyone: he wasn't as cold as he liked people to think. 'Tell me what happened, Fox.'

Fox let out a short laugh. To anyone else it was easy, but he couldn't lie to Attilla. He'd learn the truth, and it'd be better for him to know.

'I wasn't there.' He caught Attilla's gaze briefly. 'I wasn't there.'

Attilla's eyes drifted back to Catrina. The wounds had been dressed and covered; her torso was wrapped tightly in thick bandages. She might as well have been strapped to the bed. 'I see.'

Fox looked away, refusing to see that expression on his mentor's face. 'I'm worried for her,' he said eventually. His voice broke through the silence, and it was firm enough to make Attilla look back. 'Sir, I try never to doubt your beliefs…'

'…Then do not start now.' His voice was quiet but not the command behind it.

Fox rested his head against the door. 'She would've died this time,' he said, watching the smoke rise to the ceiling. 'She didn't know how to defend herself.'

'She is still a fledgling,' Attilla waited for Fox to lower his gaze before continuing. 'You cannot expect her to become so quickly. Patience, Fox, is a virtue you have never fully understood.'

Fox's laugh was hoarse. '*I* understand it,' he replied. 'But the Awakening doesn't, and Aisen sure as hell wouldn't. This whole thing isn't going to stop and wait for her to be ready. It doesn't matter about her potential or even the Genesis power. If she can't *fight*, there's nothing to stop Aisen from taking her.'

There was something else on his mind. But he only stared now, a defiant look in his eyes. Attilla moved towards him, keeping eye contact.

'Fox,' he said gently, that coaxing, resolute born leader in him showing. 'You cannot stop believing in her due to hindrances that mean nothing. There is no time to question, only to hold firm to your beliefs and understand exactly what you know.' He stared imploringly at Fox, who said nothing. After all, it was because of him that she was here. It was his fault.

There was that other matter on his mind, something that had been pressing on his conscience for a while. A quarrel with his leader was not what he wanted; counsel was what he needed now. Attilla waited a few moments, every one making Fox easier to read. The dark vampire was twitching with discomfort of a close analysis.

'What is it?'

'It's easy for you to believe in her.' He gathered the courage to meet his mentor's now curious eyes. 'You don't believe in him.'

Attilla smiled, but it was only for a moment, and the corners of his mouth trembled. 'I doubt Aisen's existence, yes. But I do not doubt that girl's abilities…' He swept his arm in the direction of the bed. 'Yet you believe in Aisen, and still *you* doubt *her*.'

Fox opened his mouth to retort but couldn't find the words. He was her maker, the one who'd insisted on having her turned in the first place. And he doubted her abilities. His head bowed.

Attilla moved his troubled student aside, reaching for the door.

'Stay with her,' he said gently. 'She needs you. Belief in herself is one thing, but without it from others…' He passed her a final fleeting glance. '…she truly does not stand a chance.'

The door closed behind him. Fox made his way back to the chair, sitting without a sound. He reached to the bedside and stubbed out his cigarette in the ashtray that had been brought in. Corey had been trying to quit, anyway. He slid it back across the table and sat quietly with his hands at his knees, and his eyes on her.

He couldn't blame himself, he knew blame made people weak, knew that guilt was one of the worst emotions anyone could succumb to. He moved restlessly in the seat, unable to find any comfort in having to sit there and watch her go through the agony that could've been prevented. He wiped over his eyes agitatedly, leant forwards and took her hand in his.

The few vampires that were in the hall hushed as Attilla entered. They glanced towards him but avoided eye contact. It was not their business to pry about what had happened to the Vessel, however much they would want to know.

Jessie was standing by the bar, her long dress trailing on the ground. She lifted it slightly as she glided towards him, speaking in a hushed voice.

'A word.' Her voice was hollow, eyes like stone circles. Whatever was on her mind, he knew discussing it would not be pleasant. He gave a brisk nod to grant her request.

There was a small room that many had not been privileged to see, to the very east of the building. A small office, pristine and organised. He held the door open for her; she did not thank him. This was where the two leaders came to discuss more sensitive, pressing matters that involved the Clan and its inhabitants.

He sat down behind the desk, but she remained standing, moving around the bookcase as though she was interested. He watched her move silently; it was a disturbing sight for most.

'Jessie?' he questioned eventually, his voice steady as always. Her face was blank, devoid of expression. On the rarest of occasions, he saw a nine-year old girl staring back at him. This was not one of those times. 'Is there a reason you wanted to speak with me?'

'There are a number of minor topics, things that should not be of consequence, that are coming to my attention.' He sat very still, unwavering to her tone. His expressionless face only ever encouraged her behaviour.

'Such as?' he inquired.

She cupped her porcelain hands at her chin, staring over tiny balled fists at him. She looked disappointed if nothing else. He had seen this before, recognising it as an endeavour for him to lower his guard.

'This girl,' she said quietly, moving towards the desk. 'Is there something I should know about her?'

This was risky; he was treading into unfamiliar territory. He would not avoid it, but telling her *anything* would simply add more deceit to the tangled web he had already created and loathed. He had managed to steer clear of the subject of Catrina for so long, because Jessie had never shown an interest. Catrina was just the Vessel to everyone else; there was no reason to care until Aisen's spirit was inside her.

'Why do you ask?'

She smiled, sweet and innocently. Nothing in her expression betrayed the darkness behind that flower of a face, except her eyes, where the deviousness of a cunning mind burned.

'I have spoken with her,' she replied carefully, finally taking the opposite seat.

She could not read him. Six hundred years had taught her many things, but Attilla was someone that most had trouble understanding, regardless of their abilities. She added, 'Was there any reason why you told her the essence of her Fate?'

He paused for a moment. He recalled Catrina telling him that she had an encounter with the child-vampire, but she had not gone into detail, and he had not asked. He could only hope that she had said nothing to arouse suspicion, which was difficult as everything that people did tended to kindle suspicion in Jessie.

'About the Vessel?' It was a risky manoeuvre to work on an assumption, but if he was correct, he could steer the conversation in a direction he knew he could control. She nodded, and his mind stopped spinning.

'I know you think that the truth overcomes every obstacle,' she said gently. He wanted to smile at the irony. 'But you are chancing the rebirth of our creator.'

'…I don't understand what you are implying,' he replied, still in a calm voice, but with the barest hint of spurned disbelief. 'Are you suggesting that the wrong decision was made?'

'I make no implication.' Her voice sliced at the air like daggers. She sighed, closing her mouth as much as she could to hide her fangs. 'She seems to have an understanding about her Fate.'

'She has no choice but to understand. She is going to die. Understanding her Fate is the first step to accepting it.'

'You are putting all your faith in this girl. If her death is inevitable, why do you insist on educating her?'

His fingers twitched on the desk. 'Simply because she is set to die is *not* a reason to disregard her.'

She smiled, thinking she had found his weakness. It broke his heart to have to willingly say that Catrina was going to die, and it was this that Jessie misread as defeat.

'You try so hard.' She smiled softly towards him. Her eyes glistened, something had skipped her mind. She leant over the table. 'But I did not come here only to speak of ill of the Vessel. The Master's tomb has been obtained.'

They stared indefinitely at one another, both with a new look of hope in their eyes. The reason for their expressions may have differed, but neither cared. The tomb was the herald of the new beginning, starting with the coming of their Master.

CHAPTER SEVENTEEN

His voice sliced through the void. 'Open your eyes.'

She had no idea where she was, but she did as the voice instructed. The pain that had burned her insides and made her sick to the point of unconsciousness was gone, replaced by only a tired feeling.

The room looked to have been taken straight from a hotel penthouse suite. She found herself on red silken sheets. The walls were full of the exquisite patterns of expensive wallpaper, a handmade oak desk and a black marble fireplace that wrapped around a genuine coal fire. Yet the scene was crafted with an air of indifference and anonymity, leaving it cold.

She caught sight of herself in a large mirror above the fireplace and made her way over. Ignorant to the warm sensation from the fire, she stared at her reflection. She was dressed in a soft, white dress. She rarely wore make up with the intention of standing out, but now her face was covered in a paling powder that accentuated the red lipstick and her beautifully long black eyelashes.

She looked like a doll.

Someone shifted behind her. The cloaked figure stepped away from the window and removed his hood. He looked tired. His black locks had lost their sheen and his treacle-coloured eyes had glazed over.

She thrust her hand towards the mirror. 'Is this your doing?' As he moved towards her, she stepped back. 'Keep away from me.'

'For *once*,' he growled. 'Listen before you speak.' He looked at her through their reflections. 'I did this to show how your 'creature' sees you.' His voice was quiet; at a stretch she would say he sounded weary. 'Despite your obvious advantages over your vampire kin, you are still no more than an innocent child to him.'

'And he wants to protect me, I get it.'

'For now,' he replied. He stepped closer. Resisting the urge to get away from him, having already witnessed his feral temper first hand. 'I would not put my faith in him.'

'I don't put my *faith* in anyone.'

She'd never heard anything quite like the laugh he returned; it was not vicious or malicious but still shook the room with its intensity. 'You can lie to your peers, Catrina,' he replied gently. 'But I can see the truth behind your eyes. Your fear over what you are becoming drives you to put faith in a protector. He will use that to pull you to him.'

'And what,' she snapped, 'I'm supposed to trust you over him?'

He shook his head. 'I am not here to form an alliance with you. I only ask that you remain wary of all around you, no matter how they portray themselves.'

'Including *you*, who uses...' She rubbed at her face, smearing the make up in an attempt to wipe it off. '...tricks and illusions to gain my confidence. This isn't what I am!'

Whatever the reason was for making her look as she did, he had gone to great lengths to perform the glamour, and he would not let it go unnoticed.

He reached out sharply and grabbed her wrist. He marched her up to the fireplace, turned her around. He hooked his hand around the back of the neck and forced her to look.

'Look at yourself,' he commanded. She had invoked primitive anger in him. '*Look at yourself!*' Reluctantly, she opened her eyes, but he did not lessen his grip. '*This* is what he will make you.'

His fingers dug deep into the back of her neck. She seethed in anger more than pain. 'Why are you doing this?'

He let go and stepped back submissively. 'I only show you what he will not. While you may not approve of my methods, I find it to be most effective with people of your conduct.'

She disregarded his answer, unable to ask whether he meant it as an insult. 'Do you know who he is?' He gave a slight nod, all anger left his face, replaced by a solemn look. 'How long have you been enemies?'

The question triggered a dejected look in his eyes. 'As long as I can remember.'

She felt a slight spasm of pity for him. He was not the strong force he was trying to be. 'You're afraid of him.'

'I would not come if he was still with you. I thank the fact that he has left you, for now.'

'He won't be coming back,' she said, feeling quite sure of herself. She had made herself clear to the creature, and despite his quite confidence in her needs, he was gone. The figure was next in line.

'You understand nothing of what you have become a part of,' he replied gently. 'He will not leave you until you have served his purpose.'

'Which is?' There was too much being kept from her; perhaps if someone were to enlighten her, she could find a better basis for judgement.

'That is the thing you do not want to know.'

Her eyes started to sting, there was a light coming from somewhere in her mind. She was regaining consciousness. The Infirmary light stung at her half-opened eyes but the figure still stared at her. She tried to hold on, waiting for him to explain.

'Tell me!' she demanded of him. He took her hands in his and held them to his chest, a desperate look in his eyes.

'It's not in my power,' he replied, holding her to him. She tried to pull away, but in his world, her strength meant little, if not nothing at all. 'Telling you would be your death.'

There was a blinding flash, and for an instant she saw nothing but his face, and the look in his eyes. She had to understand the severity of what was happening; she could not fall into any traps that had been so carefully laid out for her.

There were voices, people standing around her, all trying to speak. Her ears felt as though they were going to burst. She put her hands over her head and leant forwards; the pain returned, ripping at her stomach. The people that gathered around were no more than blurred silhouettes; someone touched her shoulder, and she jerked her head back. The clarity returned, accompanied by the pain. It was Attilla, trying to get her to lie back down.

The world took form. There were three people nearby. One was trying to move the other two away. Maria.

She glanced around the room, her eyes bringing the world back together, as her brain tried to fit everything that had happened into some sort of order.

'How long have I been out?' Her voice was little more than a grunt.

'Three days.' It was from Maria.

Catrina sighed heavily, her body ached and she felt weaker than she had in a long time.

'Perhaps we should let you come around?' Attilla suggested, ever the gentleman. Catrina gave him a nod, which he took as indication to take Maria by the shoulder and guide her towards the door. Fox remained seated, shaking his head to Attilla's silent request to join them.

She wouldn't meet his eyes at first, head turned to face the wall. She wanted him to speak; to condemn her and have done with it. When he just sat and stared, she had no choice but to start it.

'What are you waiting for?' The painkillers made her light-headed. He didn't reply but wouldn't stop staring, either. 'What? You want to have your dig at me first? You want to bitch at me for going out on my own? If that's the case, you'd better get it over with, because my interest in your arrogance has gone.' She wanted to fold her arms over her chest, but the pain in her body constricted her movement. 'You must have spent the best part of my unconsciousness planning how you were going to condemn my actions.'

'…Are you done?' he said, his voice much more powerful and consequential than she remembered. He leant forwards in the chair. 'Do you know how close you came to dying?'

'Oh, *that* would have been a shame,' she snarled. 'Who else would take all this *shit* from you people?'

'Do you think I care that you could be the Genesis?' he asked. She saw the ashtray, brimming with the butt ends of smoked cigarettes. He'd sat there a long time. Maybe he'd been too worried about her to even think about criticising her when she woke up. Her anger subsided and gave way to guilt. 'I thought you were going to *die*…what Fate wants from you was the last thing on my mind.'

He stood up and went to the door without a goodbye. She wanted to apologise. Stubborn pride forced the words into the pit of her stomach.

She couldn't tell from the way he moved whether he was angry or disappointed in her faith in him. Either way, she wished she hadn't spoken.

She thought about the figure, and she hated him. Somehow, this was his fault, whether directly or otherwise, she'd find some way to blame him. She looked up to the ceiling, the dream fading into the dull non-colour of her surroundings. The Infirmary was no hotel, and she could assume that she hardly looked the princess part. She could feel the bruises and wounds under the bandages; her stomach churned from the bullet wound.

She had no recollection of how she'd returned to the factory; she could only assume it to be the Dealer's chivalrous actions. The reminiscence of pain washed over her senses until she shuddered. She closed her eyes. Something was very wrong, but she was none the wiser. She should've died, but somehow she had survived.

At least the figure had said something constructive. She didn't trust him, nor did she believe him. His dogmatic behaviour and blatant refusal to leave her be gave a sense of claustrophobia, but one thing stuck in her mind.

'*That is the thing you do not want to know.*' The words echoed in her ears. His face flashed before her eyes, voice ringing out. '*He will not leave you until you have served his purpose.*' She didn't believe the figure any more than she believed the creature. She didn't trust them, confide in them, or lay any hopes on them. They were pitted against each other, trying to find someone to support them in their indeterminate state. She opened her eyes again, tried not to think about it, which only brought back the pain.

She wouldn't be sleeping much in the near future.

Her recovery was fairly short but by no means sweet.

Fox made it his aim to keep at her side at all times. He made no mention to their conversation. If it'd offended or otherwise affected him, he didn't say. He didn't lecture her about going out alone that night; her 'speech' made him realise it wasn't necessary. She knew her own mistake. At first, she walked gingerly with him, constantly waiting for him to do or say something, but he never did.

His mind was taken with other things, such as the small matter of the Awakening. There was a rumour that Aisen's tomb had been found. It had the Clan in a sense of anticipation; the reality of it finally sunk in.

Vampires talked more amongst each other, chat idly about the flying rumours of the tomb and of their Master. Facts were quickly distorted, word began to spread that people had seen him. The possibilities of his being were limited only by the Clan's seemingly infinite imagination.

Catrina's strength returned in a long and drawn-out process. She and Fox still trained, but he didn't want to while she was still unstable. It was only when she started going to the training rooms by herself that he gave in.

After a few weeks, she was still in some pain. But every night it faded; her mobility was barely compromised anymore.

CHAPTER EIGHTEEN

The unusual abundance of people struck her as she and Fox came into the hall that night.

Something important was happening. Maria was there; the human was rarely in the company of so many vampires. She never seemed to be out of the Infirmary. Attilla waited for the two of them to approach. Rose was playing wrestling with Sonny, her body halfway over the bar. She was in the process of winning.

'What's going on?' Catrina asked.

Rose stopped mid-wrestle, straightened her hair and made her way over. The redhead put her arm around Catrina's shoulder and turned her towards the door, lifting her finger.

'We're bringing the tomb,' she said. An area had been cleared on the far wall to the left of the bar. The tables had been rearranged, and there was a clearly set path from the doors. 'We're gonna get first peeks at the Master before the rest of the rabble.'

'The Awakening?' she asked, without knowing why her voice sounded so shaky. Rose scoffed loudly and shook her head.

'No, not the Awakening, munchkin.' She beamed, slipping her arm away. 'We just wanna have a gander at him. I mean, judging so far, he could be just about anyone. Are you in?'

Catrina looked at the others, who seemed ready to go. Realisation hit quickly, and for a very brief moment she couldn't breathe. Rose and Maria were going, both of whom believed that she was the Vessel. Rose wanted her to come. Did they want her to look at the face of the man who'd kill her? Yet Attilla and Fox waited, too. Nothing to be afraid of, perhaps?

A few cars passed them as they drove through the hollow night. The air waned, anticipating something, before picking up again. Fox's eyes locked out of the passenger window, watching the world outside. Attilla and Maria talked in depth about the notes she'd brought. Rose tapped her hand against the steering wheel, miming the song lyrics, given the company.

Catrina sat on the other side of Attilla, leaning her arm against the window, watching the streets pass, lost in thought. She began to feel light-headed, imagining how many vampires would kill to be where she was now, to have the chance to see their creator. It was like waiting to see into the eyes of God. Yet there was that haunting feeling that something was wrong. There was always the chance the tomb would be empty, or the deciphered Ritual would fail to raise him.

Everyone was expecting a miracle.

'Where is it we're going?' she asked to break her pessimistic views on the situation.

'Louis has been watching the tomb since it was recovered,' Attilla explained.

'No one knows why he got the honour,' Rose muttered.

'It was for the best,' Attilla admonished.

Rose dipped her head slightly. 'Yes, Sir.'

The car turned around a sharp corner, keeping its momentum enough to jerk forwards, as Rose slammed on the breaks. The passengers were used to her behaviour behind the wheel, so it wasn't much of a shock.

This particular part of the city was not fitting to Louis's character. It had a historic, gothic feel to it. The buildings were well-made but old, and time had not been kind to them. They loomed over the small group, as though watching the world move below. The windows weren't boarded, but no light shone through.

They stopped before one of the larger ones; an ancient structure made of the type of sandstone that weathered terribly.

Thick drapes covered the windows on the second floor—the first floor having no windows—and no light came from behind them. Fox checked his gun.

Attilla turned back. 'Is that necessary?'

'I'm not taking chances,' he replied with a shrug, placing the gun back into the lining of his coat. He cast a suspicious look about the place; not safe enough for him.

On the wall beside the door was a small intercom panel. Rose slammed it with her fist and grinned at the closed door. A loud buzzing came from inside the building; there was no doubt that the occupants had heard it. After a few moments a muffled noise came over the speaker.

'...Yes?' The voice was female, cautious and direct.

'Avon calling, I've got that order of anti-bitch cream for you,' Rose quipped into the microphone. The sound of a man laughing was distorted by the interference of the panel.

'...Wait there.' The voice was no longer cautious, only aggravated, and the panel fell silent.

Rose daintily put her finger back on the button. 'Like we can do anything else other than freeze our asses off out here.'

There was no reply; whoever had been there was on her way to the door. Rose stood back with the others and waited.

The sound of a numerous latches unlocking echoed through the silent street, chains pulled to the side, and a key turning sounded the final precautionary measure. Ebony stood in the open doorway, her deep eyes lingered for a moment on Rose. There was nothing to say; no need for formal salutations. She just held the door open and allowed them inside.

The interior fitted the gothic feel of its outer appearance. It was roughly the same size as the main hall at the factory, and the belly of the main structure was hollowed out just the same. A wide balcony ran around the entire floor, and a huge set of stairs faced the entrance. Along the balcony was nothing but shelves upon shelves of books. Louis was heading down the stairs, a smile already on his face.

The ground floor was proof that he and Ebony had been working for a long time. Star charts were strewn over tables and the floor, chewed pencils and scribbled notes were discarded everywhere.

Louis smiled at Rose. 'Avon…classic.'

She grinned back at him, moving towards the star charts. Each chart showed different aspects of the night sky. But on most was something Catrina recognised without anyone having to tell her. The strange arches that created the Mark of Divinity were everywhere she looked. The stars were connected with rough pencil lines, each one a more complete shape. Catrina followed Rose, who was scanning over the charts, brushing her hand carelessly over the sheets.

'Is this real-time?' Catrina asked.

'Pretty much,' Rose replied. 'They keep moving all the time. It's getting closer every day.'

Ebony took the folder Maria had brought, and the two moved to a more orderly table top, away from the chaos. Attilla and Fox headed for Louis, who watched them approach with just a hint of caution.

'Has there been any progress?' Attilla asked. Louis motioned them towards the largest table, as Rose became engrossed in a book she'd picked up. As she moved away, Louis scanned over the cluttered desk. He lifted the corner of one of the charts, pulling it out from under the scrunched-up papers and empty cans of soda. Resting it flat, he moved his finger over a pencil mark outlining the symbol's presence in the cosmos.

'Everything seems to be in order,' he said. 'But I'll admit it's coming in a little slow.' They both looked at him, but he could only shrug. There was no better way of explaining what the stars were showing. 'If you take the time span between the first movement and the first Awakening…' He pulled a second chart from beneath the first. 'This is where it should be.' Again, he lifted the chart to reveal the first. 'There isn't much difference, I'd say a week…two at most. But there is this one thing…' He took one of the many notepads, flitting through the pages. He held it so they could see three of the symbols, each more complete than the last, and he continued while gesturing to each one. 'This is basically how it's been going…each week we get more. But…' He flipped the page over to a scanned computer photograph of the stars. The symbol was there, but the look on both Attilla and Fox's faces was enough to say that it was unexpected.

'It's regressing,' Attilla said, taking the pad.

Fox was not so easily persuaded. 'What do you have about it? Theories, past evidence...anything?'

Louis grinned.

'Of course I have my *theories*,' he joked. Fox gave him a persuasive glance to continue, but Louis sighed. 'I don't have much to go on, you have to understand that. I mean, at the first Awakening...there was nothing like this reported. It went from point A to point B. It didn't start reverting back to point A again. The ritual book says 'the Heavens will know of his coming'. If they're retreating...I'd have to assume that the 'Heavens' or whatever powers it is *don't* know anymore...possibly that he's dying at the dividing line, that he just doesn't have the power to bring himself back.'

Catrina stood with Rose, pretending to be interested in what she was being shown. She was also listening to what was being said between the three men.

'How long have they been regressing?' Attilla asked. His eyes remained on the notebook, his hand holding the page that illustrated the right path of the stars. Louis reached over and tapped the photograph.

'That was a week ago. There are more, taken every day to as far back as two weeks.' He could read their faces; they asked why he hadn't said something earlier. He shrugged. 'I didn't think it was going to stay that way. Stars aren't the most predictable of things.' He paused; clearly talking about it was not something he had been looking forward to. 'But this...' He tapped the picture again. 'It's been that way for four days now.'

'So it *has* stopped?' Attilla clarified. This was a comfort to know, and Louis nodded.

'Maybe it's some way of telling us that he's building his strength...all we can do is wait.'

'For how long?' Fox asked.

These theories he'd tossed about in his mind since the regression had started; if he couldn't think of an answer then, he doubted he would find one now. 'I can't tell...I don't know.'

'So what happens now?' Fox asked, unwilling to let it lie. Whatever was slowly going wrong, it had to be righted as soon as possible, or it would mean more trouble than anyone was able to handle at that time.

Louis took a very long moment to build himself up to say what he had been putting off. 'It's stopped. This means the Awakening will have to be postponed.' He looked at Attilla, whose countenance matched his own. Not everyone would be as understanding. Louis voiced what others wouldn't. 'Jessie.'

They shared a glance that confirmed their anxieties.

Catrina moved towards them, since Rose had started talking more to herself. The concept of what it all meant was easy enough to pick up and she was interested in what they were saying in such hushed voices. She didn't know if she was supposed to be listening; Rose seemed numb to it. She glanced over at Ebony and Maria, clearly she wasn't able to hear it, and maybe Ebony had been over the circumstances so many times she had tuned out.

But Catrina was new to it, and everything they said only drew her further into the conversation. She didn't care if she wasn't meant to listen.

'...Jessie doesn't believe in this,' Fox said, gesturing to the entire ground floor. He waited for Attilla to make some sort of answer, but he was deep in thought and not about to be disturbed. So Fox turned to the astronomer. 'She won't postpone...'

Louis was calmer, confident in his own notion to put his faith behind it. 'It doesn't matter what Jessie thinks or says, no offence to her,' he replied, the last part intended for Attilla, who wasn't listening. Fox looked on with troubled eyes. 'You can't expect a vampire like Jessie to be able to force the Master of the entire Vampire Nation into this world just because she wants it. It's his decision at the end of it all.'

Fox's eyes drifted; for once he didn't understand what was being said. His expression was etched on his face, it was disbelief and the usual mockery, but just a slight hint of fear, something that looked foreign on his face.

Louis shrugged. 'You have to see it this way. The Heavens don't predict the future. Those stars are Aisen's way of forewarning.'

Catrina was suddenly standing with them. She *had* to be a part of this conversation. She took the notepad off Louis and patted the back of it against her hand. There was a theory of her own that she wanted to make.

'So he's doing it himself,' she said. Louis overlooked the fact that she had interrupted a discussion she was not involved in, and he spread his arms towards her.

'Exactly,' Louis said. 'See…Catrina gets it.'

'You were listening?' Attilla said, waking from his deep trance.

'It sounded serious. I take it I was right?'

'You heard what he said,' Fox replied, reaching into his jacket and pulling out his cigarettes.

'The timing's out,' Louis said directly to Catrina.

She looked at the photograph. 'Can you think of any reason why Aisen's doing this?'

The question that needed the most attention was the one there was no answer for, but there were ideas…

'He could be too weak,' Louis suggested. Attilla, who had remained silent through most of it all, finally put forth his own speculations. He shook his head, putting his hand to his face to shake that tired and weary look that appeared.

'It's not that.' His mind struggled with the burden of new information and hindrances. He held the gaze with Catrina for too long and she had to look away. Her withdrawal caused him to speak again. 'He's either afraid of something…' That caught Fox's attention, who glanced subtly at Catrina, and then warningly back at his mentor. Attilla ignored it. 'Or else he's waiting for something.'

The words worried her. Aisen would be afraid of nothing, save maybe the Genesis. But he would wait for nothing, either, save the Vessel. It didn't help the conflicting feelings about her lack of identity, since either way it pointed to her.

'What would he be afraid of?' Louis asked. Attilla's eyes drifted over Catrina as he looked at them all.

'The Genesis,' he replied. He gestured discreetly towards Maria, at which point Louis bit his lip, subduing his own humoured expression.

'Attilla, please. There is no 'other' Genesis.'

'It would explain why the stars show him as retreating,' Fox agreed, although the force he had to use in his voice was a clear indication that he wasn't happy at saying so.

Louis smiled openly. 'You don't believe that any more than I do. But this other concept...this waiting idea...I can follow that. But what would he be waiting for? This is Aisen we're talking about. He's not going to sit back and wait for it to come to him. If he wants something, he'll take it.'

Those last few words sank in silently. They may have had their theories, but putting it into practice would prove more difficult.

'I'm worried about him,' Maria said quietly, when she was sure that the others were too deep in their conversation to hear them. Ebony looked up from the notes, her usually hard face softened with concern over her friend's well being. They had spoken about the stars situation, but Maria had hardly been interested.

'Who?'

Maria sighed and closed her eyes for a moment. A presentation of personal feelings was not an easy task for her to accomplish.

'Attilla,' she replied with a heavy sigh. She tilted her head at her partner, and the way he was looking at Catrina. He held her far too highly. 'He's getting attached to Catrina...I don't think he'll be able to hand her over when the time comes. If he refuses to sacrifice her, Aisen will kill him, too.'

A silence fell; they watched the others talking, unable to catch words of the conversation.

'There's nothing I can tell you to make you feel less anxious,' Ebony said, her voice soft, calming. She had the most unusual ability to change her expression from frightening to compassionate. 'And I have no evidence to contradict your opinions, I have only my own. But I have known Attilla a long time. I know where he stands with Aisen and the Awakening. This is something he has wanted since before I met him.'

'The Awakening was never his dream.' Maria passed a pen carelessly through her fingers. Ebony was shocked, the sound she made was enough to make Maria look back up. 'I'm not saying he's against it, but it was always more of Jessie's idea.'

The vampire scoffed at the name. 'Jessica has always had plans of her own,' she replied with such scorn it chilled the air around them. 'Attilla is a very complex mind to understand, but Jessie…she is the most predictable being I've ever met. You may think you understand Attilla, and who knows…maybe you do. But Jessie…she wants the Awakening to come to pass because of one thing.'

'Which is?'

Again Ebony smiled. 'Respect. It's so predictable, yet everyone else has overlooked it. But it doesn't matter…as soon as Aisen is reborn, he will kill her for it.'

'For what?'

'For using his power and heritage to regain the respect her twisted little mind has caused her to lose for all these years.'

'Ebony,' Maria admonished. 'How can you think like that? I know Jessie isn't the most innocent of people…'

'—Others excuse her because she was made as a child,' Ebony interrupted. Her voice was getting that little louder, which she was quick to subdue. 'Regardless of everything that she has done…they still see her as such. And this girl…' She motioned to Catrina, although it was such a subtle action that Maria hardly noticed. 'If it comes to it, Jessie will kill her too, and even Attilla won't be able to stop her. If she wants the girl out of the way, she will do it.'

Again came the smile; she knew something the others did not. She'd studied the same as Louis, seen the same patterns in the stars, and she had a theory of her own.

'You want to know what I think?' she asked.

'I'm not sure I do,' Maria's voice was a touch sharper. It softened immediately. 'I'm sorry. Go on.'

Ebony shifted her weight as though deliberating whether or not she was going to reply. '...My mother always taught me that predictability is a constant...' she said eventually. She didn't have the same reservations about saying that the Awakening was painted with doubts and irregularity. Just because it wasn't going exactly to plan was no reason for Ebony to doubt it coming to pass, and she said so. When she'd finished, and before Maria even had time to let it sink in, she finished her theory. 'I don't know Aisen's reason for denying us the honour of his presence, but I know what Jessie will do as a result. As soon as it comes to telling her that it's postponed, she will mull over a new opportunity, and then you'll *know* what I mean.'

Rose rubbed her hands together, as she headed to the four of them, whose conversation had died away.

'Alrighty then,' she said, loud enough to break everyone's concentration. 'Let's get this tomb shifted, shall we?' Maybe they should have included her in the conversation. She was quickly filled in but was none too pleased about the outcome. 'So I came all this way, and you're not even gonna let us take it...'

'Rose, it's like five minutes away,' Louis pointed out.

'It's the principle, my Calvin Klein clad friend. I came here with the idea that Aisen was coming home with us. Just because his flight's been delayed doesn't mean we can't take his jet.'

'It would be safer left here, for the time being,' Attilla said. His words were enough to settle the matter. She sighed, turning her attention back to Louis.

'Then at least let me see it. Can you riddle me that much?'

Attilla gave consent and Louis headed towards the back of the hollowed-out room. There was a door under the stairs that led down into the building's lower level. Rose quickly followed him as Attilla gestured to Catrina and Fox. It was their decision if they wanted to see it.

Fox nodded and followed, but Catrina hesitated.

'I'm not ready to see him...not yet.'

'There is no need to worry,' Attilla replied calmly. 'It is sealed.'

The building's underbelly was just like the factory; networks of corridors that Catrina would never find her own way out of. The others knew exactly where they were going. Fox explained that the Clan used to live there. Slayers had attacked and they'd been forced to leave. Louis wasn't so timid and took up residence there some time later.

Louis stopped at a small wooden door and punched in an access code. It seemed pointless, as the door was practically hanging off its hinges.

There was nothing to decorate the walls, only the cement from the skeleton of the building itself, and a set of wooden stairs leading down. There was another dim light shining from the foot of the stairs as Fox and Rose headed down. Catrina stopped at the door. Louis went down next, smiling as he passed as incentive to follow.

She tried to shake the feeling that something was wrong. The air felt thick, drawing her into the darkness. The atmosphere had the same obscurity as one of her dreams, and she had the same lack of control. She took the first guarded step.

For the size of the building, this basement room was small. It was littered with debris and fickle wooden support beams. No one had thought to clean up the mess before putting the tomb there. Her eyes cast towards the stone box. She hadn't thought it to be so large. Standing upright, it towered over them all.

Fox stood a few steps away from it, taking in the view as a whole, letting that overpowering feeling of supremacy wash over him. Rose, on the other hand, was getting as close as possible, running her hands over the smooth surfaces, a mischievous smile playing about her face.

'I hate to say I told you so, but...' Louis said, moving up alongside Rose. He took her by the arm and guided her to the front of the tomb. There was not a single word carved into the stone. This box, while huge, didn't appear extraordinary. It was a wonder they'd been able to distinguish it from any other. 'Not a dot,' Louis added smugly.

She shrugged. 'Doesn't mean a thing, pretty boy.'

Fox moved towards them. 'What is it?'

Rose hurriedly filled him in on Louis's 'theory'.

Catrina stood at the foot of the stairs. Her eyes were tightly closed, listening to something much louder and more powerful than the others.

Voices rose in the air surrounding her. They were obscure and incoherent. All were ones she'd never heard before. Panicked and choked; voices of the dead. She opened her eyes and cast them around the room, but aside from the mammoth tomb, there was nothing unusual. The voices took no form, but they grew louder, until she could hear nothing else.

She wanted to be alone in the room, alone with the slab of stone that separated her from seeing who their Master was. The voices began to whisper a command in a foreign tongue. She understood perfectly.

They told her to open it.

The suggestion swayed her; she wanted to look upon Aisen in his true glory. She barely made it three steps towards the tomb and the others, before the air descended on her like a fog. She came face to face with the figure. He was adorned as always in the thick woollen cloak. He looked real. He touched her shoulder. She glanced over to the others; they failed to notice any change.

'No,' the figure said, firmly pushing her back. The shock that he had the strength to move her was enough to put fear into her. 'You are not to see him.' He motioned to the stone box. 'You are not ready to lay your eyes upon one as he. Your thoughts are tainted with your precious creature's words.'

She slipped behind a wooden support beam, so the others wouldn't see her speaking to thin air.

'I'm not concerned with him,' she hissed quietly. 'I haven't seen him since he offered to leave. But if *you're* afraid of him, I'm tempted to ask him back.'

'You would put your trust in one through spite of me?'

'I don't like you,' she spat. 'And as for Aisen…I'll see him when I want to. If I choose to see him now, you can't stop me.' She headed back to the others. The figure tried to block her path, and she had to physically shove him to the side in order to keep moving. He began to fade. He tried to stop her, but this time his arm fell through.

'Can we get it open?' she asked, breaking their concentration. Rose was examining the contours of the stone.

'It looks like the front panel's been stuck on with cement,' she said with a laugh. 'Or some bitchin' superglue.'

Catrina smiled, catching the figure a sharp sideways glance. He was struggling to stay in her world. 'Is there any way to get into it?'

'Have patience, young padawan,' Rose remarked, trying to get her fingers under the cracks in the long-since dried adhesive. 'I think we need a crowbar or something.' She glanced casually around the room for something that would suffice to break into the tomb that had been closed for millennia. 'Ah ha!' She leapt off the small platform the tomb had been placed on, picking up a metal bar that had been a load-bearer for more debris. She ignored the consequential mess she made and headed back to the platform.

Fox blocked her path. 'We shouldn't be the ones doing this.'

'I won't tell if you won't. Don't you want to have a gander?' she asked sweetly. 'Just a little sneaky peek? Please?' She pouted, but Fox remained unwavering, holding out his hand.

Catrina took the bar from her before Fox could. 'I don't know about you, but I'm sick of waiting.'

She could feel the tomb beckoning. Pushing back the thought that Aisen was drawing her in because he wanted to meet his sacrifice, she stood before it, staring at the blank front panel. She raised the bar and ran it over the edges, looking for a gap.

'Stop.'

She locked eyes with the figure and shook her head, finding a break in the slab. She felt the power behind it, the energy inside, begging to be set free. The figure grabbed her by the wrist. The others saw no one except Catrina standing there, with a shocked look on her whitening face.

Using all the strength he could muster, the figure slammed his fist into her solar plexus. It drained him considerably, because as she fell to her knees, he faded and was gone. But his job was done, as she wouldn't get to see inside. Fox came to her assistance, agreeing when Louis suggested it was too much for a fledgling to attempt.

As she was led towards the stairs, the figure reappeared at the front of the tomb, his dark eyes locked on her.

She couldn't speak, she could barely hear the others asking what happened. She managed to say she felt overwhelmed, and that was enough to settle them.

The note was solemn upon leaving Louis's home; no one had what they'd come for.

Catrina's head was aching as she leant it against the car window; the world outside became nothing more than a blur.

Thinking about Aisen and his coming, with the figure in his way, it explained why the stars had stopped moving. The figure was keeping the Master back. It didn't explain what he was hiding. He was trying to stop anyone from opening it, stop Aisen from rising.

CHAPTER NINETEEN

The only event anticipated before the Awakening ceremony was that of the Tournament final. Rose knew she was going to lose and that it'd be a brutal defeat, but she didn't care. She wanted to test her skills on someone who couldn't be beaten.

The room was overcrowded that night; Rose was standing impatiently in the improvised ring.

'He does know it's tonight, doesn't he?' she yelled over to Fox, who nodded. She cracked her knuckles and stretched; she was surprised Jessie wasn't here. She usually liked brutality.

The chatter became anxious whispers of doubt and amazement as minutes went by; was it possible Attilla was going to forfeit? She had to admit that it was petty to insist on the Tournament's final round, when the Awakening's very premise was crumbling and the Clan none the wiser. Attilla had more important things to worry about than the entertainment of his Clan.

She ran her fingers through her hair, her heart racing. If he didn't show up, it would be a first, and the match would be hers. But she didn't want to win like that; she wanted a good fight.

The opening door silenced everyone.

Attilla walked through the vampires; the look on his face was not something they could begin to understand. Fox nodded courteously. The vampires dared not speak as he walked through the pathway they created. Rose kept her posture as he approached. They faced one another; the vampires watched in awe.

Attilla removed his jacket. He carried an impressive physique beneath his usual attire. It wasn't a sight seen often; he remained somewhat reserved about his own physical prowess. He gestured to their arena.

'Combat without armament, as was your request. Do you agree?'

'Yes, sir.'

'As you have reached this point, I trust the rules need not be reinforced?'

'No, sir, I'm clear on the rules. Damn clear,' she added with a brisk and certain nod.

They raised their fists as though some invisible flag had been felled. Her body shook with excitement and a hint of anxiety. She didn't mind losing, as long as she'd still be able to walk.

Sonny approached the edge of the circle and stood with Fox, who then leant over and spoke in a low voice. 'Have you seen Catrina?'

Sonny smiled boyishly. 'Should make her wear a leash.' He coughed away the remark. 'No, I haven't seen her.'

The fight started before Fox had chance to question her whereabouts. He hadn't seen her since they had returned from Louis's. She seemed angry when she left. He tried not to think about it and focused on the fight.

Rose was on the attack; her carefully premeditated punches were knocked away without a second thought. She knew that he wasn't putting his entire force behind his movements. It was always drawn out for the spectators.

She kicked out. He hooked his arm around her knee; shifting his weight sent her spinning to the ground. She heaved back up and launched forwards, starting a dance-like exchange of punches. If she was going to lose, she may as well go down at her best.

No one heard the doors open this time, as Catrina silently took in the scene. To watch them fighting was not entertaining to her now. There was nothing incredible about it. It was brutality in its element, the instinctive nature of every living creature that fought to survive. This may have been for the benefit of everyone, something to learn from, someone to idolise. And yet she felt nothing watching it, as she leant against the wall by the door, her eyes drifted across the crowd.

What were they really watching? Did they just want to see how much pain one could put the other in? She didn't have much room to build such high opinions; the reason she'd loved her job so much in the first place was so she could kill. It was too late to go back, to change time…this was who she was.

Or maybe this was a chance to start something else. This vampire 'gift' she'd been given had been a way to go back: this was an entirely new life, one that so far—although it had been with its flaws—was not quite as shallow as that of a paid killer.

Rose tried a few strike-punches, and Attilla moved her aside without blinking. As he spun her around she kicked her legs behind her, the force spun her onto her back but it did the same to him. The entire crowd froze as he slid across the floor and she slammed onto the ground. Using his momentum, Attilla shifted himself upright, as she dragged herself to her knees. When she was on her feet, both started exchanging fierce blows again, never once getting a punch to hit its mark.

Catrina spotted Fox, who thankfully didn't notice her. She watched him carefully, that look in his eyes as he watched his beloved teacher. There was something else to him, something that ran deeply under his cold exterior. She was yet to witness it herself, but others suggested he was a good man, though not in such words. He had to be, or else Attilla wouldn't have taken him as such a close confederate. Something must have happened to him that made him this way.

Still, his behaviour was overbearing. Whether it was because he saw himself as a protector, or whether it was simply out of need to be close to her, she didn't know. Either way, she couldn't blame herself for his attitude; if he wouldn't accept her as she was, then they'd just never get along.

Her thoughts were broken as the ground shook with the force that Attilla threw Rose to the ground. She wasn't surprised at the blood she spat out, lifting her hands up in submission, knowing that any more fighting wouldn't go her way.

Attilla's face softened in an instant, as he helped her to her feet.

She wiped at her mouth and smiled. 'You've fight in you yet, old man.'

The crowd cheered and rushed forwards to comment on the brief fight. There was no need for commiserations: the outcome was expected. Fox moved slowly from the crowd, making his way towards Catrina with thoughtful and slightly brighter eyes.

It had been raining constantly over the past few nights. Fox took the Mercedes; they weren't about to walk. He didn't turn the radio on, and the car felt drained without sound. Catrina looked out of the window, watching the drops of rain trail down the sheet of glass. Although he was keeping his eyes on the road, he could not help but glance at her now and again.

They were going to another bar; she needed to feed and had wanted to be away from the Clan. She sometimes missed the solitude. She had never minded being tagged as a heartless killer. It had worked for her. It stopped people trying to befriend her, people who could be killed for having connections with her. Fox was not trying to befriend; she still wondered if he cared about her at all.

They entered the building without any difficulty despite the gathering queue still waiting in the rain. He ordered their drinks and they sat at one of the tables and waited. She was allowed to pick her choice of victim and didn't intend to move until she found someone she wanted.

Fox left his cigarette lighter out on the table after lighting up. She'd never noticed it before. It was a small, box-shaped, Zippo brand of lighter with an engraving on the side of an eagle in flight. It was difficult to make out; the years had not been kind to it, and it was covered in other marks that she guessed could have only come from the time spent in his pocket.

'Is that valuable?' she asked. He was not paying much attention; his eyes scanning the room for signs of his own prey.

'What?' he asked in a half-interested tone, until his eyes fell onto the lighter. He realised his mistake and quickly took it off the table.

She spoke up before he had a chance to put it away. 'Valuable,' she repeated.

He held the lighter in his free hand, casting his eyes over it as though seeing it for the first time. 'Depends what you mean by valuable.'

He had no idea how intrigued she was. She knew it was risky to venture further into the origins of the thing he held between his fingers, but this was the closest she had come so far in finding something more about him.

She leant forwards. '…Sentimental?'

Instead of moving away from the subject as he usually did, he shrugged and put the lighter on the table.

'It was my mother's,' he said eventually. 'My father gave it to her, and she gave it to me.'

She was stunned for the briefest of instants. She'd never thought of Fox with family, more imagined that he had simply 'begun to exist' thirty-two years ago. She immediately wanted to know who they were, where they lived, and if he ever called them.

Then it hit her. '…Was?'

He didn't bother to reply, and she regretted asking. His visage was something she had never seen from him. Behind his eyes was a stinging look of pain.

'My father died when I was very young. I never knew him.' His voice was hollow and his eyes didn't lose that hurt look. She had to have empathy for that much; she'd never known her father, either.

'What about your mother?' she pressed. His face was contorting with slow bitterness, drinking his entire whiskey back in one. 'Is she…?'

'She's dead,' he clarified sharply. She sat back in the chair. While this was months down the line of knowing and spending close to every night with him, this was the first personal conversation they'd had.

'When?' She knew it insensitive to press on a subject that was clearly so disturbing, but curiosity was in control. He knew everything about her; she held firm the belief that she, therefore, deserved to know *something* about him in return.

'When did she die?' he verified. He thought for a moment, making her wonder how many years he spent alone, between having a mother and becoming a vampire. 'How long have I been a vampire?'

She thought it was a trick question, or that he had killed his mother through some sort of confusion in his early vampiric life.

He read over her expression and smiled. 'I didn't kill her. She was already a vampire.'

She tried to picture his mother: how she looked and what her attitude was like. She doubted Fox inherited his mannerisms from a woman. Someone like Fox generally had very polite mothers; they inherited behaviours from the fathers' side. Rio had inherited his mother's charming looks, but his personality had been Tony through and through.

'...What happened to her?' she asked.

'She made me a vampire, and then...' He stopped. She guessed it was difficult for him. Although she couldn't relate to him, she could understand that his family ties had been more substantial than hers. 'The Slayers had been after her for years,' he continued eventually. 'She knew it was only a matter of time before they...' He turned away, his mind taking him back. His look turned sour in resentment towards those who had killed her.

'Did you know?' she asked, trying to break his concentration and wipe that disturbing look from his face. 'That she was a vampire?'

He shook his head. 'Not until she turned me. Until that point, I saw things the same way you did, and I didn't believe her when she told me.' He took a long drag of his cigarette. 'But...I didn't have time to question her, either.' The smallest of depraved smiles appeared as he took the cigarette out of his mouth. 'I killed two Slayers on my first night as a vampire, the ones who killed her. Took me almost four years to track down the third.'

She watched his expression change; he was proud of his accomplishments. He must've hungered for revenge, especially to uphold his mother's name. But this explanation of his vampire heritage left the question of how and why he wasn't a rogue.

'How did you get into the Clan?' She doubted there was much to that story presuming the worst had already been told.

'That was Sonny,' he said. 'When the police came to my mother's apartment, they found her and two others dead...'

'The Slayers,' she clarified, and he gave a slight nod. 'And you?'

'I wasn't there,' he replied. 'I met Sonny some time later in another Clan. That's all there was to it. I went to Attilla's Clan, and I've been there since.'

That didn't answer her question. 'But how did you meet Sonny?' She wasn't even sure why she wanted to know, but she had an inkling that there was more to it than him simply *happening* to be there. Fox looked as though his entire purpose was to be in the Clan, to work alongside Attilla, and to have been sent after her. To the question, Fox merely sat back in the chair.

'That's enough history for one night.' The silence was more awkward than usual, as he glanced towards the upstairs bar, and she refocused her attention to what his eyes were following. It was time to feed.

She returned to her room later that night unable to understand Fox any better. She didn't want to think about him or about anything. All she wanted was to be alone. Her only option was to crawl into bed, but her eyes met something far more interesting.

On the bedside cabinet was a small book. She didn't recognise it, but before she even picked it up, she knew that it was decades—if not centuries—old. The brown leather was cracked, faded on the front side and split down the spine. The pages within were yellowed; she was hesitant to handle it for fear it would disintegrate between her fingers. Upon opening it, she realised just exactly how odd this book was to be in her possession.

It was handwritten, a journal of sorts, or more field notes. Each page was scribbled in faded black ink, so obscure that she could scarcely read it. She sat down on the bed and leafed through the opening pages.

Nothing was written on the spine or on the first few pages. There was no named author or additional notes from them, only page after page of field notes on the vampire race as a whole.

She soon became engrossed in its content. Every page she turned revealed a new chapter of vampire history; their lineage and heritage, religion and beliefs...

She didn't stop to think where the book had come from, because bound in those old but preserved pages was everything she needed to know, and the things others hadn't explained.

The book hadn't been written for her benefit, and there were some things that lost her, things that were too complex, or just not appealing. It gave in-depth notes of everything the Vampire Nation had seen, and mentioned the creatures who'd been a part of it. Someone had been brave enough to document these events, and someone *else* had left this worn old journal for her to find.

It spoke of vampires whom she'd never heard of but was sure were not fiction. There was no reference to the media-created additions to the Vampire Nation; neither Nosferatu, Dracula, nor the Vampire Lestat was given mention.

The book explained the differences between the vampire breeds, of those who had once been human, and those who'd been born with the vampire gift. It explained their weaknesses, the differences between them, and Catrina absorbed all the information given.

It even mentioned Slayers, who had been around as long as vampires. The book didn't go into detail. She assumed that whoever had written it was of preternatural origin and that not many of their kind had lived to report on the inside of a Slayer Headquarters.

An innocent turn of the page brought her face to face with the same artist's depiction of Aisen's tomb she had seen before. After letting her eyes adjust and draw from its pull, she held the position with her finger and checked the rest of the book. His was the only section to be accompanied by a picture.

She carefully read over the brief historical account beneath his title:

Grand Master Aisen, Vampires' Salvation.

She continued to read, while taking in all the new information, plus enforcing the history she'd already been told of.

The power known as the Genesis had been literally *given* to him when he was human, although who was responsible for this remained nameless and without status. It was this power, paired with his lust for bloodshed, that started his reign. His three lieutenants, aptly named *the Trine* by both vampires they created and Aisen himself, were responsible for the First Blood, a dealing of powerful men and women with status already surpassing that of royalty. These vampires went on to create more vampires, until the world was packed with them.

Half a millennium after the Vampire Nation began, some of its creations started to question Aisen's true intentions for them. While it was never confirmed, they believed he was planning to kill them. The horde, headed by one of the First Blood, the Vampyr Knight Ruben, hunted Aisen down to his resting place and murdered him.

She took a deep breath. This part was new:

Attempts to raise the Master since his demise have so far been unsuccessful, the book read. *Many vampires through generations have exhumed the tomb and recited the so-called ritual. The only 'success' took place at the Crypt itself, approx. 1010AD, where Aisen's spirit took the life of the Vessel, before it was interrupted by many mysterious cloaked figures. Those present at the time believed this was the spirit of the Vampyr Knight Ruben and his horde, attempting to stop the ceremony.*

She held the book steady. Searching through for more information on this mysterious 'Ruben', she found only one line beneath his name:

The One Who Killed Him

She put the book down slowly.

Her own 'cloaked figure' guarded Aisen's tomb. He—like the history book said—was preventing Aisen's rebirth. Whether he was one of the horde or the knight himself, she neither knew nor wanted to. Either way, she was the only one who knew about it.

There was no grey area surrounding Aisen's death; vampires—or specifically *a* vampire—killed him. There was no mention of Slayers. It clearly pointed the finger to its own kind as the destroyer of their creator.

Catrina knew that the book wasn't one anyone else had access to. No one else could know, or Aisen's death wouldn't be so clouded in mystery. For more than one reason, she thought immediately to tell anyone who would listen.

But something else came to mind that crushed that instinctive desire.

She was the only one with this information. This book—likely to be a one-of-a-kind—contained information that no one else had access to, at least no one who *spoke* of it.

Perhaps there was a very important reason why the truth about Aisen's demise and the identity of who was responsible was still up in the air.

There was nothing with the book that let her know who had left it or what she was to do with it. She ruled out Fox, Attilla, and everyone else within the Clan. Since she was the only one who had a connection with the spirits—for a reason she'd still like to have explained—she was the only one with any right to know. But who else knew of her connection? It was an idea that made her suddenly want to keep quiet.

Reading Aisen's story again, she felt sorry for him. Everything that had happened to him, from his first death in the distant past, to his murder at the first Awakening: it was all so malicious.

She couldn't bring herself to imagine what it would be like to spend centuries trapped inside nothing but darkness, in a state that he couldn't escape from, and with no one to help. She rested her head on the pillow.

Maybe the creature was right. She was thinking too logically. The mere implications of vampiric life went against plausibility in its entirety, yet she was still looking for reason behind it all. Maybe if she stopped trying so hard, the answers would come more easily.

CHAPTER TWENTY

Louis burst into the conference room with an armful of papers. Having expected Rose, he was disappointed to find himself the only occupant. He went to the computer and switched it on, when the door crashed open and Rose burst inside.

'Eureka!' she yelled. 'I've done it!' She ran at him from across the room, kissed him in frenzy, and then grimaced. 'You taste like a wet dog, Louis…who *have* you been eating?'

Before he could react to her outburst, she pushed him out of the way and took control of the machine. She slid the disk into the machine and typed a few commands. The computer groaned, dissatisfied with what she was trying to do. She slammed the machine with balled fist. It whirred into motion.

'What?' Louis asked. 'What've you done?'

'The Ritual, *duh*,' she replied with a grin, accessing a certain file that displayed all the symbols and the appropriate English translation for each. 'I'm *so* fucking *good*. I rule.' She performed her own dance as she hit 'print'; the paper was chewed up. After gentle persuasion on her part, the printer was forced to give her a copy of her hard work.

'That's great, because I think I've got this into the same style,' Louis said, waving a copy of Aisen's Lament in front of her eyes.

She wafted it away. 'Don't point that *thing* at me…ooh…' Her face fell. 'Now I have to tell Jessie…'

'Right now?' he asked. He pointed to the paper she held. 'Can I have a copy of that?'

Her face contorted. 'Afraid not, monkey man. Jessie gave strict orders to take this to her when it was done, not to work it out from here…'

Louis leant closer to her. 'She doesn't have to know.'

Her face fell into a pitying smile. 'Oh, Louis…young, naïve Louis…my friend, Jessie knows *everything*. And as tempting as working even *more* than I have to is…I don't think so…no.' She made her way back to the door. 'Come on, let's go face the demon…'

He wasn't impressed by the turn of events. What he held in his hands was something he alone had worked on; it was something no one else even feigned an interest in, and yet he knew exactly what was going to happen.

They were going to go to Jessie, who would take both of their hard workings and take credit for it all. It was only to be expected, but he felt slight resentment in having started work at all. Should it be some divine light cast on the shadow of Aisen, he wouldn't be the one to discover it. She would claim the glory, as was always the case.

He expressed his feelings towards handing his findings over, and said that Rose would have to present them to Jessie alone. He handed his papers over grudgingly and left the factory soon after with a bleak expression. He didn't even rise to Sonny's passing comment as he drifted out of the front doors.

Rose's effervescent attitude dimmed in Jessie's company, as they stood at the door of the child's room. It was not decorated in a child's manner; the elegance of it was close to surpassing Attilla's suite. But not quite. Something was missing; that sense of homeliness was nowhere in her quarters.

She said nothing of gratitude while looking over the symbols and their meanings. She checked the ritual's scrambled text and the paper Louis had been forced to give, comparing the three sheets. When she was done, she took a few steps into her room, leaving Rose at the open door. Then she stopped; Rose's heart skipped a beat.

'You're sure this is correct?' she demanded.

'As sure as I can be, ma'am,' Rose replied, trying to sound sure of herself, although it was difficult while under the child's glare. She knew Jessie didn't like her; Jessie didn't like anyone.

'You may go now,' Jessie said eventually.

Rose dipped her head as the only polite gesture she could muster and closed the door as she left. Outside, she heaved a sigh of relief and headed down the corridor.

Once she was certain Jessie wouldn't hear, midway down the spiral staircase towards the main hall, she muttered, 'You're *welcome*...arrogant old bitch.'

Attilla had spoken to Jessie about the briefing they had had at Louis's as soon as he had returned. Needless to say, she had not been in the most pleasant of moods afterwards. But she had the Ritual in her hands. It was completed. That had her face slightly less aggravated than usual.

They were back in Attilla's office; she had worked her mind into several different plans over the last few days. She had come up with a theory entirely of her own deliberation. Her eyes danced intensely. She had shown him the Ritual but had quickly snatched it back.

'I think I understand.' She was talking about the stars' regression. She did not smile; in fact her face was the most expressionless it had ever been. 'I see what he is implying, and it is a strong message.' She stared hard at Attilla when she spoke. 'I'm surprised you cannot see it.' He did not retaliate. 'Your intelligence is far greater than they give you credit for...but Aisen is not afraid, not of the prospect of another Genesis. He was the first, and if it comes to it, Aisen will kill Maria.' She continued with her tirade; wanting to know his reaction. He said nothing. 'He is waiting.'

'Waiting for what?' he asked.

She placed her hands on top of the table.

'...You already know.' She scanned over the table, picked up a small gold cross that lay there. She smiled, running her fingers over it. 'You just cannot come to admit that your choice was misguided.'

He slowly rose to his feet, keeping his eyes locked on hers, trying to see what was working behind that simple look on her face. 'What is it you are implying?'

She was determined not to lose that stare but eventually backed away, placing the cross back on his table. 'So wilful,' she said. 'And so determined not to face the truth. Your choice in sacrifice was ill-advised. Aisen will not take a fledgling. One so young is not worthy to die in his name.'

'Jessie,' he said, moving around the table. He had to look down on her, but she still held the same power in everything else about her.

She turned on her heel and went to the door, beckoning him to follow.

'Aisen will want someone of a higher calibre than that girl will ever be,' she replied, turning the handle. Attilla slowly followed. 'And the Awakening will not be postponed.' She turned to him, her face more serious and dark. 'I will show you what I propose.'

She led him down the corridors, but he guessed where they were going. The first thing to strike him as they entered the hall was that the main doors were open. The rain poured into the building, but it was mostly blocked by the back-end of a truck filling in the doorway. The brake lights glared into the faces of the curious crowd gathering.

Eyes fell upon the two when they entered. Fox was with Catrina; Attilla did not want them to be here. He did not want anyone to be here.

'What is this?' he asked, his voice remaining calm though the situation was too far out of hands, as he indicated the truck edging its way into the hall.

The back doors of the vehicle flung open and two large vampires appeared. Jessie smiled at them.

'A change in circumstance.' Her eyes were glittering with excitement, her voice quivered with the same. She gestured for the burly vampires to do their job, and they hauled open the truck's back and disappeared into its belly.

Most vampires in the Clan had no idea of the recent changes and doubts of Aisen the leaders had had, and they welcomed this event gladly. The others didn't know whether to play along or stay shocked. Rose and Sonny sat at the bar and shared an anxious glance. Rose had filled Sonny in on the drama in the stars the night it'd happened, so neither were expecting this.

'She's brought it here?' he asked, although it was hardly a question worth answering. Rose's choked laugh died in her throat. What did Jessie think she was doing? The signs had been clear enough; the Awakening was suffering a setback. The look on Attilla's face said that she'd been told. She just chose not to listen.

Rose managed to keep a smile on her face. 'Smart money's on yes.'

There was an ungodly sound of stone crunching against the bottom of the truck, as the first vampire appeared. Another three came out from inside, each reaching back to lower the tomb from the carrier. It took six vampires to move the tomb from the truck, as Jessie carefully made her way towards them. She walked down the pathway that had been created towards the area that had been laid out especially. Chatter rose up; more had gathered now. They'd waited for this moment a long time.

The tomb was finally in front of them, they were going to see their Master.

Catrina made her way to the middle of that crowd, her eyes locked on the tomb as they dragged it off the truck. The figure couldn't stand in everyone's way; she would finally see who she was expected to die for.

Someone's hand brushed her shoulder, she turned to face Fox. He looked too worried to speak. She could understand; it had seemed simple enough to assume that the tomb would be staying away from the Clan for a while. This was Jessie's doing: Attilla could do nothing but stand there and watch as the six vampires fought to get the tomb in an upright position. One of them was holding a crowbar.

Catrina looked at Fox. 'They're going to try and open it.' Her voice was dry. She wanted to see the Master as much as everyone else; like them, she had only seen ancient drawings of the tomb that was now in their possession.

The vampire with the crowbar hooked it inside the gap between the front of the tomb and the main body and pulled.

Anxiety, curiosity, awe; all tense emotions that flooded the room as he tried to force the door open. A nervous chatter rippled through the crowd as he turned red with fury. The panel did not give way.

Silence fell. Attilla glanced towards Jessie. She did not want to wait. She moved forwards, wrenched the vampire aside and hooked her delicate hands around the crowbar. It was lodged deep into the gap; she pulled fiercely against it.

No one dared move.

The strain was heard as the crowbar began to creak under the force that she pulled with and still no one made a sound. There was an unholy crunch, the crowbar snapped in Jessie's hand.

A solitary gasp echoed through the midst; it was Catrina. She was overwhelmed with the power that kept the tomb shut; the figure was more powerful than he let on.

Jessie screamed and hurled the piece of metal to the ground, shattering the silence. She stormed out of the room, while the crowd exchanged confused and worried words.

Rose nudged Sonny, gesturing after Jessie. 'She's gonna kill somebody.'

He was not impressed. 'Don't joke about shit like that.' He gestured to himself. 'You know she comes after the neutral parties first.'

Fox looked at Catrina. It seemed a small glitch. There were more effective ways of opening a stone tomb that had been closed for centuries.

CHAPTER TWENTY ONE

The Awakening was put on hold.

Most of the vampires shared Attilla's unwavering patience in the event, or they had just lost interest. Those who were sceptical in believing Aisen's existence began to think that the entire event was all pretence.

A minority, however, were not so willing to let it lie.

Jessie had not spoken to anyone since the day the tomb had failed to open. More attempts came from it, all of which were without success. With all the evidence staring at her, she would still not accept that something was amiss.

Life for Catrina carried on much in the same way it had done. She went out to feed, accompanied by Fox. She doubted he would ever let her out of his sight again, and his closeness unnerved her when she fed.

Her physical training took a turn to a more advanced level.

Fox entered the training room in front of her and she was in the middle of removing her jacket, when she realised they weren't alone. She froze, coat hanging over her elbows, looking at the third person beside a basket of combatants' swords.

'Maria?'

The human smiled, lifting two rapiers from the basket, spinning them expertly over her wrists. Catrina looked to Fox for an answer. He just walked towards Maria with a malevolent smile on his face.

'I trust you're in the best of health now?' Maria inquired of her, handing Fox a sword.

He tested the blade's durability with a vicious swipe. Unsatisfied, he returned it to the basket to search for one more suited.

Catrina's face showed the confusion she couldn't put into words. Maria continued without a response on Catrina's part. 'I don't favour this kind of exercise with someone who isn't ready to face it.'

'...You mean me?' She shook her head and put her hands up. 'I don't think so, thanks all the same.'

Maria watched her face, smiled and shrugged. 'Okay. You can just watch for now.'

She and Fox took starting positions in the laid-out linoleum square. The danger was obvious to even the most simple-minded. Catrina knew how little Fox thought of the human, and there was no buffer on the blades. Maria was either an expert swordsman, very brave, or just stupid. Fox would rip her apart given half the chance.

As always, Fox insisted on defence. Despite the fact she was a human facing a vampire, Maria's skills were perfect. She didn't miss her target once, and although every attempt to catch Fox off guard was fruitless, he wasn't letting her get so close for placation's sake.

Metal clashed as Fox turned to attack. This was a short but fierce demonstration, no longer for show on Catrina's behalf. Maria kept her stance, deflecting the swings with powerful counter-attacks. But he was something else. No matter how strong or skilled, she was still human. Her bones were easier to break, her wounds took longer to heal, and her stamina was like a child's in comparison to her opponent.

He swung the sword around, slamming hers to the ground. It locked beneath his. Arrogant pride burned in his eyes and smile.

He slashed his sword aside; she dipped her head to acknowledge his victory.

'You will insist on trying,' he said with a smile.

Maria didn't react. She smiled with sportsmanship and turned her attention to Catrina.

'It's not as difficult as some make it seem,' she said helpfully, clearly aimed at Fox's performance. He made no comment. She started towards Catrina, who didn't like where this was going. Sure enough, she offered Catrina her sword. '...Learning can only be beneficial.'

Catrina took the sword doubtfully. She'd never held a sword with the intention of using it before. She didn't warm to its possibilities.

Maria stepped to the side to let her pass. Fox spun the sword around with dexterity beyond challenge. But as Maria moved her further forwards, Fox moved aside. He moved from the linoleum, replaced the sword, and headed for the door.

He stopped, gave Maria a dismissive glance, and spoke to Catrina. 'I'll leave you to it.'

The two would-be strangers faced each other. They'd spent very little time together. Catrina didn't trust herself around a human; the hunger was still its own master.

A tense silence descended; the sort that came with strangers left to get acquainted. They stood in the middle of the square, swords held idly at their sides. When training with Fox, she knew where the limits lay.

At least the anonymity meant she could concentrate on learning a new skill.

'It's not difficult to adapt,' Maria explained, lifting the sword in a preparatory stance. She motioned for Catrina to do the same.

Catrina smiled apprehensively. 'Just take it slowly, yeah?'

'From what I've heard, you won't need me to.'

She brought the sword down towards Catrina, who lifted hers upwards in uncertain instinct. The movement was so slow that the swords barely touched.

Maria was satisfied at the response. 'Good...again.'

There was a commanding tone to her voice, something that came naturally with teachers. Catrina wondered how many vampires she'd been asked to train through her evident natural flare.

By the hour mark, she'd dropped the sword more times than she'd swung it. But she was beginning to grasp the basics. She thought of the Tournament, of the speed in which Rose and Fabian had fought, and how close they'd come to killing each other.

Maria brought the sword slowly around towards the ground with the intention of knocking Catrina off her feet. There was no clear motive other than to emphasise the importance of defence. Catrina blocked the move and swung in retaliation. The sword jarred in Maria's hand. Fleetingly surprised, the woman used the momentum of the sword to force Catrina back.

'I'm sorry,' Catrina said, shocked. 'I don't know where that came from.'

Maria smiled wryly, wagging one finger. 'There's something about you.'

Catrina's mind raced with reminiscence of ideas that had been imposed on her. She couldn't move. If Maria thought *herself* as the Genesis, as Attilla had suggested, that meant she also thought Catrina was the Vessel. In her mind, she was training someone who was going to die. Judging by her skills, there was some foundation in the notion that she was the Genesis. Catrina felt her heart jump into her throat; she had to beat her, to prove that she wasn't damned.

She turned the fight on the attack; Maria accepted without questioning it. She began slowly, holding back for the sake of an amateur. Catrina wanted to win, regardless of the fact that her opponent was far more skilled.

For about a minute, it was going her way. Maria's grip loosened around the hilt. Catrina thought it a foolish move but acted upon it before thinking. She swept the blade around to disarm her, but Maria was one step ahead.

Her grip tightened, bringing the sword around in a swift uppercut. Catrina's sword hit the floor with a clash. Maria brought her leg around and knocked Catrina off her feet. She hit the ground, her head smacked against the floor. The linoleum patch may have protected the floor from scratches, but that didn't mean it was any less painful to fall onto.

Her back arched, she winced, seeing Maria's sword swinging precariously over her chest. It hung over her heart.

'I've just killed you,' Maria announced.

She'd set her sights too high. Maria must've been training since before she had come to the Clan. Whether she was the Genesis or not was irrelevant. She just had the skill Catrina didn't possess.

Maria swept the sword to the side and helped Catrina up, while saying something in a language Catrina could identify but not understand.

'What did I say?' she pressed.

'I don't know. I don't speak Italian.'

'Of course. Despite the fact that you're a vampire, you still have to learn. And though you'll learn faster than humans, as it stands I still speak better Italian than you.'

Catrina understood the implications. 'Strength doesn't mean anything, does it?'

Maria laughed. 'Not necessarily. Strength can be powered by instinct, and you have that. But you don't always need strength when you have skill. It's best to have as much of both as possible.'

The air lifted; they were fighting for the same purpose again. Maria lifted her sword.

'I see you're driven by a need to win,' she commented casually, as Catrina copied her gesture. Maria brought her blade around slowly.

'Killers can't afford to lose,' she replied. She'd learnt that lesson many times. 'I got that from Tony.' She held back a smile; it felt like years since she'd known him. She wondered how he was, how he'd taken the news that she'd disappeared. As far as he knew, Catrina Malinka was dead.

'Anthony Gostanzo?' Maria clarified. 'Was there ever much of a family tie between you?'

Catrina slowed her movements down a little, as memories came flooding back. Something struck a chord inside. She averted her eyes and focused on the blades in their hands. 'I came from a broken family before Tony.' Her tone was cold. She moved the sword back to avoid clashing it with Maria's again. 'I never had family values in my blood.'

Maria lessened pressure on her strikes. 'I was told you valued your relationship with him?'

Catrina looked through the touched blades suspiciously. She shrugged it off. 'I valued the relationship. And I appreciated the fathering he attempted...but I was ten when Tony found me. My mind was already set in its ways.' She let out a laugh; it was laced with bitter resentment. 'I wasn't exactly big on trust and the importance of family.'

Maria moved out of the way of a particularly swift strike. '...I'm sorry,' she said quietly.

'It doesn't bother me anymore,' she replied, swinging the sword towards Maria. 'I had my vengeance, and I was happy with Tony.'

'You sound as though you trusted him, at least.'

'Yeah,' Catrina said with a sigh. The memories washed away into the deep void of her mind. She raised the sword. 'I've only ever been let down by others.'

She gave Maria the gesture to continue. Her trainer didn't disagree. Aggression was something a fighter would find useful. But she didn't let the topic lie. Catrina sparked more interest than she was aware.

'You shouldn't base your opinions on a few unfortunate incidents,' Maria said. She turned the fight gently onto the attack, and Catrina moved the blade to knock the first strike away. 'You can trust some people, those who are worth your time.'

'Do you? Trust others, I mean?' She brought the weapon around quickly, if she could just get that sword out of her hand. But Maria was there already, and she spun the blades around one another, the sound of steel singing in the air until Catrina's fell to the ground.

'I trust Attilla,' she said. She sounded so sure. Catrina picked the sword back up and Maria continued, watching her carefully. 'I trust him with everything.'

'That sounds like demeaning your own ability,' Catrina commented, keeping her voice low and without scorn.

'Sometimes you need someone to trust.'

The sparring was lost in the conversation. Neither noticed that they were speeding up.

'I was always taught that trust was a weakness,' Catrina remarked casually, reciting the words she had learned from Tony. 'I had to go though Hell before I realised that was true.'

Maria analysed her face carefully, looking for signs of remorse. She swept her sword around. It was pushed aside, and the conversation continued casually.

'...You said you had your vengeance?' she questioned eventually.

'I killed them.'

'Who?'

'My mother and stepfather.'

Maria's eyes widened. Looked like there were still things that the Clan didn't know about Catrina's past. Catrina stopped and lowered the sword. She had told few people of the murder; they'd all given the same expression.

'Don't look so shocked,' she quipped sharply. 'I didn't want anyone to get away with what they did. That's the only reason I killed them.'

'That's your justification for killing your parents?'

'Eddie was *not* my father.' There was viciousness in the way she brought the sword around that time. 'Besides, they were dead in every other way. I just did what no else had the energy to do.'

Maria blinked with a flash of a smile. 'You're a puzzle in itself.'

Their comparative strikes became more rapid. 'What makes you say that?'

Maria smiled at that. 'If you were half as heartless as you're claiming, Attilla would never have brought you here.'

Catrina tried to see her comment as positive, but it just made her want to beat her more.

'I have to be heartless,' she replied. 'I'm a killer.'

The training escalated into a swift exchange of strikes, and neither registered it.

'Killing does not make a person evil if the reasons they kill for are just.'

'I killed them because they hurt me,' she replied blankly. 'They almost destroyed me.' She avoided eye contact as she went on. 'I still carry the scars…becoming a vampire won't make them go away.'

'That's because they're a part of you,' Maria said in a most informative fashion. 'You can't take away what you were by becoming a vampire. In that respect, it changes nothing.'

Catrina's eyes flashed with curiosity. '…Then why are you still human?'

The swords locked, and for a brief moment they stared into each other's eyes. There was a fear that Maria held deep inside her mind, which could only be seen when she was too busy to disguise it. She kept her hand pressed on the sword's handle; she felt Maria's grip loosening. Catrina wanted to see what it was that made Maria's eyes glint with fear.

Catrina was flung into a torrent of memories that weren't her own, something hidden within secrets and pain inside Maria's head. She had no idea what was making her see it. As though her body was not her own anymore, she leapt to the side and brought the sword around, her eyes temporarily blinded by the vision. *Vampires leaping, their fangs bared, their bodies tensed…there were fists and the sound of a gun firing, but there were so many…*

Maria lost her balance and tumbled. Catrina jolted the sword forwards and held it less than an inch from the woman's neck. The visions faded into nothing, but the sense of fear inside Maria was escalating. They kept perfectly still for a moment, Catrina with her sword at Maria's neck, and the human not daring to breathe.

A short ringing echo broke their position. Catrina realised that what she was doing. She was thinking about killing her. The speed at which she pulled the sword away said that she didn't consciously mean it. She helped Maria to her feet. She looked bewildered but unharmed.

The ringing sounded again.

Maria had hung her own jacket on one of the pieces of equipment; she walked over and pulled out her phone. She answered it with a brisk greeting. Catrina wondered how she was feeling to know she'd been beaten by a fledgling.

'Attilla's called a meeting,' Maria said, when she'd put the phone down. 'It sounds important. We've been asked to go.'

'I've seen too much,' Maria said quietly, as they headed down the corridor. 'You asked why I'm still human. It's because I've seen too much. You're a good person, and being a vampire hasn't changed that...but I've seen others, vampires so evil that the only way to understand them is to kill them. I've seen too much of the vampire world through human eyes...it's too late to start changing my perception.'

'The ones who attacked you?' Catrina asked, without considering the sensitive nature of the subject.

Maria wasn't visibly disturbed by mention of her attack; she shrugged absently. 'In part. But even the vampires who live within the Clan, some have such darkness inside them, it will destroy them. Like Fox is...' She realised her mistake, closing her eyes to wish away the comment. But it was too late. Catrina stared at her.

'Fox?' she repeated, her voice screamed offence and slight anger, no matter how she tried to hide it. At least she felt obliged to defend him.

Maria sighed. 'I've watched him over these years. Because of his past, every night he grows more detached from others.'

Seeing the look in Catrina's eyes, she spoke up quickly. 'He wasn't always that way. It's something that's grown over the years.'

'Because of his mother?'

'To begin with,' she agreed.

'So what else?'

Maria eyed her carefully. 'I don't know if I should be the one to tell you about Fox's past.'

'Please,' Catrina said. 'It's not like I can ask him about it.'

Maria found herself smiling. 'I suppose.' Her smile fell. 'Ever since the day we met, I knew Fox and I would not get along. But it was a while later, when a dying vampire was brought into the Infirmary, pumped full of Themisium, that his reason for despising me became more viable.

'Before I came here, I had some medical experience and took particular interest in toxins and poisonous substances. It didn't take me long to work out how to counteract the balance of

Themisium. I saved that particular vampire. The problem was that I was far too late in saving another, one who was much more important to Fox.'

She watched Catrina try to apply the math. 'Fox said his mother died *eleven* years ago.'

'She did.' She drew a long breath and considered stopping completely. She shouldn't be the one doing this, especially if Fox were to find out.

She laughed suddenly. What could Fox possibly do that he hadn't attempted already? 'I'm sorry,' she said to Catrina's frown. 'His attitude is not wasted on me, no more than it is on you, I suspect.' When Catrina smiled, Maria knew it was safe to continue.

'I've only had reason to ask about Fox's past once, and that was on the day I saved the first Themisium victim. I wanted to know why he'd looked at me like he wanted to kill me.'

'Why?'

She sighed. 'Fox had a partner before he joined the Clan, a young girl...strong-willed, not unlike yourself. She was his first fledgling. I don't know the details, but I heard they were close. From his reaction that night, I guessed he had been in love with her.'

She didn't have to go into much detail. 'I didn't think he'd be that way inclined.'

Maria smiled. 'No, neither did I.'

'Slayers killed her, didn't they?' Catrina said.

She nodded. 'From what I gathered, it sounded like an accident, or as much as one can be. She'd gone out alone. Fox went after her, but by the time he'd found her, the Themisium was too deep in her blood.'

She could see Catrina tense up. 'That explains a lot. What about you, though? It's not like it was your fault. He wouldn't have even known you then.'

'I know,' she agreed. 'But on the night I saved that vampire, Fox realised that *had* I been around back then, I could've saved her, too.' A sly grin curled her lips. 'I don't understand what he still has to hold against me, though. In a cruel sense, I've helped it.'

'What do you mean?'

'I don't doubt he loved her,' she said surely. 'But his true, inner pain came from losing his mother. What happened with her is a kind of emotional shield he uses to keep himself at a distance. But I pay attention.' She grinned. 'I've seen the way he looks at you.' She pretended not to see Catrina's cheeks flush. 'Then again, I've seen how he *acts*, so it's easy to confuse his intentions.'

'How he acts? You mean the mixture between overzealous bodyguard and dictator?'

'And that will probably be the most you will get from him.'

They looked at each other. Catrina's face broke into a grin first. 'I don't expect any more.'

Maria's smile widened; she paid more attention than people were aware. 'I'd believe that...' she said, as they closed in on the conference room. 'But I've seen the way you look at him, too.'

Catrina headed into the room behind Maria.

She avoided Fox's gaze for all of three seconds, before she disregarded the human's observations as ludicrous, nodded as greeting and sat down beside him.

He sat with one arm across the table, the other holding a cigarette in place, looking apprehensive. He had every reason to; this meeting—called by the Clan's leader—sounded both urgent and life-changing.

Rose sat on the table, resting her feet on the chair beneath, filing her nails like a bored secretary. Louis and Ebony had also been called; they were talking about the research they'd brought.

Maria moved silently and positioned herself next to Ebony, avoiding Fox's glare.

Catrina pressed her back against the chair, feeling uneasy. Whether something was wrong or otherwise was not the issue, it was a question of what was so important for all of them to be there.

The door opened slowly. Attilla moved to the head of the table without a word. Rose didn't move off the table, and he made no motion for her to do so. Placing a single sheet of paper on the table, he gave a greeting nod to his associates. All had come because they'd been asked, and he was grateful that they'd accepted the request at such short notice.

All eyes rested on Attilla, except for Rose's. She was still interested in the shape of her nails and would only pay attention when the time came. Louis broke the silence, handing one of the files over to Attilla, whose vigilant gaze caught his own.

'Any change?'

Louis shook his head. 'Still nothing…and with this business of the tomb, it's hard to come to any conclusion other than this isn't the time to bring Aisen back.'

'He won't be forced.' Ebony's smooth voice fell like warm rain.

Attilla nodded at them both. Catrina noticed straight away that there was something on his mind; his body rested uneasily in the seat. She also knew he wouldn't press his own matters when others had information to share.

'I don't understand it,' Fox said, his voice low and his eyes averted from everyone. He was talking to himself. 'There are scriptures that tell of nothing but his return, but it's here…everything's here, and he's *refusing* it.'

The others understood Fox's standpoint. His belief in Aisen was one of the deepest; he was one who truly thought the world would be put back into its element with the change. And it was on firm foundations. Aisen was their Jesus Christ. Vampires who honoured their founding father had nothing to fear once he was raised.

Attilla took a deep breath, cupping his hands on the table. He prepared to give them the news. Rose picked up on the shift and took her seat.

'We all have our philosophies towards the reasons for his withdrawal.' He gestured his hand to Catrina. All eyes fell on her; she stared back at Attilla. This was going somewhere; she had to remember what the present company thought she was.

Attilla put his hand back into the other. 'I made Catrina aware of her intended purpose here,' he said. She had to play the part, be the Vessel, if only for them. This would not help assuredness in herself, but it was necessary. Attilla took another deep breath. 'However, this afternoon I was given some information that will now prove her purpose otherwise.'

Catrina joined the others in staring at him, wanting an explanation.

'What?' Rose said. 'You mean the Vessel business?' Attilla looked across to her and nodded. 'What's the deal?'

After a long silence, he simply said, 'Jessie.'

Ebony caught Maria a wry sideways glance, smiling to herself. She already knew what he was going to tell them.

'She came to me this afternoon,' Attilla continued, 'with her own opinions for Aisen's postponement. She suggested he is holding back because he is not satisfied in the choice we have provided him. Jessie thinks his withdrawal is his way of saying he does not want the offering of one so young.'

Louis put his hand to his mouth, thoughtfully running his fingers over the top of his lip. He bit his finger, his brain ticking over to process the information.

His eyes widened. 'She's offering *herself*?'

At Attilla's solemn nod, the small congregation collectively sat back. Maria glanced towards Ebony, who hid a broad smile under her raised hand.

'...Why?'

Catrina's voice fell over the silence like the slam of a sledgehammer. They stared at her, but she just continued to stare at Attilla.

'Why?' he repeated, confused.

'Why has she suddenly decided that she is going to die for the Master?'

'Suddenly?' Rose laughed. 'Shorty, it's been nigh on four years now since we spotted you. She's had all that time to decide she'd prefer to get herself killed. I don't know what planet you live on, but on this place called Earth, people are generally relieved when they find out they're not a hunk of meat anymore.'

'It doesn't make sense to me, either,' Louis interjected. 'Jessie's been alive for six centuries, why would she choose to die?'

'Maybe she's had everything she can get from life,' Ebony said, offering her own well-based suggestion while holding back her smug expression for the sake of the company she addressed. 'Maybe she knows it's her time to move on.'

'It was not a simple decision for her to make,' Attilla replied, his tone ending the debate. 'What she has chosen is very honourable, and I have to respect her wishes.'

'...Sorry if I'm speaking out of turn here, Capt'n,' Rose said, starting to file her nails again. 'But until we get the tomb open, ain't *nobody* getting sacrificed.'

Everyone smiled at her comment, but they faded as they realised she was right. The problem at the moment was not that Aisen was refusing his sacrifice; it was that they couldn't get to him. It left them with bemused and anxious expressions.

Fox and Attilla looked at each other through the others; their understanding was enough from a glance. Catrina was safe. Fox looked closely at him, past that façade of quiet shock; he was nothing short of euphoric.

Catrina's mind was no longer a part of whatever the others were discussing. She was thinking about Jessie, and how wrong what she was proposing to do felt. It *was* honourable. She recalled the only conversation she'd had with the child. Why, after all she'd said about nobility and bravery being a fool's traits, had she now decided to adopt both qualities?

CHAPTER TWENTY TWO

Expectancy gleamed in the creature's golden eyes, as she opened hers to see him. He nodded a gracious welcome. It was all very natural, as though she'd just walked into the room and he was there. He just wanted to talk. They were in the factory hall, alone, except for the tomb that loomed over even him.

The creature turned, hands held behind his back, looking up towards the ancient stone box. She joined him, while wondering what he was trying to say.

'I did wonder why the vampires could not open the tomb.' He said it himself, a mere observation, a small epiphany.

'Why's that?'

He looked down at her, smiling. 'Because the gatekeeper is using you to hold the others at bay.'

'I don't follow.'

He moved away from the tomb. 'You are the only one he can relate to. While he convinces you to keep Aisen within the confines of his tomb, no one else—no matter how capable they are—will be able to get inside.'

She thrust her arm towards the tomb. 'So you're saying it's my fault he's trapped inside that thing?'

'Not your 'fault',' he repeated. 'But while you still have doubt, Ruben will use that to grow stronger.'

'I don't doubt.'

The thick skin over his eyes accentuated a raised eyebrow much stronger than any human expression was capable.

'Are you sure?'

She was about to reiterate the point, but when she tried to speak, nothing managed to form. Maybe he was right. Until recently, she'd been meant to die for the man. It was only natural to have slight hesitations about meeting him. What if he changed his mind?

She said nothing, to which the creature smiled. 'You are afraid of him.'

'Only because of what was meant to happen.'

'History has been re-written,' the creature said. 'Are you not curious to meet the first vampire ever to have existed?'

'...A little. But the thought of him scares me. He's more powerful than any other vampire in history. If he decides that he *does* want to kill me, what can I do. Deny him?'

The creature was nodding. 'I appreciate your concern. The Master is a formidable influence on his people. But you have nothing to fear. I would protect you.'

'Against the Master?' she asked.

'...Do you trust me?' he returned with the question. She shrugged but nodded all the same. There were not many people who deserved her trust, but he'd done nothing but enforce his altruistic need to protect her. 'Then trust me when I tell you the Master is not a threat to you. Once you lay your eyes upon him, you will see.' Her eyes flitted to the tomb. 'Do not fear what you do not understand. Let go of your doubts and see that there is nothing to fear.'

She looked back to the tomb, half expecting it to burst open. If the creature bared no ill will towards the Master, she had no reason to, either. Reading her thoughts, he nodded graciously, and she was awake in an instant.

She sat quietly in the bed for a moment, chewing at her thumbnail as she thought. The creature was right; after she had seen the Master, there'd be nothing left to fear.

So there it was, staring her in the face as she stood in the hall. Other vampires walked past with disregard. Whatever she was doing was neither their business nor much to their interest.

Sonny was the only one to pay her any attention, watching from the bar.

A gently divine sound filled in her ears, softly resting on her mind as an invitation. She moved closer towards the tomb. A few people looked, wondering what she thought she was doing.

She pressed her hand against the surface. The sound of screaming desperation replaced that soft caress of summons, telling her to move away. A surge of energy erupted through the stone, invisible but painful. It sank through the palm of her open hand and fed itself into her veins. She tried to back away, but it bound her to the stone. It shot through her heart, racing back towards her hand with explicit urgency.

She managed to wrench herself back, catching sight of an electrical surge shoot out of her hand. It disappeared inside the box.

A low rumble shook the ground. The vampires in the hall turned to watch, as she backed away. The tremor went through the whole building; vampires everywhere quickly made their way to the source of the uproar.

Catrina turned; a crowd was gathering. Fox pushed his way through, pulling her away from the huge stone box. 'What happened?'

She just stared back. 'I don't know.'

Jessie appeared in the doorway of the far west doors. Everybody froze. The *clip-clip* of her tiny shoes echoed sharply across the concrete, her eyes locked on Catrina.

'What did you *do*?' she demanded, her voice wretched from the pitch. Her flawless face wrinkled with fury, her brown eyes narrowed. The tomb continued to shake, some of the vampires moved closer, too curious to resist.

'I didn't do anything,' Catrina insisted. Her voice was trembling. Jessie looked as though she was going to explode, her fangs jutting out from her top lip, long and delicate but deadly all the same.

Jessie thrust her hands out to the air around her. An invisible force struck Catrina in the chest, as the child's force of will sent her flying. Fox wasn't quick enough to catch her, and she fell backwards, straight into Attilla. He gently lifted her back to her feet, but he didn't meet her thankful eyes. He glared at Jessie, who was standing before the tomb, waiting for him. He moved forwards. Catrina shielded herself behind him, moving only when he did.

He stopped on hearing a sound like foundations cracking, and every single one of the congregation stared at the trembling tomb.

It was going to fall from the podium.

Jessie stepped closer. The rest held back; they were close enough.

A boom pulsated from inside the stone prison. A thick air descended upon the hall. The sound from inside was so devastating, some had to cover their ears. The front panel of the box veered forwards, as the unknown adhesive that had bound it for centuries cracked. It was enough to make everyone move back, all except Jessie.

The panel came loose and teetered on the platform. There was a huge gap between the crowd and the tomb. The slab fell, hitting the ground with a bone-crunching thud, inches from Jessie's feet. Dust clouds billowed out from the blackness inside the tomb. All they could do was wait for it to settle. The crowd slowly moved closer, when the ground stopped trembling. They wanted the best view, the first to lay eyes on the Master.

The dust cleared after the longest stretch of a moment, and then he was there for all to see. A perfect figure, encased in impenetrable stone. His chest looked as though proudly brandishing the huge broadsword that struck straight through his body, an act of defiance towards those who opposed him.

While everyone was shocked by what they saw, no one was more so than Catrina, who stood, jaw gaping, eyes fixed on the stone replica of someone she'd already had the pleasure of meeting.

Catrina moved forwards, as the tomb towered over them all. Her movement spurred others to get closer, as their voices rose up from the silence.

'What *is* it?' someone said.

'Is that Aisen?'

'He's some kind of monster.'

'*Quiet*, all of you,' Attilla's voice shouted over the rest.

Everything turned to nothing more than static in Catrina's head. She looked up to the stone replica of that creature, and suddenly she felt drawn to him.

The only difference between this stone creature and the one she knew was that the statue had the Mark of Divinity carved into his pectoral muscle, just above where his heart was.

Unlike the rest of them, she already knew all about him. Their confusion and initial shock in the Master's appearance would come to them all in time; she was a few months ahead.

She turned to look straight into the face of Aisen himself, the creature, the thing she had grown to trust, to form a bond with. She wasn't sure how she was supposed to react.

Is this the truth I don't want to know? she asked silently, concentrating on the phrase.

Aisen, or the ghost of his memory, nodded. *Yes*, it whispered. The voice sounded like her own, but the motions were all his. *You are under the protection of the creator of your kind.*

As he vanished into the air, Fox took Catrina by the arm and pulled her away from the tomb and billowing clouds of sandy smoke. He dragged her back to the rest of the crowd.

Attilla was making the rest of the crowd move back. 'We do not know the stability of this artefact,' he told them. 'You will all keep your distance until we learn more.'

The congregation agreed, overlooking that Jessie still knelt at the foot of the tomb. They wouldn't question. She'd been waiting a long time for this.

It would all be over soon. He would be raised, and everything would fall into place.

CHAPTER TWENTY THREE

The world Ruben and his timeless adversary shared suffered a perpetual incompleteness, a lack of density and of feeling. For centuries, Ruben had longed for the ability to touch his surroundings, to feel the ground he walked upon and breathe the air, no matter how stale it was bound to be in the crypt.

He had spent years upon years walking through the desolated halls, whenever he was fortunate enough to. Aisen's presence in the crypt often meant that the vampire knight was exiled to the world outside. He wondered whether the half-life was worth its consequences; an eternity with his only company the monster who he had been forced to kill. But he always came to the same conclusion: better to stay here and withstand the constant attacks than to give in and suffer the alternative.

He did not sense the beast's presence at first. Aisen preferred to walk the crypt without the memory of his murderer. When Ruben did realise, he quickly corrected himself and readied to leave. It appeared the crypt was not the place for him now. There were other places a spirit could linger.

Aisen started after him. 'Won't you stay a while, Ruben? There is still much to discuss.' There was humour in his tone.

He turned back, the hood half hanging over his ashen face. He pulled it back down with a wary gaze covering his expression. 'Such as?'

He could tell immediately that Aisen was pleased with the turn of events. 'I wanted to commend your efforts as my constant shadow, and to commiserate your recent defeat.'

'I am not yet defeated, my lord,' he said. An arrogance that he had not dared show in some time was starting in the pit of his stomach; it had gnarled at him since Catrina had touched the tomb. 'This may pass without you travelling into their world.'

But Aisen smiled; it was as though he had already won the battle. 'I would not be so optimistic of your endeavour. The wheels are in motion. She has already shown her faith in me.'

Ruben felt his fists clenching beneath the heavy cloak. 'I cannot stand by as part of this charade any longer.' Sweeping the hood over his head—the only way he could hide his anger from the monster—he hurried to leave before he spoke out of line. From the look on Aisen's face, it appeared he had already done so.

He blocked Ruben's path.

'You will continue to play your part,' he said, pitch changing dramatically. 'I have spent too long waiting for one such as she, too much effort in earning her trust to have you wrench her away.' He reached out and ripped the hood away from Ruben's face. 'I understand that you have your loyalties against me, but I will have that girl, and your incessant need to protect her will not hold me back.'

Ruben, though feared over what Aisen was still capable of doing to him, blazed with defiance. 'I may play any role you have carefully laid out for me, but *she* will still defy you and fight you on whatever grounds you plan your battle.'

'Then why does your voice tremble so?' he challenged. 'Get out of my sight, and do not defile my grave again until this is done.'

As Ruben prepared to leave, he felt Aisen was not done. When he turned, the beast's eyes were smiling. 'By the time she learns what I have planned for her, I will not care if she *does* become my greatest enemy. I will still kill her, and not she, nor you, will be able to stop me.'

CHAPTER TWENTY FOUR

It was stiflingly humid in the hall. The vampires who hadn't gone out to feed gathered around the tomb. The place hadn't been empty since it had been opened. People gradually edged closer to the tomb; some came close enough to touch him, but no one did.

He had been in that prominent position for weeks now, they were waiting for Louis to give them the go-ahead. However, Jessie's patience was waning and the Clan knew she would act before long.

Catrina gave the statue a polite nod, half expecting him to return the gesture. There was no movement from the statuesque lord.

Fox was waiting at the bar. Sonny approached with a beer.

'Thanks,' she said automatically. No one else was around the bar, no one wanted a drink. They were all too engrossed with their Master. Sonny was staring at the tomb with what resembled jealousy.

'Is he taking all your business?' she joked.

He scowled. 'People don't want to drink because they're too busy admiring their saviour.' He shrugged to himself. 'Well, I'm more attractive than him, at least. He looks like a gargoyle.' Seeing Fox's sharp glance, he shrugged. 'Well, he does.'

Catrina glanced at the statue. 'I think he's perfect.'

Sonny opened his mouth to comment, but it was not worth his time and it turned into a tired sigh before he left them to it.

She sipped at her drink, seeing that Fox was watching her out of the corner of her eye. 'What?'

'...Perfect?'

She smiled at the look on his face from her description of their creator. 'You sound disappointed. Why did you assume Aisen would be human? Divinity may not take human form.'

'I know, and I agree that he's everything we could expect, if not more. I just didn't know *you* felt so strongly about him.'

Her smile was broad. 'We all have our secrets.'

Rose entered the hall humming the Indiana Jones theme. She perched herself on the stool beside Catrina, grinned, and slammed her hand on the bar. Sonny, who had been stacking glasses underneath, smacked his head against the wood as he came to stand.

'Mind your head,' Rose pointed out helpfully.

The door leading from the conference rooms opened with a loud creak. Maria walked through the hall, carrying a heavy-looking cardboard box brimming with scientific glassware and bottles of potentially dangerous chemicals.

Fox turned to Catrina; he was the last person who'd offer to help Maria.

'You okay over there, Maria?' Sonny asked helpfully. 'Need a hand?'

She returned his graciousness with a weary smile. 'I'll manage, thanks.'

Catrina was about to tell Fox to help her, when she realised he was on his feet, watching someone else sprint in blind panic in the opposite direction across the hall.

It was one of the vampires who acted as a bouncer. Sweat was pouring down his face, and he almost knocked Maria off her feet as he sped past. He held a two-way radio to his ear; the static echoed out in the hall and started to attract wandering eyes.

He was trying to get his gun from its holster on his belt. He pressed the radio's communication button.

'Where the hell are you, Tom?' he yelled, voice croaked from the panic he was in. This brought Catrina into the situation, and she watched with the same fascination and worry as the others.

Fox went for his gun; she did the same. Another vampire appeared from the same door from the conference rooms, his two-way radio clutched in one hand, about to speak.

There was a gunshot; everybody present hit the floor. Stray bullets were never welcomed. A second or so of silence passed.

The first bouncer cursed frantically and headed to his friend, who was sprawled on the floor. While normal bullets wouldn't affect a vampire much more than being scuffed, the way the vampire convulsed suggested it was no ordinary bullet. It was coated.

There was a Slayer in the building. Whatever initial confusion had descended was replaced with panic.

Maria put the box on the bar, but before she could move to help, the first bouncer dropped his radio and launched towards the corridor, fangs bared. He was met with a similar shot in his torso, the momentum of which forced him back into the hall, where he lay shaking beside his friend. A few of the vampires made a break for the opposite door. Despite their abilities, most of them were not fighters, and they were all afraid of what was happening.

Catrina had the opposite inclination. She wanted to investigate, but Fox held her back. It was too dangerous to run blindly into.

The sound of footsteps approached the hall. Catrina listened; there was more than one set, which meant the attacker was not alone. Either they had a hostage, or they were part of a team. From the way they sounded, she assumed no one was struggling.

Four Slayers burst into the hall, guns blazing.

A lot of vampires went down with the first round. While one Slayer reloaded, the others provided ample backup. Fox took one out straight away, but then the Clan vampires moved in on the attack, and he had to hold back.

While the vampires fought the enemy who'd unexpectedly arrived in their midst, Catrina didn't move. Fox left her by the bar to help the others and vampires were arriving from around the building, but Catrina remained transfixed to the thoughts that were suddenly ploughing into her mind.

They were not her thoughts; it was happening just as it had when she and Maria had sparred. This was different. These were not memories but rather *thoughts* as the human created them. She had to sit down; it was crushing at her temples until she could hardly see. The thoughts came quicker than she could register.

She looked to Aisen, but his stone eyes gave no comfort. He couldn't explain what she was experiencing, or why it was choosing now to do so.

The thoughts steadily grew more clear, but the fragments of forgotten voices were too fast for her to comprehend. She slumped to the ground with a thud. She backed up against the wooden panelling, pulling her knees to her chin and gritting her teeth. Something was forcing its way into her mind.

Rose grabbed one of the male Slayers from the crowd and hurled him to the ground. When it came to skill, she was one of the best. The Slayer kicked as he fell, and Rose went down after him. She rolled to her feet, wrenching the man with her. The complex manoeuvres she eloquently displayed in the Tournaments were gone; she was brutal, and proud of it. She pulled out her gun and shot the man in the face. Another Slayer tackled her; she went down again.

It was a mangled mess of fighters and dead bodies; to say that only two Slayers were left, they were hardly defeated.

Vampires were falling; their blood spilled and created a sickly pool at their feet. Fox grabbed the remaining male Slayer from the side; he moved so quickly the Slayer's neck was broken before the other vampires realised he'd been attacked.

As Fox dropped the fresh corpse, the most distressing cry stopped all other action. It was the sound only one such as Rose could make, as the last Slayer rammed the stake into her chest.

It gave Catrina her consciousness again, and her eyes travelled upwards to see Rose die. The blood spilled over her white shirt. The other vampires just stepped back. To lose so many of their own in such a short amount of time was disturbing, but in having to watch their most vivacious vampire die was beyond expressed emotion.

The vampires backed away from the girl. She was outnumbered, but shock at seeing Rose's body slump to the floor was enough to keep them at bay. The Slayer raised her gun to any who would challenge her; her ears picking up the sound of the door behind her being opened.

Attilla and Jessie entered a subdued room, with Sonny trailing close behind. They froze on seeing what lay before them. Judging from the smile on her face, the Slayer liked the reaction. But she wasn't looking at them. She was looking at someone standing by the bar, someone who hadn't moved throughout the entire fight.

The vampires moved further from the Slayer, now with a sick curiosity as to with whom her attention was taken. They parted way for her, while that wry smile remained on her face.

Fox had his gun raised at the Slayer's head, but on seeing the look in her eyes as she stared at Maria, he didn't pull the trigger. He saw that look every time a vampire spotted him across a crowded room.

It was recognition.

Maria pulled an immaculate 9mm pistol from her jacket and pointed it at the Slayer's head. The Slayer let out a small titter, shaking her head in pitied wonder.

'Maria la Graziano.' She said the human's name slowly, savouring the feel of the words in her mouth, while the air thickened, and a viscous leer marred her otherwise pretty face. 'I *always* wondered what happened to you.'

Maria wrapped her other shaking hand around the gun's handle.

The vampires whispered murmurs of shock and revelation. Jessie slowly walked through the small crowd, which no one acted upon. Fox lowered his gun and just watched the story unfold. They all did. Attilla bowed his head.

The Slayer raised her hands in surrender. 'I don't want to fight you, Maria.' She addressed the others gathered. 'She's a traitor to both your kind and mine.' She faced Maria, gave the smallest dip of her head, and addressed the vampires again. 'Without her guidance, I could not call myself a Slayer.'

The world closed in around them, filled only by the sharp intakes of realisation.

'...A Mentor.'

Jessie's voice broke the silence. She stared at Maria, who looked helplessly back, her gun still fixed on the Slayer. There were tears in her eyes, but she didn't deny it. Her former pupil took a few steps forwards, not timid but taunting. She was close to her now and did lower her voice. 'If I don't kill you then they will.'

The gun in Maria's hands fired, her face not registering the sound. The Slayer was dead, but the damage was done.

She lowered the gun, her gaze fell on the hateful ones surrounding her. It reflected on their expressions… cold, biting, vengeful, confused, hurt; a myriad of emotions on a sea of faces. She heard the vampires whispering her name in disbelieving, sharp tones.

She saw Attilla. He was staring back; his eyes said it all, her betrayal of his trust and even his love. She couldn't have expected anything less, but it didn't make the pain inside any more bearable.

Fox raised his gun like lightning, sighting up Maria's head. Catrina wanted to stop him, but he had every right to do it.

'Fox…stop.'

It was a wonder Fox heard the command at all; the voice was quiet, torn, and wretched. Fox looked at Attilla, his mentor, friend…and more than ever wanted to kill Maria. His finger hovered over the trigger, catching Maria's helpless gaze.

Maria started to back away. She stopped at the Slayer, tears streaming down her face. She knelt down, perhaps to say a parting ritual, then she fled.

Fox couldn't let this happen. His grip tightened again and he knew he would fire.

The shot rang out but she was gone.

He didn't realise the intervention until he saw that Attilla was standing next to him. His grip on Fox's wrist had deflected his perfect aim.

'I said *no*,' the authority was back in the leader's voice but it was laced with something darker.

Jessie was standing by Aisen's tomb, looking up into his eyes. Spinning on her heel, she went through the crowd, shoving aside anyone who was not quick enough to move. When the crowd had parted enough for her to see Attilla, she forced her hands out. The invisible force threw him to the ground. He didn't try to fight it. He didn't have the will to stand and face her as she glared down at him. Her face was pure white, the trace of colour she possessed was stripped with rage.

'Harbouring a Slayer Mentor!' Her voice frayed. She lifted her hand and struck him across the face. The sound stung the air. 'How long have you known?'

The vampires muttered further shock. They never thought he would protect a Slayer Mentor. He put the safety of his Clan above everything.

'I did not know,' he replied, his voice as firm as ever.

'Is this why she would not become one of us?' Jessie snapped back. Whether he knew or not was anyone's deliberation, but his face was sincere. It was their choice whether they would trust the vampire they had known for so long. 'She could not stand to become something she helped to *destroy*!' There was no hint of a question in her accusation.

He just stared, unable to answer, or perhaps unwilling. When he gave no reply, her eyes narrowed and she stormed out.

Silence swept through the hall. It had been so quick, they did not need this, not now. Fox was the first to move. The others literally leapt out of his way. Catrina didn't go with him. Attilla stood to look him in the eye.

'*Did* you know?' His voice was devoid of emotion.

There was hesitation in his voice. 'No.'

Fox bit his lip. A long, hard stare put them on firmer ground. 'I believe you,' he said, 'but I still want her dead.'

Attilla nodded at him before addressing his Clan. 'I will find her. No one is to take this matter into their own hands.' His eyes returned to Fox. 'No one. Anyone who decides to will answer to me.' Authority still burned in his eyes.

They watched him leave without a word.

Fox was left standing in the middle of the room, one hand held the gun, the other balled into a tight fist. He went to Rose's body, knelt down and closed her glassy eyes. He cast Aisen's statue a quick glance but didn't look at anyone else as he left.

When he'd gone, nervous chatter sprang up.

Sonny knelt down beside Rose's lifeless body. He gripped Catrina's hand when she came forwards and offered it. There were tears in his eyes that he didn't try hiding.

The vampires that were left started to move the bodies of their allies from the blood-spattered floor with an uneasy air sweeping amongst them.

CHAPTER TWENTY FIVE

Louis awoke to the sound of his front door being pounded in. Leaping out of bed, he hurriedly hauled his jeans on and grabbed his shirt.

Raised voices rose from outside. Someone in heavy shoes stormed up the stairs. He rushed, buttoning his shirt wrong, to his bedroom door. It flung open before he managed to reach the handle and he was lucky to avoid being hit.

Fox stood there. Rain soaked him, dripping from his hair, streaming down his face. It formed a small pool at his feet. It could have boiled from the look in the vampire's dark eyes.

'What the hell happened to you?' Louis asked, confusion and worry covering an otherwise blank expression.

Ebony stormed into the room.

'Manners are something you *seriously* take for granted, Fox,' she spat at him, rubbing her arm from where he had wrenched her aside.

He dismissed her with a sharp glance. 'Get out.' His voice had never been so low and threatening. Ebony stood firm. Fox thrust his hand in the direction of the door. 'Get *out!*'

Ebony was a born vampire. Regardless of Fox's abilities, she could easily beat him if demanded by circumstance. But something was very wrong; she knew better than to provoke him in his current state. Glancing briefly at Louis, she reluctantly and angrily left the room. The door closed with a heavy slam.

Fox's attention fixed back to his purpose. He was seething, pent-up anger tearing him between advancing or pacing back and forth.

'What's with you?' Louis frowned with consternation. Fox stepped towards him, and unconsciously he matched by taking a few steps back. Fox would back him up against the wall if he had to; his anger wouldn't be subdued.

'Did you know?'

'Know what?'

'About Maria.' This time, he spat out her name like a bad taste in his mouth.

There was suddenly a wary portrayal in the way Louis stood. 'What about her?'

Fox could see it in his eyes, hear the inflection in his voice. He knew. 'Have you known since the start?'

'What's happened?'

'We were attacked by Slayers. One of them knew her…she'd been her *Mentor*.'

'Is she…?' He was unable to drive out the last word.

Fox shook his head. His tongue rolled over protruding fangs. He waited until they had drawn back. 'If I had it my way, she would be.' He followed it with a demeaning glance. 'You should thank Attilla.'

He did so silently and wondered what her lover had made of the revelation. Everyone knew that Louis had brought her to the Clan. Fox might not be the only one to break down his door.

'She left the Slayers,' he insisted. 'She's not helped them in a long time.' Louis was always a good judge of character; for Fox to doubt her he had to doubt the integrity of someone he'd trusted for years. 'She's not like them. I know her.'

Fox laughed again; it sounded so cynical, so sour. 'No, you *think* you know her.' He waited for that to sink in. 'You don't know what happened to her, she would have been trained to deceive people. Are you saying you're the same person you were when you were human?'

'It's not the same thing.'

Fox stopped too close to him, his body tensed so much it trembled. 'You put my life at risk, and Attilla's. The entire Clan's, in fact.'

'She was dying on me,' Louis protested.

Fox felt his hand tighten into a fist. He had to physically hold it back, having to move away to do so. He was past caring that Louis was a friend; now all he saw was a traitor. 'You brought an enemy into my...*our* home, and did nothing while she nestled up to our leader!'

'All I did was try to save her,' he said, feeling himself getting angry now. 'I didn't know she'd stay. I didn't tell you, because you would've killed her.'

'Are you trying to convince me that she's as weak as she makes out?'

'She's not like them.'

'She's been playing a role since the day she came to us,' Fox growled. He'd never trusted her; now it made sense that his inherent mistrust was so strong towards her. 'She worked them all around her little finger, lying to them all...she lied her way into his *bed*! Everyone trusted her and put their unquestionable faith in that *bitch*.'

Louis's eyes sharpened a fraction. 'But not you, right?'

That thoughtless comment cost him. Fox punched him in the jaw, knocking him to the ground. His face brushed against the carpet, burning his cheek. Fox loomed over him, as he rolled onto his back, coughing up the blood he'd swallowed. He glared up at Fox, who remained completely motionless.

'People like her trained Slayers to kill people like my mother,' Fox said. Louis felt his jaw throbbing; the blood was dripping down his neck. He wiped it away. 'And Rose is dead.'

Watching Louis's face cloud in shock and dismay lessened Fox's anger.

'...Because of Maria?' He was numb from both pain and shock.

Fox stepped back to let Louis stand up. 'The Slayers just *appeared*. Don't you think it's a little coincidental?'

'You think she led them to you?'

'Why don't you tell *me*, since you know her so well?'

Louis grabbed a cloth from the dresser and wiped at his mouth.

'If she'd died that night, it would've been on my head,' he said, catching Fox a sharp look. It was his turn to be angry, and to justify his actions back then. 'Maybe you can live with the guilt of someone else's death, but I sure as hell can't. But I couldn't turn her.' He saw the question in Fox's eyes and went on to explain. 'Yes, I knew about her past, but I also remembered the girl I had loved before that…and still love.' He sat down on the edge of his bed, the stained cloth gathered in his hands. 'I wasn't about to let her die in my arms.'

'Your reconciliation with her didn't go as planned.'

He let out a small laugh. 'No. She sees me as a diseased version of someone she once knew. But she loves *him*.' He looked up. 'I hope Attilla remembers that.'

'He may kill her because of it.' Fox's body lost its tension, his arms fell limp at his sides. 'I wanted her dead. I still do. But I have to stand by whatever Attilla decides. It's not my decision.'

Following the misfortune that cost Rose her life, Attilla went after Maria. No one challenged his orders, and no one disobeyed. Most of the vampires went out. They had to escape the terrifying revelation that they'd been sharing their home with the enemy.

Attilla returned alone, and was greeted by Jessie. The cold rain ran into his eyes. His face was just as cold, devoid of expression. He had found Maria, and she was not dead.

Jessie folded her arms as he told her.

'You may hold respect over the rest of them, but not over me.' Her voice was bitter. 'I will not allow her back here until Aisen is raised. I suggest you take her away. After he is raised, you may both return and it will be the Master's choice what will be done with her…possibly with you.'

He had no choice but to comply. No one spoke to him. No one knew what he was thinking or going through. He spent a long time standing at the tomb whispering words to their creator.

Then he left the Clan.

They didn't know if Maria would come back alive, whether their leader loved the Slayer Mentor regardless. There was pain and vehemence in him that suggested otherwise.

The vampires didn't know what to think. She hadn't been a Slayer Mentor to them. She was a physician and a friend. Most were divided in their opinions. The one feeling they all shared was that sense of betrayal.

Catrina was mixed in her feelings about Attilla leaving, but took her anxieties up with no one.

In the days after he'd left with Maria, the mood changed. Anger subsided into abandonment. With Jessie as their only guidance and Attilla giving no time when he would return, the Clan anxiously awaited the Master's coming.

To make things worse, Fox had gone to the laboratory to check with Corey about the situation without their leading practitioner, only to find that he wasn't there. Neither—when Fox checked his room—were any of his belongings. No one knew the reason for his departure, but guesses were made. They assumed it had something to do with Maria and how long the two of them had worked side by side. Whatever his reasons, the Clan was now without medical assistance.

Those days were long, and the nights—when they were forced to continue their lives as though nothing had changed— were longer. They tried to be optimistic. The Awakening was approaching; the arrangements were set.

Jessie prepared to give herself to the Master. She didn't spend time with others, instead became more of a recluse than ever. The vampires weren't worried about this behaviour; if anything they were thankful for her absence.

*****

Catrina hadn't dreamt since she'd opened the tomb. There was a burn mark on the palm of her hand from where she had touched the stone. It had scarred over but showed no signs of disappearing.

She thought of Attilla, confident that he hadn't known Maria's secret, despite Jessie's accusations. She understood the severity of the woman's secret. She'd taught Slayers, people the vampires both hated and feared. She could be dead by now. Just because Attilla had left with her didn't mean she would return to face the judgement of the Master. Catrina could understand if he killed her himself.

She didn't get changed, pacing the room in the long grey t-shirt she slept in, holding the old reference journal in her hands. It had provided most insightful.

That familiar grating of claws filled her ears. The creature, Aisen, their Master, everything the Vampire Nation held in the highest regard, walked towards her. She lowered the book.

Now she knew who he was, he looked different. There was now a reason for that strange glow in his eyes, the power that emanated from his very being was not only the instinctive power of a demon, but the energy that came from the Master vampire. He was not monstrous, simply compelling beauty in its purest form.

She couldn't speak to him in the same doubting, uncertain tone. And now that she couldn't question him on his presence, or his drive behind protecting her, there was very little to say.

'I have a question that I could not wait until our worlds unite to ask,' he said.

'What is it?' she asked, at once at ease that their conversation wouldn't be a confused exchange of mutterings or her showing her unwavering faith in the one that created them all.

'That book...' he began. She presented it to him. 'It contains my so-called lament, does it not?' She nodded. 'Find it.'

She did as was asked, leafing through the pages until the only illustration in the book came up. He stood behind her and looked over her shoulder like a curious child at the depiction of his own resting place.

'What about it?' she asked.

He ran one claw thoughtfully over his tomb. 'I am curious as to the meaning of these symbols.'

She turned her head slightly and craned her neck to meet his eyes. 'Can't you read it?'

He paused but gradually shook his head. 'It was written in a language I am unfamiliar with.'

Her eyebrows furrowed. 'But the Trine...your children wrote it.'

Again he signalled disagreement. 'They wrote the commands for my resurrection. This seems to be the nonsense of an unknown author.'

'I think Jessie was looking into their meaning,' she said. She had spoken with Louis; he'd been very unimpressed at that fact.

'The self-proclaimed Vessel,' Aisen said with a shake of his head. The look was unfathomable and was gone quickly. He reached his palm over the back of his neck, rubbing the aching muscles beneath. He acted so human sometimes, it was unusual to see it coming from him. He craned his neck. 'If it is something of importance, surely it would have been discovered by others?'

His comment sparked something in the atmosphere, it thickened, and the cloaked figure, Ruben, appeared. She saw Aisen's muscles tense; it was frightening to see something over seven feet tall with a girder-like biceps getting angry. His justification was simple, and it explained his aggressive behaviour in her dreams. Aisen was facing his killer.

'Or perhaps you hide it from them,' Ruben said, moving forwards. Catrina moved aside. Aisen stood firm, the burning in his eyes could've killed. The man was not deterred. 'A beautiful weave of lies is still lies.'

'Leave us,' the Master hissed. 'Do not defy me, leader of the rebellion.'

Ruben's laugh pierced the thick air. 'Is this what you tell her? I have been eager to learn why she looks so coldly towards me.'

'I tell her only the truth.'

'You tell her *your* truth.'

'Do I lie when I tell her that you destroyed me?'

'And what justifications do you give me?'

'None, as much as you deserve.'

Catrina stood beside Aisen, listening to them argue. She stood there, watching the two fight with their equally powerful words. Any faith that Aisen suggested she had in Ruben, the gatekeeper, the figure, the killer, was gone. She stepped forwards, standing in Aisen's path, staring at the knight.

'I know what you did,' she said. From what she had experienced, Aisen—for all his power—didn't have the ability to

force Ruben to leave. But she held power over the both of them;
she was still alive. 'It's *your* sword in his heart, and you've been
trying to stop me from understanding since I was turned. You've
been guarding his grave from the day you were killed, haven't
you?' He gave no reply. 'I had to listen to both of you, because
you both fight for different causes. He wants to live, to return
equilibrium…and you want to stop him.' Aisen stood behind
her. 'You've tried to turn me against him, because I'm the only
one who can make you stand aside. I don't know why you both
chose me, but I know who I'll side with. The choice between our
Master or his killer, there's no question. If you are the only thing
holding him back, and I am the only thing binding you to this
world, then I will do everything in my power to destroy you.'

When she was finished, and Ruben was sure she had said all
she felt was needed, he stepped back. He held his hands at his
chest. He gave no retaliation. Instead, he bowed to her.

'That is not necessary,' he said gently. 'If it is your request, I
will do so and leave it in your hands. You will live in the
knowledge that you are the one who released this plague on the
world once more.' His voice was growing sharp again, spiteful to
Aisen's being. He kept his eyes on Catrina. 'Moreover,' he
added, as he began to fade into nothing. There was a worrying
smile on his fang-bearing face. 'Your heart beats with his now.'

He was gone as quickly as he'd appeared. Catrina looked up
to Aisen, sheer pride still gleamed in his eyes. She nodded
solemnly.

'Is this more of what I didn't want to know?' she asked.
'That I was a tool for the both of you? That I was the one
keeping you from being risen because I held a trust in him?' She
gestured to the space where Ruben had been.

'Do you understand it?'

She paused. 'I don't understand why you chose me.'

'Do you accept it?'

After a long pause, she nodded. 'Yes.'

He bowed and was gone. The air lifted as it did when
spiritual presences were no longer at hand. She sat down on the
bed, wanting to go back to sleep. She had no worry about
dreaming anymore; the spirits were out in the world. It wasn't as

comforting as she would've thought. Now they could come and go as they pleased. At the end of it all, neither was there for her benefit; they both had their own plans.

The rain fell in harsh droplets; the dim luminosity of the oil lamps shed the only light over the cemetery. There was not a large congregation, just a few who had known Rose well. Sonny stood beside the priest, a man who looked more wizened with time than afraid of this impromptu night-time burial. Catrina doubted he knew vampires existed, but they had to lay Rose to rest, however they went about it.

Fox stood beside her, his eyes locked ahead at nothing but the emptiness that stretched out before them. She could not bring herself to look at him. She'd barely known Rose, yet it still hurt, and Fox had known her for years.

Four vampires carried the casket towards the freshly dug grave. The last funeral she'd been to was that of Tony's son, Rio. They had been friends for close to seven years, and he'd been taken away so young. She had cried in Tony's arms, while he and his associates planned revenge. She didn't want to think what was going through Fox's mind.

The priest stepped forwards, holding a small bible in his hand. He began to speak, but Catrina couldn't hear him. The rain padded on the top of the coffin, drowning a single white rose that someone had thoughtfully placed there.

CHAPTER TWENTY SIX

The factory had never been quieter. Not a breath was heard through the corridors, barely even a heartbeat. But the anticipation was there; it soared as highly as any emotion could over the group as they flocked into the main hall. After all the waiting, it was becoming a reality. The statue of Aisen stood magnificently on the platform, it hadn't even been removed from the tomb. No one wanted to touch it; there was a sense of unparalleled reverence and the undiluted essence of fear that came from getting too close.

The crowd parted for Jessie. She was dressed in a black dress, fitted with precious gems, thick weaved lace covered the material; a funeral garb. Some of the vampires bowed their heads. She stared blankly ahead. Her shoes clipped across the stone, as she walked willingly to die.

The tapping rippled through them like the ticking of a clock. She headed towards the waiting tomb, to the sword forced into their Master's heart. She turned, her head held high, stopped. The statue waited for her.

She held no papers, having learned the translated ritual by heart. She presented herself before him, her hands held firmly by her sides, and she opened her mouth to speak. The language was not English or understandable. She spoke so quickly that each syllable fell into the next.

She stepped up to the statue.

Catrina's eyes flashed open.

She hadn't wanted to be there for the Awakening. For all the nobility in seeing Aisen reborn, she didn't want to see someone sacrifice themselves.

But it seemed someone *wanted* her to attend. The pounding in her head grew like a tornado. In the background, there was a faint sound of screaming, an unknown voice from deep inside.

She tried to stand but fell to her knees. Her head pulsed with a burning sensation. She could feel her heart in her throat. Her blood drove through her veins, giving a new realness to everything. The world consumed her, the screaming intensified.

A sharp pain shot through her spine, forcing her head up. She came face to face with Aisen. His eyes were vigorous, alive. She tried to get up, but the pain kept her incapacitated. His mouth was moving, but all she could hear was screaming. Tears streamed down her face. It must have been the pain he had lived with, everything he had been surrounded by.

The gates were open.

The congregation was spellbound. The thickness to the air wasn't through emotion for once. It was a physical density, a profuse cloud of supernatural presence. Jessie screamed the words.

Fox stood with his hands behind his back, watching the power descend, passing into Aisen's stone shell. His eyes drifted. He thought how Attilla would've wanted to see this and what he'd given it up for.

Jessie held a ceremonial knife. She unwrapped it from a red silk cloth and let the material fall to the ground. She held the blade over her hands, the ritual still spilling from her lips. It was as though Aisen had already taken over, when she slowly ripped the blade over the palm of her open right hand.

The blood dripped over her pale skin, as she continued to recite the words without flinching. Her bloody hand reached for the sword's handle. She stopped, stared in the stone-coated eyes of Aisen. Her arm shot out with inhuman speed. She hooked her tiny hand around the hilt.

The dark cloud above them spilled into the sword and the lifeless body it impaled. Pain shot through Jessie's spine, standing her rigid. The cloud sank entirely into the statue, as a dull boom echoed through the building. The tomb shook, the statue shuddered as though it was going to crash to the ground. Collective fear ran through them. Jessie trembled, her hand locked around the weapon. The blood spilled from between her fingers. There were tears in her eyes as she looked up at him. People could only assume what she was seeing. All that he had seen, his suffering, his beliefs, all passing into her.

A shot of cold light consumed the statue, gaping through the cavity in his chest, still behind Ruben's sword. Jessie pulled as the light grew brighter. It spilled through the room, filled their hearts with an understanding. They all shared his pain, his everything.

There was an explosion from within the statue, it sent a shock wave through the building, out into the city, and further beyond. Humans stopped in the street, shuddered, and dismissed it. Vampires city-wide shared an instant feeling of oneness; but it was too fleeting to assume it to be anything other than a freak coincidence.

…Catrina only just found her feet, before the pressure sank into her mind. The screaming reached full pitch, and she felt the darkness surround her. She collapsed, her body shuddered as the screaming and burning pain receded into the void, taking her consciousness with it…

The explosive force catapulted Jessie across the room. Her little body tumbled over the stone; the vampires could only move out of the way. The dark cloud sprung back from the statue and sank through her skin, she shook on the ground, and her eyelids flickered in rapid succession.

She jerked and twisted involuntarily, but no one went to her aid. They were transfixed with the manifestation of absolute power, and they dared not stop what was clearly Aisen's doing.

They watched the cloud settle and dissipate into the air around them. Her body stopped struggling and lay very, very still. Nothing happened. The cloud was gone. They looked to the statue, but there was nothing new; it was as dead and silent as it had ever been.

Suddenly, Jessie's body lifted itself into a sitting position. She screamed an unholy wail of a child and a beast in agony. Her fangs shot out, somewhat longer, and her eyes slowly opened, a deep topaz tinge to them. She breathed like a ravenous beast that had spotted its prey.

'The darkness...such black, limitless void...what we have become.' Her voice echoed out through the silence, the timbre was no different, but more deadly.

Someone stepped forwards. 'Jessie?'

Such a fool. She was on her feet in an instant, her hand outstretched towards the man. He froze. The little girl's golden-tinged eyes narrowed.

'I am your *Master*, child,' she hissed. She held out the bloody hand, palm open for all to see. The wound had healed before the blood had even dried. She stared at the vampire, who tried to move away, but his feet were locked in place. Something was holding him there, and from the look in the eyes of the child, it was she.

She clenched her fist into a ball, eyes burning into him. He clutched at his chest. His hand scraped over his skin to reach something he could not touch. She tightened her grip of the air. The man brought up blood that painted the floor. He fell to the ground. The wound came up clearly from under his skin, a discoloured bruise. His heart had been ruptured without a touch. A steady stream of scarlet ran down the corpse's mouth.

Jessie straightened, eyes falling on her followers. 'This power you see, there is only one who is capable of such influence. In the darkness, we will wander...all the screams will die with the coming of the night.'

Another vampire stepped forwards, bowed graciously. 'Master,' he said. There was no hesitation or doubt in his voice.

The child turned to him, still unimpressed. She brought her arm around, some stepped back thinking this man would suffer the same fate to the other. Invisible power forced him on one knee; he did not fight it and his head bowed more.

'You will address me as such,' she said, eyes scanning over the crowd. 'I am your Master. You will bow to my presence, you will cower before me, and you will do my bidding without question.'

The vampires immediately fell to their knees, heads bowed, without question. The little girl watched them, nodding slightly.

'What do you request of us, Master?' one asked.

The girl opened her mouth to answer, but nothing surfaced. It was beat by another scream. Her body fell on all fours, fangs protruded, eyes wide. The sound echoed through the building. They all watched with a growing uneasiness. Perhaps the Awakening was not over. Perhaps something was wrong. Faster than lightning, she was on her feet and fled.

Fox was the first person to stand, noticing that the attention was on him. Without Attilla there, and with Jessie—or whatever inhabited her body—in that state, he was assumed to be in charge. He ran his fingers through his hair, craned his neck until it cracked, and went for his cigarettes.

'I don't know what to tell you,' he said. The others slowly lifted themselves off the ground. 'But we can't question Aisen's actions. Bear in mind he hasn't been a part of our world for a long time. His mannerisms can't be expected to match our own ethics.'

His words were taken as suitable explanation.

Now that Aisen walked amongst them in this erratic and brutal form, the vampires finally braved touching the stone statue. They ran their hands over the stone, recoiling if they touched the bloody sword. There was nothing reverent about it now; it was useless. One of the bouncers suggested destroying it. Louis intervened, suggesting that he would take it as he had done before, and they didn't argue. He could do whatever he wanted with it, now it was just a shell.

The Master walked amongst them.

Fox knocked for a third time on Catrina's door. When there was still no answer, he went in to find her unconscious. He roused her, her eyes darted wildly as though it was the first time she had used them.

'What happened?' he asked, helping her sit on the bed.

She veered forwards, her hands clutching at her temples. She frowned as though she didn't recognise him. He remained steadfast in front of her. 'Catrina, what happened?'

She tried to laugh, but the dull memory of the pain still stabbed at her head. She gestured to the room. 'He came through this way.'

Fox lifted her to her feet, but she wasn't quite ready, and she sat back down. Her head lolled, twisted strands of hair fell over her eyes. Her breathing was heavy but hurried.

He didn't know what to do. '...Aisen?'

Her head bobbed slightly, she winced at the pain, forcing herself to look up.

She tried to focus, the pain wasn't there, just the memory of it, which was enough. It was unlike any pain she'd felt before; the memory of a life lost. She'd been with him in that tomb, feeling the agony as he was wrenched from it. Now it was slowly fading. She knew the Awakening had come to pass.

The time that followed was eerie. The Clan spoke little of the Awakening, almost as though it had not happened. The Vessel had not been seen since. It remained locked inside Jessie's room. The vampires didn't know how long this uncertainty would last, but they were without a leader. Fox was given the role without much need to consider alternative possibilities. During this time he instructed the bodyguards to watch over Jessie's room; the Vessel had to be guarded until Aisen had finished with it. Fox took charge as best he could, until one night, without prior warning, Attilla returned. Maria was with him.

Fox brought Attilla up to date with the situation of the Awakening and the fact that the Vessel hadn't been seen since. The only thing that suggested it was still there was the sound of screaming that echoed every now and then from Jessie's room. At the request of the Clan's majority, Attilla had to hold Maria in confinement until further notice. When Aisen had finished whatever he was doing to the Vessel, he could judge her. None of the Clan wanted to be the one to guard her, either afraid she would turn on them or unable to trust themselves with her imprisonment. It appeared she would fare no better in their company than she would in Aisen's.

In the end it was Attilla who took the responsibility. He did so without comment. The time away had changed him. However, the warmth and cheerfulness that had been removed at his departure was beginning to take shape again. Perhaps the arrival of Aisen had conjured up hope.

It took Catrina a few more nights of self-assuring words to make a decision towards how she would approach the change.

The playing field had been levelled; the Master was amongst them. There was nothing to stop her simply walking into the room and talking to him.

The steps she took that evening were cautious; she approached Fox, who was sitting, as usual, at the bar with a half-spent cigarette hanging from his lips.

'Are you ready?' he asked, stepping back off the stool.

'I won't be coming out tonight.'

'Are you alright?' He moved closer, what passed as worry veiled his expression.

She smiled to ease him. 'There's something I have to do.'

'...What?'

CHAPTER TWENTY SEVEN

'I want to talk to him,' she said, as Attilla blocked her path to the upstairs and Jessie's room.

Attilla looked over her expression, but there was nothing he could discern from it. 'May I ask why?'

'I want to know what he thinks of me.'

'You should know that the transformation has not been easy for him,' he replied in warning. 'I understand you have your questions, but he will be drained and may not wish to divulge in conversation.'

'Have you spoken to him yet?' she asked.

He hesitated. 'Not in length, no. His responses tend to be short and his idea of conversation is not more than a few questions and answers. And he seems to tire of anyone's company in a matter of minutes. I assume he is still adjusting to the setting.'

She doubted that; he wasn't the kind of creature to find anything difficult to adjust to. 'Can I at least try? The worst that can happen is he refuses to talk.'

He considered the question for a moment. 'Very well.' He stood aside; if she were to go, she would have to go without him. With a grateful and obedient nod, she passed him and ascended the spiral staircase.

It was darker up here now; the lights had been dimmed at Aisen's request. She edged her way along the corridor. There was an ominous air about it; something that told her to retreat while she had the chance.

The room smelled odd, it was the first thing that struck her once she was inside. It was darker than it should be; the only light was barely shining from the desk lamp. It was too dim for her eyes to focus. But through the darkness, she could make out the silhouette of Jessie's animated corpse standing like a mannequin by the boarded window. The second odd point was that Aisen didn't turn on hearing her enter.

The atmosphere was tense, and for the first time in a while, Catrina felt anxiety turning her stomach. Her heart quickened its pace, palms felt sweaty. She held them to her chest and padded softly across the carpet.

Aisen turned when the door clicked shut. Stepping from the window, he guided the body of the child around and set eyes on Catrina.

'...Yes?' he asked, the word soothed through the little girl's voice box to hang like treacle in the air. But he sounded agitated, as though she had no right to share his company. Perhaps the Awakening had changed him; perhaps his spirit inhabiting Jessie's body was picking up and feeding from her mannerisms. 'Why are you here?'

She shuffled on the spot, not expecting the cold reception. 'I...I...'

'Out with it, *girl*,' Aisen spat.

'I wanted to talk to you,' she said, with a hint of both desperation and agitation. He'd always been so accommodating. 'That's all.'

'That's all?' he mocked with an unpleasant laugh. 'You and every other creature here wants my company. What makes *you* any different from the others?'

'Aisen...' She made a start across the floor; barely two steps and an invisible force was holding her at bay. The child stood a few feet away, with one arm raised; the sheer power inside him was enough to keep her away.

'Where do you find the audacity to address me so?' he snapped. She felt pressure collect around her wrist; the same force twisted her arm around her back. She stumbled forwards, but the pressure only grew. She looked towards Aisen, whose hand had not moved, but a slight sadistic pleasure was evident on his angelic face. 'Your first lesson I will teach you is to know the meaning of respect.'

She bit her tongue and forced her mouth shut to stop an agonised cry from escaping; she wouldn't let her weakness show. Doing so was only making him angrier, and it began to feel as though her arm was going to break. Another weight shoved itself into the small of her back, such a vicious action was what brought her to her knees. From this angle, she had to crane her neck to see into the small child's eyes; the eyes that looked back were dark and menacing, the face—though pure in appearance— was marred with the dark undertone of a twisted and troubled mind. She could only assume that all this happening with the Awakening had exhausted him; Attilla may have been correct in saying Aisen would not be one for holding conversation in his current condition.

The pressure didn't lessen from either around her arm or in her back; it was starting to hurt. She writhed on the floor, trying to stand. He looked down on her, holding his hand out to maintain pressure.

'How did you get here?' he asked with a suspicious tone. 'The vampire Attilla guards my quarters.'

'He...he let me up,' she said, trying to keep a patient head on her shoulders. It was slowly dwindling; there was a limit to how much she would freely take from anyone, and Aisen—regardless of his status—was no different. 'I wanted to talk to you. I wanted to know what you thought of me now you were here.'

His grip lessened, a little look of wrong-footedness glossed his eyes as he moved backwards. '...Now?' he asked. 'What '*now*'?' Catrina was about to stand up, when the pressure came back with a vengeance. Aisen swooped forwards like a wraith, his use of the child-vampire's corpse was next to flawless; the child's body twisted with his every gesture. 'Stay where you are.'

Catrina felt her eyes narrow, unable to keep her anger at bay. 'What's *wrong* with you?'

The tension fell like lead; Aisen stared at her. 'I do not wish to divulge in pointless conversation with one as unworthy as you.'

A moment of silence passed between them, when the darkness that surrounded them echoed with the sound of resonant growls. The pressure again lessened again from Catrina, only this time she was not so quick to try to rise. Aisen became visually irate; she wasn't sure what caused it, but something triggered the expression of white rage he was giving. The sound of roaring filtered through her ears; she knew it as Aisen's call, and looking at him, he wasn't best pleased.

Coming here had been a mistake; that realisation hit as Aisen clenched his fists by his sides. He was angry; she should've left it a few more days to let him adjust to this new world. 'Have you no respect for the one who created you?' he demanded.

The noise increased a few pitches; Aisen stepped back and clutched at his head. Something was happening to him; he leant forwards and let out a scream. Catrina was amazed the child's voice box didn't shatter. She had done something wrong; the question was merely a case of what it was.

'Leave,' he snarled. She remained fixed on the spot; the closeness that had developed between the two made her resolute to find the root of his evident problem.

'You need help,' she said, moving closer.

His eyes became narrow slits; she reconsidered her actions. Perhaps she should've worded that better; the last thing Aisen needed to hear was that he was somehow inferior. He raised one hand, the door behind Catrina flung open. By the time she realised what was coming, she was already on her way; Aisen's force sent her flying through the air and out of the door. She hit her head hard on the opposite wall, looking up in time to see the child standing in the doorway before the same indeterminate force swung it shut once more.

She remained still for the moment, huddled by the wall; her elbow hurt but she ignored its sting. Aisen wasn't well, and he was too self-sufficient to ask for help. His uneasiness was understandable; this world was by no means the same one he left all those years ago.

Aisen was acting as though he didn't know her, and she didn't like how lost she felt with that in mind. She didn't want to think that she relied on him. She eventually found her feet and walked with a dead expression and numb motions back downstairs.

She didn't even look at Attilla as she passed him; it was he who stopped her and brought her attention back to reality.

'How was he?' he asked.

She held back the bitter smile, shrugged. 'Not in a talkative mood. I don't blame him, really. This has been hard on him.'

Attilla looked confused. 'You empathise with him?'

'I...don't know,' she replied with furrowed brows. 'I try to, but he's not acting like...' She checked herself quickly before saying more. 'Like the Master should.'

Attilla nodded. 'The change has hit him, I assume. It will only be a matter of time before he adjusts to it.'

'What until then?' she asked with a worried face.

'Until then,' he said, 'we have to accept the fact that he is our Master and not question his actions.'

CHAPTER TWENTY EIGHT

It had been almost a year since Catrina had been turned into a vampire. She could say she'd discovered what the world hid through human ignorance, but she'd have been lying.

She'd discovered that deception was a constant through immortality, just as it'd been for human existence. And she'd learned that a life without much fear of death only brought more confusion, and that there were things out there better off not known.

She'd come no closer to knowing what she was. She'd hoped with Aisen's rebirth she'd have the answers she needed to know, but there was nothing.

It wasn't that she couldn't find them if she looked hard enough, but there was a sense that it just wasn't time to know. Since Aisen had shifted into Jessie's body, Catrina didn't dream again.

Catrina headed for the bar. It was a Feed, an event Fox had explained many times and tried on numerous occasions to get her interested in. Catrina made it an aim to avoid them. She didn't see the point in bringing humans into their home in order to feed off them, when the Moderator bars were designed for the exact same purpose. Many of the Clan saw it as a test of ability; she saw it as a meagre attempt to exercise skills that were suited more to the streets.

She didn't plan on staying at this one, either. She wanted to go out on the hunt. It had been a while since she'd hunted someone instead of finding them in a bar. She had hunter's instinct; she considered killing whoever her victim was that night.

The hall was packed, and as a result Sonny was extremely busy. He darted up the bar to get a clean glass, while someone else motioned for their change. These were the worst times, but was still a job he adored.

Catrina didn't feel awake. She had the feeling she should've stayed in bed longer. She sat down on a stool that had just become free, shooting a spiteful look at the man who tried to take the place first.

Sonny scooted over. 'What can I get you?'

'A beer, what else?'

'You're such a *sophisticated* woman, Catrina.'

She spread her arms. 'You can take the girl out of the slums…' she started.

He waved the remark aside with a smile and slid an open bottle across to her.

She passed a cardboard coaster through her fingers, mouthing the lyrics from the song playing in the background. She'd been there too long; now she knew the words. It was heavy music, chugging guitars and a soul-wrenched singer. The mournful cries echoed through the amplifiers, dotted in various locations around the room, none of which she could see. It must've taken hours to get the music system set up, but it was pleasing the crowd and therefore doing its job. Anything to make people believe the place was a popular night spot…

She straightened in the seat. Fox's arrival had a way of striking her senses; she caught traces of his cologne. She nodded as welcome, as he took the seat beside her. Sonny came over, gave Fox one look and went for the whiskey.

'You look tired,' Fox said to her, trying to make his observation sound neutral.

She returned his observation with a shrug. 'I always look tired.'

He shook his head, taking the drink Sonny was offering. Sonny leant forwards, about to strike up a conversation, when someone from the opposite end of the bar shouted for a drink and he was called back to duty.

'I could do with an assistant,' he said to himself as much as to the two of them. 'Preferably a woman, preferably young...'

Catrina turned back to Fox. 'You don't look so great yourself.'

That was a lie. He looked the same as always. He shrugged, tipping half of the whiskey back. He was reaching for his cigarettes before he had even put the glass down.

The music faded into the next track, and for a split second all she heard was the gas hissing from Fox's lighter. It reminded her of her first night outside as a vampire, when everything had seemed more 'real'. It shamed her to admit that Fox had been right yet again, but the world had lost its spectacular façade in a relatively short time.

It had only been a year, and already things didn't surprise or enlighten her. She didn't want to think how she would see the world after years behind vampire eyes. She wanted to believe that it would be a more fulfilled existence, that the vampiric gift would finally make her realise the world's possibilities. But she doubted it.

She didn't mind this life for its similarities to her previous one. But she would never have to retire from this, never step down when she was no longer capable. This life was near enough the same as being human, only with a more fanciful background and a lifetime of forever to go through.

'How's Attilla?' she asked, breaking her own thought. Fox looked over his raised hand, drawing it to his lips to take a thoughtful inhalation. He didn't reply immediately, letting the smoke rise slowly from his mouth. Catrina leant closer to remind him that she expected an answer. 'Have you spoken to him?'

'...Not much.'

'What do you think will happen to Maria?' She knew how Fox felt about Maria, but she was also trying to imagine what Attilla must have been going through.

'I don't know,' he replied, his voice slightly agitated, but she disregarded it, giving him a more imploring look. 'I've let him have his time. He needs it.'

That didn't answer her question. She presumed he didn't know. There'd be certain topics, such as love, that Attilla wouldn't share. She sipped at the beer, it had a refreshing taste and began to wake her up.

It was going to be a long night; she could feel it. The music drifted on to its own beat. At least the crowd was entertained. This dark, gothic, old industrial factory was a novelty to them. Catrina watched the double shot spirits being sold in dozens, people leaning over the bar to catch the barman's attention.

'It's almost been a year,' she said, throwing a casual glance in Fox's direction.

'I know.' His face sported a dry smile. 'Can you feel it yet?'

'Feel what?'

'Divinity.'

She thought on this for a second or so, shook her head boldly and continued to drink.

'I won't be able to see it the way you want me to,' she said with a tired yet sincere smile. 'Not until I know why I'm here.'

'You know why you're here,' he remarked self-assuredly, taking the whiskey. Smoke trailed from his lips. 'You just can't bring yourself to accept it.'

She was about to come back with a biting comment at his observation, but the look on his face made her stop. He was starting to turn on the seat while reaching for his gun.

The main doors were open and strangers stood there. The vampires in the crowd began to back away anxiously. Everyone's attention fixed on the doorway. The music scratched to an abrupt halt, anyone who'd been engrossed by the sound was now looking at the new company.

Attilla was suddenly in the room. Fox took the gun out while walking towards him. Catrina wasn't asked to follow, but that didn't stop her.

There were fifteen or so. She could smell their blood over the overwhelming sense of the humans. Slayers. It left the question of why they were there, and how they'd found them. Maria. If this had anything to do with Maria, she'd die. This had to cross the line.

The Slayers parted ways at the doors, as Nathaniel Rae entered. His stride was arrogant, the most vindictive smile settled on his face, and he rested his shotgun against his shoulder. The humans started to panic first, thinking this was some kind of gang warfare. Nathaniel let a single shot go into the ceiling. Some people screamed. The vampires' eyes remained locked on the Head Slayer.

He walked through the parting crowd like the shadow of a demon. The fact that he was mortal was insignificant. There was evil beating in that heart.

Attilla's face was blank, as was Fox's. Catrina, however, was neither willing nor able to hide her feelings towards the man. She glared ravenously. His Slayers advanced into the hall, filtering across the room to cover all possible exits.

Nathaniel threw Catrina a quick look of recognition, but his attention focused on the Clan leader. He could tie up loose ends when business had been tended to.

He pointed the shotgun at Attilla. 'I've waited too long to bring this arrogant masquerade to its end.'

Attilla made no motion. The fact he was there was hindrance enough. It was obvious Fox wanted to raise his gun and kill the man standing before them, but he would and could not do so without his leader's consent.

'We will not yield to idle threats, Nathaniel,' Attilla said eventually, keeping his stance firm, his hands at his sides.

'Yes, you will.'

His fist struck out and caught Attilla a blow across the face. It was quick, but Attilla had had time to dodge it. He simply chose not to.

Fox took a step forwards to retaliate, but he felt Attilla's arm move across his chest, withholding his assault.

Nathaniel wanted the advantage, but his approach didn't have the effect he intended. The vampires followed their leader's example; there was no need to cower. They moved forwards, closing in around the Slayers.

Fox's grip tightened around his gun. Catrina continued to glare. She remembered the pain Rae put her through, how close she'd come to dying. She wanted to fight him. He'd prayed on a weak fledgling then. Circumstances had changed…sort of.

'I offer you the opportunity to leave now,' Attilla said, running his hand under his lip to wipe away the blood. He was composed, and it was making Nathaniel angrier.

'Do you?' he retorted slyly. 'That's very thoughtful of you. But what if don't take that opportunity? Are you willing to fight us, or are you trying to save your Clan from falling into submission?' His smiled became broader. 'Until now, we've let you be. Your Clan has been united for years in the thought that numbers will protect you. I give you a choice. Either you hand over what we have come for, or you will *all* die.'

'What have you come for?' Attilla grew more wary.

'A proportion of your vampires,' Nathaniel replied, more as an instruction. '…and the traitor you have. We intend to deal with her, as well.'

Attilla shook his head. '…Maria's already dead.'

This wasn't true, but nevertheless the words were startling. He was still protecting her.

The Head Slayer didn't seem pleased with that; no doubt he wanted to kill her himself. The smile crept back onto his face. 'Just the vampires then. You can hand them over or else we will take them by force and kill the rest.'

It was Attilla's turn, and Nathaniel, for all his ability, could not have seen it coming. A hand shot forwards, hooking around his throat. Startled, he dropped his shotgun. There was no time for the Slayer to give his orders as he was thrown to the ground. If he had broken any bones it didn't show, as he rolled back into a stand and lifted the second gun—a smaller but by no means less effective 9mm—in one fluid motion. Such agility in humans was unknown; it was understandable why he was Head Slayer.

His eyes burned with bruised pride. He let a few shots fly. They all missed Attilla by inches; this display of violence ordered the advance.

The room was filled with a swarm of bullets echoing through the spacious room. Humans screamed, packing towards the door. It became easy for the fighters to recognise one another.

Catrina backed up against the bar, reaching for her gun. As she looked up, she caught sight of Fox slitting the throat of one young man, his eyes already on his next target. Someone leapt over from behind the bar; she raised her gun.

'Sweet Jesus, woman!' Sonny yelled, using one hand to cock the shotgun he held. 'The fight's out there!' He pointed his gun out into the crowd, picking off one Slayer without looking. The fight was in the middle of the hall, for a very short time they were safe by the bar. He was about to move off when she grabbed his arm.

'Why do they want some of us, Sonny?'

'The Slayers?' She nodded quickly. Someone shot out a bottle from behind the bar; the glass showered down over them. 'The prime rule for any assailant is to know your enemy. In their case, the only way to know their enemy is to take them.'

'That's why they have the Themisium.' The Slayers were outnumbered, but they each had weapons that rendered vampires incapacitated with one successful shot.

Catrina looked at Sonny. He cocked the shotgun again and they parted ways.

She fired a few warning shots. The bullets flew into Slayers' arms, legs; no major arteries were hit. She would not shoot to kill yet. She heard someone approach from behind so swiftly that she was surprised at sensing them. As the stranger leapt, they were met by her gun barrel and the bullet inside. The body hit the floor with a dull thud.

A few vampires were already down. Some flinched from the Themisium, others didn't move at all. She watched, her vigilance still high. The Slayers were breaking down the side doors and getting into the rest of the building.

She raised her gun and tried to block their way. It worked until someone flew at her, tackling her to the ground. She kicked out, the sole of her boot contacted flesh, and the attacker was sent back down. The Slayer grabbed Catrina by the shoulder, hauling her to the ground. Her gun was flung across the floor, all she had left now was her fists. She hit the floor hard, but there was too much adrenaline shooting through her to register any pain.

The young man she faced smelled of fear. He may have been trained well, but when it came to ending a life, no matter what kind, he didn't seem capable.

Catrina had no sympathy. He would either fight or die. She hooked one arm around his neck. The fear was potent now. He knew he was going to die, these were his last moments in this world. She pulled back until she felt the crunch.

She spotted her gun across the floor, started across the room. She bent down to pick it up, when she was met by a fierce kick under her chin. She flew backwards, felt her neck crack under the strain as she rolled. She had the Beretta back in her hand. As she scrambled back to her feet, it was already raised.

Her opponent was Nathaniel, and he just smiled, raising his own pistol. 'It had to be me.'

They were in deadlock. Catrina had never tried to dodge a bullet before, and she didn't favour her chances. However, if she managed to get a shot in first, it would be all over. She pulled back the safety catch, and for that moment, it was just the two of them.

'Come to finish business?' she snapped, gripping her other hand around the handle. She wasn't afraid. He smiled, shaking his head.

'Audacious *and* self-centred.' He held his gun in one relaxed hand. 'What makes you think this is about you, Catrina?'

He'd remembered her name after all this time. She must've been one of the few who'd faced him and lived; maybe it wasn't wholly about her, but nevertheless she was a valuable extra to be removed. She didn't take her eyes from him but assessed the situation around them.

'Your people are dying,' she stated.

He couldn't deny it, although some of the vampires were unconscious, there for the taking, there were a fair number of Slayers who'd lost their lives.

'Casualties of war.' He turned his head slightly. She was right, his people were falling. At this rate, they'd lose. He moved away slowly from her, gun still aimed.

She just stared.

'Fall back!' Nathaniel yelled to the Slayers, and every single one of them stopped in their tracks and began to retreat. Some took the time to haul convulsing vampires they had managed to injure over their shoulders, heading for the main doors.

Catrina was willing to let them leave, as the others seemed to be.

'Catrina, get down!' The command was direct; she did what she was told and hit the floor.

Fox ran across the room, his gun raised. As she ducked out of the line of fire, he unloaded the entire cartridge. Nathaniel let out a loud scream, as he fell backwards and hit the ground with a heavy thud.

The Slayers continued to heave their prizes out of the door as though it hadn't happened.

Catrina rose to her feet, catching Fox's equally wary stare. 'Is that it?'

A single gunshot sent him to the ground. Her eyes widened as he crumbled, his body began to react to the Themisium instantly. She thought Fox would be the one person who could survive such an attack. Judging from the way his body jarred, there was nobody above it.

Nathaniel was standing again, his shotgun resting against his shoulder. He had the gall to wink at her. The rips in his shirt showed a few glimpses at the bullet-proof vest he wore underneath.

She ran at him, too fast for him to turn the gun on her. She threw her entire body against his, sending the shotgun half way across the room and the both of them to the hard concrete floor.

She rose up like a viper and punched him hard in the face. His jaw bone cracked. She lifted her fist and struck again. He tried to lift a hand towards her neck, but she thrust it away and punched him again and again...she felt the warm blood on her knuckles and it only drove her to hit him harder.

There was nothing for her now but the two of them. If no one stopped her, she was going to beat him to death and lavish every second of it. She didn't see the Slayers carrying Fox away. She didn't see the rest of the fighting cease, while everyone else stopped to watch the Head Slayer be beat into a pulp. The only sound was that of her fist smacking against his skin with a soft and repetitive thwack. Her hands were wet with his blood.

She didn't feel him slide his pistol up to her chest. The sound of the coated bullet ripping through her flesh echoed in the silence.

Nathaniel staggered to his feet in a bloody mess; he could barely see. He still managed to throw her writhing body a look of contempt. He caught the gaze of two of his men and gestured them to get her with a rough cock of his head. He wiped his palm over his face; it came away deep red. A thick river of blood streamed down his face.

This time, it was Attilla who intervened. The two Slayers considered taking him on. When this number had reduced to one and the first to attack lay dead at his feet, the other backed down quickly and fell back behind Nathaniel's guard. The Head Slayer was naturally less coy, but as he stepped forwards Attilla's hand shot out and caught him by the throat.

'No,' he commanded. 'You have all you came for. You will *not* take her, too.'

Nathaniel tilted his head as much as was granted, to sight his one good eye to Attilla's dark and dangerous stare.

'What does it matter to you?' Nathaniel asked, his voice was too quiet for the others to hear as it was choked and grated through the streams of blood he swallowed with each intake of air.

Attilla dragged him close enough for his breath to sweep through the Slayer's hair. 'Everything,' he whispered. 'I have let you live in this city for these years, Nathaniel, because I pity you. I trust another to end your life, not me. You don't *deserve* to die by my hand. But you try my patience. This one is mine. You will *not* have her.' He pushed Nathaniel back. He almost fell, but conceited pride kept him standing. 'Now get out of my home, and take your dogs with you.'

After a long pause, and with nothing to retaliate with, Nathaniel spat his blood onto the ground at Attilla's feet and instructed his people out of the building.

The others watched them go. Attilla was breaking on the inside; the Slayers had Fox. He tried not to let it show, as he scooped Catrina up in his arms and headed for the Infirmary.

*****

The light burned her eyelids when she came to. She lay still and tried to remember what had happened. She'd been shot with Themisium. It'd been so direct, it was over before it had begun. The pain was still there, scratching as her blood fought to pump around her system. She opened her eyes, greeted by nothing but the low buzz of the Infirmary lights.

She wasn't alone; all the beds were occupied by other injured vampires, those not unfortunate enough to be taken.

Fox.

She couldn't focus on the people recovering alongside her. If he wasn't one of them, he'd either been taken, or he was dead. Or both.

She ran her hands over her face, pulling through her mangled hair. She dragged herself into a sitting position, feeling nauseous.

A thought came to her.

Corey had disappeared, and in any case he hadn't known how to treat people shot with Themisium. There was only one person who was able to heal the wounds. Had Maria not helped, they would've died. She was the only one with the knowledge and ability to save them.

If Catrina had been in the woman's position, she would've let them all die. She wouldn't provide remedies for people who hated her. It was a matter of principle.

She winced as the blood rushed to her head but forced herself to get out of the bed. She wanted to know how long she'd been unconscious, and what the Clan had been doing in that time to get their allies back. She held the bedside table for support. Her head hung between her arms, heart pounding against her chest.

She forced herself to take the first steps, and her body fought against it. She didn't remember it like this the last time. Maybe this time was different because she was trying to move when she shouldn't.

She reached for the Infirmary's door; the handle turned before she touched it.

Maria looked momentarily shocked, but it passed them both by. Neither knew what to expect from the other, natural enemies who'd been something in the way of associates. Catrina folded her arms slowly. Maria didn't avoid her gaze.

'I don't want to try and understand your reasons,' Catrina said, her voice hoarse from the time without using it. 'But I can't hold what you were against you. You've saved my life…twice, if this is anything to go by. I don't know if you helped because you were forced, or because you wanted to. I'd rather not know, if it's all the same to you. Just so you know, I'm not your enemy. I have more important grudges to stomach.'

Maria's eyes glistened, although she didn't smile.

Catrina's head tilted to one side. 'I want to know, though…if they hadn't found out, would you have been willing to let it go untold, living here as a human until you died?'

Maria's eyes lost their sparkle. 'Everything happens for a reason.' Her tone was bleak. 'But if I had the choice, I would've taken the truth to my grave, yes. I was happy with the way things were.' Maria *was* happy; what was she now? She was only out of confinement to facilitate those injured. She'd go back once they recovered, called on only when someone was hurt. 'I'm still looking for the reason behind this,' she added. 'Some things that people do are so hard to forgive. I was something that your kind hates. But it all made sense to me then, just like my choice makes sense now. I broke my allegiance to the Slayers a long time ago, because they aren't worth fighting for.'

She was helping the vampires because she wanted to. Catrina couldn't grasp that concept. '…And *we* are?'

A lingering look of happiness crept onto the human's face. 'I'd do anything to take away what everyone is going through. Some forgive more easily than others, I might have had a very different outcome if not.'

There was something else. Through the light-headed nausea of Catrina's recent return to consciousness came a perfect moment of clarity.

A view from inside a commercial flight…surrounded by the hum of happy holiday-goers…looking out of the window to the pure blue sky. There was a sense of euphoria with only the trace of regret of what was left behind…

Catrina didn't want to think of the reasons or implications of being able to read the human's thoughts. The image was very clear this time. It was the only thing Maria had on her mind.

Catrina blinked. 'Don't take him with you.'

'What?'

'When you leave,' she continued, 'don't take Attilla with you.'

Anxious surprise consumed her; she swallowed. 'How did you know?'

Catrina just shook her head. 'Don't ask. *I* don't even know. But I'm right, aren't I? You're leaving the Clan?'

'I don't want to die,' Maria said in a frighteningly calm voice. 'Aisen will rise to full strength soon. He'd kill me without so much as a second thought. And the Slayers are after me now.' She smiled. 'Don't worry, Catrina. This is something I have to do alone.'

'Will you tell him?'

Her nod was solemn. 'He has a right to know.'

Catrina parted her lips, wanting to say more, but the words never reached past her throat. She stepped to the side, allowing Maria inside the Infirmary to do her job.

'How long have I been out?' she asked.

Maria took a fraction too long to think. 'Fifteen days,' she said. She saw the bewildered expression. 'You were shot very close to the heart. The poison didn't set so deeply, because you were treated very quickly. But it takes time for your pulmonary system to heal…'

'—What's happened?'

'Did you see who was taken?'

'I don't see Fox anywhere,' she replied to answer the question.

'Attilla's in the hall,' Maria offered. 'You should go talk to him. He'll be glad to see you're alright, at least.'

Catrina nodded thankfully and left.

She was venting worry mingled with anger as she headed into the hall. It'd been two weeks, yet the Slayers hadn't been ambushed, and their allies were still in danger.

Attilla was talking with a dark-haired male vampire. He looked to be in his mid thirties, but his aura suggested he was much older. A finely-tailored midnight-blue suit complimented the long black hair tied sleekly down his back. She could sense power on him, as well as slight audacity. She didn't recognise him and wasn't interested who he was. She wanted to speak to Attilla. He hadn't acknowledged her arrival; his attention taken with the new guest.

Sonny slowly made his way over to the end of the bar, as Catrina drew her eyes away from the conversation. 'It's good to see you're okay.'

She didn't say anything immediately. All she wanted was to talk to Attilla, but the conversation was obviously too serious to interrupt.

'Tell me what I've missed,' she said. Sonny was overcome with reticence for a moment, not wanting, or not being able, to discuss the events so close to the heart. Seeing this, she gestured to the stranger, making it subtle enough so that he wouldn't notice. 'Who's that?'

Sonny's face slipped into a smirk. 'Oh he's some real bigwig in the rogue community.'

'I thought we didn't associate with rogues?' Her voice was suspicious, catching the gentleman a sharp look, which he didn't notice. There was a constant look of disinterest on his face however imploringly Attilla was making his point.

'We've never needed their help before,' Sonny replied. He leant forwards as though it would stop anyone from listening in. 'Can you imagine how humiliating it is to have to stand there and watch your enemies take part of your team?'

'You mean no one's tried to get them back yet?'

He put down the glass he was holding. 'Well, of course not. We don't attack the Slayers. That's suicide. When these things happen, usually the only thing that gets done is a farewell ceremony.'

'Why?'

'We don't go looking for violence.' A slight aggravation rose in to his tone. 'Jesus, you sound just like Fox.'

The conversation between leaders was over. The rogue shook Attilla's hand politely, but he left without any sign of returning. Catrina headed towards Attilla; he sensed her approach, turned and smiled. His hand was up before she opened her mouth.

'I understand your concern, but this is the most we can do,' Attilla said, lowering his hand.

Her expression shifted from aggravation to worry. '…They're going to die, if they're not dead already. *Fox* is going to die.'

He shook his head firmly, certain in his own ideas. 'I won't risk any more casualties. I must know that everyone who is sent out will return alive.'

'Is that why you're asking rogues for help?'

He nodded the comment away. 'You seem to imagine this as a simple task, Catrina.'

'How many were taken?'

'Seven.'

'And where is this place?' she asked.

He wanted to smile. 'That isn't important yet,' he insisted. 'A Slayer was held hostage, we had Maria talk to her. We have the location, but we don't have the support to head an attack.'

'It's only seven people,' she reiterated.

He must've known her nature; must've seen the schemes ticking over in her mind.

'…You need more rest,' he said, stopping her from planning something that she simply had not thought up yet. He touched her shoulder, an imploring gesture. His eyes glistened with the sympathy that said he understood exactly how she felt. 'We have this under control, and we will get them back.'

Her expression softened; she valued his judgement, and the gentle tone in his voice calmed her fierce spirit. She nodded, her face full of understanding.

'I should get back to the Infirmary,' she said. 'I can't help if I'm not in the best of health.'

She flashed a quick smile in his direction, which didn't drop as she walked away. Instead it became something more wayward, her eyes glistened with the new information. Since he wouldn't give up the Vicinity's location, she would try another source.

She re-entered the laboratory. Her legs went from under her; she just managed to haul herself into the nearest chair. Her head tipped back over the headrest and she stared up at the tiled ceiling. Her body wasn't ready for anything, let alone a solitary infiltration of a Slayer Vicinity. But the longer she waited, the more her conscience ate away at her.

She heard the Infirmary door close and used her feet to turn the chair on its pivot.

'You weren't gone long,' Maria commented, as she headed across the room, placing a dish of used syringes in the sink.

'He's being elusive with his information,' she replied nonchalantly. 'So where is it?'

'Where's what?' she asked. Catrina braved to raise one eyebrow at the woman's poor act of naivety; it hurt to do so. Maria sighed. 'You know I can't tell you.'

Catrina could understand Maria's situation, but she could also feel her emotions rising. She closed her eyes and swallowed to force them back into her stomach, where they churned and made her feel sick.

'Do you think that they'll be okay?' It wasn't much of a question. 'You must've been inside that place, or something like it. You know what happens to them. Tell me where it is.'

'You're still weak,' she stated as a defence. 'I know you're strong, Catrina, but…'

'—Then help me with that, too,' Catrina interrupted, finding the energy to stand. Her head was screaming at her to sit down. 'Give me something for it. Adrenaline, painkillers…anything.'

'The best remedy is time.'

'I don't have time. Neither do the others.'

The human looked at her for a moment; a feeling of helplessness came over them both. She knew the girl was right. They wouldn't be saved by weeks of planning; something had to be done.

Maria was the first to break the stare. She moved around the worktop, gathering materials. Catrina watched but decided not to say anymore.

She stood up straight with a small needle in her hands. 'Roll up your sleeve.'

Catrina looked at her with slight hesitance but did as she was told. It could be a trick, some form of sedative, Maria's attempt to subdue her. Guiding her back into the seat, Maria took her arm by the wrist. She tapped at the inside of her elbow to bring up the vein.

Catrina continued to stare. 'What is that?'

Maria smiled sincerely as she pushed the plunger. The contents were released into her system, and the effects were instantaneous. Her heart raced, as though battling with itself for superiority. Catrina gasped, feeling the energy rush through her in one vast pulsation. It reminded her of the substance both Fox and the Dealer had given to her.

'It's temporary,' Maria said. When it came to the contents of the serum, she was as elusive about it as the Dealer had been.

Catrina, in all fairness, wasn't interested. Her eyes came into sharp focus. They went from seeing blurred images to seeing everything in more vivid detail than ever before. '...Thank you.'

Maria turned away, placing the needle into the sink with the others. She helped Catrina to stand. While Catrina remembered how to use her legs, Maria took a small scrap of paper from her pocket. It was decorated in spots of blood, and written on it was an address. Maria handed it over without hesitation.

Catrina pocketed the information. 'What time is it?'

Maria checked her watch. 'It's still early. If you're insistent on going, I'd go now. Most will be out on watch.'

Catrina went to the armoury and spent quarter of an hour flitting from her room to the weapons area, taking a rucksack to carry ten or so weapons. She was out of the building within the hour, refusing to waste any more time.

CHAPTER TWENTY NINE

She felt uncomfortable driving the Mercedes alone. She turned the radio on and browsed the stations. She had to distract her attention from what she was doing and the overwhelming sensation that it was the wrong thing to do.

She held the scrap of paper over the steering wheel. Devlin Street. She took a deep breath, checking that she still had the bag of guns on the passenger seat.

She turned the music up; the quick-paced beat made her press her foot down on the accelerator, or maybe it was through urgency. She slammed the pedal, and the car roared forwards.

The streetlights were blurs as she weaved around the slower drivers, ignoring the blaring horns and verbal abuse they gave in response. She swerved down streets, missed turnings, ran stop signs, sped through red lights…she wasn't going to stop for anything.

She imagined how angry, or rather disappointed, Attilla would be in finding she'd broken his trust. She could only hope that he understood, that he realised how important this was.

It wasn't as far as she'd thought, or maybe she had just been driving so fast she hadn't noticed. But there she was, she could see the turnoff for Devlin Street. The lights were red before she approached, and she slowly applied the brakes. She was just thankful that the police hadn't pulled her over.

She looked through the window to the people outside. They had no idea about the world around them in its tragic entirety.

She checked her rear-view mirror, catching a glimpse at her own face. She looked ill, but her eyes blazed with the energy the serum had provided.

The car turned onto Devlin Street, a fairly large road with very few buildings. The ones that were there had that same gothic quality of those around Louis's place, as though the buildings had spirits of their own.

She didn't need direction as to which building the Vicinity was. She sensed it as she drove by. It was so overpowering, her foot was on the brake before she realised. Outside, the rain fell heavily.

She sat for a moment, looking over to the building across the street. She knew nothing about what was inside, how many people would be waiting for her, whether Maria was right in saying most would be out.

She considered turning back. She was walking blindly into this. She didn't know what she would come up against.

Prising her fingers from the wheel, she turned off the engine and grabbed the bag. She needed the extra firepower, something to give to the people she managed to save. If there was anyone *to* save. She took out one gun and screwed on the silencer while kicking the car door open.

She moved as quickly as she could across the road, backing up against the building wall. This was a basic retrieval; any threat would be killed.

Again came that trace of doubt; maybe someone already knew she was there, she hadn't exactly made the most stealthy of approaches. But she couldn't go back now; the task in her mind played over and over. If it came to it, she'd kill them all.

She gingerly tried the door, the fact that it opened without protest alerted her suspicions. But a thought came to her, something Sonny had said. How truthful he was being was anybody's guess, but he made it sound as though the Slayer Vicinities were never attacked. How defensive could an organisation be if they never had to fear attacks?

Her confidence overran her hesitance as she softly pushed the door open.

Emptiness met her, save a cold chill that ran up her spine. Ahead of her was a long corridor, moss-green and black tiled floor, a greyish colour painted the walls. It reminded her of an old hospital, or an asylum. Everything was so impersonal; no paintings on the walls, no sense of homeliness, nothing. Yet there was something faintly familiar. The organisation of the building was like the factory, only this place felt cold, deserted, and dead.

Along each side were wooden doors, each one manufactured identically, whether by coincidence or choice. She had to check them all; it was going to take a while.

Her first plan of action was to hollow out one room; she needed a point of sentry.

The corridor forked at the end, with no indication how many more rooms the building accommodated. The oak-wood double doors in the centre of the junction was clearly the central point of the building. She didn't want to go in there; instinct drove her away already. She pressed her body against the first door, listened as best she could through the wood. There were no voices, only the sound of the rain outside.

She flung the door open and readied her gun.

She threw herself back from the sight that greeted her, forcing vomit back down her throat. She didn't close her eyes, knowing that she would still see it. She took a deep breath, steeling herself to check inside.

Determination forced her to look at the vampire's corpse whose insides had been gouged out. She didn't want to know what had happened to the rest of him. His eyes were still open, but a white film had long since covered them.

She closed the vampire's eyes. His fangs had been ripped out. She couldn't think what the Slayers could possibly have learned from this butchery. She didn't want to know, praying quietly that this end had not met the rest.

Going back to the entrance, she heard voices. They sounded suspicious. She slipped behind the open door, gun ready against her chest, waiting. Her heart brushed her skin against the metal. She needed to know how many there were to deal with before she could strike.

There were two. As they headed towards the corpse, their backs now to her, Catrina raised the gun. The first heard her move, but as he turned, all he met with was a bullet. She couldn't tell what his face said, whether it had been shock, fear or anger. She didn't care, and the second fell just as easily.

The rooms she investigated were all similar. The dissection table was empty in the next room, but bloodstains covered the metallic surface. Anger began to rise up; she couldn't understand the reasoning behind what the Slayers were doing.

Every room she went into, the anger gnarled her. She wanted to destroy the entire place and the monsters inside.

People dared call vampires 'monsters'. They'd never seen places like this, what methods were used to wipe out a species that was only trying to survive. It was sickening. Tattered corpses lay everywhere, one of which she recognised as a vampire from the Clan. She had never spoken with him, not even known his name. Waiting had proved fatal for at least one.

The oak doors of the Vicinity's core faced her. She could brave the doors ahead, or she could go down either side of the junction. She decided to go right, work her way around, and back to the core, when there was nowhere else left.

As she neared the turn towards the new corridor, she heard footsteps again. She pressed her back against the wall, her fangs protruding. There was only one set of footsteps; Catrina slid her gun away.

The young woman was too slow. Catrina grabbed her by the hair and forced to her knees. Catrina felt slight retribution in draining her life out of her. A scream tried to inch its way past the victim's throat with no luck.

She dragged the body into the nearest room and shackled it to the dissection table. It in no way had vengeance against what the Slayers had done. They'd been doing this for years.

She took in a few deep breaths. There were six to find now, Fox included.

She tried the next door.

Two vampires were tied in a spider web of surgical tape. This room looked more like the innards of an insane asylum than the rest of the building. One vampire was dead, the stake still embedded in her chest. There was another Slayer, a mature, dark-haired woman, injecting something into the arm of the other.

Catrina raised the gun and fired, moving forwards in one sleek motion to check for no pulse, before she tried to get the vampire down. They were both Clan. He was a strapping, muscular man, but as she tried to move him, it was obvious that he had little if any control over his body. He stared at her; one eye was missing. Blood spilled out of his mouth. Through the tears in his shirt she saw the mess left of his chest. Stake wounds spanning the two weeks he'd been here throbbed as he wheezed. No strike had hit the heart. This wasn't 'knowing the enemy'; this was torture.

She freed him from the restraints, catching him as he fell. He fought to get out of her grasp and crumbled to his knees. Again, she went to help him, but he shoved her aside. He hooked one hand on the table top with all his mustered strength and pulled up. There were stakes on the top, his hands gripped one, shifting his balance caused him to hit to the floor. His one eye was full of tears. He whimpered like a wounded animal; she could hardly look at him.

He found the strength to get up on his haunches. A few seconds passed as he focused his one remaining eye onto her face. He held the stake out to her.

'I'm here to help,' she insisted, her voice desperate.

He just continued to hold the stake out to her. She stepped back. Realising that she wouldn't do it, he took it upon himself to drive the thick piece of sharpened wood through his own chest. She didn't stop him but fought back tears in having to watch him struggle and die.

Her circuit of the building's inner perimeter was without success. Aside from the Slayers she came up against, there was nothing living. They themselves were not so for long. She accounted for the other Clan members, each one tortured and butchered in the Slayers' own horrific manner. She also found numerous carcasses, some fresh, some weeks old, belonging to vampires she'd never met. This place was nothing more than an abattoir.

Hatred rose in her throat. She felt it like the taste of blood, but more venomous, wicked.

There was no sign of Fox. She tried to remain optimistic; he could've escaped. But in her frame of mind, the idea passed by without much consideration.

She would bring this place to its knees. The anger was more than she was used to; it felt different somehow, like its own intelligence. It didn't so much evoke emotion as it did *agree* with her. It, too, wanted to see the Vicinity crumble. Her heart raced; she was back at the junction, the oak doors loomed over her like gates of Pandemonium.

She had to go inside; a sick sense inside wanted to see what beat at the Vicinity's core.

It was a sight to behold. The room was huge, perhaps two thirds the size of the factory's hall. The ceiling towered into a huge dome with the artistic masterpiece, Michelangelo's 'Creation of Adam', recreated exquisitely on its surface. It would have been beautiful, had it not been such an ungodly place. Catrina wondered if the Slayers thought that displaying such religious icons would forgive them their sins.

The room was dimly lit, the furnishings unlike anything else in the building. It was a totally different place. The carpet was plush burgundy, renaissance decorations adorned the expensively papered walls. There were a few chairs at either side of the room, set in rows towards a pedestal at the far end. It was empty, a cold draft came unexpectedly from the ceiling as Catrina moved further inside. Tapestries hung from the walls, reminding her of biblical allusions and prophecies. She didn't want to read it, her eyes were taken by the amount of religious trinkets scattered about. An altar to the left, full of unlit candles, and a small ornament of the Virgin Mary in the centre.

This was how the Slayers justified themselves. They thought they were working for God.

'I *knew* you'd come...' The voice sent shivers up her spine. Instinctively, she turned with her gun raised towards the pedestal. Nathaniel stood in front of it, holding Fox's battered body with one arm. 'No one else would be so stupid.' She held the gun steady. Nathaniel shifted his shield upwards, drew his 9mm to Fox's temple. Unconscious, barely alive, Fox didn't struggle. 'I wouldn't, if I were you. I kept him alive for you, I can change my mind pretty quick.'

Fox was covered in bruises and thick knife wounds; his hands were bound behind his back and he was gagged. His eyes barely open; she didn't know whether he could see her. The sight made her lower her gun.

'You were healed,' Nathaniel commented, 'Interesting.'

He let Fox slip out of his grip. He fell to his knees, the force he landed with made his eyes open wider. Through the two weeks' worth of beatings and torture, he just stared at her. She couldn't tell what his face said.

Her gaze shifted to her enemy, whose gun was now on her. She was close to firing regardless; if she died, too, so be it. She shook her head.

'You *bastard*,' she spat, making her way across the room, a bare-faced challenge. That third-party anger was urging her forwards, begging for provocation. She waved her hand swiftly to the décor. 'You paint yourself in this worthless picture that you fight for the good of all humanity. This isn't a research centre. It's a place for you sadistic sons of bitches to have your *playtime*,' her fangs protruded as she spoke, 'with innocent people.'

Nathaniel stood very still, gun cradled against his athletic chest and listened. The smile crept into the corners of his mouth. 'Finished?'

The accusations rolled off him without so much as a flicker of remorse. It couldn't have been the first time someone had screamed indictments to his cause.

The thick air descended as Nathaniel raised his gun. She felt this external presence start to form around her, slowly at first, but it became thick enough to touch…

Time ground to a crawl as Nathaniel kicked Fox in the back and rested a boot on his injured shoulder. He took aim at Catrina from across the room. Fox looked up in time to see the bullets flying towards her.

Then this iridescent force took her body under its guiding motions. She felt the surge of raw power slip over her arms. It raised them. One by one, the force guided her hands to bat each tiny piece of Themisium-coated metal away like flies. The power meant the bullets didn't even touch her.

This wasn't the same as the Slayer attack in the Moderator bar. No one was doing this *for* her. This thing was rising up from inside her body, growing stronger with every beat of her heart.

Nathaniel unloaded the entire clip, his face growing steadily redder with every shot.

Her heart felt like it was about to burst. As his gun clicked on empty and the final bullet was discarded like trash, she collapsed on her knees. Her insides churned for sharing presence with such strength. She keeled over, seething, fangs in show.

She heard Nathaniel approach, his boots padded over the soft carpet and the noise echoed in her ears.

She forced herself to stand and face him. He wasn't so far away now; she caught Fox trying to get up from the corner of her eye. At least he was still alive. The look didn't linger. She didn't draw attention to him for chance Nathaniel would kill him out of spite. It was enough of a challenge to pit herself against the Head Slayer; she couldn't protect Fox as well.

Every step he took brought that residual anger to the surface. It whispered in a voice she recognised as her own; the power still coursing through her veins whispered with it. *Do it*, it said. *Show him what you are.* The power was simmering just below the boil. It wanted the challenge like the hunger wanted blood; she couldn't hold it back for long.

Nathaniel looked at her with clear confusion masking the deep-set fascination behind it. She knew in that instant he wouldn't kill her. She was the most precious specimen he'd ever found, and for the sake of a friend, she had walked blindly into his open arms.

He was barely twenty feet away. The power pumped like battery acid, begging for its own fill.

Nathaniel was without a gun now; his cartridge was empty and they both knew it. Morbid curiosity brought him to speak. 'What…*are* you?'

She replied with an unblinking stare and wry smile. 'What...*am* I?' She mocked his question, laughed blatantly at it. This was not her; the force was controlling her now. 'I'm the Genesis, Nathaniel.'

His eyes widened, and hers wanted to, too. Where'd that come from? The Slayer's eyes glazed with fear. She glanced to Fox; his expression was about the same.

Ruben appeared like a dark angel hovering beside the Slayer. He raised his right hand, the index finger and thumb motioned the universal hand gesture for a gun.

Catrina's eyes flitted; Nathaniel sighted her head up with new, fully-loaded weapon. The power inside erupted. Ruben swept his hood over his head and vanished. All that remained was a whisper of his command: 'Stand alone.'

She had no choice but to do so; there was no one to protect her, aside from this alien being that settled in her blood.

Nathaniel pulled back the trigger.

Energy slipped through her blood like syrup, warming her heart and filling her with a taste of divine power. Was this her doing? Her arms shot out to deflect the hail of ammunition. She just stood there, arms and fingers spread. The bullets washed over her without a touch.

Her eyes remained locked on his. She saw primal fear and unparalleled rage burn back as he began to scream. It was a helpless sound. Behind his eyes she heard his thoughts; they were screaming, too. The desperate cacophony of one who knew he was dead.

He turned and put Fox in the line of fire, who was just about on his feet. A single shot left his barrel before a shot to the back ripped through his spinal cord and sent him crashing face-first to the floor like a lump of meat.

She leapt over the body and went to Fox's side.

He lay motionless, the fresh blood seeped over his ripped shirt and covered the rust-coloured bloodstains already there. She didn't want to imagine what he had been subjected to in their hands. She shot the chain that bound his hands and rolled him onto his back.

She pressed her ear against his chest; a dull and singular thud said his heart was still beating. Something was odd; he wasn't convulsing. She tore his shirt open. Overlooking the initial shock at seeing the severity of the beatings he had endured, she saw the bullet in his chest. It had hit his sternum and was easily retrievable.

The feel of her fingers on his skin brought him around. He tried to sit up. She put one arm over his throat and forced him back. He mumbled something; it came through the gag as nothing more than a muffled protest. After considering leaving him in a position where he couldn't pass comment, she pulled the gag away and looked down on him.

Her eyes smiled. 'What did you say?'

'I said...I'm alright,' he replied. He looked back with one black eye and another that looked fortunate to still be intact. A thick slash drew a fresh scar from the top of his right eyebrow, all the way down his cheek. He tried to move again.

'I need to get this bullet out,' she said, pushing him back down.

He fell back with a huff. 'It isn't coated,' he commented with a fairly casual tone, looking at the room from his less than advantageous vantage point. He tensed when she touched him again.

She ignored the flinch; it had to be done. 'How can you tell?'

He let out a laugh; it pained him to do so, and his body quivered. She had to sit back and wait for it to pass.

'I'd *know* if it was,' he commented.

'Hold still,' she said. 'This might hurt.'

She pressed her hand firmly against the top of his stomach muscles and hooked the metallic fragment between her other hand's fingers. He bit his lip to hold back a yell. She wanted to tell him he could let it out, but she knew he wouldn't take up the offer.

She pulled back sharply. The bullet came loose; Fox jolted and seethed, gritted his teeth and showed fang without intention. He fell onto his back and began to breathe.

She sat back and watched him in quiet, unspoken admiration. He slowly leant up on his elbows and returned her gaze. He was thanking her silently; his eyes, though wounded, were the softest she'd ever seen them.

There was no need for words. He was welcome.

She stood up and held out her hand. She helped him up and kept her hand around his wrist for chances he might stumble. 'We should go.'

His eyes fell on the body of the late Head Slayer. 'Catrina...you killed him.'

'You make it sound like a mistake,' she said, her eyes narrowing.

He still didn't look at her; his eyes scanned all about the room. His injured face frowned when he saw the red light blinking at him from a darkened corner. 'Shit.'

'What?' she asked, unable to follow his look.

He backed it up with a motion in that direction and explanation through a worried face. He started to move. 'A surveillance camera.'

She saw it, too. It was there, recording everything. It had them on film; it had taken account of Nathaniel's murder. 'Oh *God.*'

They fled the building as fast as Fox was able, which was still faster than most humans. The soft breeze and thick lashes of heavy rain welcomed them back into the night.

Fox was not as composed as usual; perhaps because he hadn't smoked a cigarette in days. He ran his fingers through his hair, they drew back with flakes of blood from where one Slayer had hit him over the back of the head with the blunt of a hunting rifle.

'They'll find you,' he said. He spoke to the sky, perhaps praying. He felt the side of his neck, the only place to have been bandaged. He had been conscious when the Slayers had drained him...

She wasn't listening to him, either. While he looked to the stars and begged them for her safety, she stood facing the Vicinity feeling a cold rush of frustration.

She could almost *see* the lurking evil emitting from its walls; killing its resident owner was not enough. It had to be destroyed.

Fox was still talking to himself, occasionally looking her way. When she craned her neck to look back at him, he stared as if looking into the eyes of a corpse.

'I had to do it,' she said. As he turned away and continued his excessively useless mumbling, she looked at her hands and began to wonder. 'Didn't I?'

She looked again to the building; its ominous exterior in no way compared to the horrors that took place there. She had seen only a snapshot of their enemies' nature that night. This had been happening long before she was turned, for as long as vampires had existed. Her gut tightened; she felt sick. That power that had so recently saved her life was still coursing through her veins. It shared her pain, and it was angry. One Head Slayer and a few underlings wasn't enough. She wanted to hurt them as much as she was able. The power agreed.

There was a slight delay from the sound of the explosion to when the ring of fire burst out from the Vicinity. As though a volcano had erupted inside the building, the explosion burst through every crack they could to escape. Windows were blown out, shattering glass onto the street, it wouldn't take long before there would be nothing to recognise. And no video evidence to find.

Fox came up behind Catrina and started to drag her away. She was just watching the building crumble like a dying colossus, bewildered by her own actions as much as transfixed by the magnificence of the fire. The dome crumbled to the ground, smoke billowed from the foundations. The Vicinity was engulfed in flames. The glow went far into the night, it danced across their faces, through Catrina's eyes. The smoke spread into the sky and chased the wind. She fought to get out of his grasp, wanting to see the revolution in all its glory.

He spotted the Mercedes that she hadn't bothered to conceal. He pushed her into the driver's seat, but only because he was in no condition to drive himself. He pulled himself around the car and with his last ounce of energy threw himself into the passenger seat. Someone would alert the police soon. They had to get out.

'Catrina!' he yelled.

She snapped out of the spell, eyes averted from the beauty of destruction. She fumbled in her pocket for the keys and slammed it into the ignition. The engine roared beneath them. Her eyes drew back to the burning rubble and the slightly shadowed figure of Ruben standing before it. He was smiling. She felt drawn, as though she was supposed to get out and talk to him. Why was he happy all of a sudden?

'Catrina!'

She slammed her foot on the accelerator, jerking the car into an uneasy pull out. She swerved off the sidewalk as quickly as she could. She checked the rear-view; Ruben was walking from the scene and into the road, eyes fixed on hers. He dipped his head, knowing full-well that she was watching him.

Fox found Rose's stash of cigarettes hidden in the glove compartment. He relaxed considerably once the nicotine rushed through his system.

Catrina's eyes locked on the road, ignoring the looks Fox kept throwing her way. It was his turn to be curious and hers to be elusive.

'What?' she snapped eventually.

'You admitted it.'

'Admitted what?'

'That you're the Genesis.'

She laughed and shook her head. 'I didn't mean it.'

'Didn't mean it?' he questioned in a tone too sharp for her taste. 'After what happened back there, how can you *still* not accept it?'

She didn't, couldn't, reply. It was so easy to cave in and say he was right. A large part of her wanted to. She'd felt it in her veins, through her fingertips. It had warmed her heart and made her feel complete for the first time. Why, even now, did she not believe it? Because the Genesis was *Aisen's* power. She couldn't assume control of it when the man who first owned it still lived. She couldn't assume it was hers when its true owner was also her guardian.

'It's not that simple,' she muttered.

'I watched you do it,' he argued. 'I know what I saw. Why can't you bring yourself to accept that you have something that verges on divinity?'

'It's *not* that simple,' she repeated, her tone sharpening. She gripped the wheel that little bit tighter, silently asking him to keep quiet.

He did not pick up on her request. 'Why?' he challenged. 'What could possibly complicate it?'

Aisen, she thought. 'I don't want to talk about it.'

That only made him hostile. 'You really are *incapable* of asking for help, aren't you?'

She snapped like a twig. 'Shut up,' she growled. 'I'm dealing with this in my own way. I'll work it out, and I'll do it by myself. You don't know what I've been through...' She should have stopped, left it there. His face said he had heard enough, but she was not quite finished. 'I'm *sick* of people trying to be there for me. You people don't know the half of it. Believe me...' She caught his stare. His was dark; hers was darker a thousand-fold. '...you don't. You wouldn't know how to react to the things I'd tell you if I thought you'd understand. If you'd seen the things I'd seen, you'd never sleep again.'

For once, Fox had nothing to say. He sat very still and took deep inhalations of the cigarette that was almost spent. He didn't know whether to be angry or worried.

She didn't know what he was thinking, and now she truly didn't care. The confused ideas of what she'd done plagued her, mixing with the horrors she'd seen there. Even though it was destroyed, it was not the only one by any means.

It enraged and sickened her that those places went without a single attack, safe behind the defence of vampiric mentality and the fact that they were, in all honesty, cowards.

She gripped at the wheel tightly, and a question began to repeat itself in her mind.

If she *were* the Genesis, was there any point being the divine representation of a race too afraid to fight for its survival?

She considered the possibility, while she drove with unerring preciseness, that if the Genesis power *was* hers, what she would do with it. She already knew. She would show the rest of the Vampire Nation *what it meant* to be divine.

*****

The Clan was held in chaos, confusion and worry after Catrina's latest exploit. Knowing that she had saved Fox and destroyed the Vicinity—the *fundamental* information of how a single person could destroy an entire *building* was overlooked—had raised their spirits, but it made them worry to what the Slayers would do in retaliation.

Maria left the Clan once the last Themisium victim was tended to. She disappeared at sunrise to ensure no one would follow for the longest possible time. Attilla was the only one to say his goodbyes. Rumours passed of how the parting had gone between them. The only thing that really mattered was that she was gone, and this, too, brought a variety of emotions from the Clan. But she diminished in interest as the notion of Aisen's reign was brought to the foreground.

There had been no movement from Jessie's room. People who passed just stood in front of the child vampire's bedroom, listening to the ungodly sounds that the Vessel screamed through the thick wood.

The Clan never spoke out loud about it, but they were all thinking the same thing. It had been a month now since the Awakening, and yet nothing had come from it.

Perhaps it had all been a mistake.

CHAPTER THIRTY

The music blared as always, the bouncers guarded the doors. There would be no humans at this gathering. The atmosphere was joyous yet tense. Apprehension hung constantly in the air. Rumours passed about Jessie, Maria, and of the vampires who had died at the Vicinity. Fox refused to talk of his experience.

No one had seen Catrina at all since she'd returned the night that the Vicinity had fallen. People wanted to congratulate her, but she kept in her room. Attilla had even approached to apologise and admit that he had been wrong. She'd ignored him. Fox had spoken to her on a few occasions but she had kept the door closed.

There was something about this night, something everyone could feel but no one would admit to. The rain felt colder, the wind more harrowing, the sounds the old building made were that of confused anticipation. Nature itself was trying to pass on a message, and from the way it spoke, it was something important.

It had been three days since she'd turned the power to destroy the Vicinity. It had not only been for her own protection; she had wanted revenge on the soulless creatures that had killed so many for so long without a single uprising. Now she was disgusted by the cowardice of her kind.

Fox had spoken to her quietly on the other side of her door on a few occasions, telling what was happening, but she had refused to open it. She didn't want to see him. He had said that the Clan were having a celebration; she wouldn't attend.

She opened her eyes from a dreamless sleep to see Aisen standing at the foot of her bed. She sat up and looked at him, not quite sure how to feel. While his unusual face was a welcome surprise, she was innately angry at the fact that his presence in this world had changed nothing.

He looked sick; his eyes dulled to the colour of his skin, head bowed, and arms still attempting a proud stance behind his back, which was hunched more than usual. He turned a tilted glance her way, expecting something.

'What are you waiting for?' she asked.

His head tilted more. 'Why do you ask?'

She rose slowly out of bed, taking her time in approaching him. Despite his haggard and even more monstrous appearance than usual, he seemed strangely human at the same time. He looked vulnerable.

'Because we're waiting, too,' she said.

The thick skin over his eyes knotted. 'Waiting?'

She tried to hold back the residual anger. It was not enough to have destroyed the Vicinity and killed Nathaniel Rae, because in their position they were still fighting an unbeatable enemy.

'It's embarrassing being part of race that doesn't even try to take a stand against its enemy.' She sighed heavily; it was weighting as such on her mind.

'My children have become weak,' he said. 'If I were alive, I would show them the way.'

A deep onset of confusion washed over her eyes. 'But you are alive. Jessie...' Her voice trailed off in seeing his brow knot more.

'The self-proclaimed Vessel?' he questioned with a confused smile.

Unsure, she was ready for anything. An outburst, or for him to vanish, but instead, he stood there, expectancy painted strongly on his face.

She heard the truth whispering through her ears, broken souls screaming at her, telling her something she had to say out loud. She almost choked on her words. 'You never took Jessie's offer?'

He blinked, his intangible look was gone, and he shook his head. 'I fought against it.'

'Why?'

'Because I am the incarnate of true salvation,' he replied, knowing the child's nature. He had seen everything the vampire world had seen, possibly more. 'Her heart is dead, beating dead blood for a dead soul.' He stepped back, shook his head again, this time with defiance. 'I will not share my life with her.'

'She claimed it'd worked,' she said, still in a state of unsure shock. The Awakening had never happened. Aisen was still dead.

Slowly, the pieces of Jessie's twisted strategy came into perspective. The Master hadn't risen, yet the child-vampire had convinced the Clan that he had. She'd wanted the respect of the creator of the Vampire Nation. And chances were it would have worked, had it not been for Catrina.

'Did she?' A sinister smile broadened his jaw, but it quickly degenerated into a scowl. Even a scowl was disturbing to see from one such as he. His eyes narrowed. 'Did she indeed.'

'She lied,' Catrina said, without noticing Aisen's shoulders hunch. Perhaps he hadn't known the child's guise. But he had to have done. He'd been watching her, too.

He looked down to Catrina with a soft expression. 'You are a good child,' he said, cupping her chin in his hand. She let him lift her face to look him in the eye. His eyes brightened now. 'Do you trust me when I say everything has a reason, everyone their purpose?'

She did not feel confident at first, but his sincerity was palpable. 'Yes, I do.'

'Then let me guide you first,' he replied. 'We will set this to rights together.'

An instant passed, and she was dragged away from that world with no pain. She knew this feeling before; the end of another dream. The world flooded her system, along with the knowledge that Aisen was still dead.

His last words ran through her mind: 'Everything has a reason, everyone their purpose.' It was not a question but an instruction.

It was telling her something was intended for her. She forgot her simmering anger at the disgrace the Vampire Nation's innate cowardice marred its reputation with, because under those words there was meaning. Aisen was saying she was above them.

She was on her feet, heading to the door. She had something to do, something so important it couldn't wait another second. She went to the underground parking lot: less people would see her leave that way. The bass from the upstairs music pounded the concrete over her head. By the time she was outside she broke into a full sprint with the sun having barely set behind the skyline.

Her feet took a path they unconsciously knew, a path that had always been there, waiting for her to take. She was none the wiser as to where it was leading, or why she had to get there so desperately, but there was an overpowering sense that every question would be answered if she would just get there.

Fox entered the hall; only Attilla was watching him. He made his way to the bar; Sonny had a whiskey at the ready. He took it gratefully, lighting his latest cigarette. He didn't look at Attilla, but he could feel his eyes pressing for him to speak up.

He turned his head slightly, holding the glass to his lips. 'She isn't there.'

He didn't mention the state the room had been in when he had gone to check on Catrina; it was enough to know that she'd disappeared. His hand held the cigarette over the ashtray in preparation.

'When did you last speak to her?' Attilla asked uncertainly. He could feel the shift in the atmosphere and knew something was coming to pass.

'Last night. Maybe she just needs some time to herself.' But his words were jagged by the sense they all felt. Something was moving around them, too fine to be seen, but too powerful to ignore. He saw his hand quivering involuntarily over the ashtray. To shake the feeling, he raised the cigarette again to his lips.

Catrina could no longer feel the ground under her feet, as the Heavens opened and brought down a chilling storm. She couldn't stop moving, turning frantically down alleys and out across busy roads. People moved aside for her as always, but now from fear rather than her preternatural aura. Water sprayed from passing cars; she didn't feel it soak her. Every step she made, she came closer to liberation. All the answers waited in the distance.

Her leg muscles didn't strain. She was not gasping for air. Even as a vampire, she'd found herself breathless, but not now. The streets grew quiet as she approached the city outskirts. No clubs, no bars, no life. There was a convenience store still alive; its cheap neon light shone out into the darkness. She caught a glimpse of the people inside purchasing their miscellaneous scraps from an apathetic store clerk.

And then there was nothing. Darkness, aside from the streetlights that were of little use. They flickered as she turned down another street, and then she stopped.

Her body was back under her instruction once she realised where she was heading.

Her eyes drifted up through the lashing rain to Louis's home. The building looked more menacing than before, but that didn't stop her from moving forwards. The door was ajar. She pressed the intercom anyway but let herself in when there was no reply.

The place had been tidied since she had last been there, the star charts folded and stacked on shelves, all the notepads had been moved. There was only one thing out of place.

There was one book laid open on the main table. Curiosity drew her closer, despite the spiteful sensation surrounding her that said to ignore it.

It was the book Louis had essentially stolen from the Clan. Rose had hardly given much argument; the less work for her, the better. After Jessie denied him the chance to decipher Aisen's lament, he had taken it upon himself to work it out. In the privacy of his own home, he'd made a startling discovery, which had now been written on a scrap piece of paper sandwiched between the pages.

Louis had finished packing the last of his belongings into his silver convertible and had been about to take the ritual book, when a mysterious cloaked figure had appeared before him. The power emanating from the presence had proved too much for the astronomer; he'd been unconscious for six hours. He had wanted to take the findings to Attilla, but Ruben had a more important role for the information...

There was a sharp pain in Catrina's hands as she tried to touch it. She recoiled and took her hand to her chest, head tilted. The air was shifting. A claustrophobic awareness pressed against the back of her neck. She took a deep breath and moved forwards. The pain started slowly, trying with all its might to push her back. She winced but carried on, taking the book and opening it on the first page. The piece of paper fell from between the yellowed pages; she bent down and scooped it up.

Again she forced the external influences aside and read over the words beneath the famous symbol. Each word she read caused her heart to beat more fiercely and the helplessness grew:

> *...he will turn on those who raise him,*
> *the descendants of his killers...*
> *...with his birth, all will die...*

Now the force lessened its grip; it made little difference at this point what she was enlightened with. She opened the book she was holding and found what she knew was there.

Ruben emerged slowly from the shadows, his expression echoed through each lacklustre step. Angered and afraid, she threw the book at him; it passed through him like falling through mist.

'I want to explain,' he said abruptly. 'And I don't have much time. He will soon be one with you.'

She thrust the deciphered lament towards him. 'What is this? Some sick joke?'

He shook his head. Whatever spiritual realm he was from was losing him. Or he was dying. 'It was the warning left behind by *my* Clan and the First Blood. The descendants of those who were first to fall by Aisen's hand wanted to protect their future by dispelling the myth of its creator. But the attempt backfired.'

'Who wrote it?' she demanded. He was close enough to touch her; his attempt to do so left her with a cold shiver.

Despite the fact that he was fading steadily into the thickening air that was surrounding them, he managed to smile. It was pure, honest. 'The man who wrote it disappeared before his intentions were passed onto future generations. The knowledge of him was lost in history, and its purpose because such a moot point that it was forgotten entirely. That was when the Trine knew it would be safe to grant vampires access to Aisen's tomb, to try and bring him back.'

Catrina could feel the rise of emotion in the back of her throat. 'They knew the tomb was taken.'

'Of course. Had they considered any danger to their father, no one would've returned from the tomb's retrieval.'

She felt the presence of another being making its way into the room. They had to be quick.

'So why wait until now to tell me? You've left it a little late.'

'Aisen would not have allowed it,' he explained. 'I played the part he wanted, to save my soul from damnation. That and to protect you. Had I told you his intentions directly, he would've killed us both.'

'What's changed?'

He smiled more broadly, though by now he was barely more than a whisper in the air. 'It appears to be too late for you. His plan is in motion and cannot be stopped now. He is too close to his goal to care what you know. The hard part is over for him. Now you will endure the fruits of his labour.'

The air descended like thick fog. Aisen was coming for her. She sighed at him, remembering how she looked when he had forced her to look in the mirror. An innocent child.

The dreams flooded over her memory, too many to recall. The two spirits had fought so hard for her to side with them, she had chosen to side with the Master, just because he was the heralded saviour of their kind. It had been so carefully planned, each time he'd visited her, she'd put more faith in him.

'It was all planned,' she said with no hint to a question.

Ruben nodded all the same. 'He has waited for centuries to find one such as you. Every step he took was a carefully laid trap to lure you in his debt.'

Her smile turned sour. 'I owe him, don't I?'

The smile he returned was the saddest expression of emotion she had ever seen. 'You owe him your life.'

She had to repay him. She had to die for him. He had saved her to bring her to this place, to awaken him, to begin the end.

She wasn't as shaken by the revelation as she should've been, but the anger was rising in her system and was forcing a few tears to fall.

Ruben felt the black smoke creep over his arms. It felt as real to him as it did to her. He put the hood over his head. She looked at his eyes; they glinted through the darkness of his shroud.

'Don't let it end here,' he said, stepping into the smoke that enveloped him. 'You do not have much time, but you must stand alone and fight him.'

Aisen took form behind him; the two spirits passed through one another, and Ruben was gone. She had no *choice* but to 'stand alone'. Only now it was against one who had truly betrayed her.

She thought about the tomb in the basement. Her eyes sharpened.

Aisen was smiling. 'You will forgive my prudence, I'm sure, but I couldn't bare to lose your trust. I credit to the man for his efforts.' He swept one huge arm over the space where Ruben had been.

She backed up against the table. Aisen's skin was ripped, his eyes were darker. Blood dripped from his mouth. He stepped closer, and she wanted nothing more than to flee. But it was too late for that, she'd made her choice by trusting him.

'Why me?' she demanded, holding back the fear with the incessant anger at the prolonged charade he had dragged her along with.

His head tilted; he blinked once, taking her thoughts and expression in. He had never looked so cold, quite so evil as the thing she was staring at now. This was what hid behind the beautiful lies, false trust, the deception; he was truly *just* a creature.

'You still look for reason,' he said. 'My reasons are tangled in circumstances beyond description, unless you have centuries to ponder them. Which you do not. You are strong, but not in a way that can protect you. Mentally, you are easily influenced.'

He moved closer, she could feel the cold air envelop her. This was what the underworld felt like, of pure depravity and nothing more.

'You are a part of something you could never understand.' He laughed briefly, hollow and dark. The blood from his injuries seeped down his huge biceps, down his neck. 'And *still*,' he spat, growing angry. 'You look for reasoning. Remember why you are here.'

She shook her head firmly, eyes full of scorn. He had lied to her since the beginning. 'I'm not here for you.'

'Then why do you not run?' he challenged.

She held the stare with him just long enough to realise that he was right. *This* was the thing she had not wanted to know. And all at once, she fell into submission. He motioned towards the back of the room, to the door that led to his crude mausoleum. She had no choice, and as he vanished with a breath of cold air, she headed towards the door.

The factory atmosphere was growing more tense, though they tried to ignore it. The music was blaring. Other sounds began as a gentle murmur, creeping along the factory floor, rising with the humidity from inside the building, blown along with the breeze. They took material form, as they slipped under Jessie's door.

She lay wrapped in satin sheets, a restless sleep that she had been cursed to suffer since she had tried to awaken Aisen. It was never sleep, just the trapped feeling inside the abyss, with only the spirits of Aisen's victims for solace. Now they were outside; Jessie could see them through Aisen's eyes. Although the passage from him to her may not have been completed, a part of him was pumping through her blood. It darkened it, drew her further into the insanity she had lived in all her vampiric life.

She sat up, a single tear streaked down one cheek, fangs dripping with her own blood. The whites of her eyes were black. Throwing her head back, she let out an earth-shattering scream. Aisen was going to live. She knew her sin. She had lied, and she would be the first he would kill.

Desperation consumed her.

She went to the fireplace. A crossbow hung above the ornamental marble hearth. She reached out her tiny white hands to it and wrenched the weapon from its clasps. She refused to die, even to him.

Catrina took the last step into the underbelly of the old building, all the while transfixed on the tomb. The front slab was propped back up against the huge box. All she could hear was the sound of her own heart slamming against her chest.

This was Fate; she'd been damned from before she had been turned.

Ruben had tried to warn her. She had ignored him, allowed herself to be taken in by the idea that Aisen had been there to protect her.

She felt so used. She'd asked for this, allowing herself to be watched under the eyes of the Master vampire, believing his lies, disregarding all slanderous remarks that the knight had tried.

This was the only reason she did not try to stop herself from wrenching the stone slab from the tomb. Jessie's dried blood was still on the sword.

The voices came quickly, echoed through her head and the haunting sounds of death that came with them. Catrina could do nothing, just staring into the stone eyes of the 'forsaken'.

Her mouth opened; she began to recite the ritual. She had never learned the words, never even heard them, and yet she spoke the language as though it was her mother tongue.

The fear only came over her when she put her hand on the sword's handle. Blood spilled through her fingers from a cut that wasn't there. Electricity shot through her. Her hand remained locked around the hilt. There was an almighty scream from the Earth itself; black smoke filled the room, congealing around the tomb. It sank into the sword and into Aisen's stone body.

The third desperate heave and she broke free from the statue, but she took Ruben's sword with her. She fell from the platform. Her head hit the ground with a thud. The tomb that surrounded Aisen spilt and fell. She could taste blood in her mouth, backing up on her elbows, but that was as far to moving as she could get.

The statue started to crack, beginning at the heart in thick jagged lines. She heard him screaming from inside. All that time in the dark, finally he was free. The stone split and she saw Aisen for the first time.

His skin was an ashen sand colour, stained by the blood he had died covered in. He freed his arms, his legs, everything but the head. He fell forwards, roaring.

She gripped the sword in both hands, trying to back further away, her boot heels scraped along the floor. She'd plunge the sword straight back into his chest if he came any nearer...

His body hit the ground with such force that the ground shuddered. She was mesmerised by the pain he was in; she could feel it. The blood dripped over him, his chest expanded to almost double in size, as he breathed for the first time in a millennia. He reached his clawed hands for the stone that masked his face. It was tattered and torn. What she'd seen of him until that moment was a majestic and proud creature. This thing staring back with wild and hungry eyes was anything but.

He knelt up, the skin was close to tearing in holding the colossus muscle structure in place. Throwing his head back, he opened his mouth and let out a sharp and unnerving scream. She felt her hands shaking as they gripped the weapon.

His head jolted forwards, eyes opened wide, and he looked down on her. There was no way of telling what was going through his mind; the feel of the ground under his body, the musty scent of the basement air. The look of her, wide-eyed and moving away.

He found his feet, watching her with a certain curiosity. One swipe of his marred arm through the air, and the sword flew out of her hands. He closed his eyes, breathed in the world around him, let himself be taken in by its essence.

Then he offered his hand. 'Come.'

Awash with defeat, she slowly stood up and put her hand into his. He did not feel cold or warm. He felt of nothing.

He took her in his arms and tilted her head. She felt his fangs sink into her neck, her eyes widened in shock, which overtook the pain. This was really happening. No trick of the mind or vivid dream. Reality hit hard. She was dying. She couldn't see the monster that held her, just the abyss he was sending her to.

His own weak and fragile body turned to smoke as he drained her, thick black clouds engulfed him, until there was nothing to hold her up. She toppled to the ground, too lost to feel the pain. The cloud sank through her skin and into her veins. It beat her organs into surrender, pumping Aisen's blood through her. Her body convulsed with every beat. The blackness of Aisen's heart consumed hers until only his blood pumped through her shell. She was gone in an instant, and her body lay still.

A dull thud echoed through the factory. The vampires stopped trying to hide their inner anxieties; their eyes drifted to Attilla for an explanation he could not give. In the limitless void, something was rising. Something with more power than any of them could remotely compare to or even fully comprehend.

Their hearts, for a split second, beat as one.

Broken pieces of the statue that had held Aisen for so long rolled across the uneven floor. The rain padded from the world above, as he sat up in Catrina's body. He leant over, raising his hands to look at them. He turned them over; the scars had gone. It was not Catrina's body now; everything that had been hers, her past and the marks it had left, were no more.

He waited a moment longer, letting the purity of the world that he was now a part of sink in. Eventually he stood up, the air itself shifted aside with a close to conscious effort. Very slowly, he made his way to the stairs. He spotted the sword. He took it with him. He would use it to kill them.

Catrina's soul was lost with the thousand other vampires he'd killed. Her spirit sank into black water, with no release, no hope, just the numbing pain in knowing the truth.

Aisen walked the streets in Catrina's body. His eyes wandered in amazement at the purity of it all. He couldn't bring himself to kill the humans walking by. Their ignorance filled him with ancient wonder. He didn't care that those he passed turned and looked again, dumbfounded at the sight of a young woman carrying a heavy broadsword in one hand.

He walked out into the road and looked to the Heavens. Stars that formed the symbol, *his* symbol. It was immaculately pressed against the sky of ink-black; he smiled at it.

A car horn blared to his right, and he stopped nonchalantly, turning his head to face the fast-approaching vehicle.

The golden glow of the girl's eyes caught the glare of the headlights. The driver slammed on the brakes, but the state of the road only made the tires spin. It was an all-purpose, family car, all members of which were screaming, as they ploughed into the girl standing in the middle of the road.

The car crashed into him and yet did not touch him. The seven-seated saloon would had fared better if it had driven into the side of a tank. The hood crumpled, smoke flew out from the engine on impact with the air between it and Aisen, and he tilted his head inquisitively at the attempt on his life. When the car had stopped and the family inside were dead, Aisen continued onto the opposite sidewalk, oblivious to the gaping jaws and shocked cries of the passers by.

Every second he walked, he took in more of Catrina's power that resided inside of her. He had waited for this moment. It had taken time, persistence and patience, but he could not have taken her unless she had accepted it.

If she had had fought against him, he would have died.

Catrina's soul was wrenched from all sides from deep within the waters. Every second she almost died but was dragged back just before the final point. She was surrounded by others, all swimming into oblivion. One grabbed her leg; she ferociously kicked it away. They had been there since before Aisen had died, driven into insanity with only the memory of their own death for company. She tried to swim upwards, but the current dragged her back down.

She knew exactly where Aisen was heading.

She writhed against the current, which only sent her further into the abyss.

As he walked through the streets he did not know, he reached out his mind for the sensations of his descendants. It had been so long, he had close to forgotten how a vampire sensed another.

There were two very close by; he could smell traces of his own essence diluted in centuries of disgraced humanity. He turned a corner and saw the two in a passionate embrace.

These will be the first, he thought. He took a step closer, calling out to them from within the mind.

They stopped being so interested in one another and turned to the girl watching them.

'You got a problem?' the man asked.

Aisen looked up at him; the man was taken aback by the wild golden glow in the woman's eyes.

'No problem,' Aisen replied. His voice was no longer the deep, hoarse bellow of a beast, but just because it was through a Vessel made it no less disconcerting.

The man stepped further away, reaching his hand out for his partner. Aisen took a step back also, and fixed his attention on the woman. His eyes took the woman by surprise, but then she was mesmerised by them.

As her partner moved towards her, she ran at him, fangs protruding, and eyes blazing. The man ducked out of dodge. The woman hit the floor hard but barely noticed, and she was going for him again in seconds. He turned to the strange girl in their company, but suddenly his mind was filled with voices charging him into a blind rage.

Aisen watched his puppet show unfold. The two continued to fight amongst themselves; she flung her fist into his face with a loud crunch as his nose broke. He was stunned but more angry, and they continued to hit, kick and garrotte one another. It came to a climax when the man took the twelve inch knife he kept in his jacket 'just in case' and—as though carving a prize bird—slammed it into his partner's chest.

The rage that had burned so brightly in his eyes turned to utter shock, as his partner fell out of his reach. He screamed 'What have I done?' over and over, while Aisen stood to the side, laughing in absolute delight.

The man, still distraught, turned to the girl who was laughing at the tragedy. Unsure and afraid, the young vampire wretched the blade out of his girlfriend and charged at the stranger.

Aisen stopped the deranged man without touching him. They stood opposite one another; the founding father of the Vampire Nation and one of the latest streams of the vampire gene. He was disgusted with what they had become.

'I am your maker,' Aisen spat at the man. 'You have no control over me. On your knees.'

The man was even more confused, when his legs gave way of their own accord and he was forced to do as the woman commanded.

'I tire of your ignorance,' Aisen said, and with that, he gripped the man by the hair and pulled. His screamed echoed through the empty street, but Aisen did not stop until the head was clean off.

He stood there, with the man's decapitated head, the beginning of spinal cord, blood, muscle and sinew, and felt it was not good enough. He threw the head down and continued on his way.

His mind emitted constant waves of hypnotising control. The vampires it touched were filled with rage and turned on any other vampire in their reach. If they could find no one, they turned on themselves.

Aisen headed towards the factory, listening to the sounds ten blocks away of a woman bludgeoning a complete stranger to death with a rock. Their only connection was their race. Aisen revelled every bloody second.

The doormen outside the factory passed Catrina a look of vague recognition. They realised too late that evil danced behind entrancing gold-tinted eyes.

Aisen struck out, the first guard hit the ground, neck broken, heart torn out. The second guard backed up as Aisen hooked his hand around his neck. He dragged the bouncer effortlessly to his knees, sinking his teeth into the exposed neck. He was drained in an instant without a drop spilt.

With the pitiful defences down, Aisen turned slowly to the doors of the factory.

CHAPTER THIRTY ONE

The music shook the amplifiers with the bass it pumped out, the sound was there to try and drive away the growing fear in them; it was not their imaginations. They looked curiously at each other. Someone *had* to know what was happening.

Attilla moved away from the bar; Fox watched him go but didn't follow. The leader of the Clan walked through his people, drawn towards the main doors, but he couldn't have imagined what was about to face him. The doors gave a slight groan, then were suddenly thrown from their hinges crashing to the ground with a dull metallic thud.

The music stopped.

Aisen took his first steps into the building, watching the shocked faces with a peaceful excitement. He could feel their hearts beating, every one of them was his. They parted ground for him; no one dared speak.

Disbelief filled Attilla, his eyes darkened; he knew what had happened and that Catrina was dead. Thoughts of Jessie flitted through him, but what he saw before him now was a true god. The creator he had doubted the existence of was standing there in flesh and blood. Fox started forwards, but Attilla took him by the shoulder. This was no time for impulsiveness.

Aisen walked through the crowd that parted for him, enthralled by every pore in their skin, every follicle of hair, the essence he had given birth to.

Weight slid around Catrina's legs, pulling her further into the void. She didn't want to die in this precipice, surrounded by the screams of his victims and the haunting memory of the Master's words. Ruben had been right. Nothing hid behind Aisen's eyes but the lies and deceit that had consumed him for centuries. He'd never wanted turned vampires in the world. And yet, they'd been the ones to kill him. Now he wanted every single one of them dead. It wasn't only the need to rectify his mistake that drove him. It was revenge. If only someone had noticed it. If only someone had cared.

She fought against the current, trying to reach a surface that she couldn't see.

Jessie marched into the main hall, dragging the crossbow like a stubborn animal behind her. A face so naturally without expression was covered in fury. She raised the crossbow as she walked, and Aisen stopped, turning towards her. Her finger trembled. The vampires shifted. They could hear sounds falling around them. Nothing but screaming, waning with the sweeping breeze and rain outside, then escalating again.

Aisen opened his arms, baring a heart that was still Catrina's, beating beneath that perfect sheath. Jessie released an arrow before anyone could stop her. Aisen welcomed it. He had taken all he had needed from his Vessel. Catrina had served her purpose, he would let her fall limitlessly in that abyss with the rest of them.

The arrow pierced the skin and hit the heart dead-on. Catrina's body went down for the second time that night.

A rush of expectancy filled the air. Smoke rose through her open mouth. As it grew and pulsed, swirling within it was the body of Aisen; wraithlike, tormented, reborn. This was what he had been waiting for, the thing he hadn't experienced since Ruben had plunged the sword into his heart. Life that was his own. The cloud settled over Catrina's lifeless body in a dome, settling too slowly for anyone's patience.

Curiosity overcame the initial shock. The vampires felt exquisite power emanating from the darkness, calling to them. Jessie stood there and watched the smoke clear. The crossbow slipped from her hands, but Aisen's roar drowned the sound of it. As the smoke trailed to the ground dissipating into the atmosphere, the Clan became the first of the Vampire Nation to lay eyes on Grand Master Aisen.

He raised himself, his muscles slid over his shoulder blades, his jaws stretched to reveal that magnificent set of fangs. He stood with his head bowed, eyes closed, dragging every inch of energy he could muster. From what he had been when Catrina revived him, this sight was quite different. He was still that powerful beast, but without a drop of blood or even a mark.

That was, of course, save the Mark of Divinity branded just below his left shoulder, the emblematic scar of what he was. Whoever had branded him, whether it had been Ruben, the Trine, or another entity, it was something that even Aisen could not remove.

The complex network of his system was visible in parts; tiny veins protruded under his new flesh. He stood as straight as his body was able. His back had a slight hunch; his only imperfection. He stood over Catrina's corpse, listening to the *thud, thud, thud* of racing heartbeats.

The intensity of his eyes was unparalleled as he finally opened them. While most did not know what to do, some managed a smile. They could not mistake him; he was there to redeem them. He returned the gesture, but there was a dark undertone that no one noticed.

Fox tried to move towards Catrina. He had not believed Aisen would do this; to Fox, Catrina had never been the Vessel. Attilla put his arm out quickly, again holding him back. They both knew she was gone.

On a subconscious level, Catrina felt Aisen leave her body. She kicked upwards. Her body was uninhabited. If only she could find her way back…

Aisen was going to kill them all, and with how much they trusted him, chances were they'd just *let* him. She fought wildly against the current. There was an abrupt knock in her chest.

She opened her eyes. Was she in the void or her body? She kicked at the water, it tried so hard to pull her back but still lessened its hold. She was too strong.

Aisen looked down at his torso. The arrow had missed his heart by a fraction. His eyes narrowed as they locked on Jessie. He twisted the metal out from under his skin. It cracked against bone, he tore it from his chest, and the wound healed immediately. He turned, pointing the sword's glinting blade at the child. He threw the arrow to the ground and began to advance on her. Jessie stood still, a veil of fear masked her face.

Aisen pointed the sword at her, moving closer at a very drawn-out speed. He was enjoying the fear spread into her eyes, widening them, making her tremble.

'Where do you find the audacity to take my power and name for your own?'

He towered over her and lowered the sword. She couldn't run, for all the need to. She just stood there. She was in his power the same as the rest; her age and influence was nothing in comparison.

He wrapped a huge hand around her neck and lifted her clean off the ground. She screamed as he sank his teeth into her neck to take back what was his. He drew out her death longer than was necessary, still revelling in the feel of fresh, warm blood slide down his throat.

He drained the child-vampire of every drop. Catrina's body flinched; no one noticed. All eyes were on their Master, as he dropped the body and turned to them. Arrogant supremacy narrowed his eyes, and the sword in his hands ached to kill.

Catrina took a deep breath, feeling the black water fill her lungs, but something else with it. Power in its element, raw and primeval. She could see the surface. As she kicked ferociously upwards, she saw Jessie's limp body falling into the abyss. She was not struggling like the rest of the lost souls; she knew her place. Catrina turned and forced herself upwards, starting to feel her heart beating.

Her body stirred. Aisen may have left her, but a part of his blood had been assimilated with hers, and it enthused the heart into motion. Aisen's blood pumped through her body, so slowly at first, no one could have noticed.

She broke the surface, throwing her head back in a struggled gasp for air. Her hair flew in a cartwheel and slapped harshly against the water. The deadness of the void around the water was smashed with a delicate prism of light. The power shook her heart, she felt as though she was about to die.

She was free.

Aisen scanned the life through the room, his eyes still narrow. These creatures were the source of his torment, descendants of the ones who had killed him. And now they were so weak, they would not stand a chance.

Together, they could've defeated him. But they would be divided, and he knew how to make it easy.

He opened his mind of influence. The feelings washed over them, and that same primeval rage overcame them all. They all flew at one another, fangs protruding for the kill.

Aisen fell under as much attack as the others; precedence meant nothing to the anger that flowed through their veins. But there was no one even close to a match for him, even in a group. He took each that charged for him with a welcoming smile, but every one was met with the sharp blade of Ruben's sword. It was not long before the Clan had been halved.

Sonny trembled from underneath the bar, clutching his shotgun to his chest. Being not of vampire blood, he didn't understand what was happening, but he was too afraid to be out there. He leant out gingerly over one side of the bar. No one noticed him. They were too busy killing one another.

He noticed Catrina's body jolt.

Fox broke Fabian's neck and dropped his student's body. He looked around in barbaric desperation for his next victim.

A huge weight was suddenly upon him, as Attilla wrestled his own student to the ground. He lifted the vampire by the collar and slammed his head repeatedly against the concrete. He was screaming, feeling the blood pouring from the back of his head and wanting only to kill the vampire above him.

Fox kicked Attilla in the stomach, throwing him into the bar. The two threw themselves at each other, neither willing to back down, and the older of the two looking as though he would be victorious.

Aisen moved faster than his descendants could dodge. One by one, they fell, without a chance for their emotions to catch up with their own death.

Catrina's eyes were open. She couldn't move. She blinked occasionally. She was deaf to the sounds of abhorrent death. A particularly sharp beat shocked her heart into regular motion. Her chest expanded, fingers curled against the stone floor.

Ruben's voice echoed in her ears. It was a simple command: 'Fight him.'

Realisation hit her like stingingly cold rain. She had to get up. She had to face him.

She saw him standing across the room, throwing his latest kill to the ground. His body trembled with ancient power. The fact that she was still alive may not be enough to stop him.

Compared to Aisen, what was she?

Aisen felt alive in a way he had not for centuries. The smell of fresh death filled his senses, and the fighting continued. These creatures were too weak-minded to challenge the influences he was emitting. Even now he could hear the city's vampire population slowly turning on itself.

But there was something else, and it made him stop. The fight continued without him, as he listened to something alien, something out of place. One of his descendants was breaking free from his influence, or they had not been caught up in it at all.

'*Aisen!*'

He turned to the scream, eyes falling more fierce than they had ever been, on Catrina, who was trying desperately to keep upright. Even from across the room, he could see she was more angry than all of the others.

Her body staggered this way and that. She struggled to breathe. She drew her head back and raised her gun at Aisen's head. She looked as though at any moment she could fall. She was only alive because his blood pumped through her veins. That and her will to fight him.

'Fight *me*, Aisen.' Her voice was jagged.

His head tilted; he dropped the latest carcass to the floor. The fighting was suspended, as Aisen's constant influential train of thought was interrupted. 'You'll challenge me now? I've killed you once...'

'—You're not likely to again,' she growled, still pointing the gun in his direction. She wasn't quite sure where she was going to take this; bullets would do nothing to him. She just wanted to stop him from killing, regardless of what happened to her. This was beyond her life and the Clan now. 'Fight *me*.'

'Why?' he asked. 'What gives you the honour?'

'No one else will face you,' she replied, fangs protruding. She did not meet anyone else's gaze. 'But I will. I'll fight you.'

The circle of vampires that surrounded him stood aside to let him through. He went towards her, she swayed. He stopped and took a breath, closed his eyes. With a sweep of his hand through the close air, the vampires fell. They thought they were individual; in reality, they were all his creatures. It was in their nature. It was in their blood.

Catrina was still standing, her gun poised, neither trembling nor at ease. The closest way to describe her feeling was more a complete lack of it. Her body was alive, but the abyss had a lingering hold over her spirit.

Aisen didn't move straight towards her. First, he knelt down and lay the sword on the ground. The thought that he wasn't willing to fight did not sink in. She remained vigilant; each motion could be a carefully planned trick.

When he *did* approach, he did so slowly, magnificence burning in his stride.

She knew this would be how she died, but still her gun remained on him. He stood before her, as he always had done, the icon of true immortality, something she'd never noticed but had always been there.

Her hand trembled. She was losing control, and she couldn't tell whether it was through her lack of belief, or the power of influence he held over her. She needed help, but her allies were littered like corpses around the room. They were alive; the collective dull thump in her ears was their heartbeats.

'Why do you insist on fighting me?' the Master asked with a curious note.

She moved forwards, tipped the gun furiously. 'What choice do I have? You were meant to be a saviour...'

'And I was,' he insisted. 'They repaid my efforts by murdering me. Can you imagine my life since then? Living beyond death...with nothing, only the memories of their betrayal...' He swept his arm around the room to indicate his enemies and his creation.

Many were dead, strewn around a circle he had been standing in. It reminded her of the sketch. This had been what had happened at the first Awakening; the sketch itself had been someone's effort to warn those of the future.

Her eyes wandered over the bodies, and she could not help but smile. It was a defeated gesture. 'Why have you come back? To destroy us all?' A laugh slipped out, but she made no motion of apology.

He smiled with dejection. 'Life is not something I pride myself in taking. But vampires formed from human skin was a transgression never meant to be, let alone to get this far.' He seemed sincere.

She shook her head. 'You don't belong in this world. It isn't the place you left.'

'They were never meant to live.' His eyes narrowed. 'I created this bloodline. It is my right to rectify this mistake.' This wasn't the way he'd planned his return. His Vessel was alive and challenging him. She was stopping him from starting the shift in vampiric order. 'I have waited all this time...'

'—You'd kill them *all*?' she asked incredulously.

He didn't reply. It was an answer in itself. He had no qualms in wiping out an entire race.

A rush of anger propelled her forwards. Purely as a reflex, Aisen took a step back. She would have moved again, but a thought struck her and held her steady.

Stand alone.

It started to burn in the pit of her stomach. It was the reason she had not fallen with the rest of her vampire kind. It streamed in her blood along with Aisen's, and it held him at bay.

She looked into his eyes; something wept behind impenetrable armour. Facing him was not done by his will. This was either someone else's doing, or it was her own.

A fraction of a smile came over her face. 'Is that fear I see behind your eyes? Are you afraid of me?'

The words barely had time to pass her lips, let alone to hang in the air. He grabbed her shoulders, dragging her off her feet, eyes narrow with rage, and she didn't try to defend herself.

'Your resolution to live is the only thing that holds you here.' His muscles tensed, and she prepared for him to sink his fangs into her skin. 'Let it go.'

A breath caught in her throat; she wanted to gasp. If he wanted her dead, surely he could've done it without hindrance of any kind. Yet here she was, held in his arms, still standing in his way. He couldn't sink his teeth into her. She was fighting against it, and the coil in her stomach was unwinding up into her heart.

It was the same power she had known when facing Nathaniel Rae; the same force that protected her then was still with her. It was not his power at all. It was hers. And he wanted her dead before she realised what she had become.

The Genesis.

She had Aisen's power inside her, pumping through her veins. And he could not take it back while she was alive and with the will to be so. She would not let him have his wish. She would *not* die for him again.

She felt the pressure increasing around her shoulder, as the other arm went around her neck. She slowly began to choke. Defiance brought her gun around to his temple, and she shot him. He reeled back. The blood that poured ghastly down his face only did so for a few seconds, then it was gone.

He glared at her and threw her across the room like a rag doll. She crashed into the neatly lined bottles behind the bar, tumbling to the floor in a shower of broken glass. And as she lay there in the pool of spilled liqueurs, she felt no pain. All she could feel was her heart growing stronger, the power surging over her like a drug.

Aisen moved with unerring grace towards her as she leapt over the bar and readied herself for the attack. If he could not kill her with mind games, he would *have to* fight. But this was not a Slayer, or even a Head Slayer...this was Grand Master Aisen. He was the thing that ultimately made her what she was, and now what she knew she was meant to be.

He moved with such a swift motion she didn't realise what he'd done until it was too late. He grabbed her by the neck, hauling her from the ground and suspending her at eye-level.

Inside, the power shifted. It was unsure, hesitant. The only reason she had time to ascertain was that this power had once been Aisen's. Now it was fighting against him, and it could not quite bring itself to do it.

Her neck began to hurt. He closed his eyes, she felt his mind prying hers open, delving into her deepest thoughts. 'You have been conditioned, as they always are. The thoughts and ideals of those around you have been embedded in your being. You are no different from them now.'

He flung her to the ground. She hit concrete with a loud crack. She scrambled around on her knees feeling the pain shooting through her system. She trembled, it was starting to hurt as it tried to take over. She could not hold back a power so immense for long.

'*I* am the purity of this world, regardless of your ideals...' he said, moving towards her as she stood. He hauled her across the floor. She could feel blood pouring from her temple, as she skidded to a slow halt. His only intention was to kill her. He stopped for a second, watching her crawl back to a stand, hanging his head in shame at her insolence. 'But you are different from the others in another way now,' he continued. 'You are no longer a part of me, but *I* am a part of *you*. You are the one who gave me life again. My spirit will never leave you now.'

He growled again, eyes narrowed to slits, his inner anger was clear from his stance. He reached his arms out, shoving her by shoulders. Her feet left the ground as she sailed across the room.

The pain inside grew ever stronger, the force of energy battling against her system. She screamed in agony as it coursed through her veins, the same way the blood of her victims did but with a white-hot fire. Aisen was hurting her with intention to kill. The Genesis would not let this happen to its host.

As he reached out to grab her once more, the power jolted through her heart like an electrical current, forcing her arm up.

She blocked Aisen's attack, seeing it pass his thoughts, and kicked him with forceful exertion in the stomach. He keeled over but grabbed her arm and flung her to the ground. She rolled and landed hard on her back, her head followed with a loud smack.

Dazed, she could only see the lights above her, shadowed by the silhouette of Aisen's advance. As she backed up on her elbows, something cold brushed up against her arm. She turned to see Ruben's sword within reach.

Aisen leapt forwards. There was a brief instant when all she saw was into his eyes. Time slowed to a crawl to show the pain he was already in. It was beyond his eyes, something this power was letting her see. They were his memories. She saw his life, everything he had done, the horror that followed his mere existence. She couldn't see what it was that made him this way. She wasn't ready to understand that much.

Time stopped waiting, and as Aisen leapt, she spun to her feet, gripped at the sword hilt, and brought it upwards. Unable to fight gravity, Aisen impaled himself on the sword that had been the product of his first demise.

They fell together. His immense weight fell against her. The sword split his skin, cracked through the bone and sank into his heart. He jolted, suspended only by her raised arms, and the blade that pierced his heart once more. She could feel his heart breaking. He heaved, starting to crush her until she rolled out from beneath him.

The supreme power that had taken over diminished before it even had the chance to erupt. She could still feel it, but it fell docile. It drained her energy, so all she could do was sit beside Aisen, watching and waiting for him to die.

His head dipped to the ground, resting on huddled knees and elbows. The sword protruded his monstrosity of a torso, precious blood spilling from one wound that wouldn't heal. His eyes were tight, he collapsed, landing hard on his back. He used what little energy he had left to watch his blood spill around the glinting blade. Slowly, he turned his heavy head towards her.

Her blue eyes swelled with tears, and she couldn't understand why. He'd been the cause of all her confusion, the one who'd stopped her realising her destiny. It made her angry, yet without energy to move, she just sat there and looked back at him.

He'd waited for so long for his revenge. Now they knew his intentions, vampires wouldn't be so naïve again. Catrina would make sure of it.

'Now you shed your tears.' The slight laugh he gave was choked from the blood rising in his throat. 'Do you know why?' Regardless of the situation, beyond the thought that she'd defeated him, she knew that he still had control. She shook her head. 'Because this is not where I die,' he continued. He scratched the stone floor in agony, the blood spilled over his bare chest. Watching her face, and seeing the sad realisation wash over her, he managed to smile through the pain. 'Is this your moment of clarity?' he asked, his eyes, while dulling, were still staring at her with the same spark of knowledge they always had. 'Now do you understand and accept that you are here for me, and I am now a part of you?'

To know that she was weeping over his death only made her more angry, and that only made her cry harder. She huddled closer to him, reached her hand to his chest.

'My blood pumps through your veins,' he said. 'Now you will never be free of me.'

Her fingers ran down the thick blade touching the wound in his chest as he let out a wretched cry. His body trembled, as she gripped her blood-covered fingers around the hilt and pushed down with all her might.

It was only when his heart stopped that she let herself crumble. She collapsed against the hideous monstrosity that he had become, crying angry tears onto his cold, leathery skin.

CHAPTER THIRTY TWO

Catrina watched herself in the mirror. She put her hand to her cheek; it was like touching ice. She stared back through the reflection, the blue in her eyes was dim. She looked past herself through the mirror at the room behind her, scanning the room for her expected companion.

Ruben stood in the far corner, completely covered by the cloak that had hidden him for so long. She turned in the seat, trying to see into the darkness of his hood that concealed his eyes. He didn't move, but he had brought her to this place once more, and she was still made to look like a porcelain doll.

'What's left to say?' she asked without raising her voice or rising from the seat. Slowly, he made his way across the room, removing the hood so she could see his face. He was smiling; an expression had never looked so comforting. 'I had a feeling you'd come back…I just didn't know why.'

'I do not expect you to understand everything.' He helped her gently to her feet, gesturing to the mirror. 'Can you see what he did to you?'

She looked carefully; her eyes narrowed. The doll looking back was not who she was. This was the deception Aisen wanted her to believe. She shook her head. 'I feel it every time my heart beats. His blood is inside me.'

'As is your own.' Ruben said. 'Look again.'

He stepped back. Hesitantly, she turned back towards her reflection. At first, the only thing looking back at her was the perfect porcelain figure, with glassy eyes and pouted crimson lips. She noticed something. The white makeup was starting to flake, showing the pale yet effervescent skin beneath. The mask fell from her face. Her eyes became wider and lost the sheen. It came away like an entire layer of skin, as she ran her hands over her new face. She looked no different to when she had become a vampire, perhaps a little more energetic. She stared, admiring herself for the first time.

He was momentarily taken by her new appearance, waiting for it to pass before preparing himself for the first and last real explanation he'd ever give her.

'Three lives,' he said. She turned away from the mirror. 'The first, a human life…not lost, but reborn, into the second…the vampire life.' Again that smile. It came before he spoke up and died by the time he had finished making his point. 'Will is a formidable force, Catrina. Aisen wanted your blood, the power that you hold inside. The Genesis power.' He pointed to the mirror, and she caught sight of herself again. 'This is now your third life, with Aisen's blood as your own. It is not a hindrance, but a gain…and a new beginning.'

She took a moment to speak, gathering her energy as though to force it out of her mouth. She wouldn't understand it yet; it'd happened too quickly. '…The Genesis.'

He nodded gently. 'The only vampire in existence to live with the Master's blood. You will not understand your power yet…it comes with time, and you will learn to harness and embrace it.'

She gave a final thought to Aisen and how through all his lies what he had said between the lines was true. They were the same, kindred spirits, but in a way *he* would never be able to understand or accept.

She turned back, only then realising that she had been walking away. 'You won't be back, will you?' There was a sadness in her tone. After all he had tried so hard to show her, he was not intended to stay.

'The privilege of teaching you is not mine. It was within my power to protect you from him as best I could. Without him, I serve no purpose. You have learned all you need to from me. The rest lies with you.'

She headed without noticing towards the soft light that flooded the room.

Everything happened for a reason, and everyone had their purpose. Protecting her had been that of the knight. As for her own purpose—why she had been blessed with the Master's gift—it was at least worth searching for.

*****

She woke up that night as though it was the first time. She climbed out of bed, got dressed and grabbed her bag bulging with everything she owned. The room was left bare, all trace of her gone…

The repercussions of Aisen's death had been harrowing. Many vampires had lost their beliefs. Their creator had tried to kill them. What remained of the Clan members after that night was divided; many left to find their own answers. The few who stayed had listened to Catrina explain Aisen's underlying cause. She led them to believe that she'd learned this while Aisen had been inhabiting her body, not throughout her entire time there. They had no reason to doubt what she said.

Catrina walked through the desolated corridors, taking each breath with careful precision. She wouldn't miss another moment in this world. She reached the door leading to the main hall and pulled it open…

The Clan assumed that her killing him had been pure luck. She couldn't possibly have fought the Master and won of her own ability. But she was fabled with strength some of them couldn't know, her 'destruction' of the Vicinity had led to her credibility in this matter. She was willing to let them believe what they wanted, all she did was make sure that they knew Aisen's intentions.

She didn't mention the fact that she now harboured the power of their creator. The discovery of a new Genesis to the Vampire Nation was not advisable, especially when she was still so unsure.

Attilla was standing in the middle of the hall. He guided the remaining Clan vampires outside. They carried boxes and various objects that the Clan held most dear.

While he had spoken little of it, Attilla was one of the most affected by the Awakening. Catrina watched him for a moment before going to the bar.

Those who stayed agreed that Aisen's body was to be buried, as was only fitting. He may have wanted them dead, but their entire bloodline came from him, their ancestry and abilities were still his. The ceremony was short and few tears were shed. Catrina didn't cry; she had lost the ability to do so over him. The tears that did fall came out of hopelessness. They'd put their hopes in him, and he'd turned on them. They could not let him win by giving in, and the new life started as the final nail was hammered into Aisen's box-coffin.

Sonny still manned his post. There were no bottles on the shelves. Most had been broken in the fight and the rest were packed away. Sonny had been conscious when Catrina had faced Aisen, although he was the only one who knew. He hadn't told anyone of what he had seen and heard during the fight, and he planned to let it die with him.

'Last drink?' he asked her.

She gave him an encouraging nod. Fox was sitting as he always was, with a cigarette in one hand and a glass of whiskey in the other. He had hardly spoken since Aisen's death.

He had been the first one to break out of Aisen's trance after Catrina had killed him. He'd found Catrina huddled over Aisen's dead body.

'I never thought I'd miss this place,' Catrina said casually, as she sat down beside Fox, his ashen face brightened a little.

Sonny returned with her beer. He finished packing the remaining bottles in the last of the boxes and left the two to talk.

Catrina pivoted on the stool and watched the vampires heading to the trucks outside. 'Will you miss it?'

Fox took a long drag. He let the smoke rise slowly from his mouth, watching it vanish into the air. He was considering saying something, she could see it rising in his throat, but he silenced himself.

'What?' she pressed.

'Some things are more difficult to let go of than a building.'

He'd been one who had truly believed that Aisen would return equilibrium to the Vampire Nation, and seeing the event from Fox's perspective, it was a severe disappointment.

The vampires had been working through the night, and as the moon rose up towards midnight, everything the Clan owned was ready to go.

She sighed one more time. 'It proves one thing.'

'...Which is?'

'We're no more divine than he was,' she replied. He looked offended. After all, that was his entire basis for arguments. She didn't stop. 'We made the mistake of raising a monster, *we* made a mistake...there's no divinity in mistakes.' He frowned, it should've been enough to silence her, but she just smiled. 'You could say we're too human. It's their blood that runs through us. Maybe humanity affects us more than we know.'

He stared at her for a moment. The tiniest smile crept into the corner of his lips. He let out a sceptical laugh. After drinking what was left of the whiskey, he stood and made his way across the room, saying something to Attilla before heading for the door. Attilla turned his attention to Catrina, and she smiled, finishing her drink and going to join him.

A brief moment of definitive understanding passed between them. She watched as Sonny gathered what was left of his stock and joined the others outside. The factory was empty now, save them.

She motioned to the factory. 'Something to miss?'

'Something to remember,' he corrected.

They walked towards the entrance.

A truck horn blared and the road was filled with the cars that had been in the underground parking lot. The Clan had been forced out of their home and stripped of their beliefs. But all was not sour, and the future was to be rebuilt.

She stopped for a moment, he noticed and faced her again. She couldn't be certain, but she had a feeling she wasn't the only one who had known Aisen's true intentions. She read over his expression, for once it seemed to tell an entire story. She smiled warmly.

Her eyes fell unintentionally to Aisen's last resting-place. She shook the images away, letting them fade into nothing. That was history, all she had to do was let it go. Her eyes were bright as they caught Attilla's. She nodded and moved forwards.

The engines from the cars outside roared. One by one, led by the trucks that contained their belongings, they departed. The factory was more than just a building, it had been a home full of memories that would never leave them.

Attilla reached out his hand and took her by the shoulder. Fox stood by the entrance door, impatient as ever. Attilla gestured gently for him to wait outside. Fox gave her a final glance as he turned, flicking his cigarette out into the street and heading to the parked Mercedes.

Attilla waited until Fox had gone. 'How long have you known?'

'Not long enough to understand it.' Her words caught in her throat; it was impossible to keep things from him.

He nodded, cupping his hands, as though he understood. But he couldn't understand this; it was *her* gift, not his. She waited for him to speak. When he didn't, she asked him where they would go from here.

The question ran much deeper than that of the Clan moving its location. With only a fraction of the associations, and those who had remained with destroyed spirits, it was a long journey that was to be faced. He understood the underlying questions within a question, and he replied in a way he'd always done.

'Without the façade of Aisen's deception to blind us, the true path is all that lies ahead.'

'Everyone believed he'd save us, to give us something we couldn't achieve on our own,' she replied, her brows knotted as she tried to find the words. It was too difficult to explain how centuries of beliefs had been uprooted and destroyed, until only the smouldering ashes remained. 'Our own creator wanted to destroy us...that's something that'll take a strong force to overcome.'

He was humoured by her comment. 'You still believe he was like us? Because he was the beginning, that made his actions just? Our salvation lies close at hand. The first step is believing in the definitive nobility that beats in the heart of the Vampire Nation.'

'How can we?' she asked, her sceptical side mounting. 'He was the Genesis, the Master, everything we're supposed to *want* to be. Without an ancestry worth following, what nobility is there to search for?'

'Nobility is not something given by those who have fallen before us,' he replied gently. 'We earn it from those who surround us, and in ourselves. Aisen's deceptive intentions have not stripped us of our dignity, simply given us something more to strive for.'

He escorted her to the entrance where they were welcomed by the perfect night. Fox pulled the car up to the door; the other vehicles had gone. Attilla opened the back door for her.

She watched the never changing city lights through the window as Fox drove out. Attilla was right. Although it was not intentional, Aisen hadn't brought the death and suffering he had intended, but a new sense of hope.

This was the beginning now, whatever happened could only be known when it came to pass, and answers would come when the basis for this new hope was established. The beliefs may have been broken, but it would give the foundations for something new, something more precious.

In the Precipice, the Wanderer Returns…

The spirit tore through the crypt so quickly, the inhabitants did not notice. It retreated to the coffin of its material self, angry for being defeated so easily.

In the dark, quiet solace of its resting place, the spirit calmed. As it readied itself for a long period of sleep, it recited an old wives' tale to ease its troubled mind:

Not a word is spoken,
Not a thing is done,
Not a movement made,
For all is yet to come.

For all the latest news on the
VAMPYR SNYPER series and its author,
visit the web site at:

VAMPYRSNYPER.COM

Lightning Source UK Ltd.
Milton Keynes UK
16 November 2009

146307UK00001B/248/P